A Plague of Rats

By

Lazette Gifford

Copyright 2020 Lazette Gifford

An ACOA Publication

www.aconspiracyofauthors.com

ISBN: 978-1-936507-96-2

Dedication:
This book was completed during the Covid 19 epidemic. We could not gather, except online, and there we shared our time and our work. Thank you to all my fellow writers who made the days not so long and lonely.

A Plague of Rats
A Conspiracy of Authors Publication
www.aconspiracyofauthors.com
Copyright 2020, Lazette Gifford
ISBN: 978-1-936507-96-2

Cover Art Copyright 2020, Lazette Gifford
Editor, Steph Eastman

TABLE OF CONTENTS

CHAPTER

ONE

The Most Holy Priest of the Temple of the Ten, Cedric the Benevolent, pounded his beefy fist on the tabletop with a resounding crash, the impact sounding as though the very doors of paradise had slammed shut. His bloated face, already dangerously red, now turned nearly purple; his bulging, muddy colored brown eyes fixed on the young priest standing across from him.

"You will be *silent*!" Cedric ordered, his voice a rumble of power and rage.

"I will *not*."

The other priests present, a full twenty sitting around the carefully polished table, had kept silent during the tirade between Cedric and Koya, but this time Koya heard an audible gasp echo around the room. Koya paid no attention, his gaze fixed on the man before him -- the Most Holy, the Most Wise ... and the Most Blind.

Koya had hoped for better. Against all the odds, he had expected some show of sanity from the leader and highest-ranking priest of the Temple of the Sun.

The candles flickered as though a cold wind had suddenly blown through the room. The strong scents the Most Holy favored -- expensive and wasted perfumes -- nearly won another sneeze from Koya. He fought it back with a grimace that probably looked like a snarl. No matter. Nothing he did or said would improve the man's attitude. Still, Koya knew he dared not give up.

"Trouble is coming," Koya said and not for the first time, even in this last hour. He dropped his voice from the near shout of moments before. Cedric's mouth clamped shut, but wouldn't stay that way for long. Koya rushed onward, reciting what he'd already told the man who sat there in his exquisite white robes, flaunting expensive jewels on his fingers while Koya stood in his simple blue robe and hand-made sandals. Maybe if he repeated what he knew enough times, someone would hear him. "There is a great welling of magic to the north and east, and this comes from nothing good --"

"No one else has seen this trouble!" Cedric snarled with his glaring eyes nearly closed behind layers of fat. "Not even so much as a sign at the Forbidden Valley. We have priests always tuned to watch the Dragonkin and the east, boy. I'm not stupid."

Koya took three quick and calming breaths, hoping this line of conversation might yield at least a closer look at the trouble he sensed. "I never meant to imply you were stupid, Most Holy, but neither did I say this trouble was with the Dragonkin. I don't believe it is." The statement won a snort of derision as the Most Holy sat back in his chair. The wood creaked under the strain. "I can't tell you exactly where or how ... but I can feel the trouble growing, leaching magic from the land, and growing stronger with each day. It pulses --"

Koya lifted his hand, feeling the faint touch of such a pulse, and he looked to the Most Holy, hoping -- but no. The man noticed nothing. Koya could feel the power like a dark, oozing sore upon the land, and he almost felt ill from a mere brush of that evil. Compounded by knowing the Most Holy would never listen to him.

Kenning had told Koya that this would happen. His friend, and the High Priest of the small Temple where they lived, had told him there would be problems with the Most Holy, but Koya hadn't believed the person who stood closest to the gods could be this blind!

"The problem grows, Most Holy," Koya said, though without any power in the words knowing the man didn't believe him. "There is going to be trouble, and we of the Temple of the Sun should spread the word so others can prepare."

"And you -- you *alone* of all of us -- can feel this trouble." Cedric's mud eyes blinked in a face grown round and soft with too many easy years in the capital.

"I can point the way. Maybe if you tried --"

"I will not take orders from a Norter bastard!"

Koya flinched backward as though he had been physically struck, shocked by the personal attack and the venomous hatred in the Most Holy's voice. Yes, he had been born in the magicless northlands, and it showed in his paler hair, blue eyes, and taller statue. Was this the real problem? Koya had been born in a small Damarian village but blessed with more magic than many of the southern priests. That blessing had created problems on both sides of the border. To the north, he'd risked death at the hands of those who thought all magic a curse from the demons. Here in the south, many people treated him like a demon for having been born in the north. *Norter bastard* was not the worst he'd been called over the years.

Cedric's taunt shouldn't have surprised him, though he

never expected such an open attack from the man. The words also drew looks of shock and dismay from his brother priests who must have thought the Most Holy would be above such mundane pettiness.

Koya only gave a belated snort of disgust, which hardly helped the situation.

Nothing would.

"There is a problem growing," Koya said, his voice calm as he stood straighter again. He would not be cowed by this bigot, no matter what his standing. "And if you can't feel the danger, that isn't my fault."

"You have come here, you --" Cedric stopped himself from repeating something impolite, but Koya could see the words in his glaring eyes. "You have come here, bringing your northern ways to our Temple, demanding our attention, fabricating trouble --"

"You can't really believe --"

"*Silence!*"

So, they were back to this again, were they? Koya caught a warning look from Kenning and knew he had gone beyond any hope of understanding. He turned back to the Most Holy in silence, but not with any respect; he could not school his face to such a lie.

Cedric leaned forward, his right fist pounding the table, not ready to give up his own tirade even though Koya had stopped arguing with the old fool. In fact, Koya was already turning his thoughts to other ways they might stop the trouble before something dire happened.

"I will not have such behavior in a holy Temple!" Cedric gasped in rage, his flabby face trembling. "I will not have your contamination ruining the sanctity of this place! You lack the humility needed to be a true priest --"

"Well, I'm not going to learn humility from you, am I?"

Cedric's face moved to another level of red, and Koya

feared the man would have a convulsion. Cedric stumbled to his feet, his mouth moving as though he gasped like a fish and his fists coming up. Kenning stood to reach for the man, to try and calm him --

Koya realized he was in trouble a moment too late.

The Most Holy was not having a fit. His hands moved, the fists opening as magic flew outward like a dark cloud. Black lines and baleful spots swept over Koya before he could even yelp in protest, let alone raise any shield of protection. The darkness struck and seeped into him like water into cloth. Koya's legs gave way as he tried to grab at the chair, but he tangled in his own robe and fell, his head swimming. The world moved out from under him as he went down, hitting the floor hard enough to win a surge of agony through his body.

"I will not be insulted by Norter rabble! I will not accept this piece of trash that was flung out by his own people to curse us! I will teach the bastard humility!"

Others drew the Most Holy away, his white clothing conspicuous in a cloud of sky-blue priests' robes. Koya watched the sandaled feet heading toward the dining hall's door, voices soothing the Most Holy as they left Koya lying on the cold floor, stunned, hurt, and angry.

Once they were gone, Koya tried to sit up, but his right arm gave way with an agonizing pain that spread from fingers to shoulder and left him hissing for breath. He tried again and fell. And again --

"Careful, Koya. Careful." Kenning knelt beside him. Koya was not alone, after all. Kenning cautiously helped him sit up and shook his head with disbelief. "Didn't I tell you not to annoy the Most Holy? Didn't I warn you that he had no patience for anything but what he believed and what he saw?"

"I --" Koya began, but then he hissed in pain as he tried to straighten his right leg. It couldn't be anything serious; he hadn't fallen that hard. "He wouldn't listen. Why wouldn't he listen?"

"Because he is a stubborn old bigot," Kenning replied with a snarl, this man who had always been gentle and kind. "He's come to Templeton to find trouble he can exploit, Koya. If you had been a southern-born priest, Most Holy likely would have embraced you and your message about the darkness -- but he has always hated Norters. He wants a Holy War against them so he can be powerful again."

Koya stared at Kenning in shocked disbelief, but that emotion disappeared as he became aware that his body still didn't respond the way it should. His right arm and leg felt weak and sent a shock of agony through his body whenever he moved either of them.

"What -- what did he do to me?" Koya whispered as fear overcame his anger.

"The spell was one I'd never seen before," Kenning replied with a frown. "The others are talking with him, trying to keep him calm and appeal to his better nature --"

"Hell. He has no better nature."

"I did try to warn you, Koya."

"I didn't listen to you, and he didn't listen to me." Koya felt panic building, layer-upon-layer of trouble rushing through his mind. "We are facing serious trouble Kenning, and we have to prepare --"

"On your word alone."

The four small words struck like a knife, a pain that overlaid any physical discomfort. He turned his head and tried to sit up on his own. "*Even you.*"

"That's not what I meant! Only that no one else feels this magic you say is out there, Koya. No one else can sense anything wrong, and too many are going to be like the Most Holy." Kenning stood and pulled Koya to his feet, where he stood in breathless agony, not able to defend himself with any words. Koya could still hear the Most Holy shouting with anger from somewhere down the hall. He was not going to lift the spell.

Angry and feeling betrayed, Koya pulled away from Kenning and took a step forward.

The pain sent him falling again, but this time he was unconscious before he hit the floor.

CHAPTER

TWO

A frantic brown rat, sides heaving from exertion, tumbled down the hillside and slid across the mud at the edge of the scum-filled pond. He scrambled back to his feet and shook the muck from his head, splattering it everywhere. A chorus of frogs protested as they leapt from stones and sticks into the safety of the murky water. The rat circled, trying to run one way or another -- but he always turned back to the south, where something unnatural called to him.

More rats had appeared on the hill's ridge, squealing in protest as they, too, followed that abnormal call. One rolled down the hill, and then another lost his footing and rolled as well. The first rat now spun and darted away from the onslaught, finding his way along the edge of the pond while the hill behind him became covered in squealing rats. Birds screamed in surprise, small creatures raced for cover, and the frogs, wisely, began to abandon the pond for branches and ledges above the path. Rats slid and were shoved into the mud and deeper water. Those that could swim made quickly for the southern shore -- but more came, and more, until the pond filled with rats. A hundred or more drowned and as many more were trampled into the mud.

And still, they came, wave upon wave of frantic, squealing rats that tumbled down the hillside and ran on across the bodies that had piled up.

The first rat still ran ahead of the others, staggering now, but still racing through the dark night. He collapsed once, twice -- but something drew him onward. Other rats joined him from different directions, and now he must continue or be trampled. Some part of his primitive brain knew the only way to survive was to keep moving.

He was the first to reach the village walls and scramble over the top, down the other side, and into the pre-dawn streets of the small settlement. The call that had propelled him fell silent, but he still rushed onward before the others caught up. They were not far behind.

By the time the townspeople awoke, there were already twice as many rats as there were people. By noon the streets ran brown with rats. Townspeople hastily herded larger animals away to whatever safety they could find. Children and chickens were kept behind bolted doors, the windows secured, except when someone stood guard to knock the rats back with shovels and pans.

The frightened townspeople hastily created a rat-battling militia that guarded the walls and patrolled the streets, fighting back the creatures as best they could.

The numbers still grew; the fields outside the town, which had only just been planted, swarmed with even more rats. Eagles and hawks took up the battle with glee until they satiated their appetites, and then they hung on tree limbs and roofs, watching the glutton's feast pass by below.

Master Alcrew, old and arthritic, hobbled to the Temple of the Sun with the help of his cane and with his young assistant, Malin, at his side, a steadying hand when they crossed rough ruts and stinking mud. A guard of six fought away frantic rats on all sides while Alcrew climbed the five stairs, mumbling under his breath about old bones and uncommon haste, though he dared not curse in this place where the gods might really listen.

Alcrew silently regretted that their priest had gone missing in the dead of winter during one of his trips to the smaller villages higher up in the hills. They needed old Galt now. This infestation couldn't be natural, and no one else in Ziven had magic to confront the trouble. The only power left anywhere lingered in the old stone Temple building, a potent residue that had built up over two hundred years while the Temple stood in the middle of Ziven. The small town had grown out around it and later compacted back to a hillside village of barely four hundred. They no longer rated more than one priest.

Only Alcrew could open the massive wooden doors to the Temple, having been the assistant to the Priest Galt and curator of the building for most of his life. The magic of the place recognized Alcrew and trusted his good intentions. Galt had often spent long weeks away, traveling to different villages and sometimes to a lowland Temple. He had always left Alcrew to dispense medical supplies or to let someone in to pray at the altar. They should have reported the disappearance before now, but everyone in Ziven had hoped -- and prayed -- to see the old man hobbling along the road, bells ringing on his staff, and his bright laughter greeting old friends.

Alcrew knew no magic of his own, of course. He couldn't even feel the power of the building the way Galt could. Nonetheless, he reached the top step and pushed open the door, where all the battering in the world by the others wouldn't get the heavy, carved wood to budge.

The door felt reluctant to move today, and Alcrew had to shove harder than usual. Was that his weakness or a reaction against whatever evil power sent the rats against them? Such a plague of rats could not be natural, though why would anyone choose Ziven for such an attack? He feared they were only caught in a more significant problem, but he didn't say so to the others. They had to believe help would still come to save them.

Alcrew stepped inside as spots of fire flared not only in the sconces on the walls, but also along the dozen candles placed around the altar at the far side of the room. Everything suddenly glittered with golds, blues, and greens. Alcrew accepted the magical light as the first good sign he'd had all day; the gods had not forsaken them. He had the second good sign when one of the rats got through the door with them, then stood, dazed, while Malin grabbed the creature and shoved it back outside where one of the others could kill it. Wise boy, not to kill the rat in this Temple, which was sacred to all creatures of the earth.

Alcrew and Malin had made it safely inside while the rats milled around at the opening and retreated down the stairs when one of the guards stepped out. Better still. He left the door open in case anyone else needed to come here to pray, or the guards needed to retreat to safety.

Master Alcrew had never sent a message to the high Temple before, but Galt had taught him what to do, just in case anything happened to him. Galt was an old man -- older than Alcrew -- and had never doubted his own mortality. In fact, in the last few months before he disappeared, he had seemed more aware of it than before. The priest might have had a vision that he would not return home. Alcrew didn't like to think it, but no one could find Galt, and he'd never reached any of the villages on his trip.

Alcrew slowed as he crossed the room and gave a slight bow to the altar. No time for more, though he would have liked to stop and pray. Instead, he hurried to the plain wooden door to the right of the altar. Only Malin followed behind, curious to see a bit of magic he would never have been allowed to watch at another time.

Alcrew pushed open the second door and went into Galt's private rooms. No need for locks here where no one could enter without the consent of the magic present. Other rooms could be reached by a similar door to the left of the altar and there was even an extensive basement complex -- but all of those had been locked up and abandoned a hundred years ago or more. Little Ziven didn't need so large a complex.

The room inside, with one candle lit, looked neat and dusted despite how long Galt had been gone. Alcrew never let the place get dirty. Malin had helped do the cleaning work just yesterday morning. Now Malin looked around the room as though he'd never been here, his bright brown eyes almost lost behind a fall of gold and brown hair that needed trimming. The boy's thin face looked as pale as it had the first time that he'd set foot in here, three years ago.

"That one," Alcrew said and pointed to an ornate wooden box on a shelf to the side of the door. He went to the table and pushed the candle to the edge, the light flickering and shadows dancing everywhere. The room felt stifling, but he didn't try to open the shutters to the two small windows for fear the rats might come through after all.

Malin brought a box that was the size and shape of three very thick books, and carefully placed it on the table. The old maple wood had been polished to a glowing luster. The glyphs had been carefully carved and then filled with gold paint. There were worn marks along the lid; this was not a new box, having passed down through four priests even before Galt's very long residence in the position.

This was the Temple's own set of runes, unlike those that a priest made for himself. These had been part of the Ziven Temple for more than two hundred years, assigned to whatever priest held the position -- a sort of back up in case of a problem.

Alcrew carefully lifted the lid. Inside he saw the familiar white cloth embroidered with more glyphs and signs of power. He reached in and twitched back the edge before he sighed with relief. Malin sucked in his breath at the sight of a hundred or more neatly stacked dark rune stones, all of them glowing softly. They were ancient and had never entirely lost the cantankerous feel of Priest Trefin, who had served here before Galt. The man had never been happy with his backwater assignment, and though no one knew for sure, the villages had suspected he'd been sent away from the High Temple of the Sun for political reasons. Here he had stayed, a good enough priest, though he clearly had thought himself better than any of the locals.

Alcrew would have welcomed even that pompous bast -- he stopped himself with the reminder that he was still inside the Temple. He would have welcomed that unpleasant man back right now.

He stared down at the stacks of runes, seeing mostly symbols for animals and plants carved into small square pieces of brown limestone and each imbued with some magic with which it glowed. If Alcrew had known which rune represented rats, he'd have been tempted to do something unwise and use the magic in the stone to try to get control of the animals. However, he was saved from that temptation because of the few animal runes he saw, he couldn't have told a cat from a rat or a fox.

Instead, he picked up the one rune he did recognize because Galt had made certain he knew this one and always left it on top of one the stacks. The stone linked to Galt's central Temple and would carry a message back to the priests there.

Malin leaned in closer. "Is this safe?" he asked softly, a wise boy to recognize dangers over the lure of power.

"Safe enough," Alcrew mumbled. He picked up the stone and held it in his hand, welcoming the warmth. "Galt showed me how to do this years ago when he was too ill to even call for help. I did what he said, and the Temple sent a young priest to help for a while. The poor boy had never been out of the Temple before, and he could hardly wait to return."

"I remember him. I was just a child."

Alcrew suppressed a smile. Malin, at seventeen, thought himself a man already. How quickly they wanted to grow up.

The rune drew Alcrew's attention again. He wrapped his gnarled fingers around the stone and held it tightly while the stone grew warmer. He wasn't really feeling the magic, but rather the residue of heat it left behind. The warmth told him that the rune was still capable of one act of magic. He had to be careful and not waste the chance.

With his eyes closed, Alcrew focused on the runestone and leaned closer over his fist. "Rats," he said aloud and felt the stone pulse. "We have an infestation of rats here in Ziven. Priest Galt never came home this winter. We have rats everywhere. Please send help!"

The rune pulsed one more time before it went cold. Alcrew had hoped someone might answer like they had the last time, but Galt had said incoming messages were usually gathered and held by magic at the Temple.

With a sigh of relief, Alcrew carefully put the stone back in the box.

"Is that all?" Malin asked, trying to hide the disappointment in his voice.

"Not all, no. We have no idea if the message actually got through, though it felt as though it did," Alcrew said. He felt tired, which might have been the magic, but was more likely the troubles of the day catching up with him. "We have to take it on faith that if they do hear the message, they will send us a priest to help. Pick up the rune I just used, Malin."

Malin looked startled and then carefully reached into the box. He drew his hand back in haste when a spark leapt out at his hand.

"Ow! Why did it do that to me and not to you?"

"The runes don't know you," Alcrew said, brushing the cloth back into place before he put the lid back on the box. "Galt introduced us, so to speak so that in an emergency, I could do just what I did here. And yes, if you continue as my apprentice, you'll be introduced as well."

Malin nodded thoughtfully. Sometimes Alcrew believed the boy thought too much. No one that young should be so concerned with the what-ifs and whys of life.

"Is that why the Temple only opens to you and Galt?"

"Not entirely. The Temple has come to know me. I've been here for a long time, boy. The place trusts me. I was the one who first gave Galt access here, in fact. He didn't have a feel for the place yet."

Malin's eyes darted around the room with a new worry. "The building makes decisions."

"The magic in the building, the touch of the Gods," Alcrew answered with his own look around the room. "The Temple is ancient. Older than anything else in this region."

"Yes, sir," Malin said and seemed to take comfort in those words for some reason. Maybe it was the permanence of the place that had surely withstood other dangers. "And now we wait?"

"We will wait for the Temple to send someone, or until some stranger gets close enough to the village to see our problem and they send help. Put the box back."

Malin carefully placed it back on the shelf, unconsciously

wiping a little dust from the edge. He had always taken his work seriously. They left the room, closed the door behind them, and both paused to pray by the altar while the guards looked in from the open door.

"We are not helpless," Galt said suddenly with a glance around the large room. "Go tell the others to bring the women and children here. The rats cannot enter, and I think this will be the safest place. We also need to start moving food in here to keep the rats out of the supplies. I'll open the other rooms. We're in for a siege, my lad. A long one. Even if the Temple heard my call, I can't believe we will see anyone soon."

Malin stared out the door where rats still ran through the street. "I hope they have someone to send. I hope they have someone *powerful.*"

CHAPTER

THREE

Koya awoke, blinking slowly as his eyes focused on the familiar shelves in Kenning's small private office. Someone had placed him on the bench by the open window. From here, he could see several leather-bound manuscripts, a gathering of pretty rocks, and a shelf of holy carvings in stone and wood. Koya had always loved this room. The Most Holy had taken it over whenever he pretended to work, but the man was not here now.

Koya had a pillow under his head and a blanket over him. He accepted the peace and remained still as he listened to the chatter of birds outside. A slightly cool breeze smelling of dust and distant rain brushed past him.

Fool, Koya finally told himself. Fool and worse. Kenning had warned him to be careful around the Most Holy. His worry about the darkness no one else detected had overcome any small amount of good sense he'd ever possessed in his entire life.

Koya could feel the dark power still, gathering and growing a little each day. Something would happen soon and not anything good. If he alone felt the darkness growing, then it was up to him to do something to stop it. The Most Holy would not send help.

Koya started to sit up, but any movement of his right arm and leg proved to be just as painful as the last time, and he barely held to consciousness. He had thought the spell would have worn off by now!

Koya closed his eyes and breathed carefully, trying to call back the calm of a moment before. Then he became aware of a shadow standing over him. He looked up with a start of fear, something that hadn't happened since the first year he'd been here in this beloved Temple, having just escaped from the north and those who had tried to kill him.

He'd felt safe here. Koya didn't want that feeling to pass. He didn't want to mistrust everything he'd come to believe --

"Let me help you sit up," Kenning said and leaned forward, brooking no disagreement. "We must talk."

Koya didn't want to move, but Kenning wasn't going to listen to him. No surprise there; it seemed no one listened to him lately.

Kenning helped Koya sit and put the pillow at his back so that he almost felt comfortable, though oddly weak. Kenning brought a chair from the desk and sat down before him, his hands in his lap, and looking worried enough that Koya felt his heart miss several beats.

"We have a problem, Koya," he said softly.

"We?" he demanded, his temper starting to get the better of him again. Then he shook his head and calmed himself again. "What did he do to me?"

"I don't know," Kenning replied, calm still and his own

anger in check, though Koya saw a flash of emotion in the priest's eyes. "The Most Holy is very powerful, Koya. I'd even forgotten it, but he is the Guardian of the Gate, and Cedric can touch that place where the others sealed themselves away behind their magic wall. He's privy to powers that none of the rest of us know. Every priest in this Temple has come by to test the spell he put on you, and none of us can begin to unravel what he's done."

"You have to talk to him," Koya said and hated the sound of panic growing in his voice. He couldn't stop the feeling, though, nor the trembling that started with his hands and threatened to spread. "You have to get him to reverse the spell, Kenning. He can't leave me like this!"

Koya started to lift his right arm and fell back in a wave of agony and fear, unable to control his emotions.

"Drink this."

Koya looked up at Kenning who had crossed the room and come back with a goblet in hand. Koya was ready to curse and stopped himself. Kenning had warned him. Kenning hadn't done anything stupid. Koya started to reach for the goblet and stopped at the slightest painful twitch of his right arm; Koya took it in his left instead. The silver felt cool under his fingers, and he sipped the sweet cider. The taste lingered in his mouth, chasing away the sour taste of fear. Koya drank more, forcing calm through his mind. He finally handed the goblet back with a nod of thanks.

Kenning settled in the chair and sat the goblet on the floor. He leaned forward again. "Are you ready to listen to me this time?"

"Yes," Koya said and bowed his head, half in apology and half in acceptance.

"Good. I have talked to the Most Holy. I pointed out that what he did was far worse than you losing your temper."

Koya winced this time, both at the reminder of how

stupid he'd been and at the idea of Kenning saying such things to the Most Holy. "Did he react badly?"

"Oh, not as badly as he did with you," Kenning replied, but his face colored, so it must have been an unpleasant conversation. How could it have been anything different? "The Most Holy started to shout in rage, and then he stopped. He almost smiled. And he said he had not been the one who cast a spell on you --"

Koya stared, stunned by the impossibility of those words. "How could he claim such a thing when we all saw --"

"He said the gods themselves worked through him, and they left their mark to show your evil."

Koya still stared, feeling himself going cold and ill as he understood the depth of his problem. "If he doesn't admit that he had cast the magic ... if the Most Holy claims this as the work of the gods, then there is no way he will release me from the spell. Oh hell, oh hell."

"Calm Koya. Calm." Kenning put a hand carefully on Koya's shoulder -- the left one, because any touch on the right was painful, and Kenning understood the depth of the spell. "We're not done yet. And the magic will, eventually, wear off no matter what else happens."

"That might take years," Koya replied and tried to measure such time in his mind. The room had gone cold.

"Yes," Kenning agreed. At least he didn't lie. "However, some of us think we can dispel the power behind the spell, as long as the Most Holy isn't fixated on you. If you remain in his presence -- or even near him -- the Most Holy will reinforce the spell just with his wish. Obviously, we can't send the Most Holy away, so you are going on a journey, Koya."

Koya thought his heart would stop this time as he felt an old fear he hadn't experienced in years. "Going? You are sending me away?"

Kenning ignored the reaction except for a slight squeeze

of his fingers before he took his hand from Koya's shoulder. "This is a legitimate assignment and one that will suit you. There is a village that seems to have a problem --"

"I can't help anyone! Not like this!" He lifted his right arm, welcoming the pain this time. Kenning couldn't expect him to help others when he couldn't even cross the room on his own.

"*Listen to me.*"

Koya stopped moving, stunned by the tone, and let his aching arm rest in his lap. He said nothing of what came to his mind, so maybe he'd learned at least a little wisdom from his encounter with Cedric.

"Koya, you stumbled into the Temple ten years ago with your magic nearly fully-fledged. You were far more powerful than a normal acolyte would have been. We worked hard in those early years to help you learn control. We skipped most of the early exercises because they would have been dangerous in the hands of someone as powerful as you when you had so little control. However, you do know them, Koya. Lift your left hand call up a small light."

He almost refused, stubbornness trying to take hold again. However, Kenning watched and waited until, with a sigh, Koya lifted the left arm without pain, though it did tremble. That was a reaction to emotions and not weakness, though.

Koya paused, afraid to try any magic and learn he'd lost that gift from the gods. No, if the gods gave it to him, then Cedric couldn't take it away. He moved his fingers and whispered words, still half afraid --

The light came quickly, a flash of bright blue and yellow, glowing brightly.

"Good!" Kenning smiled with delight, which helped. "I had hoped your magic was unaffected. We'll do a couple more tests tonight, just to make certain of your abilities before you leave in the morning --"

"Morning?" The world seemed to drop out from under him again. He didn't want to leave this sanctuary to which he had fled so long ago. He wanted to go to his room and stay there until the spell went away. Yes, years if necessary. "I could go beg forgiveness of the Most Holy, Kenning. I would crawl there if necessary --"

"Oh, and I'm certain he would love to see you do so," Kenning replied, his face gone hard with anger this time. Kenning stared out the window for a moment, and Koya could see his friend regaining his self-control. A breeze blew past them, and a bee flew lazily through the room and out again before Kenning turned back. "Going to the Most Holy would win you nothing, Koya. He said the spell is the work of the Gods. By saying so, he made certain he could do nothing to help."

"What am I going to do, Kenning?" Koya felt fear surging again, the whirl of emotions taking a toll. He trembled this time, unable to stop.

"Listen to me, Koya. You are going to this village and help the people there."

"I can't help anyone!"

"Then you can no longer be a priest of the Temple of the Sun, can you? We are chosen to help others."

The words hit like a blow, and Koya fell back and lifted both hands -- despite the pain -- in a gesture of protest, unable to find the words to speak. Kenning couldn't turn him away now! Kenning wouldn't --

Kenning fetched the goblet from the floor and stood, crossing back to his desk, where he poured more cider and carried it back. Koya was no better for the moment of calm, and his hands trembled so much he didn't dare take the goblet.

His heart refused to settle this time, and the fear that Kenning would turn him out overrode any whisper of logic that said his friend would never do such a thing. What if the

Most Holy ordered Kenning to dismiss him from the Temple? What if the Most Holy crippled him with pain and then sent him out into the world?

"I'm sorry, Koya. I had to shock you into realizing things could get far worse unless we find a quick solution to get you away as long as Cedric is here," Kenning explained. He held out the goblet again, looking contrite, and Koya forced himself to calm down enough to take it and sip. "If the Most Holy heard you say you couldn't help others, he'd have every excuse for kicking you out the door."

Koya sipped again and then shook his head. "He's already said the gods have struck me down. What more does he need?"

"Something that the rest of us believe is true. If you say you can't help, it is so."

"They don't believe the Most Holy? You really don't believe what he said?" Koya asked. He hated how pathetic those words sounded, but fear of the Most Holy's sacred station had lingered in the back of his mind. The man was the most influential person in the Temple of the Sun, and inevitably some would believe him --

But not here. Not where they knew Koya.

"No one believes him, Koya, and least of all the Most Holy High himself. We can see it in his eyes every time he makes the claim, and I think he's going to learn, eventually, the price of his bigotry. You are going to this village, Koya. You will help them get rid of a few rats and remain there for a bit. The place is in the mountains. I know you've longed to return to the highlands for a while. Ziven is near the border, too. You having been born a Norter bastard won't mean anything to them."

Koya felt a ghost of a smile flicker across his face. He closed his eyes for a moment and focused not on his problems but instead on the part of him that had been touched by the gods; he was gifted, and he quickly found his inner peace once he looked for it. The gods had not really cursed him, after all.

"I am not opposed to going to this place, providing I can move at all." Koya shifted his arm, trying not to wince. "I think I would like it. I just don't know if I can help them, Kenning. I really don't."

Kenning walked across the room and came back with a cane. He held it out. "Let's do the one test we must before we go any farther with this plan. If you can't walk, then you can't go. That's not a good answer. I fear the Most Holy will demand that you go with him back to the capital to face charges based on nothing more than where you were bone. I saw him writing something out, which is why I am rushed, Koya --"

"I can't believe this keeps getting worse."

"It hasn't yet -- but we have to move before he can. I'm sorry, Koya. If I didn't know your innate strengths, I wouldn't even try this. I don't want you stripped from the Temple, even if I think I could eventually win you back. Stand. Keep the cane on the side opposite the injured leg."

He didn't argue this time. Understanding of the entire situation seeped through the panic and pain. He pushed himself up, wincing at the movement of the arm. The leg didn't seem as bad, though, and even stood a little weight.

"Maybe something to brace the knee," he said after a couple steps. "And a sling for my arm, so it doesn't move much."

"Yes. Good ideas." Kenning looked much relieved. "We'll get you through this, Koya. I am not giving you over to the Most Holy. The call for help from these people of Ziven is a gift of the gods, you know. It is a place I would have sent you anyway, because you are perfect for the job -- yes, even now. They lost their priest sometime over the winter. Galt was older than the Empire, I think. You can rid them of the rats and stay to offer some rites."

Koya took a few more steps. He felt better for it, in fact. Not helpless. "The Most Holy cannot stay here forever."

"Oh, he could if he wanted to," Kenning replied and covered a snarl with a shrug. "He's already spoken about remaining through the winter to be certain we have not been led from the true path. You wouldn't want to be here with him because he's not going to be happy. We are going to be so perfectly rigid in our rules that he'll be running back to the soft, comfortable Temple in the capital before autumn, let alone winter. I wonder how long he'll manage to live on gruel, rise at dawn for prayers to the sun and the gods, tend the gardens --"

"Oh, you wouldn't order him to, would you?" Koya said and thought that might be fun to see.

"As soon as you are on your way, I am going to pull out the rules of the order, and we are going to adhere to even the most out-of-date, unpleasant practices. Oh yes, I'll gladly suffer along with him, just to see the damned Most Holy get this shoved back into his face. And then I might just start demanding a look at his own Temple."

"Carefully, Kenning," Koya whispered. He came back and sat down, feeling less frantic now. Koya didn't want to go, but he couldn't stay. The mountains would be lovely, and as long as he didn't have to walk far, he thought he would be happy there for a few days while Kenning sorted out the trouble here. "I did this to myself --"

"You could have been wiser."

"And shown more humility."

"But neither would have helped," Kenning finally admitted. He sipped the cider this time and then handed the goblet over to Koya again. "Cedric came here intending to have you thrown out of the Temple, probably as the first step to something worse in your future. You gave him an easy answer for what he wanted, but he would have found one anyway. We just have to move before he can finish his plan."

The sun slipped low on the horizon, shadows growing across the room. Evening prayers would start soon. Koya felt his hand take tight hold of the cane as he prepared to go to the altar, even with the Most Holy there watching him. He might show physical weakness, but he wouldn't display weakness of spirit. That had never failed him.

When the bells rang. Kenning nodded, and together they walked through the shadowed stone corridors and finally to the central room and the altar, just as they had walked this path on so many other days. The others gave him looks of regret and worry, but Koya felt the same serenity he always did when he came into this room. The simple altar, surrounded by candles and glowing with power, filled the room with peace. Koya knelt there, his head bowed, whispering prayers with the others long before the Most Holy finally arrived.

He did not even glance at the man. The pain would pass. In the meantime, he had work to do that would help those in need and serve the gods.

CHAPTER

FOUR

Koya slowly made his way down the path that wound from the hilltop Temple of the Sun to the small town of Templeton below. His body had started to adjust; while the ache remained, the shock grew less, and he only had to stop twice along the mile-long trail. Kenning had found a way to wrap the right knee and ankle, and his arm rested in a sling. Koya still felt crippled, but he refused to let that fear win over him. He refused to let the Most Holy win.

Kenning walked with him, silent as they listened to the birds and the whisper of words from the townspeople. In one respect, Koya was glad to be leaving. The Most Holy had been late to prayers again, and although no one made anything of it, the man could not have missed the looks of disdain.

The bag slung over Koya's shoulder felt heavy, though he took only a few possessions; he owned very little, after all. He shifted the strap with a slight shrug and kept moving, hearing more and more sounds from below. Templeton was not a large town, and he'd enjoyed helping the people there once they had gotten used to him. He hoped he had no trouble at Ziven, though Kenning was right about one crucial fact: they were close to the border where northern blood would be more common.

"You shouldn't have come down here with me," Koya finally said. "He's going to be looking for you -- and probably for me, too. This isn't safe."

"Sometimes, one must court danger in the path of doing what is right, Koya."

"I can walk down the path."

Kenning said nothing for the next few steps that took them around a curve and past Koya's favorite ancient tree. They paused there. "I need to see you able to walk from the Temple to the road below," Kenning admitted. "I need to know, for my own peace of mind, my friend. Then I can face the Most Holy with the calm that I will need."

Koya nodded and focused on making sure he didn't fall for his own sake as well as Kennings. They walked a few more steps in silence while he listened to the familiar sounds of birds and squirrels. A rabbit darted across the path, and somewhere far outside the Temple grounds, a dog barked frantically while people yelled. These were the sounds he had come to know; this was home.

Koya had to go somewhere else. That wasn't the worst of the problems, really.

Koya stopped within view of the gate, and Kenning looked at him, worried perhaps that he'd lost his nerve.

"Do you really believe that you sometimes have to court danger to do right?" Koya asked.

"Yes."

He lifted his head and stared into Kenning's face. "Then, I

did the right thing. Something evil is growing out there, Kenning. Something dangerous is lurking just beyond our borders. I can feel it, even still."

Kenning blinked several times and then bowed his head, as though he had forgotten the larger picture. Or had he never believed? Koya couldn't be certain, and he decided not to ask. He had warned them, even the Most Holy. Koya could do nothing more, expect to go to the little village of Ziven, and help rid them of some troublesome rats.

Koya took the last steps forward and pushed open the gate with the edge of the cane, determined to prove he wasn't helpless both to Kenning and to himself. He almost paused before he stepped out into the open where others would see him, but he had never been vain, and this wasn't the time to fear what others would think.

People gave him startled looks as he limped past the gate and down to the road. They'd gotten used to him, even though he was from the north and still held a bit too much of his old accent, though he'd tried very hard to lose it over the years.

He hoped the locals never learned why he walked with a cane today. He did not want them to anger the Most Holy and put themselves in danger. The less he made of his current problem, the better.

"I hope the coach isn't late today," he said softly and barely caught himself from tripping on the rough stone walk. Kenning hovered nearby, reaching out when he faltered and pulling back again. "You might as well relax, Kenning. If I do fall, I had better learn how to get back up again."

Kenning gave a reluctant nod and then frowned. "Koya ... please don't be bitter. You have always served joyfully, from the first day you came to the Temple. Perhaps you have never been really tested, Koya --"

"Never had my faith tested?" He looked at Kenning with disbelief. "Not even when I gave up everything I was to go south and join the Temple? You know, from the number of times you have said something like this since yesterday, I am starting to think you believe I needed this."

Kenning paled, his eyes wide and his face shocked. "No! Gods of all, Koya -- I never meant anything like that. I think -- I think I'm trying to convince myself there is a reason the gods *allowed* this to happen."

Kenning meant those words, and Koya felt a new pang of worry that overlaid all the anger, pain, and fear that troubled him. He stopped and leaned against the stone wall, ignoring the morning dampness that seeped through the edge of his blue robe.

"Don't let Cedric get more from this than he already has," Koya said softly, glancing to make certain no one stood nearby. "We cannot blame the gods for what he's done. I certainly haven't. The Most Holy has just as much choice as you and I have had in our lives. Shall we say we made our own decisions, but he didn't make his when he did this? I will not blame the gods for his bad actions."

"Yes, you're right."

This was like many conversations they'd had. Koya would miss them over the next few days. "I had the choice to shut up, too," he reminded Kenning and then frowned. "I can't remember when I have ever been so rude. Ha. Maybe the gods did have their hands in this. Maybe they needed me to go to Ziven because they really, really dislike rats."

He made Kenning laugh just as they heard the coach coming and saw it take the turn at the edge of town. Kenning looked worried again, but he only gave a nod when the coach stopped. Koya climbed up and settled onto the hard interior bench.

For the moment, at least, he sat alone inside. He put the cane where he could reach it and let his hand rest on the satchel where his clothing and runes were packed. Koya had spent the night searching his soul for understanding. Before the dawn, he had realized that nothing lasted forever, not even the corrupt wishes of a petulant man with too much power.

The driver climbed up top, the carriage bouncing slightly. Koya tried not to wince.

"Time to go, sirs. Make your blessings, and we'll be on our way."

"Yes, good idea," Kenning said and stepped back. Then he did, truly, bless Koya; his hand raised, and he a whisper of words (one never shouted at the gods), and the magic swept over him, soothing his soul. Kenning was a priest of true and extraordinary power.

Before Koya could say anything, the coach began to move with a quick jerk that set him falling back against the hard seat, pain redoubled for a moment. By the time he recovered, he could no longer see Kenning and regretted the loss already. The road turned slightly, and he caught a glimpse of the Temple gate and the stone portico, high up the hill, the white stone sheathed in green trees and morning light.

Paradise, Koya thought, just as he had the first day he stumbled into town, having walked for weeks, following the call of the Gods to a place of safety. He resented the Most Holy for having tainted that feeling for him.

Koya hadn't rested the night before, and now the movement of the rolling wheels lulled him into snatches of sleep caught between painful ruts and potholes. He felt better for the rest, though, and the long morning alone with the silent driver helped settle his nerves. They passed through several small hamlets where the coach barely slowed, and no new travelers boarded. That would change, he knew, at Partla, which was a larger town and always busy. Koya had reconciled himself to the idea of other passengers. He'd always been gregarious, and too much time to himself only made his problems seem worse.

Coming into Partla woke him with a cacophony of sounds: men and women shouted their wares from street-side shops, children ran and screamed at each other as they played on the village green and somewhere he couldn't clearly see, a group of dogs barked and growled viciously.

He didn't like that last sound and lifted his left hand -- getting used to using it already -- and wished the animals calm and to disperse. They grew silent a heartbeat later, and he liked to think that was his work, though he couldn't be sure. He'd always been good with animals, though.

The road was worse in town, the stones in bad need of repair. They passed row after row of shacks where nervous people watched the carriage. Koya gritted his teeth, giving a sincere prayer of thanks when they came to a slow stop before a large stucco building. He looked out the window, noting the rush of people everywhere. The town had recently started growing after an impressive silver strike in the hills nearby and was now five times the population of Templeton. They had only a single priest and a small Temple, but that was likely going to grow soon along with the town.

While Koya liked people, crowds were a different problem. He'd never been comfortable in groups of strangers. He watched the people moving along the edge of the road with misgivings.

The building beside the coach looked like a haven from the people and the dust. The façade had been painted in pale blues and greens, a well-kept place, with a dozen small glass windows at street-level and an open, inviting door.

He'd never been to Partla before, and the place appeared far different from the quiet, peaceful Templeton. Everything seemed alive, loud, and energetic. He'd grown up in such a city to the north, though he rarely thought about those days.

The driver, having secured the reins, leapt down beside the door and hastily reached to help Koya down. Koya accepted the help with gratitude. The ride had been challenging for him, and parts of his body ached that had nothing to do with the spell.

Koya went slowly up the five steps to the door that stood well above what was likely a muddy street sometimes. He could smell food from here.

"We'll be here for an hour or so, priest, while I get the horses changed and eat a bit meself," the driver said as he came up with Koya. "There's good food for travelers inside there if you care for lunch. We won't be stopping for a long time after this, so best have a meal."

"Thank you. That sounds like a good idea."

Koya wasn't sure why the driver stayed with him ... until they stepped inside the main room. People went quiet, except for a whisper he had not heard in a long time. Norter.

They were even closer to the border than Templeton. The driver, however, waved over someone who clearly worked here. The tall, bald man came closer, his eyes narrowed.

"What have we here, then?"

"Come in from Templeton, Carter," the driver said with a pat on Koya's arm. "Priest Kenning himself brought him out to the carriage and blessed him on the journey."

Carter looked at him with a quick nod, no doubt seeing the blue robes of a priest for the first time. "Ah, you be that priest, then. The one what caused such a stir, a decade or so ago when you turned up."

"You know about me? You remember?" he said, stunned by the idea.

"Come take a chair," the man said, less worried now. "Fresh bread and cheese?"

"Yes, thank you." He bowed his head in thanks to the driver and followed Carter to a nice table by the window. The seats had stuffed pillows, a comfort after the hard bench of the coach. People stared, but he ignored them and leaned back, resting. He wouldn't be here for long.

Carter brought back the food and refused any coin for it. "No, sir. Priests always eat free here. And more so you, since I was so ill-graced when I met you at the door."

"There's no need --"

"It's my place and my rules," the man said with a bright smile. "Ah, and there's Brother Slade. I wondered if he'd be about!"

Koya smiled to see the man coming through the door, the priest highlighted by the light for a moment before he began to cross the room at a deliberate pace that seemed at odds with the blue robe he wore. Slade was a big man, older than Koya by a decade or more, and probably the son of a farmer. He settled into the chair across from Koya, which seemed too small for his big frame.

"Koya, lad," Slade said and reached out a hand. Koya clasped it awkwardly with his left hand. "Gods of all. I heard about your ... accident. Kenning messaged me this morning and said you would be this way, and I should check and make certain you were up to the rest of the journey. If not, you can stay here with me."

Koya looked at the man, startled by the idea. He was almost tempted to at least rest a day or two more -- but he shook his head. "It might be wise --"

"Kenning told me what happened. Don't worry. I've had to deal with the Most Holy before." His voice had lowered to a near whisper as he leaned forward. For a moment, something very dark crossed his face and then disappeared again in a shrug. "I've reasons of my own to avoid him. Why do you think I didn't go back to Templeton for the Blessing of his presence? It's not like it's a long journey."

"I hadn't thought about it," he admitted. "From the moment the man stepped into the Temple, I knew there was going to be trouble. At least it's not just me that he hates."

"He is a powerful man with bad manners and too much power." Slade sat back in the chair and sighed, clearly letting his own anger go. "Stay with me awhile, Koya."

He considered accepting the offer but found himself shaking his head. "No, I'll go on. I need the journey for many reasons, Slade. The power of the spell seems to be less already. I want to go the rest of the way."

"You are pale as a ghost, Koya. You don't need to suffer through this --"

"But I do need to accept and to keep working. It would be too easy to rest, Slade. It would be addictive. So, I'm going on to Ziven."

Slade gave a nod of acceptance and poured them each water from a pitcher a woman brought. Carter brought them more food, including bowls of soup. It smelled wonderful.

"Going to Ziven?" Carter asked. "Then you be going to help with the rats?"

"You've heard about the rats?" Koya asked, surprised that news of something so inconsequential should have reached this far.

"Oh, yes. Had a trader through here early yesterday, said he couldn't get through to Ziven because of the rats," Carter said. He paused, frowning. "Something of a storyteller is old Isaac, so I didn't take him seriously. But if you are going --"

"I'm sure it's not anything so dire," Koya said and even tapped his cane, hanging on the edge of the table. "They would have sent someone capable if it was true trouble. Is Isaac still around?"

"No, sorry. He went on yesterday."

"Ah well," Koya said with a wave of his hand. "Thank you."

Carter nodded and headed off to deal with others. When Koya looked up, Slade was staring at him, pensive and worried.

"I'm going," Koya said before Slade could say anything more. "I am probably the best person for the job anyway, you know. I've always had a good touch with animals."

"Like stopping a dog fight when you came into town, and without even seeing it? Oh yes, I felt that one. Good work, too."

"Thank you. I'll go on, and if this is more trouble than I can manage, I'll send a message to the Temple."

Slade graciously gave way in the argument, and without ever saying Koya wasn't capable of the trip or the work. He did still look worried, but likely because Koya had trouble slicing the cheese. Neither of them said anything about it.

Slade saw him off on the carriage in much the same way Kenning had at Templeton. Others were traveling with him now. The couple eyed him with obvious suspicion, but the older woman appeared to accept him with a better grace. Her servant even helped him into the coach before the man went up top to ride with the driver. No one seemed interested in conversation, so Koya settled into his corner, keeping his aching arm in his lap, and slept again as best he could.

The first hour proved pleasant enough until the couple began to complain about the roads, the weather, and the general sloth of priests. Koya pretended to sleep through their incessant complaints, and he wasn't sorry when the couple took their leave at a small village.

"They were not very polite," the older woman said as the coach pulled away. She sounded relieved to have them gone as well and now took the bench across from him. For a while, they would both have more room.

"I have learned to ignore people who are so unhappy with life that they'll see nothing good in the world." Koya tried not to wince at a slight movement of his arm. "We'll have a far nicer journey without people who dislike everything they see."

"Are you really a priest?" she asked suddenly, head tilted

to the side, a strand of grey hair escaping her hood of silver and silk. A few gems decorated her clothing, and he wondered what a woman of such means was doing traveling almost alone and by coach.

"Oh, yes." He fished out the emblem of his station, the gold catching a little light and the chain making a soft bell-like sound. Magic made and magically imbued: this was a sign that none but priests could carry.

She leaned forward to look at the circle, the rays of gold wire representing the power of the gods and the sun. She leaned back with one eyebrow raised. "That is a lot of rays for someone as young as you."

He smiled despite the little jab at his age. "I am blessed."

"And injured."

"Unfortunately, yes, but still blessed." He realized the truth of those words.

They had a pleasant conversation about the countryside, the weather, and the world. She didn't seem to care that Koya came from the north, and looking at her, he wondered if perhaps she had some northern blood of her own. He was sorry to say farewell at her village, and the coach felt empty.

He looked out to say one more goodbye, but the woman was nowhere to be found. A small chill went through him, but then a feeling of peace. Koya had the feeling that he'd been tested.

He slept once more and woke again when they stopped, surprised to find full night had come upon them. He heard the boisterous sounds of an inn, but out his window, he could only see open fields and a few trees -- apple, he guessed -- tucked up by a low wall. The world smelled of spring and life; they had left the edge of the drylands behind and were moving up into the highlands.

The driver came around the side of the coach, but he was already out and on his feet.

"We'll be spending the night here, sir," he said with a bob of his head. The man had driven all day and looked dusty and tired. "I'll go in with you. They're not used to priests traveling through this area, though it happens now and again."

The place had been rowdy when he went in and calmed down immediately. Koya gave a quick blessing, ate a light meal, and retired to the room the innkeeper provided. He'd had a long, hard day of travel and had two more ahead of him. He ached, but he thought the ache of the spell might have eased. He really couldn't tell.

He did sleep well, though.

CHAPTER

FIVE

The next morning, as the travelers prepared to board the carriage, Koya wandered down by one of the apple trees. There were two loud and anxious children in the group, and keeping away as they raced around, even startling the horses, seemed wise. The parents had been rude and not pleased with the idea of a priest in their midst, so Koya kept his distance as long as he dared.

Stablemen began preparing the carriage for the day. Four other people milled around, which meant they were in for a tight fit. Koya tried not to think about his arm and leg being jostled by people who didn't know any better. He would manage.

Koya started to limp across the yard to join them when he heard an odd sound, like a distant caw from a very loud group of birds. The sound grew progressively closer --

"All Gods save us! Dragonkin!" A man shouted and

pointed down the trail to the east. The others raced back into the building where shutters were already closing with loud bangs. Koya took a faltering step in that direction and stopped. He'd never make it across the wide yard before the Dragonkin were on them. Instead, he flattened himself to the side of a substantial oak tree and waited. Even the stablemen took the horses and carriage back to the cover of the barn, moving so quickly that the horses protested.

Koya worried for a moment, and then he wondered if this was so bad. Such Dragonkin processions took place every few years, and Koya counted himself lucky to be here when one went through. They did not go through Templeton, or else he probably would have found a way to watch them before now.

Koya glanced around the side of the tree, watching the high poles and fluttering banners of the Dragonkin as they neared. He quickly counted a dozen different flags, all bright reds, greens, blues, and yellows. Dust rose to obscure the scene in a brown haze, but a moment later, Koya could see the first of the people.

Many claimed the Dragonkin weren't people at all and never would be, no matter what magic had made of them. Myth said they had been dragons in another age, but they'd suffered an ancient curse by a powerful mage who took away their dragon forms and made them human. Another tale said this was the work of the Gods to make them equal to the humans whom they had oppressed. Koya had even heard that the Dragonkin claimed to have made the choice themselves to fit into the changing world where humans had become more prevalent than magical beings.

If the last were true, the change hadn't worked. They still did not fit in.

While the other magical beings had gone through The Dark Gate and into the Forbidden Valley, sealing themselves away from humanity hundreds of years ago, the Dragonkin had remained. As they drew nearer, Koya could see that while the Dragonkin had assumed human shape, they were not human. As they came up the last rise beside the inn, Koya could clearly see what drove the two peoples apart.

The Dragonkin moved steadily forward, the ranks filled with tall people -- thin, and oddly colorful. A quick count showed about two hundred in the group. Hair, looking more akin to feathers, rose in bright arrays on each head -- blue here, gold there, a striking emerald green on one in the middle. She -- yes, he could tell the genders were as well defined as with humans -- stood at least a foot taller than him, even without the shock of hair that rose like a crest above her narrow face. Her eyes were large, her nose and mouth small. The others were much the same, an array of long necks, narrow shoulders, long arms, and slender legs. The Dragonkin people wore close-fitting clothing that appeared to be knitted armor and fit like a woolen shirt, though it sparkled with silver and gold. They wore weapons, too, including swords longer than any Koya had ever seen, but then they had the longer bodies -- and arms -- to use them.

They all carried the famous -- or infamous -- Dragonkin bows. Koya had heard that each bow had a personality, and no two were alike. The last, at least, appeared to be true. Koya saw each bow had its own design and runes, and Koya discerned some with the shapes of animals carved into the broad curve of wood. They were longer than any human could likely draw, and the power behind those long pulls could put an arrow straight through a wooden wall.

Or straight through a human.

The fletching on the arrows matched the color of the hair for the person carrying them. Odd that no one had mentioned that in the past, but Koya filed the information away, intending to add it to some notes back at the Temple where they favored such little tidbits of knowledge.

The Dragonkin marched on while keeping beat to the pad of drums from somewhere in the line. He couldn't see the end yet. Nor were they making the cawing sound of earlier. He wondered if that wasn't a way to scare the humans out of their path. It had certainly worked here.

As the first line neared, those in the front turned as one to stare at him. The suddenness of the move took Koya so much by surprise that he didn't even think to step behind the tree. They slowed.

The emerald-haired woman gave him a nod, and he returned the gesture; magic calling to magic, he realized. They didn't stop, and he watched her head turn at an unnatural angle to look back at him, more flexible than a human's neck. Something else to note.

They kept going, moving a little faster now. Koya saw a blur of colors, and then a group with particolored hair, all of them carrying banners. Behind them came the drummers, their beat-matching the marching feet so perfectly that he couldn't be sure which mimicked the other.

Koya felt gifted by the Gods to have seen such a spectacle. This moment broadened the world he had watched from the Temple where he'd been hiding for so long. Koya was glad to be here. He was about to take a step back when the second group arrived, moving out of the dust of their larger companions.

Lesslings.

Koya hadn't seen them behind the taller Dragonkin. The creatures came into view, some of them running on all fours, some striding along on two legs, though they looked nothing even remotely human. The scaled bodies, long-reptilian heads, and clawed hands and feet plainly showed their lizard ancestry. Glossy black scales covered most of their bodies, and they were long-necked and squared mouths. The Lesslings reminded Koya of the much smaller black monitor lizards of home.

But wrong ... they were just wrong, and the sight of the twenty or so creatures marching with the Dragonkin sent the kind of chill through Koya that others seemed to feel at the view of Dragonkin itself. He even took a stumbling step backward --

The movement drew every Lessling head to turn in his direction. Yellow eyes narrowed as brown slit tongues danced into the air before the long snouts. Hisses rose among the group, and they slowed, a couple already moving out of the line and towards Koya.

Koya had nothing but the cane to protect himself. He leaned against the tree and raised it, thinking he was about to be the cause of a significant incident no matter what happened now --

Emerald, the woman from the first line of Dragonkin, suddenly arrived and faced the creatures down with a set of barking and hissing orders that no human voice could have made. Lesslings fell back into place in haste, and the entire group began to move faster. She waited, her back to him until the last of the creatures had passed. He could see how the crown of green hair grew longer in the back and seemed so fine that the slightest breeze sent it fluttering. Her shoulders, set in a steady straight line, showed delicate bones leading down to thin arms. Standing just behind her, he could see that the top of his head barely reached her neck.

The Lesslings went onward with the sound of hisses and claws on the dirt and rock. He could see the slits of yellow eyes still turned his way, and he didn't move from behind Emerald. He wasn't a fool.

The entire group passed and disappeared in a haze of dust before Emerald turned and looked at him with large green eyes -- catlike slits for the pupil. Not human: that was even more evident standing this close to one.

"Never show weakness around us, human," she said, her green eyes narrowing as she looked him over. Her accent was unlike any he'd heard before, but she spoke the language well. "Not before those of the Dragonkin nor to the Lesslings. It is our way to go for the weak and injured."

She glanced at the cane in his hand, then back into his face. Her green eyes seemed too bright and the face too narrow; for a moment, Koya felt what it must be like to be a mouse standing before a hawk.

She bowed her head. Koya returned the gesture, all perfectly civilized before she turned and hurried to catch up with her group. She passed the Lesslings with long-legged strides that quickly took her to the front of the line.

Only then did Koya sigh with relief. Maybe this hadn't been wise, standing and watching as they passed. He could have remained hidden behind the tree, though they might have sensed him anyway. This moment of curiosity had come very close to starting the kind of trouble that led to long wars.

The encounter was also something Koya would never forget. Blessed, he thought and smiled.

With the strangers finally gone, humans -- and dogs -- began to appear again. They slipped out of doorways and peered out partly opened windows as though they feared members of the Dragonkin still lurked in the shadows.

A boy started to dart away from the building towards him, but his mother grabbed him back, a look of fright turned towards Koya as though he'd suddenly sprouted Dragonkin hair of his own. They might be wary of him, but he'd deal with it. He walked slowly back to the inn while the others milled about, anxious and worried.

The carriage arrived from the barn not long afterward and with a new driver for the day. The man's age-lined face didn't show any of the worries that the passengers did as they filed past Koya, who waited patiently while the group loaded in --

five now, which meant they would be even more crowded.

"Maybe want to ride up top with me, priest?" the driver said, noting his reluctance to climb in with the others.

"That would be wonderful. Thank you." Koya prepared himself for the uncomfortable climb to the top, but he didn't have much trouble and settled in comfortably enough. Being on the upper bench allowed him to avoid the two children who already alternated between yelling and crying. He didn't want to think how long that would go on.

Koya took a deep breath of air as they left the little village, and the road dipped into the low hills and up again, aiming towards a long stretch of steppe lands beyond. He could see the faint shapes of mountains far beyond, an odd view that tried to pull him home. They snaked their way through a short, narrow valley and then up a rather steep hill and finally into flatland that stretched on ahead.

Hawks flew in circles as they passed: very many of them and in large groups, which Koya had never seen before. He watched for a while and then saw the driver lifting a hand to shield his eyes and nodded.

"That happens every time the Dragonkin come through here," he said. "Birds act odd, they do. Won't see little ones for a few days, and the raptors all act like they need to band together against danger. Kinda' unnatural, all of it."

"You've been here when they came through before?" Koya asked, both curious and hopeful for more information.

"Yes. They come every decade or so, heading towards the capital, apparently ta' swear allegiance to the Queen."

"But you don't think that's the real reason," Koya said noting both the words and the tone. He shifted a little trying to get comfortable, but still found this far better than what he could hear from inside the carriage.

"I don't know," the man admitted. "But seems a long journey for no real good reason, don't you think? Not like the

Queen, or anyone else, is likely to trust them. At the Inn, there's always talk about how they be sizing us up for invasion -- but that makes no better sense to my mind. Why'd they always take the same path then? Seems to me they'd want to see more than some backwater inns and rundown farms."

"Good points," Koya agreed.

"It worried and thrilled me when I was younger, thinking there might be a war with the old enemy again after so long. But I've seen them pass through three times now, and never with a bit of trouble. I'm older now. I wouldn't wish for a war."

Koya, who had seen skirmishes back when he'd been growing up as a Norter, gave a frantic and emphatic nod of agreement. He tried not to think about how close he had come to starting that war. He'd been a fool and shook his head, trying to get that worry out of his mind. "So, do you have your own ideas of why they go so often to the capital of the human lands?"

"My grandda' -- him long dead now -- said they went because the capital is built on their own holy ground, and they still go to say prayers at the place of their old Temple."

Koya looked his way, intrigued by the fascinating thought. "That's something I'll try to look into when I get a chance."

"If you find it be true, send back this way with the answer, will you?" he said and gave a smile with several teeth missing. "They use ta say my grandda' was a fool, thinking about such things, trying to learn stuff what had nothing to do with his life. But he was a smart man, he was, and I always listened to him tell the tales by the fireside at night. Only suitable for children, the others would say ... but I think maybe he passed on knowledge when others didn't know it."

"He sounded like a wise man. I'll get you word if I learn it's true."

"Names Teldin. I work out of the inn, so you can always

send word there. I can read a bit, too -- grandda' found I liked it and taught me." Teldin shook his head, apparently at the thought of better days. He'd be a grandda' as well now, and Koya thought he probably told such tales around the fire as his own grandfather had in that past age. "You being a priest and all, I thought you might be interested in such things. So, what made you stay and watch them go by when all sane people ran?"

"I could pretend that I couldn't run because of my injuries," Koya said. "But I won't lie. By the time I even thought of getting out of sight, it was too late. I was already caught. I longed to understand something of a legend, I suppose."

Apparently, he gave the right answer. Tedlin nodded. "Where are you headed?"

"Ziven."

"Not much a place for legends, unless you be interested in rats these days."

"So, I hear. You been there?"

"Not lately."

They talked about many things, he and Teldin; about the world, the weather, Dragonkin, and rats. The day went too quickly, and Koya was sorry when they stopped at a rundown inn in a village where nothing looked any better. Wilon -- Koya had never heard of the place and didn't like what he saw.

"Get yourself a room," Teldin said softly as he helped Koya down and before he got the luggage for the others. "Don't trust the common room here."

Koya nodded his thanks. He paid dearly for the room, but he was grateful for it when late that night he heard a fight break out down below. He moved his bed -- what there was of it -- up against the door, no easy job when his arm and leg ached. The pain was not so bad as before, though. Getting far away from the Most Holy helped.

People tried to sneak into his room twice that night, but the bed against the door saved him. A slight spell kept him from the infestation of insects in the bedding, too, so he slept rather well, despite not being comfortable.

They were much closer to the border here. This area had always been a wild place, though not entirely lawless. Koya didn't like what he saw, and he'd report it back to the Temple as soon as possible. The local lord would want to get some guards out this way, if possible. If not, the crown might have to step in.

As he stepped out of the building, Koya felt the problem growing in the north again, and he said his prayers with more fervor than usual.

Koya was only a few hours from Ziven and would be there probably before noon. A good night's rest would have been helpful, but given the trouble he'd heard, Koya considered himself lucky to have gotten through the night without his neck slashed. Teldin bade him farewell, which was nice. He felt as though he wasn't completely alone out in this strange place. He took the next carriage on to Marchland with no one inside except him. Koya was only about ten miles from his destination now. He looked forward to reaching Ziven and getting some rest. He would be there soon.

Or so he thought.

CHAPTER

SIX

"No, sir." The boy twisted his battered hat in his hands and moved from foot-to-foot as though he feared a curse and would try to outrun it. He even glanced at the barn's opening and back again. "No carriages, no wagons, no horses. Nothing goes on to Ziven. It's the rats, you see."

"Yes, I know about the rats," Koya replied and tried to sound reasonable, though he had begun to lose his patience and maybe his temper. He reigned both in with what he hoped at least looked like a sincere smile. "The rats are the reason I'm going there to help take care of the problem."

"Huh." The boy looked Koya over -- no more than twelve, but obviously someone who was used to running the little livery in town. His eyes lingered on the cane. "You think you can help."

The boy had apparently gotten over his fear of a curse,

though when he looked back into Koya's face, a hint of worry ran through his hazel eyes again. He started fidgeting from foot-to-foot once more.

"The Temple sent me to take care of this problem," Koya replied. He had begun to doubt the rat problem existed. Koya had only a few more miles to Ziven. He had found nothing out of the ordinary, except for a marked lack of rats rather than too many. "And that is where I am going."

"Not in a carriage or on horseback," the boy said.

"Fine."

Koya turned and walked back out of the barn and into fresh air filled with the scent of pine. Home, he thought, with an odd wistfulness he would never have expected. He'd come close to being murdered before he left the northern highlands where his family lived and had never felt an urge towards home before. He hadn't thought about the old scar on the back of his right shoulder, where his uncle had swung an ax, trying to take off Koya's head. Magic had deflected the weapon and scared the others enough that he'd been able to run, even wounded. Koya had kept running until he left his past and the Damara far behind. He'd never looked back. Koya couldn't begin to imagine what his life would have been in the north, even without magic.

Koya realized he still loved the area, even if he feared the people. He no longer thought of the place as Damara, the winter lands. Most of the southerners in Kasprin called the odd alliance of scattered tribes the Norters, a term that covered the entire mountains and beyond. He'd become accustomed to it, now that Norter had drifted from rude slur to common slang, just a shorter name than the Northern Tribes.

Except when used by a few like the Most Holy who held to old angers.

Oh, there had been times when he missed the cold of

winter and counted himself a fool for doing so. He'd lived more than a decade in the dry plain of Kasprin, where the rains came soft and sweet in spring, but the rest of the year turned dry, and dust blew like the snow had at home.

He shoved those thoughts away. No winter snow here, and very little dust, either. The path out of town towards Ziven was well-marked and well-traveled. Early spring flowers dotted the hillsides, and though the trail went uphill, it wasn't a bad walk. Koya had to rest often, his leg aching worse, but not so much that he couldn't go on. He stopped at the top of each rise, catching his breath, letting the pain ease, and listening to the world around him.

Here Koya finally began to get the feel of something out of place, though he couldn't quite guess what it might be yet. Rats? Maybe, but he hadn't seen any so far, and he was already nearly halfway to the village.

Koya glanced up at the higher mountains, still some ways off, and for a moment, he wished he could climb there and touch the snow again. Sled down the hills into the valleys, gather wood and watch for owls in their trees -- harbingers of danger, those owls that could fly like ghosts through the night.

He smiled a little at the thought and then started back along the trail towards Ziven, which he decided would be trek enough for him. He really wasn't up to mountain climbing, and there was no other way he could have gone to sneak a look at his old home. The roads would be too well patrolled.

On the other side of the hills stood a lovely stone bridge arching over a pleasant little stream. Koya paused at the edge, uncertain why. The bridge was certainly sturdy enough. He started across --

The force of *wrongness* hit Koya so suddenly that he almost went to his knees despite his cane. He grabbed at the railing, gasping for breath as his vision clouded and panic alone got him to take a step back --

The feeling went away.

There, at the far edge of the stream, he'd found an intense wall of unnatural magic. Koya stood still, letting the cool mountain breeze brush over him, washing away the taint of what he'd felt. He needed to be clear-headed. Koya wondered why he hadn't listened to anyone on the way here. Everyone had said there was a problem, but he simply had not believed it because the Temple had no real sign except for one message about rats.

Someone should have felt this wall. For a moment, Koya wondered if this might not be the trouble that he'd been feeling all along -- but no, he could still sense that problem somewhere to the North, and not very close.

Koya hadn't taken the problem seriously because he hadn't felt it. Too much pride; he admitted as much now as he faced something so odd and distasteful. There had been something dark to the feel of that magic.

He still saw no rats.

With his hand carefully held out, Koya felt for the invisible wall, touched it, and drew back in haste again because it still felt wrong. It would not stop him -- he could have walked through the last time if he hadn't been caught by surprise. However, this magical wall spoke of more power than he'd realized he would face, and Koya was not prepared to take on anything serious.

So, should he turn around and go back to Marchtown and then wait for another priest to come and take care of the real trouble? What did that make him? Nothing more than a scout, and no one the others could depend on against any critical problem.

Koya prepared to go on.

Before he passed through that wall, though, he had to warn the others that this truly did represent a magical concern. He took a few steps away from the bridge, cleared a fallen log of insects and frogs, and sat, making sure the cane didn't slide away. Then he pulled his small pack around to his lap and found his rune box.

It settled nicely into Koya's lap, a familiar weight, and a welcome reminder of his powers given the kind of trouble he faced here. A touch of his hand on the edge of the lid was enough for it to pop open. Within sat row upon row of white stone runes, rare stone and rare power. He'd made them himself, and they answered to his presence with a soft glow and a slight hum of power.

The rune on the top right corner represented the Temple. He had made certain he could easily find that one in case he needed Kenning's help. Now he tuned the rune specifically to his friend and not simply to anyone at the Temple as most would have done. He didn't want to accidentally call upon the Most Holy or any of his traveling companions. Kenning did not answer the slight tingle he would feel from the crystal in his office, but the stone would hold a quick message.

"Kenning, sir, there's a bigger problem than we thought," he said. Careful because someone might hear the words. "I am only a couple miles from the town and just found a stream used as a magical barrier, and there's something bad on the other side. People have been telling me that Ziven is filled with rats." He stopped and caught his breath, but held tight to the connection, despite the drain. "I'm going on. I'll let you know what I find."

He closed his cold hand around the rune and felt the connection drift away. Koya had hoped to hear Kenning say he'd send more help because, despite getting this far, Koya wasn't prepared for serious trouble. The message would wait for Kenning to enter his office. Maybe his friend would contact him later if he could through that barrier.

Koya had trouble getting back to his feet, and he stopped once he stood, uncertain ... but no, he had to go on. He couldn't walk away and leave these people in trouble. Something had purposely turned the rats against the town, and that meant they needed him more than he had expected.

Before Koya put the box of runes back into his pack, Koya pulled out the one that represented rats and the one he had just used to contact Kenning. They might be handy if he ran into trouble, though he still couldn't be sure what would work on the other side of the stream. He carefully put both in the small pouch on his belt where he could get to them as quickly as possible. He thought about holding them in his left hand inside the sling, but he didn't want to risk dropping either. Koya went prepared, as though he could be ready for something like this, even at better times.

Koya took a deeper breath and stepped carefully onto the bridge again, looking down to judge when he crossed the deepest water. This time Koya was prepared. He forced himself across the bridge and onto the trail beyond, despite the chills that came over him. He had barely been able to hold on to the cane at the end.

After he left the bridge, Koya could breathe more easily again. He kept moving until he no longer felt that wall of magic at his back, like something about to crush him. He could feel different magic on this side ... something strong. He suspected the spell at the bridge kept strangers out -- people without magic would simply feel something wrong and turn around.

Nothing stirred but a slow breeze. Koya could, however, see vultures circling in the sky not far ahead. He swallowed back a surge of illness. He could smell death in the air, and a sense of dread grew with each step as he took up the next incline.

At the top of the hill, Koya had his first view of what had to be Ziven -- a small town, with sound walls. They needed such protections in outposts like this, where barbarians were apt to come looking for any easy pickings. He even saw people moving along the walls, and occasionally sweeping limbs down on the outside and knocking down ... rats.

Rats swarmed everywhere in the clearing between him and the town. Rats yowled and screamed as they attacked each other since they had clearly stripped everything else from the land. They swarmed over the fields and road and up to the walls of the town. The people inside had no choice but to beat them back, but even from here, Koya could see a few get through.

They needed his help.

Koya pulled the rat rune from his pouch and wrapped his fingers around it, forcing his will into the stone, which quickly grew warm in his left hand, a good sign. At another time, he wouldn't have had to hold the rune so tightly, but he tried not to think about his personal problems now -- except to wrap his other hand tighter around the cane, determined not to fall.

Koya grew angry, seeing the creatures so misused; he could feel the magic that had pulled them here as he broke apart pieces of the spell. He started down the path, ordering rats away with a touch of magic so that they scattered on all sides. The animals fell back in disarray as Koya spread his power as wide as he dared. Many of the rats headed toward the North as he broke the spell. Koya hoped there wasn't another wall of power in that direction. He wanted the rats to go far and fast.

Dead rats lay in piles at the village wall, and he often had to kick half-gnawed bodies away from the path as well. Magic had driven the animals here, and he kept disrupting as much of the spell as he could, while he tried to figure out why someone would do this. Why Ziven? This was not, after all, a very important town.

The people in the village saw him coming and realized he had begun scattering the rats before him. A shout of pleasure went up and heartened him, even as he felt the strain of having come this far on foot besides using magic. However, he made it all the way to the gate with the path cleared. Glancing back, he saw many rats still running for the woods and freedom. He couldn't be sure they wouldn't be back. With a wave of his hand, he divested the village walls of more rats, and they too went running.

The townspeople let him in very quickly.

"Sir! We're so glad you came. We'd about given up hope!" An old woman wiped tears from her eyes, even though she smiled, showing a row of crooked teeth.

"I came as quickly as I could," he said and managed not to moan when someone patted his right shoulder. "Please be careful. I've injured my arm and leg, and they're quite painful when touched."

"Oh, your pardon! Your pardon!" The woman looked horrified, even though she hadn't touched him. She drew her hands back in haste, though.

"It's all right. Spread the word, though, will you?" Koya said and smiled. Quite a group was gathering.

She did better than simply spread the word. The woman took up a spot as a guard on his right, and no one got near his arm or leg as he moved through the town, sending rats scurrying at every turn. Most of the rats in this half of the country must have come converged on Ziven.

The people led him straightaway to the Temple in the middle of town, rushing down dirt-packed streets past piles of rats and rats skulking into the shadows. The town stank of rats, and even as he sent more of them away, he saw others slinking along to take their places. This was going to take thought to best use his powers. The work was not going to be easy.

They brought Koya to a beautiful Temple, well-tended, and larger than he had expected. This must have been a prominent location at an earlier age. The Temple was unexpectedly packed with crying children and yelling women. A dozen men stood by the steps and door, weapons (often just shovels) in hand.

Everyone fell silent as he worked his way up the steps, doing his best not to show any sign of his genuine distress. He ached. His head began to pound, likely from the use of so much magic.

"A priest! Praise the Gods!" a woman called out, and the words echoed around the large room with growing fervor.

"He's already sent many a rat runnin'," announced the woman who continued to keep her place as his guard. "Make room for him now. He needs room! Let him to the priest's quarters!"

People scattered, many weeping with joy, both men and women. Koya worried because they put so much faith in him, but they also gave him the courage to try harder. He still had the rune in hand, and he put it in his pouch, feeling the magic of the place that repelled the animals. He needed to think this out and find a better way than brute force to break the evil spell.

The woman got him across the room and to the door to the private office, where he hoped he would find solitude and a chance to think. Instead, he found an older man and a teen, both leaning over the desk and reading -- of all things -- one of the sacred books.

The woman left him there, going to deal with the people outside. The two looked startled by the interruption, clearly so involved in the reading that they hadn't even heard the change when he entered the Temple. The old man leaned back in the chair and took a deep breath as though he hadn't dared to do so for days.

"Praise the Gods; praise all the Gods," the man said, his old voice wavering slightly with emotion, age, and exhaustion.

Koya could clearly see the weight of the town's troubles in his lined face. "You came quickly, priest."

"Koya," he introduced himself with a bow of his head and walked to the desk, limping a bit worse now. The teen got out of his chair in haste, and he gladly took it. "Odd reading for laymen."

"Dangerous reading, I'm sure," the older man admitted, and the boy paled a little. "But we were desperate, you see."

"Yes, I understand. This is a desperate situation, and to be honest, far worse than I had expected to find."

"I'm Alcrew, and this is Malin." The man waved a thin, wrinkled hand at the boy who backed up a step, as though he expected to be struck by lightning. "What can we do to help?"

"I would like a glass of water if there is any to be had."

Malin moved to the cupboard, where he withdrew a glass and a pitcher of water. The boy looked steadier now that he hadn't been struck down by the wrath of the Gods. Good. Koya thought he would need someone he could trust in this mess, especially to do the little errands that would save him from having to hunt for things in this strange place.

Koya placed his pack on the floor and fished out the rune to contact the Temple from his pouch. He deposited it on the table beside the huge, ancient book the two had been studying. He could see it now and realized they'd been reading the *Codex of Wiscon.*

"Gods all, you couldn't have chosen a more boring book to read. You understand any of it?"

"Barely enough to realize we knew nothing at all," Alcrew admitted, closing the cover and pushing the book aside. "But it helped to pass the time and to pretend like we might have learned something to help, sir."

"Koya."

"Koya," Alcrew replied with a bow of his head. "We passed the time and hoped for something to help with this mess."

"You'd have had better luck holding out pieces of cheese and clubbing the rats over the head with that book," Koya told them.

Koya won laughter from both of them. Koya nodded his thanks to Malin for the water. He drank deeply; it had been hard work making his way from the hilltop and through the town gate -- and little better once he got inside. He could feel exhaustion digging at him and knew he'd have to rest soon. He could call on a bit of reserve to help tonight, but after that, he'd have no choice but to rest.

He did need to contact Kenning, though. He leaned over and let his finger run over the cold, smooth surface of the rune, feeling it start to warm as he called up the contact. He could feel the connection with the room again, the warmth and calm that spread out from the rune. He suspected Alcrew and Malin might perceive it as well.

"Kenning? Are you there? I need --"

"Gods all!" Kenning shouted back, startling him. "Are you all right, Koya? I've been worried sick!"

The other two had leapt at the sound, but Koya smiled, relieved to have connected with his friend this time. "I'm fine. I'm in Ziven. Kenning, we really do have a rat problem here. I think every rat in this half of the country is in this town, and it's not natural."

"So, I gathered from your last message," Kenning said, sounding calmer now. "Your link is weak -- are you tired?"

"Exhausted. I must have freed at least a thousand of the rats already --"

"A thousand!" Kenning sounded startled again.

"Kenning, we have *a lot of rats here.*"

"Oh. Sorry. I thought you were exaggerating."

"I thought much the same thing when people told me about Ziven," he admitted.

"Koya, do you need help?" Kenning asked and sounded as though he feared insulting his friend.

"Kenning, even at my best, I would need help with this one."

"Ah." That must not have sounded very reassuring. "I'll see what I can do, Koya. This is a problem. The Most Holy is still claiming --"

"I am not alone," he said in haste before anything unwise was spoken.

"Well, best to keep Temple politics to ourselves then, right?" Kenning tried to sound cheerful, but anyone who knew the man would know how forced that humor seemed. "I'll send someone your way, Koya."

"Perhaps Slade? He's not involved with anything at the Temple right now, and he's a bit closer since he's in Partla."

"Yes, good choice," he agreed. "How are you holding up, Koya?"

"I'll be fine," he said, though he shifted slightly and winced. At least Kenning couldn't see it. "I don't have the power I did, Kenning -- and this needs power. And it needs looking into, which I can't do while I'm dealing with the rats themselves. Someone has set this in motion, and we'll need to learn how and why."

"Excellent points."

"I am cutting the connection now, Kenning, and going to get some rest. I'll be back later after I see if I can get the town cleared and maybe a ward set on the walls. But the fields are a mess, and this is going to take more than simply clearing the rats to get the town back on its feet."

"I'll contact Slade and then start looking at what the Temple can do to help. Contact me when you can. I'll try to listen for you, rather than trying to contact you and possibly upsetting something you're doing."

"Thank you, Kenning. Take care," he said with a smile.

Koya closed his hand again and cleared the connection. A wave of exhaustion washed over him, and the reaction must have shown. Alcrew looked worried.

"I'm all right," Koya reassured them both and sat up straighter again. The small room was warm with a friendly fire lit in the hearth: a clean, well-kept room. He liked it, and that helped. "I had a long journey here, and I wasn't really up to it. We didn't know, you see, that the problem would be this serious, or I wouldn't have come here alone."

"You've done well for us so far, sir," Malin said. "I can hear what they're saying in the other room. There's hope now, and there was none this morning. We thought the rats would kill us all before they was done."

"We can clear the rats out, but the problem goes deeper," Koya admitted with a frown and saw Alcrew nod agreement. "That's trouble for later, though. The rats first. I need to rest before I can deal with them again."

Alcrew nodded and stood; then hobbled across the room and pushed open a door. "The priest's quarters. They haven't been used since Galt disappeared, but I keep them clean and neat. Go sleep for a while. We'll do fine for a few hours more. You've already helped."

Koya levered himself up out of the chair, grabbing his Temple rune, the pack. and the cane before he followed the man to the door, limping worse than he had since the first day. The bed looked inviting, and he crossed and sat on the edge, dropping his pack on the floor beside him.

"Is there anything else you need, sir?" Alcrew asked.

"Nothing. Thank you."

Alcrew bowed his head, waved Malin back from the doorway, and pulled it closed. A bit of light came from a slit of a window, high up on the wall, and he could hear the other two in the room beyond, which felt oddly reassuring.

He also heard rats in the streets outside, and close to the

building. Koya pulled out the rat rune and put the other away. He wished the rats to leave. He didn't put a lot of power into the magic this time, but he still managed to send the animals fleeing from around the Temple. That would help him and the others.

With that bit of magic, calm seemed to settle around the little Temple. He put the rune away and laid down, closing his eyes and drifting quickly to sleep.

CHAPTER

SEVEN

Kenning hadn't slept well through the night. He worried about Koya, and he had already started Slade on the journey to join him. He wanted to contact Koya and knew that was unwise. He didn't want to interrupt any work the priest might be doing, and besides -- he didn't dare call Koya when the Most Holy might happen along.

Prayers did not calm the anger that Kenning barely kept from his face whenever he had to sit for more than a few minutes with the Most Holy. The man was impolite, bigoted, and he ate like a pig.

Kenning passed over another breast of chicken, a smile frozen on his face as the Most Holy ranted and raved, the words not really clear with the food in his mouth. Just nod and say nothing. He hardly dared a glance at the rest of the priests, either. None of them were happy with the man's visit, and it wasn't just because of Koya.

Every time he thought about his friend, impious ideas crowded closer into his mind. Maybe the gods would be kind, and the man would choke to death.

He'd have to pray forgiveness for that thought.

Later.

Bells rang. Kenning kept the sigh of relief from his lips, but he stood with a bow, just as the others did.

"What? More prayers?" The Most Holy glared at the priest and focused -- somewhat -- on Kenning. He'd drank almost all the ale that usually lasted the local priests at least two meals. "You don't pray this much when I'm not around. I won't put up with this kind of pretentious show."

"We pray for our souls, sir," he said and bowed his head. "But one who has attained such a state as you would have no need to beseech the gods for mercy as we do."

Most Holy's eyes narrowed then he glanced around the table and at all the food they left behind. "Go."

Kenning bowed and left, the others falling in behind him. No one said anything. They dared not because the Most Holy had not arrived alone for his visit, and his servants were apt to follow them everywhere they went. Kenning almost looked over his shoulder to see which one trailed along behind them today.

There'd be no food left by the time they were done with prayers. The glutton would eat everything and probably get into the wine as well -- and this was only the noon meal.

Kenning had never in his life hated someone as much as he did the Most Holy, and he knew he had to get that anger under control. This was not a good reaction for a priest, and he knew ... knew he was the one being tested as much as Koya.

So, he prayed quite fervently through the service, and it must have helped. He felt far calmer when he left the altar. He helped clean up the dining hall, the Most Holy having already retired. Most Holy had taken over Kenning's room, of course -

- not that it was any better than the cells for the rest of the priests. In fact, they had guesting quarters that were far better appointed, but no one had mentioned it to the man. Kenning supposed it was childish, but even now, he kept such things to himself.

Kenning had spent as much time as he could doing things to keep the Most Holy happy should the man get back up in need of a snack. It had happened, and he complained of every dish they served. The Most Holy had, praise the Gods, given one service for the people of the village and would do another tomorrow. The locals were thrilled to have such an important man in Templeton, but they didn't have to deal with him. In fact, Kenning did his best to make sure they had minimal contact with the man. He was anxious that they did not lose faith over someone who should have been their model.

Kenning quietly walked past his room, his head bowed in his cowl, just another priest heading for more work or prayers. Most Holy was snoring through his afternoon nap. Loudly.

Good.

"Armath," he said softly when he found the man nearby. "I think the floors need to be cleaned badly, especially by my office."

"Yes, sir."

The man knew Kenning wanted a guard to warn against the Most Holy rushing in unannounced. Kenning went on to his office and sat down at his desk, starting to sort through some paperwork. As he expected, one of the Most Holy's weasely little servants opened the door without a knock and stared at him, eyes narrowed in mistrust.

"Yes?" he said.

"I was looking for the Most Holy," the man said, a growl of words, as though he would have dared burst into a room where the Most Holy worked, and without even a knock. Kenning smiled at the thought.

"The Most Holy has retired," he said, as the weasel knew, since the Most Holy retired after every meal.

"Then what are you doing?" the servant demanded.

Demanded. For a moment, Kenning considered what he could do to this servant, whom he suspected the Most Holy would never truly miss among the dozens he had brought with him. Instead, Kenning sighed and waved a hand at the book before him.

"I'm updating our supply list to make certain everything is ready if the Most Holy wishes to do a review."

As though that was going to happen. It would require the Most Holy to do some actual work.

The prissy little man dared to come across the room and look down at the paper. "Huh."

"Do you keep the books for Most Holy?" he asked with a note of hope in his voice. "We could use help with the work right now --"

"I am not your servant." The man turned and stalked out of the room, almost tripping over the priest who had come to clean the floor. He did slip on the wet spot and nearly went down, but he caught himself, cursed loudly, and kept going.

Armath went back to work with silent diligence, scrubbing without notice of anything around him. The silent priest kept at it for quite a while and then moved slightly farther away. Kenning worked at the numbers. Most Holy's visit was going to set them back quite a bit. He didn't care.

Kenning glanced at the priest and saw the signal he'd been waiting for. The servant had finally stopped standing around, listening, and hoping for some tidbit to take to his master.

Kenning didn't close the door, just in case, someone needed to warn him. He put his fingers carefully on the crystal, but he held the quill as well in case someone walked past the window, though the priests working in the gardens would warn him.

Kenning had trouble focusing at first; every little sound made him think that Most Holy was back up or his servants spying. Dear gods, this had to end soon.

He focused, finally, because he knew he didn't have much time.

"Koya?"

"Kenning!" he answered almost immediately. "Are you all right?"

Worried about them when he was the one in a dangerous situation. Kenning smiled. "We're fine, though there may be a shortage of food in the area before the Most Holy leaves."

Koya made a sound of amusement. "I've got a good amount of the rats cleared from town. I still haven't found what's directing them, but it is powerful magic. I don't think it is what I've been feeling, but I suspect it's connected."

"Be careful of it. Slade will be heading your way. You're handling this well, but --"

"I want help!" Koya said and sounded panicked for a moment. "No matter what, I'd want help with this one, Kenning. This is so far beyond normal that I'd even ask for the Most Holy if I thought he could help sort it out."

"Instead of making it worse," Kenning said with too much of a snarl. He shook his head and concentrated on Koya. "No matter. We'll do all we can."

"Yes," Koya said and sounded distant for a moment. Then the connection came back strong once more. "We've another wave of rats, Kenning. I best get back to work, or they'll be in the town again."

"Take care, my friend," Kenning said.

The connection drifted away. Kenning sighed and regretted they couldn't talk longer. He'd be dealing with Most Holy again soon. How could things be so difficult at a time when they needed --

He started to pull away from the crystal, but it suddenly

grew warm. He thought Koya was contacting him again --

No. Something --

Kenning had only been granted a vision by the Gods once before. This time the power spread up through the crystal and into his head so that he fell back in the chair, frozen -- forever. For a heartbeat. He couldn't tell.

Armies, trouble -- but also a place of green and peace, beauty and danger.

He didn't understand ... but that was the way of visions. Kenning didn't know precisely what he'd seen, but he knew it meant trouble for all of them.

CHAPTER

EIGHT

S tanding on the village's outer wall, Koya could see all the way to the hilltop where he'd first arrived the day before. He still saw rats everywhere, but noticeably fewer than there had been even this morning.

They had far fewer rats left in the town, as well. People moved through streets below, some piling rat bodies in carts and wagons to be taken beyond the walls and buried as soon as possible. He hated to see so many dead animals and knew this entire problem upset a balance that was going to be hard to fix later.

From here, Koya could feel a bit more of the power that set the rats on them, a pulsing sensation in the air, too steady to be held by a human; the spell must have been put in place and powered, and then let run. If he could find the source --

Koya reached out and tried to follow the line of power, but the feel nearly overwhelmed him, and he swayed. Malin caught hold of his arm -- his left one -- and looked as though he had gone pale white.

"Careful, sir. You nearly fell there!"

"Thank you." Koya looked distractedly towards the woods but tried not to think about the power just now. His inability to deal with the magic spell annoyed him, though. He turned that annoyance to a positive effect, setting another hundred rats free from the spell that had kept them throwing themselves at the wall, trying to get in. They darted away into the nearest underbrush to hide. "I suspect by the time I'm done, you won't have a rat in this town for a decade or more!"

Malin looked surprised, apparently more at the humor than the idea of being rat-free. Evidently, the boy thought priests had no sense of humor at all, though from what he'd heard in town, Galt had been a friendly old man. He hoped the priest's disappearance had been age catching up with him, and not something related to what was happening now. Koya kept those thoughts to himself. The locals seemed to have revered their old priest, even though they sometimes commented on how much better Koya was with magic.

Koya had twice talked to Kenning and learned Slade would leave to join him in the morning, having first done what study he could from his place. Koya felt such gratitude at knowing help was on the way that he hardly knew how to express it to himself, let alone to Kenning, Slade, and the Gods. He feared the locals relied on him too much, and in his weakened state, he still might fail them.

Koya hadn't thought much about the Most Holy since he arrived in Ziven, even though the weakness came from his curse. He had thought more about it during the night when he had trouble getting comfortable, but not while he was awake and doing his best to help people.

Kenning had been right to send him. This wasn't merely an excuse to get him away, or punishment for being such a fool, though he had been the last, beyond any doubt. Koya thought back to that moment when he had faced the Most Holy with disbelief at his actions. He would have been half-tempted to claim his actions as the work of the Gods if he hadn't been afraid the Gods would take offense for being portrayed as that stupid.

They went back to the Temple. The streets were safer this afternoon, and even some of the local cats began to show themselves. People kept close to their homes. There would not be much rest for a few days still, but things would go back to normal.

Malin brought him dinner and went back to work with Alcrew, setting the Temple back to rights now that the others had left. The peaceful silence gave Koya respite at last. He'd gotten too used to the quiet, peaceful life of at his own Temple. Even the people of Templeton had seemed more subdued than those who lived here.

He still felt strange to see so many people with lighter hair like his, and a few with blue eyes as well. Border people -- there was enough northern blood here that Koya didn't stand out for that reason.

The food here proved to be excellent, too. Alcrew apparently knew the right baker for the best bread, and he'd chosen three women to cook for their new priest. Koya had done his best to make sure they knew he wasn't going to stay ... but it felt oddly reassuring to have people want him around.

Oh, he would need to nip that little feeling of paranoia in the bud right away. He'd gotten along well with nearly everyone at the Temple, at least after the first few months when he finally stopped fearing they'd turn him out or cart him back off over the border to Damara. The other priests had become his friends. Being sent here was not, he reminded himself again, punishment. In fact, Koya imagined the one person who was not his friend -- the Most Holy -- would not want him to be here where he proved that he could help others against an evil.

A breeze blew through the high window, and Koya finally caught a better scent than that of rats. Koya was closer to the northlands than he'd been since he ran over the border ... and he hadn't thought much about it until he smelled pine and wood smoke. Koya wondered if his family thought him dead, or if they'd heard about the Damara priest living in the south. There were, after all, a few merchants trading between the lands, despite hostilities.

Odd thoughts. They probably came with the tasty bean soup, so much like what Koya's mother used to make. He'd been a middle son, welcome into a family where strong hands were needed to do the work.

Koya pushed the stray memories away, determined not to find himself trying to sort out his odd life at a time like this. He needed a plan that he and Slade could handle to clear out the rats. Then there would be the big question of why this had happened, and Koya was not going to leave until he had an answer and a way to stop it from happening again. Koya had been accused of being stubborn often enough. Now was the time to prove the others were right in that assessment of his personality. Tomorrow he intended to hike toward the forest and see if he could find some other link to the magic. He had his pack ready, and he'd thought of a few tests to try.

"Sir? Do you need anything more tonight?" Malin asked from the doorway.

"Nothing -- oh, do you see my pack? I need to put away my runes, so I'll be ready in the morning."

"Yes, sir," he said and crossed the room, a tall, lanky boy with long legs and hands he hadn't quite grown into yet. He brought back the pack and even handled the rune box with care, lifting it from the table and settling it into the bag on the floor by the bed. Koya watched him, not out of worry, but out of a sudden wonder of what would become of the boy as he grew older. He had the patience of a priest, and perhaps even the interest ... it wasn't often that a sixteen-year-old spent so much time at the Temple, after all.

"Anything else, sir?" Malin asked as he gently nudged the pack into the corner by the bed.

"No, thank you." Koya couldn't get used to being called sir, but it seemed to help the others. "Go home and get some rest. We'll be up and at it early enough tomorrow."

"Thank you." Malin moved off to the doorway again, but he paused once more and drew his attention. "I don't think we can tell you how grateful we are."

Koya looked up again and smiled. "I'm only doing my duty, Malin. I'm glad I can help. It gives me a purpose."

Malin tilted his head and frowned, as though the idea of having a purpose had never occurred to him. Well, he was young, and it was hard to think about such things at that age.

"A couple more cats turned up at the Temple door, come out of hiding," Malin said. "We got them fed and all. We think there might be others in hiding still -- but seeing them is a good sign, I think."

"An excellent sign. Cats are wise. They knew they couldn't take on that many rats, so they took to cover. I'm glad to hear they're showing back up to help with the problem now."

"Could you use your runes to call more of them out?" Malin asked, a bit braver than he had been since Koya arrived. "It might help if they could patrol the streets at night."

"Not quite yet. I don't think it wise to add another form of animal control to what's already out there," Koya said with a nod towards the world outside. "It's always best to let nature recover at her own speed."

"Yes, sir," he said with a nod and a brush of hair from his eyes. "Yes, that does sound like a wise decision. Who knows, but someone was trying to fix a problem elsewhere that set all the rats on us, right?"

"That could well be," he agreed. Very astute boy. "Sometimes, things get out of hand, even with the best intentions."

Malin left looking contemplative. The boy pulled the door closed behind him, and Koya could hear the muffled sounds of Malin and Alcrew talking. Soon the front door to the Temple closed with a definite thump, and Koya knew he was alone in the building.

When was the last time he'd been alone in a building? It might have been years. Koya had spent time in his room at the Temple, but there were always others just a wall away. There had always been someone close by who could help him or share prayers with, or --

Koya had taken them, and his life at the Temple, for granted as though they owed it to him.

With a hand on his broach, he felt out the lines of power radiating from the sun and bowed his head in prayer. "Gods give me strength and make me wise. Let me handle this well."

He felt a little warmth from the symbol of the sun, and the power did not come from his hands. He felt better again for the reminder that the Gods did watch over him. He finished his food, wiped out the bowl leaving it ready to go back to the owner in the morning. Time to rest. He took off his robe, no easy work with an arm that didn't want to move -- and the chain of the broach caught and broke.

Koya stared at where the symbol of his status had fallen to the bed. One of the links had snapped in half, and the sight brought a wave of worry and fear. However, when he picked up the broach again, he saw the glitter of light in the sun and felt a surge of warmth and euphoria that surely had to mean he shouldn't worry.

He served the Gods, but he had never pretended to understand them.

Koya put the broach on the shelf by the bed and would get the chain fixed in the morning. Despite that odd sign, he went to bed feeling content and hopeful. He slept very well.

CHAPTER

NINE

Sometime in the darkness and not long before the dawn, Koya heard frantic shouts that pulled him from his deep sleep. He awoke startled and uncertain of his place. Then he realized the rats must have come back, and he got up as quickly as he could move. His leg gave way on the first step, and he went to his knees, gasping in pain until he could find the cane and get up again.

Flickering lights danced outside his window. Koya thought he heard screams this time. The small window stood too high in the wall, and he couldn't see out. He threw his robe back on -- not for the covering or the warmth, but because he had tied the small pouch to it, and he could quickly grab the two runes he most used, despite his injured arm.

Koya moved as fast as he dared through the office and to the door that led into the sanctuary, but he paused there. The sounds outside were growing worse, a cacophony of yells and screams. This was something more than rats. Koya had barely stepped into the sanctuary when the outer door burst from the hinges, and the attackers swarmed in. Though nearly lost in the dark, Koya caught glimpses of the bright colored hair and the waving banners outside.

Dragonkin.

Koya called on his powers and threw the people backward. Some of them tumbled outside. He rushed back to the office and threw the bar down over the door, and then on to the sleeping room where he put the next bar into place. They wouldn't hold for long, so Koya knew he didn't have much time. He could hear more screams and yells as he fumbled for the rune. Not the rat one, the other.

He sat on the bed with the rune grasped tightly in his hand. He could feel the indentation of his fingernails in his palm.

"Kenning! Gods, Kenning -- answer! We need help!" He could hear the enemy pounding against the first door. It wouldn't take them long to break through into the room. "Kenning!"

"Koya?" a sleepy voice asked, uncertain.

"We're under attack! Dragonkin, Kenning. They've attacked the town --"

"Get to cover, Koya!"

"There is none." He heard the outer door splinter and then the rush of feet to the next door, whispered words, and the pounding again, loud and incessant. "They're almost in. If the Dragonkin is attacking Ziven, they must be preparing for more --"

The door splintered, sending shards of wood everywhere. He saw the shapes outlined in the opening, the flickering light of torches casting light and shadow everywhere --

"Koya!"

One of the attackers leapt into the room with a curse and grabbed at him.

A curse he knew too well and a language Koya

remembered.

Norters.

"Kenning! They aren't really Dragon--"

A fist caught him in the side of the head. The rune went flying, and he could feel the connection break at that moment. He tried to throw himself after it, but someone caught hold, twisting his arm and kicking his injured leg.

They carried him through the sanctuary but did him no more injury. For a moment, he thought he'd been rescued until he heard grunted words in the Northerner's tongue. He shoved an elbow into the stomach of the one to his left, for all the good it did him. They dropped him, finally, on the Temple floor.

Koya tried to sit up. He could still hear screams, shouts, and crying outside. Through the ruined door of the Temple, he could see a half dozen bodies on the stairs. He feared one of them was Alcrew.

"Damn you all," he shouted and meant those words on very many levels and in a depth of feeling he had not touched ever before. Kneeling there in the Temple, he thought the curse might even mean something.

One of the men nudged him with a foot and growled something unintelligible. Koya glared at him, considered how much he looked like one of them (without their disguises), and decided he dared not pretend to be anything else. News about the Norter priest would have reached home.

"You can stop with your act," Koya said in Damarian. The man took a hasty step backward, betraying himself. "I heard you speak already. You will not get away with this."

The man leaned down, the flickering light clearly showing his face -- to blunt and ugly for a Dragonkin. "We already have won. We know you sent the message. And we have you, and you are a northerner besides. That's all the better."

He may have thought so, but Koya wouldn't cooperate

with these animals, and he didn't care where they came from.

"Get up, priest."

"Not without my cane," he replied with a wave back towards the room. "And my boots."

The man who was clearly in charge glared at him, but he waved someone back to the room to get the things. Another came from the back with his wig of bright yellow slightly askew.

"I have the runes, Captain."

"Good."

The man carried Galt's box of runes. Better still. Chances were that they wouldn't even find his own runes tucked into the pack by the bed. Koya knew he could use Galt's runes, but no matter what they did to him, he could not work these runes with his true power.

Oh, and yes, he had seen what Northerners could do to their prisoners. He had seen it twice, even in the little village where he'd grown up, and that nightmare came back with full force now. He swallowed back a wave of illness and did his best to remain steady. The man came back with Koya's cane and boots, but not his pack, which gave him hope again.

Koya pulled on the boots and got to his feet without their help -- not that they offered any. The sounds outside had died down -- not a good sign, not at all. As they reached the broken doors of the Temple, Koya saw dead everywhere, and if there were any others still alive, they were hidden as well as the cats.

Koya would only have one chance.

He took a deep breath and shouted. "They're Damarian, not Dragon --"

His shout ended in a woof of pain as someone hit him in the back of the head. He tumbled down the stairs, landing up against the still body of Alcrew.

"Damn him! If anyone did survive --"

Someone grabbed Koya by the arm, jerking him upward.

After another blow, he didn't hear any more of what they said. Nor did he see any more of the dead as they carried him away, unconscious.

Lazette Gifford/92

CHAPTER

TEN

M alin woke up. It surprised him.
He remembered the hideous, green-haired head appearing before him as he hurried out of his father's cottage, ready to face down the rats again and get to Koya. Malin even remembered the swing of the sword that should have killed him.

Malin had grabbed the shovel he kept by his bed, a useful weapon against rats and one he'd learned to keep at hand. He'd lifted the handle, and the sword had bounced off of it, and then cut deep into his shoulder.

The sword should have taken his neck, but even so, he didn't expect to live. He fell in silence, his eyes closed -- but that didn't stop what he heard. They killed his father, the older man cursing them to the end. He listened to the family in the next cottage die, the baby crying out in fear and then silenced.

The enemy screamed their inhuman war cries as they

rushed through the streets.

Silence later.

And then, suddenly, another voice.

"They're Damarian, not Dragon --"

Koya's voice; Koya alive. Malin lifted his head and could barely see a group at the Temple, so far away, he could make out none of the shapes and faces. He saw them lift Koya, his blue robe catching the light as they carried him away.

Malin tried to get up, but true darkness took him.

He awoke later as agony swept through his body. He sat up, retched, coughed, and retched again. Blood caked the side of his tunic and flowed again as he carefully pulled his right arm inside his tunic, fearing he would pass out at every movement.

Malin glanced into the cottage. The light from the hearth gave just enough illumination to show his father where he had sprawled half out of his bed. His head had tilted unnaturally, and his dead eyes staring at the fire. Malin looked away as quickly as he could, but he knew the memory of that scene would be etched forever in his mind.

After a while, with the sun fully up, he struggled up to his feet. Malin stumbled to the Temple, not daring to look at the bodies along the way. He wasn't sure why he turned to the Temple. After all, there could be no help there. He didn't really believe Koya had survived.

Bodies everywhere. Malin tried not to see them and listened with growing worry when he heard nothing but the breeze and the movement of animals. No sounds of anyone else, and he shivered at the thought of the ghosts he walked past today. Were they why he was so cold?

Alcrew hadn't survived. He looked down at the old man and felt a welling of tears that mixed the fate of his mentor and his father in a single memory. Then he walked up the stairs, moving up and up again until he was inside.

They'd broken the doors into the Temple, and the doors to the office and the sleeping room beyond. Malin took each step, expecting to find Koya's body. He wasn't here, and he hadn't been on the steps. The memory of the damned Dragonkin people carrying him off came back --

They're Damarian, not Dragon --

Was it true?

Malin reached the sleeping room. The priest's robe was not on the edge of the bed, and the priest was not dead where he had slept or elsewhere in the Temple. For whatever reason, they'd taken Koya.

There could be no good reason they would want him.

Malin thought he should follow and find a way to help the priest. He sat on the bed instead, unwilling to go back out of the building and face the dead, even to save someone else who might have survived. Were there others out there? He wanted to go and find them. He didn't want to be the only one.

He leaned his head back and close his eyes. Waiting, he thought, though he neither knew what for nor really cared.

CHAPTER

ELEVEN

Just before noon, Slade reached the bridge that spanned the little stream, panting and his head pounding from the exertion. He hadn't even bothered to try for a horse from Marchland since he'd heard about the problems Koya had faced there. He'd gone through the town, past the horse barn, and on to the trail without even slowing. Startled people had looked his way, but he had kept going, too worried to stop and say anything that might have calmed them. If they'd known about the trouble so close at hand, they wouldn't have been so calm -- and he was torn between telling them and seeing a panic start or making certain of the trouble first.

Slade didn't stop or slow until he reached the bridge. Yes, this was the one Kenning had warned about, where Koya had reported a spell while he was on his way into Ziven. Slade could feel the lingering evil touching there at the water's edge, though most of it had dissipated. He could even feel Koya's strong hand in destroying most of the line, though he'd worked from some distance. There were holes in the magic, as though Koya had driven spells through it.

"Slade!"

Even after all this time, Slade still leapt at the sound of a voice coming out of nowhere. He wasn't the only one this time. Birds took to flight at the sudden shout, and a deer, unseen until that moment, darted back away from the stream.

Slade fumbled for the rune and nearly dropped the damned small thing; it was not fit for a man with hands as big as his, despite that he'd made them himself. "Kenning?" he asked, his fingers wrapping around the rune, though not too tightly. He'd broken one in half that way, and it had taken him more than a month to make a new one.

"Just checking on you," Kenning said, his voice softer now, though no less harried. "Some of us are starting to get ... well, bad feelings from that area."

"No surprise." Slade looked up into the sky and at the distant circling of vultures. His skin went clammy, and he nearly lost his connection. Slade fought to keep his voice steady, calling up controls from another life before he had gone to the priesthood. "I'm at the bridge. I can feel our Koya's work here, where he first found the trouble. He obviously tore holes in the magic, whatever it was. I can't really feel more of it."

"Anything else?"

He looked up at the vultures. "Nothing yet, sir. I still have some distance to go."

"You've made good time, though," Kenning said, sounding worried.

"I'll be there soon enough," Slade said and started walking. Despite the jokes made about him -- a big, lumbering bear of a man -- he could both walk and talk at the same time. "I just ... I don't think this is going to be good, sir."

"No, I can't see how it would be."

"I'll contact you when I get there and have had a look around. It'll be soon enough."

"I'll be waiting."

The connection slipped away. Most times, Slade would have enjoyed talking to Kenning and would have spent all the morning discussing anything from vegetable gardening to the history of Kasprin. They had done so in the past on several occasions. Not today. This time, Slade wanted the silence, the emptiness, and the seclusion to react without sharing his emotions with others.

Slade did wonder what the Most Holy was doing right now. If they were fortunate, he'd hear about the trouble and turn tail, rushing back to the capital and out of their way.

Slade knew what he would find before he reached the gate. He could smell the death from that far away, the combination of old blood and the start of decay in the warm morning air. This wasn't the first time he'd seen large scale death, or even a battlefield, though few but Kenning knew about that past. His previous life made him a better person for this journey than any of the others. He had lived this horror before and survived, and he could do so again.

Even so, having gone to serve the Gods, Slade had thought he would never face something as terrible as this again. The village had been prosperous. Perhaps as many as three hundred had lived here, but the only things alive now were the vultures and the rats.

Just inside the gate, he stopped and sorted through his runes and sent both sets of animals fleeing, at least while he was here. He understood about nature and the places of such creatures, but he could not bear the sight of their work today.

Slade headed straight for the Temple, which was not far across the little town. He went quickly up the steps into the surprisingly beautiful building. Bright fledged arrows from

Dragonkin bows had dug into the exterior wall, marring the brightly painted sun symbol of the Ten.

He found little damage inside the Temple except for ruined doors. The simple charm of the place came like a whisper of relief, as long as he didn't look over his shoulder to the outside. Even the air tasted fresher in here. Slade paused by the gilt covered circle sitting atop the altar, offering a prayer for the dead.

He moved on to the office, seeing a few things knocked over, and finally into the sleeping room, seeing a body there, his heart pounding with fear this time --

He hadn't expected to find anyone alive, and neither, apparently, had the boy who suddenly sat up.

"Koya?" the boy whispered hope in his voice, a bittersweet thing to hear, that the boy would hope to see their lost brother.

"No, not Koya. I'm Slade."

"Slade. He spoke ... spoke of you."

The boy fell back again, energy fled with consciousness. Slade nearly cursed aloud at his own slow reaction and hurried to help this single, young survivor.

Slade found a bad wound in the shoulder and back, and one that had not bled as much as it should have, he thought. He grabbed runes out of his pack, sorting through the little things with some haste until he found the one that would help him do at least a little healing magic. He'd never been very good at this work, but he tried his best.

Then Slade settled on the hard, cold floor and waited with far more patience than most people would have given him credit for managing. He'd learned the need for quiet thought and meditation.

Something was not right here. Something more than the killing of defenseless villagers. Something more, even, than the plague of rats that had brought Koya to this highland village.

He could feel it.

Something wrong -- and hadn't Koya been saying the like for several months now? Something wrong and Slade feared Koya had been inadvertently put right in the middle of that trouble when things turned worse.

He hadn't found Koya's body yet. He would have to go and look soon, as well as do the final rites as they should be said. He was putting it off by sitting here with the boy.

No. Tending to the living always took precedent over memorials for the dead. He stepped out of the room and quietly contacted Kenning, briefly telling him what he'd found. Neither of them dwelt on the conversation this time, except that Kenning would arrange for others to get there quickly and help with burials. After that discussion, Slade checked the boy on occasion and reinforced his little magic. Late in the afternoon, Slade was rewarded with the boy opening his eyes and turning his head, blinking several times before the loss, anger, and fear came back.

"Why are you still here?" the boy asked softly and started to sit up.

"You needed help," Slade replied, trying to hold him down. "There was nothing more important --"

The boy looked shocked, then frightened again. "You don't know. They took Koya --"

"Took?" he said, suddenly on his feet, surprised and shocked. Hopeful? He dared not let that in yet.

"I'm sorry. I should have said. I thought -- Gods forgive me --"

The boy started to panic. Slade gently rested a hand on his uninjured shoulder and drew the young man's attention. "No, it's all right. Look at me. You are certain they took Koya?"

"I saw them. I had turned my head to see the Temple. He said something odd, sir."

"Slade. My name is Slade. Who said something odd?"

"Koya. He shouted the words, or tried to, but they stopped him. He said they were Damarian, not Dragon. That's all he said. Could it be so?"

Slade stared at the boy, not caring about anything except that Koya might still be alive. Then he realized the real import of what the boy said. Damarians?

"Koya contacted the Temple. He said they were Dragonkin," Slade said softly.

"Yes, sir." He looked more awake and more troubled. "That's what I thought they were, too. Never seen the Dragonkin before. They had colored hair that stood up, and they shot bows."

Slade stood still, his eyes closed, trying to see the dead in the village without feeling the overwhelming grief and anger. Slade didn't want to ask the boy more questions if he could find the answers himself, and not burden him with memories he shouldn't have to face just yet.

"Lesslings?" Slade asked. "Did you see them?"

"Are there really such creatures?" The boy's face paled. "Giant lizards what walk like humans?"

"Yes, somewhat. I've seen them before. They're guards and servants, and probably things we don't understand at all. I've never heard of a Dragonkin without at least one."

"Maybe they don't take them to battle."

Slade looked back at him and frowned. "In the old days, back in the wars, the Lesslings were feared more than the Dragonkin. You could deal with a member of the Dragonkin on the battlefield, but not a Lessling. They were scavengers, and they always went for the weak and injured."

"But they weren't here. If they had been, I wouldn't have survived."

Slade looked back down at him, startled.

"I was attacked by the cottage." He stopped and closed his eyes and then shook his head as though to remove that memory from his mind. "They would have found me if they'd been through. I was in plain sight, even when unconscious."

Slade nodded and reached into his pocket to find the rune and contact Kenning again. He didn't want to give false hope about Koya, but just the same, odd things were going on here that he needed to relate.

Norters pretending to be Dragonkin? Trying to stir up trouble between the humans and the Dragonkin? No, not between humans and the Dragonkin -- between the magic-using humans and the Dragonkin, two groups they held equally evil and tainted. Slade wrapped his hand around the rune and felt power come quickly this time, fueled by what he feared and what he'd learned.

"Kenning, sir, are you there?" he asked, his breath unaccountably short, as though he had just run a long way. Panic played up through his heart and head, and his hand trembled, and all the more so when Kenning didn't immediately answer.

Patience, he told himself. Patience was something he had always lacked, and he fought, to breathe slowly, to wait.

"Slade, my apologies," Kenning suddenly said. "I had to come from the dinner table with the Most Holy."

"I've found someone alive, sir --"

"Malin," the boy said softly. "Koya spoke of me."

"Malin!" Kenning replied, surprised.

"He says they carried Koya off, sir. He said that maybe Koya was trying to warn others that they were Damarians and not Dragonkin. It might be so, Kenning. No sign of Lesslings anywhere, and though I saw arrows everywhere, none of them looked extraordinary to me."

"Koya and Damarians. This is troubling, Slade. If this is true --"

"I think the only way to know for certain is if I start tracking them, sir. I can do that. I don't think they'll have moved far. They must have brought a considerable force to do this work so quickly and without the villagers having any chance. A force that size can't move quickly. If they killed any of the Damarians, I suspect those bodies will be gone. I'll keep an eye open to see if I am wrong."

Kenning said nothing for a moment, but Slade could feel his attention as a slight throb through the rune like the irregular beat of a heart. "What about Malin?" Kenning asked. "We must always help those in need, Slade, even above helping our own."

"Yes, sir."

"I'll go with him," Malin said and was already throwing his feet over the edge of the bed. "I know land about here very well, sir. I can help."

"You're hurt, lad --" Slade said, worried as much about the boy's injury as the fear of taking someone else off to a battle. He'd sworn to the Gods he would never do such a thing again.

"I can help you find Koya, and that way we can find out the truth. And I can't stay here. Neither of us can."

That was true enough. Slade sighed and looked at the rune. "Kenning --"

"I leave this in your hands, friend." Kenning sounded worried, but Slade had the distinct feeling that was not about having him in charge. "We need the truth. I fear things are already getting out of hand. When I tell the Most Holy the new development, I can guess exactly what he will say."

"That if they are Norters, then Koya was obviously in league with them," Slade replied with a snarl. He should have considered that part. "Or that Koya is lying to throw us off the track of the Dragonkin."

"Exactly."

Slade saw Malin blink, the boy's face reddening in a show of anger for Koya's sake. Slade shouldn't have been surprised, and he tried not to wince at what the boy thought of their Most Holy. Then he decided it wouldn't matter. The Most Holy wasn't ever going to come out here to the edge of the Empire and preach in a border town.

All dead now anyway.

"We'll go as soon as we can, sir," Slade said to the rune. "You take care. Don't let the Most Holy push you into doing something that annoys him, and that will make this worse. We need you to help keep things steady there."

"I'll do what I can. Report to me whenever you can. I won't contact you unless it's absolutely necessary. I don't want to put the two of you in any more danger than you'll already be in."

"Thank you, sir."

"Get him back if you can, Slade. There are a dozen different aspects of this that I don't like, not the least of which is that Koya is normally the most powerful priest I know. I don't like that these people have already used magic on the rats --"

"If they're related."

"I don't believe in coincidences of that large a scale," Kenning replied. "That includes their former priest disappearing and these people now grabbing Koya. I fear it is all related and I don't like any of it. Be careful."

"We will."

The rune went dead in Slade's hand, and he put it away, already looking around the little room, judging what things could help them.

"Koya is a powerful priest?" Malin said. He held his left arm close to his chest, plainly trying to ease the pressure on his shoulder. A sling was the first order of business.

"Oh, yes. Quite powerful," Slade said, somewhat distracted. "Took us all by surprise, him being from the north."

"Is he? We --" Pain crossed his face again, but this was a pain of the soul, not the body. "Some of us wondered, and thought it both strange and wondrous, that such a man should come to our little village."

"Koya is a good man," Slade said, still distracted. He pulled a small knife from his pack and began to cut up the bed cloth, startling Malin. "There were people, both in the Temple and out, who mistrusted Koya's power and his place of birth. Most of us got over it."

"But not the Most Holy," Malin said, and met his look this time.

"Not the Most Holy," Slade agreed. He wouldn't lie. "The Most Holy is an old man and has held power in the capital for more than thirty years. Usually, though, the Most Holy sits in the Temple of Tralista, and only his local priests and the Empress deal with him regularly. However, now and then, he leaves to check on other Temples. We don't know why he came to Templeton. I think it may just have been to give Koya trouble."

Malin looked bothered, but then he seemed to decide it wasn't a real problem. His eyes cleared, and he began to look around the room as well and with anxiousness that surprised Slade.

"Here, this will help," Slade said. He settled the sling over the boy's neck and gently lifted the arm into place. Malin paled a little and then nodded.

"What do you think happened to Galt?" Malin suddenly asked.

"Your previous priest? I'd like to think that the poor, old man died peacefully somewhere. I don't know that it's true. There are supplies here in the Temple?"

"Enough for you and me to carry," the boy said. He stood and looked steady enough. Slade thought his magic must have worked better than usual. "Ah. And there's Koya's pack. We can use that to carry things."

"Yes, good." Slade grabbed the pack, surprised by the weight as he carried it out to the table in the other room. Malin followed, glancing once towards the sanctuary, and beyond to the street. Crows had gathered there. Slade sent them away with a subtle little twitch of magic.

The boy needn't to see such things.

Malin opened a cupboard by the wall and handed out bread, dried meat, and some cheese. "We kept food here because of the rats, you see," the boy said. "They were getting into everything, but not into the Temple. There's some dried fruit, too. And a few herbs for tisanes."

"Better and better," Slade said, hefting the pack onto the table. "You are a Godsend."

Slade wondered if that wasn't literally true but said nothing more. Malin had enough weighing on him already, and it would get worse when they left, and he saw the dead. He would know that he, alone, had survived.

Unless they found Koya, of course.

Slade found Koya's rune box inside the pack, the lid slightly off. One of the runes, to contact the temple, had fallen partway across the floor. Slade put it back and sealed the lid. Malin looked at the box and then frowned, glancing at one of the shelves.

"The Temple's rune box is gone, sir."

"Slade."

"Slade," he repeated but didn't sound as though he paid much attention. "It was there on the shelf."

"Galt didn't take it with him this winter?"

"He never did, sir, not at least since I knew him. Galt had his own that he took when he went to visit the outer homesteads or headed up to a couple small settlings higher up the mountains. I think he went mostly to get away from us for a while. He liked his solitude, did Galt."

"Most priests do," Slade replied and saw Malin's nervous glance. "But not me. I never did take to the meditation as well as I should have."

"Ah." Here's a bag of winter berries, dried, but they're good if you soak them in a bit of water. And a water pouch there in the cupboard by you."

"You know this room well."

"I helped Alcrew here during the last few months. Alcrew had served Galt forever, and I think he wanted to make certain there was someone who knew enough about this place to help Koya or any priest." He stopped and leaned his hand against the table, looking Slade entirely in the face this time. "They're all dead."

Slade wouldn't lie to him. "Yes, they are. The Gods have them now, Malin, for what little solace that may seem to you."

"Some screamed and screamed." The boy had gone white, his voice too soft as he turned away and stared at nothing Slade could see. "Screamed and then went so silent."

"Look at me, Malin."

The young man reluctantly looked back. His grey eyes were bloodshot, his face pallid, and Slade could see panic as the eyes darted to the door they would be going through soon.

"I'm going to do something that will help," Slade said. He put down his pack and opened his own rune box. What Malin needed was near the bottom. He hadn't had to use this one in the last few years. "I can make bad thoughts distant for a little while. Long enough for us to leave Ziven and get into the hills. You won't forget. Everything will come back to you, but not with the force of suffering that you'd feel walking through this town today."

Malin winced at the idea of passing all those dead, but he looked at the rune Slade held with some trepidation. "I thought priests only had runes for animals and for things like contacting the Temples."

"Mostly, that's true. However, we also use some aspects of animals for special controls. Peace we take from turtles, Malin. Turtles sitting in a pond, sunning themselves on fallen branches. Peace, but alert for trouble. I can give you that peace for a little while. This will help because -- Gods forgive me -- we don't have time to grieve for Ziven right now."

Malin looked at him, eyes round with a bruised look about them. He finally nodded. "Yes. This is wise. We need to go, and I couldn't walk out there and just ... leave. I knew them all, sir."

"Slade," he said again. "And I know how you feel, Malin. Yes, I really do. I was a soldier once, long, long ago. I was in a battle with the Damarians, and of all my company, I alone survived."

"Ah." Malin nodded and looked toward Slade with a little kinship he had not meant to foster, though maybe it helped. "Damarians then, too?"

"Yes. We were told we were safe." Slade stopped that memory there and drew the turtle rune into his hand and tightened his fingers around it. Very few used the power of the turtle, but he'd become quite adept at it, turning that peace to himself in the early years before he learned to control his own emotions. "Close your eyes, Malin. I'll do this, and then we'll leave."

Malin swallowed, looking ill, but did as Slade ordered.

Slade brushed the power down over Malin, a gentle little pulse of blue light that didn't rush in to shove the boy's emotions away and frighten him. Slade saw the boy's muscles slowly relax, the tightness in the shoulders loosen, and even his breathing ease. The spell took very well, which good because they didn't have time to waste.

"We need to go, Malin."

"Yes, sir."

He sighed but didn't correct Malin this time. Instead, he

picked up Koya's pack and put Koya's runes in it along with his own. His own pack was filled with food, and he let Malin carry that lighter one. Malin stood and followed him out of the room, his eyes dulled, but his step even. They went out into the bright sunlight and down the stairs. Malin only paused a moment, and even the magic could not ease the flicker of pain in his face.

"Goodbye, Alcrew," he said softly as he paused by an old man.

And then they left.

CHAPTER

TWELVE

Koya awoke with the right side of his face pressed against damp dirt and a rock beneath his cheek. He moved, uncertain about what had happened and where he was, trying to ignore the pain in his right arm and leg.

Someone yanked Koya upward without any apparent effort. The world spun, and the pain in his arm and leg tripled. Shock, though, overcame everything as he stared into the face of something not human at all. The creature was enormous, towering half a body taller than Koya, who dangled in its hold. The squat and wide body had a loose, folded covering of coarse dirt brown skin, though mottled with grey and beige across the shoulders and head. The bald, flat head held grey-on-grey eyes in a squat, frog-like face. The nostrils of the blunt nose flared as it bent its head closer to him.

Large creature, the free hand -- or something like a hand -

- that suddenly pressed against Koya's chest covered most of his body.

Koya thought this creature would kill him. He didn't know why the others had left him with it. He didn't care. He had failed to protect the people of Ziven -- and he feared he had started a war for the Damarians. The creature leaned closer, and Koya realized it radiated a tainted, dark magic so strong that Koya feared it would contaminate him and probably had tainted the men it traveled with. This *thing* was the heart of the trouble he had sensed back in Templeton.

It had hold of his injured arm, reminding Koya of his previous stupidity with the Most Holy. When Koya measured the things he had done wrong, he found himself a failure at every turn.

"Well?" a human voice demanded from behind.

The word startled Koya, and he tried to look, a half moment of hope ... until he realized the voice had spoken Damarian.

"Mashic," the creature replied, a purr of a word, at odds with the misshapen face, the stone-cold stare. "Mashic made pain."

"Excellent. Well done."

The creature drew back it's thin, almost non-existent, lips into a caricature of a smile, showing two rows of greenish-brown teeth. Then it tossed Koya aside; he landed at the feet of a man who dropped down on his heels and smiled, though he hardly looked human for it either.

"You are a Godsend, you know," the man said, nudging Koya with a booted foot. "The old priest ... well, we drained him far too quickly. You are young, you're strong, and you come ready-made for our work."

"I will not --"

The man grabbed him by the arm and pulled him up. Koya's breath caught in pain, tremors passing through his body.

"You will do any number of things before we're done, friend."

Koya denied those words with a shake of his head because he couldn't get a breath back to speak. The man laughed. Failed everyone, and feared, now he would do even worse.

The world went dark, and Koya welcomed unconsciousness.

Koya awoke, lying on the dirt and staring up through ancient pines. Peaceful, in that single heartbeat before he tried to move, and memory returned. He bit back a moan and stayed very still.

The creature with the Damarians had been magical -- something of the deep earth, a long time from the lands of man. He couldn't name it, but Koya knew this one meant trouble, especially allied with the magic hating Norters.

At the sound of others nearby, Koya turned his head slightly, blinking away dirt. Knowing was better than staying blind, after all. He found they'd put him into some sort of cage, several yards wide, and made of poles shoved into the ground and wrapped in lines of magic. Though not covered at the top, there was no way he would ever get up the tall poles to reach the opening.

He wasn't alone in the enclosure. The site of the other brought a snarl to him -- someone pretending to be Dragonkin --

Only a heartbeat later, when the face turned his way, Koya knew this was no act. The thin face, the multicolored hair, the dark green-eyed glare: this was indeed a Dragonkin member, and he belonged here no more than Koya did.

Seeing Koya conscious, the man stood and stalked to him. The stranger limped and had his arms secured close to his body, so he could only move his elbows up and down. He knelt and leaned down, hawk-faced and angry, staring into Koya's face.

Then he blinked and pulled back.

"Why are you not afraid?" the stranger asked, his voice harsh.

"You are not my enemy."

"Oh, you are wrong, Norter. You are very wrong."

Ah, now there was a problem. "I am not -- I was born in the north, but I ran for the south when the Gods touched me with power."

"You lie."

"I do not."

The other wouldn't be convinced so quickly, of course. Koya couldn't say he cared, except they were trapped together, and they might have a better chance if his companion had been willing to work with him.

Koya finally forced himself to sit up. He felt bruised from the top of his head to his toes. He thought about the creature that had sniffed out the magic on him -- and tried very hard not to curse the Most Holy in that thought. What was happening? None of it made sense.

He wanted to ask, but the other had already walked away to his other side of the little cage. Fine. Koya could, perhaps, practice a little patience.

Could he use magic to break through the wall they'd put around them? He tried to feel it out and knew he hadn't the strength to take this on. He'd have to conserve every bit of energy he could if he had the chance.

The camp lay all around them, though not a long-term site, so the Darmarians couldn't have been here for long. Koya tried to guess the number of people and realized there might be as many as six hundred or more. They'd had enough warriors to kill everyone in Ziven before the locals had a chance to rally their own people. Koya had put a ward along the Ziven walls, and he should have felt it breached. Ah, but they had a power of their own, didn't they? That creature might have simply dug his way in. The others had probably been lax that night since the guards weren't needed to hold back the rats.

Koya couldn't see the hellish creature anywhere, but a sense of magic told him it was off to the right and down the curve of the land. He had confirmation of sorts when he noticed that the others avoided walking down in that area. Koya wanted to know how this creature came to travel with people who hated everything magical.

It marked a change in the world, and under different circumstances, Koya would have welcomed the idea of Damarians finally accepting magic.

The other prisoner glanced his way, measuring him. What would Koya do if attacked?

Nothing.

If the Dragonkin killed him, a good many problems would be solved. Koya feared far more that he might survive in the hands of these people and their pet. He feared he would eventually give them what they wanted. He did not want to fail again.

Koya worried when three soldiers passed close by, but they only grumbled about the lateness of their food again as they walked on. He nodded with relief.

"You understand them," the Dragonkin said, a snarl of words in Kasparian.

"Yes."

The other prisoner said no more, but he still glared sometimes.

The night fell. They had no food, of course, and no one offered a covering from the deluge that broke, drenching them both. Koya shivered and very nearly cursed the Most Holy aloud this time. He would have suffered enough without the added problems created by the spell ... and problems it would be since the Damarians had learned about the magic curse.

Koya slept, curled up as best he could in the mud. The night seemed too long, but he didn't wish for the dawn to come.

CHAPTER

THIRTEEN

Malin settled against a stout tree trunk and watched as the clouds blew in. "We can't go on in this weather," he said softly, uncertain of his place, even though he'd been the one doing the tracking. "We'll need light to follow their path when the rains come."

Malin had expected the priest to argue. Instead, Slade looked up at the sky and nodded, his face grim and showing lines of worry and fatigue. "Yes, you're right. We need to find what cover we can."

No one had ever really listened to him without question before, not on something this important. It gave Malin a little shiver, thinking he might be making a mistake. What if the Norters camped over the next hill, and by the time they got there in the morning, they'd already killed Koya?

What if, what if...

"How did the Norters get into Ziven?" Malin asked

suddenly, trying to bury away other worries. "Koya had a ward up to keep the rats out. We could feel it as well, and he said he'd know if we went in or out of the town."

"Ah, now there's an excellent question," Slade said. He came over to the tree as well, digging through his pack as he sat down. "There are several things we're going to want to learn. I suspect they used some magic."

"Not them!" Malin said, shocked by the idea. "The Norters don't have any magic!"

"Koya does, and he was born in the north."

"Was he?" Malin felt ill at the idea of magic in the north and how the possibility upset everything. "I never thought about it. He looked northern, but a lot of people around here do."

"True. But Koya has an accent still --"

"So do you. It's a different accent, is all," Malin said, looking at him. "We never thought about such a thing. He was a priest. That's all that mattered."

"As it should be," Slade said with a bow of his head.

"But isn't that way for Koya."

"No, not always," Slade replied and shifted slightly. He plainly didn't want to talk about this aspect of Koya's life, and a day ago, Malin would have bowed his head and kept his silence, respecting how the others felt. Today, though, all the world had changed, and Malin suddenly felt desperate for answers. Everything that had been sure in life was gone now and finding a new path ... he didn't know if he could.

"The others don't like him because he's from the north," Malin supplied, having fit that much together.

Slade looked at him, startled. "Oh, no! Almost everyone likes Koya, both in the Temple and in the town. There was mistrust at first, but that passed quickly, and there's been no sign of it over the years."

"Then it is only the Most Holy who doesn't like him?"

Slade frowned and clearly didn't want to answer this one. Malin didn't back down. Slade said nothing as he got out a rune, and then cast a little magic that blunted the wind and drove the first drops of rain away. They'd be comfortable enough under the small shield.

"Beaver for protection," Slade said, holding out the rune so Malin could see. "They build good homes for themselves."

"Oh. That makes sense."

Slade nodded and sat back against the tree. He did not look at Malin. "The Most Holy does not like Koya at all. The Most Holy, for reasons none of us can perceive, has decided Koya is working against the Empire of Kasprin and our Gods. It is his spell that is causing Koya so much pain."

Malin shook his head, not so much in denial as simply disbelief. "He never said!"

"No, he wouldn't. Koya is far too loyal to the Temple and the Gods."

"How can he be after what the Most Holy did to him?"

"Because the Most Holy is not the Temple or the Gods, Malin. He's just a man with his own agenda, and who has too much power -- secular and magical -- for his own good. That happens sometimes, you know."

Malin remembered such instances at Ziven -- painful memories, but true ones he could measure this truth against. Malin had known such people as the Most Holy, but he had never thought of them in higher ranks.

Naïve.

"Yes, I see," Malin said at last. Slade looked relieved, and Malin appreciated that he'd told him the truth of the matter, even though admitting the truth had worried the older man. Malin leaned his head back against the tree and didn't consider the idea of getting comfortable. He didn't think he would ever find comfort in the world again, now that his place in it had been destroyed.

Oh, he could go back to Ziven. Someone would come and clear away the bodies. Others take over the houses and the Temple. They would use his father's tools, and sleep in his bed --

"Malin?" Slade asked softly.

Malin had started trembling and couldn't stop. He couldn't see the future, and he didn't want to look at the past. Malin could only see now, sitting here by this tree, in a dark, cold night, with nowhere to go. No home.

"Malin?" Slade repeated his voice more forceful this time.

He looked at the priest and swallowed back the wave of illness that nearly took him. "What am I going to do?" Malin whispered. "What am I going to do now?"

"You're going to help me find Koya."

"But afterward --" Malin waved a shaking hand towards the world around them. "I can't go back."

"No, you can't," he agreed, and Malin took unexpected comfort from those words. He'd worried that the priest would say he had to go back and face what had happened, or fix it, or do something else beyond anything Malin could understand. "But you do have to go on."

"Go on," he said, trying to work his thoughts around those words. He didn't want to think too far ahead, and the mere idea set him shivering. "I was going to marry Calina. We were going to take over her father's lands since he had no sons of his own. I was going to..."

The words drifted off, and he lost what he meant to say, although the image of Calina stayed with him, her smiling face, her eyes bright with joy as they talked about the future.

"I hate them. I hate them all."

Slade nodded.

"What am I going to do now?"

"You're going to help me find Koya and get him safely away from these people."

"Why? Why should I care?"

"Because if we save him, you won't be the only survivor."

Those words struck him like a blow, and he jerked back, frightened by the thought, frightened by the future and the idea of being the *only one*. Koya hadn't been one of them, though. Koya had only been there ... but still, this was better than no one at all.

"Find Koya." Malin gave a quick nod of his head, probably more decisive than he'd been in his entire life. "Yes. In the morning."

Slade said nothing more. Malin liked him the better for it. He couldn't have stood lectures, sermons, or tales of how the Gods did what was right for reasons humans could not readily see.

Though, secretly, Malin hoped that was somehow true.

He didn't sleep much.

CHAPTER

FOURTEEN

"Supplies, Kenning," Most Holy said, looking up from behind Kenning's desk where he had settled an hour before. He'd made a mess of the paperwork, of course. There was nothing this man did that didn't become a problem for someone else.

"Supplies?" Kenning dared ask, forcing calm still.

"I am leaving to return to the Tralista," Most Holy replied. Kenning forced himself not to smile. "I must have adequate supplies and a company of guardsmen to keep me safe during this time of trouble. I must go straight to the Empress and tell her what has happened."

The man stared at Kenning, daring him to say anything to the contrary, but Kenning had learned that lesson. Most Holy listened to nothing that contradicted his vision of the world, which currently meant the Dragonkin were attacking, and maybe in league with the Damarians, or at least with one

Norter priest.

Kenning began making his own plans, even while he bowed his head to the Most Holy. "What shall you require?" he asked.

"My man will tell you," Most Holy said and waved him away. Kenning wondered why he'd bothered calling him to the desk then, but he supposed it was a show of being in charge, like everything else. "I expect it all in place by tomorrow."

"Yes sir, of course," Kenning replied and didn't have to pretend to look bothered. Most Holy smiled and dismissed him with a nod. Kenning wasn't even allowed to do the work from the place where he could see the paperwork on what supplies they had on hand.

Fine. Kenning didn't care. Kenning would do whatever he could to get the Most Holy out of the Temple. Afterward, he would do his best to counter whatever mess the Most Holy was about to create. He remembered the vision of the battle and suddenly felt a chill. Most Holy was going to start a war.

Out in the hall, Kenning snagged Armath, saying nothing until they were all the way to the dining hall where other priests were preparing for the next meal. None of the Most Holy's people were here. They didn't help.

"He's heading for the capital to start a war," Kenning said without any preamble. Priests looked his way, worried, but none of them surprised. "We need to get his supplies ready, and he'll be gone tomorrow. Armath, I'm sorry, but you are going to have to deal with his people and find out what they expect us to come up with on such short notice."

"And you?" Armath asked, knowing Kenning planned more.

"I will be getting my own supplies," he said. "I'll have to leave right after the Most Holy. He'll go by the south road. I'll head north and then south again, so we're not on the same path. Mine is a much longer journey, but if I'm fast -- and the

Gods are with me -- I'll reach the city no more than a day behind him."

"Sir -- that's dangerous. If there really is trouble along the border, and you are heading northward --"

"Then I'll know the Most Holy is right," he said. His hand tightened on Armath's arm. "But we know he isn't right, and I can't let his voice be the only one to reach the capital to tell of this trouble."

"Yes, sir. You're right. I can go with --"

"No. I want you here. The Gods know there is going to be trouble enough no matter what is really happening. People already think there's a war brewing, and all of you, my friends, are the ones who know the truth and must do your best to tell the others. I'm going to speak with the Headman here in Templeton as soon as I can slip away. If Most Holy asks, tell him that I have gone to the town to buy -- no, to demand -- the supplies that are needed for him."

"Yes, sir," Armath said with a bow of his head. "A little lie to make our lives easier."

"Exactly. It will also keep the man from harrying any of you. Make certain everyone looks very busy."

"We will be busy," Armath replied. "I had better start baking now, don't you think?"

"Oh yes," he said. "All kinds of work -- that's bound to keep the Most Holy and his people away if they think they might be asked to help with something."

Armath made a sound of agreement and went on his way. Kenning didn't wait any longer. He headed out of the building and straight down the path to the gate. He hadn't been in Templeton much since Most Holy arrived ten days before. How could so much have gone wrong in so short a time? Koya, the rats, the war --

The people in town knew there were problems. Their greetings were subdued, worried -- and Kenning tried not to look as though the world might come to an end at any moment. He didn't need to make this worse for the locals. He stopped scowling, but he made it plain he had work to do for the Most Holy.

Headman Fywarth saw him more quickly than usual. The older man sat behind a desk as littered with paperwork as Kenning's own.

Neither of them had time to waste.

"Most Holy is leaving in the morning," Kenning said.

That got the man's attention. He pushed back papers and frowned. "That's rather quick -- ah. Running for the capital, is he?"

"Yes," Kenning said. He saw no use in playing games with this man. "He wants to be there to tell the Empress what is happening."

"What happened to Koya?"

The question caught him off guard. "Sir?"

"People saw that he was injured when he left -- an odd time for him to be packed off to some remote village when you have so many other priests. You were getting Koya out of the Temple and away from the Most Holy, weren't you?"

"Yes," he said. Honesty seemed the best idea here. He trusted that Fywarth wouldn't go straight to the Most Holy with what he had to say. "And I will be leaving shortly after the Most Holy in hopes of reaching the capital and countering any evil he starts to spread. We have problems, Headman, but they are not with the Dragonkin. Norters are trying to start a war between us and the Dragonkin, no doubt hoping we'll destroy each other and wipe the evil of magic from the face of the earth. I cannot stop the Most Holy. He is very powerful, and we don't want any trouble with him here. So, he'll leave in the morning by the southern route. I will go by the north. He'll travel slowly. If I move as fast as I dare --"

"Do you want guards?"

"Not for me. Most Holy will be demanding them, though."

"Will he?"

"Don't toy with the man. Don't annoy him. We want him on the road because, quite honestly, he'll do less damage there as he heads to the capital. I need you here to help keep matters as calm as possible, not only in Templeton but also in the entire area. We will have panic when the rumors start. We might have war. I hope not."

Headman Fywarth had always been touchy about his power, and he had never been very cooperative with Kenning. However, the Most Holy had been less than polite to the man, outright ignoring him on the few occasions when they were in the same place. That played into Kenning's favor now. Fywarth wanted the man gone as much as he did.

"Yes," Fywarth said with a nod. "Let's see what we can do to get him on his way. You never did say what happened to Koya ... but in your own way, I think you gave me the answer. We've noticed that the Most Holy doesn't care for anyone with northern blood."

"No, he does not."

The man nodded and asked no more. He pushed away his paperwork and stood. "Let's get the man ready for his trip home then, shall we? And then we can get to work on the real problems."

Kenning didn't argue.

CHAPTER

FIFTEEN

The Damarians broke camp with quick, practiced moves and in relative silence. Torches moved, flickering fitfully in the damp grey of a near dawn morning and letting off more smoke than light. Koya watched as the faint illumination danced through the lines of trees around them.

Then the thing came up the hillside, a lumbering dark shadow in the predawn dark. Torchlight only vaguely outlined the creature, making it seem even more monstrous. The humans moved away in haste; they were not comfortable allies, then. Koya didn't think the fact would help him, though.

The creature let out a growl that must have been heard for miles and startled him enough to move back from the edge of the cage. He only belatedly realized the sound had been words of power. Magic swept in, and the poles lifted from the ground and dropped down into a ragged pile. Men hurried to gather them up, while others came for the two prisoners. They were leery of the Dragonkin, but not too worried about handling a human priest. Koya would have been embarrassed if he hadn't been more anxious about what would happen next.

They soon left camp, but Koya couldn't keep pace with the guards. Within a quarter of a mile, he'd fallen so many times that crawling might have been preferable to trying to stand again.

"Get up!" One of the men viciously kicked him hard enough in his right leg that the world went red with pain and then black. He wasn't going to walk or crawl anywhere...

He came awake with a splash of cold water across his face.

"Get up," another guard said, leaning down close to his face this time.

Koya saw no use in arguing over something he could not win -- and thought about his unfortunate conversation with the Most Holy once more. This was not the time for any disagreement. He got back to his feet and walked as far as he could. After the first couple of miles, he saw the Dragonkin looking at him with confusion rather than distaste.

Koya went down again on the rougher part of the trail, and this time his leg wouldn't hold him at all. The guard grabbed Koya -- left arm, they'd learn that at least -- and cursed.

The creature ambled towards them. Guards froze everywhere, and fear shown clearly in all their faces. The thing tossed a stripped branch at Koya's feet, just the right size for a walking staff.

"You walk," it growled in a voice that made the very stones tremble beneath him.

Intelligent -- more so than Koya had expected.

The soldier grabbed the staff and shoved it into Koya's hand. No kindness on his part; the creature wanted Koya to walk, and the soldiers would do what they could to make certain he did so. Koya thought about purposely still slowing them, though nothing obvious. They appeared to be in a hurry, as though they worried about something following. If he slowed, there might be a chance of rescue.

They walked all through the grey and dreary day, heading mostly eastward along what had been no more than deer trails, but soon became wider and trampled down by so many feet. They crossed snowmelt brooks, but never anything deep enough that Koya might have thrown himself into the water and escaped, one way or another.

The creature moved with the army, which proved to be a distraction for Koya. He studied it, trying to make sense of what such a magical beast was doing with Norters who never should have allied themselves with something of magic.

Were these men outcasts? He would have hoped so, but he thought them too well-disciplined and too well supplied. Several of his cousins had served in the border patrols, and he knew the look of army weapons, clothing, and gear.

They stopped at midday while the soldiers ate, and the scouts came in with reports. The creature settled on a huge boulder, blending in so well that Koya shivered, thinking such things might have always been around and not seen.

Koya wanted to ask the Dragonkin, but his fellow prisoner purposely took himself as far away from Koya as the guards would allow. Koya tamed his annoyance since he didn't have the energy to waste. He settled in the only spot of sunlight he could find and lifted his head into the waning light, feeling the warmth brush against his face.

Koya whispered a prayer to the Gods, giving thanks for the day, as he had every other day since he went to the Temple, though he usually would have done so at dawn. He was not where he wanted to be, but Koya began to think maybe the Gods had placed him here because he understood the guards, and he had magic of his own.

Koya let himself relax and accept this bit of respite that he knew wouldn't last long. His leg and arm ached, settling into a steady pain, rather than the sudden jolts he'd felt every time he took a step. His body could adjust to constant pain, rather than the shocks of movement on uneven ground. Koya thought this might help him survive.

Did he want to survive? Nothing good could come from his capture. And what about his unwilling companion? Koya glanced at the Dragonkin, who sat much like Koya, though with his head back and his eyes closed. His head turned a little eastward, and he sniffed and sniffed again.

Could he smell home? They weren't far into the mountains, and the lands of the Dragonkin lay on the other side. Maybe the Dragonkin could scent freedom out there or the way home. Koya didn't ask.

The guard soon forced them up and moving. Koya used the makeshift staff and struggled back into line with the Dragonkin. They walked in silence, the soldiers spread out around them and grumbling. They were not happy, these northern soldiers. They didn't like where they were, and they didn't like their ally, which was the best hope Koya had that the deal with magic was not widespread.

The trail became rougher, and with his arms secured, Koya's fellow prisoner began to take more falls. Koya finally moved to where he could put a steadying hand out now and then. That won glares at first, but later grunted sounds of acknowledgment and even a nod of thanks.

They walked long into the dark, even the soldiers starting to trip and fall more often -- and if they knew where they were going, no one said.

The creature stayed with them.

CHAPTER

SIXTEEN

Malin had more than proved his worth by early the next day. While Slade could do some scout work, Malin knew the short cuts through the mountains and was far better at reading the signs. The group had broken camp before they caught up and had headed up the long trail over the visible pass that headed into a wilder area where humans rarely went. They had heard strange noises but hadn't dared get close enough to see what was happening.

Malin showed him a path better fit for mountain goats than humans, but by the time they reconnected with the main trail, they'd cut out several miles from the trek and saved themselves hours.

As they came down on the main trail, Slade worried about what would happen if they caught up with the people who had taken Koya. He paused there, frowning, and Malin looked back with sudden concern.

"We need to slow down," Slade said softly.

"We've almost caught up with them," Malin protested, waving a hand to weeds bent over, not yet dying. "They're not moving very quickly."

"What do we do if we catch up?"

Malin blinked several times, obviously trying to figure out what the two of them could do against what had to be several hundred of the enemy. "Can you use magic?" he finally asked.

"Some, but the magic I use is meant to help and heal, and it's not a good idea to use that to hurt others. The Gods wouldn't be pleased, and we don't want to add their anger to our current list of troubles."

"Should I care?" Malin asked and meant those words quite honestly. "What have the Gods done for me? They let the village be destroyed."

"Malin, I'm not going to tell you how the Gods do things for a reason, because I'm not always certain that's true. I think sometimes things slip past them, or people find a way to work so that the Gods don't notice until too late. Maybe these soldiers have found the backing of Gods who are not our Gods. I'm not certain what might have happened, but I do know this: you should never have survived long enough for me to help you. I think, truly, there is some outside purpose in that part."

Malin vehemently shook his head, showing more emotion than he had so far. Shadows danced across his face, like something alive moving over him. Slade shivered, wondering if Malin had been given to him as a gift to help, or if there might be something else entirely at work here. The Norters had taken Koya, a priest. What if they wanted another one? What if Malin led him to the enemy, whether willingly or not?

"We need to slow down," Slade again said. This time

Malin didn't argue.

He had to trust the boy, and he put his fears aside as they began to walk on. Slade hoped he could come up with something they could do when they did catch up with the others. To that end, he began to look around the woods. Slade hadn't traveled much in this area before, having come from the south and the flatlands. The mountains had interested Slade, but his work as a priest had taken all his time and energy, and he'd only spent a few days in the mountains over the last ten years.

A priest would be stupid to go blindly into any wild area where there might be trouble. The Gods he served were aligned with life. Once he considered the situation, he could feel specific shifts in the natural world and gathered information just by sensing it.

What Slade had seen at the village had knocked all awareness out of him, and he had suddenly felt like a soldier again. It had taken nearly a day to remember new resources learned since the last time he had walked away from a battlefield.

Slade listened instead of rushing around like a wild boar on a rampage. He could hear birds and animals in the underbrush. The breeze brushed against his face, and when he closed his eyes, he could even feel the pulse of the enemy, still moving steadily ahead of them.

Then he felt something else. Something wrong. Dark magic, like a storm cloud, brought to earth.

"I need to contact Kenning," Slade said very softly, signaling Malin to stop and step off the trail. He feared that if he could feel this thing of magic, it could feel him as well.

"Sir?"

"They have something with them, Malin. Something magical -- far more magical than Koya. Something different."

"Dragonkin?"

He thought for a moment and shook his head. "No, I don't think so. When I was a soldier, we fought the Dragonkin. I couldn't feel them the way I can as a priest, but even so ... no. This doesn't belong. Sit down and rest. I am going to contact Kenning, but I'll do it with as little show as I can manage."

Malin settled on a fallen log, staring at him with open worry before he turned away and stared off into the woods. Slade suspected the boy might not truly be watching the forest, but he said nothing. Malin needed time to deal with his ghosts. Slade knew that very well.

Slade pulled out the rune for the Temple, holding the stone in his palm and practicing some turtle-calm before he tried to make contact. He didn't want to draw the attention of whatever else lurked in these woods.

Calm. Quiet.

"Kenning?" he finally said when the felt the thread connect to somewhere else.

He didn't know if the priest would hear him right away, but he knew Kenning would have some link to the two of them and would know about the contact. He waited. Patient, oh, so patient.

And then he heard a voice.

"No, Most Holy. Of course, it's not Koya. I told you, he's been captured."

"So, you said," another voice growled.

"This is Slade. I do have several priests in my district, sir. And they all have problems of their own."

"This one is in the area of the traitor priest."

Malin's head turned to stare at the rune with his eyes narrowed in anger. Slade held up one hand and stilled any outburst, though it was hard enough for him to keep his own temper. Kenning had given him all the warning he could, though. Whatever Slade reported, he must not set the Most

Holy off.

Slade covered his own annoyance, knowing that no matter what Kenning said, he'd know Slade had contacted him for a serious reason. He'd have to play this stupid game for now, though.

"Kenning, sir? Are you there? I think I can hear you --"

"I'm here, Slade," Kenning said, his voice calm. "Did you reach the village? Are they dead?"

"Yes sir," he said and didn't have to hide his feelings there. "All dead."

"I'll send others to help with the rights and the cleansing. Did you learn anything else?"

"No, sir," he said, assuming that Kenning wasn't really asking for information since he kept leading the conversation to areas they'd already gone over. "I don't think there's anything more we can learn from the village."

"Then make peace with the Gods, Slade, and take care. I'll talk to you again later."

"Yes, sir."

The connection went dead.

"Gods rot that impossible man!" Slade growled and startled Malin probably as much for their intensity of his anger as the words.

"That was the Most Holy? Why ... why would he be so...?"

"Unhelpful," Slade offered the most charitable word he could find as he tamed his own anger. "Because he is a man who has come to believe too much in himself."

"What are we going to do?"

Slade glanced around the area, trying to find calm again. The Most Holy's words had not helped him in this problem. He needed to anchor himself here and link to what was happening. There was one more thing he could try, but not if he radiated anger, worry, and fear.

"I'm not good at communicating with the animals," Slade

admitted. "It takes the kind of patience that I haven't ever held for very long. However, I think it's time I call on something more than our eyes to tell us what's going on here."

"You can do that?" Malin asked and looked around with a start. "Galt always said the wild ones were more hindrance than a help."

"Ah, now, Galt sounds like someone far too much like me," Slade admitted and won a slight smile from the bit. "Koya ... Koya, on the other hand, could sit with rabbits and squirrels for hours and listen to them. He is truly blessed by the Gods."

"Is that why the Most Holy doesn't like him?"

Slade considered the idea. "I'm sure that's one of the many reasons. Koya is very good at being a priest. The people soon came to accept him and came to him for help. And he's powerful. The Most Holy doesn't trust anyone from the north. A Norter priest with powers that probably rival his own did not settle well with him. Kenning kept Koya safe and close, at least until the Most Holy came for a visit."

"The Most Holy won't help Koya."

"No, he will not," Slade agreed. He began to lift runes from his box and looked them over. He had become good with tame chickens and dogs, but neither of those was available here. What else? He stopped and looked back at Malin, remembering the other conversation. "The rest of us, though, believe and trust Koya. We'll do what we can, even working around the Most Holy, to help Koya. And in assisting him, it's plain that we will be doing some greater good. There are too many things out of balance, Malin. This is about far more than just Koya."

"Yes, sir. I know."

Slade wished he could find the words to help the boy. Though, perhaps, the words didn't exist. He'd never found any that comforted him, back in that past life. Perhaps only action would help -- and having a reason to move forward.

Slade looked at the runes and focused on what to do next. Squirrels were too anxious and jittery for him. Rabbits were too shy, and he scared them by being impatient. There were rats about, probably more than there should be, but Slade didn't trust them considering their part in what had already happened. There were even hints of some of the lesser magical creatures that humans rarely saw in the more settled areas. He didn't want to try to call too any of them because the other thing out there might feel such a movement. Besides, some of them were dangerous in their own right. He had also heard that they were often fiercely territorial, though Slade thought they were all on the move as well.

Fox.

Foxes were much like dogs in some ways, and probably the closest he could come to something he'd touched before unless he dared to call in a wolf. No, he didn't trust he had that much control.

He looked back at Malin, the rune in his hand. "I'm going to try to call a fox, but I don't know if it will work. I'll have to do it softly, because there's something else out there that might hear the magic, and I don't want to draw that attention. If the fox does come, the two of us may talk for a while, but it will mostly look like we're just staring at each other and making odd noises."

"I'll be still, sir," Malin said. Slade thought he saw something unexpected in Malin's face just then: curiosity mixed with excitement.

Slade hoped this worked as he settled on the ground, sitting cross-legged and cupping the rune in his hand. The first step had to be forcing calm into his thoughts, and he did that with relative ease this time, helped by exhaustion.

Next, he had to think himself into fox terms. Slade had to see the world through a fox point of view, which meant low to the ground, not bound to trails, the scent of life everywhere. Slade carefully reached out, first towards the camp of the enemies, hoping to find something along the way ... but he dared not go too close in that direction. So, Slade turned from the northeast to the east, and moved slowly, slowly along the ground. It was long, tedious work, even though he didn't stretch out more than two miles.

The late afternoon passed into twilight.

And he found the fox. It startled them both.

"Come to me, friend fox," he said aloud, his voice a mere whisper. The words helped him to concentrate after nearly losing touch in that moment of surprise. "Come to me. I wish only to converse."

The fox didn't want to leave off his hunt. Food had been scarce with the others here.

"I wish to know about the others."

A feeling of revulsion, a hint of fear -- and the fox turned and started darting through the brush, heading straight for him. Slade wanted to tell Malin, but he didn't dare let go of the little thread that brought the fox to him. He only nodded and hoped Malin understood.

The fox eventually parted the brush beside a tree. The animal blended into the shadows, the fur molting from winter grey to red. He spotted Malin, and his head went down and his back up.

Friend. A boy. No harm.

Priest.

Not him. But me.

Others.

I wish to know the others. I wish to see them.

There had been too many words for the poor fox, who made a yipping sound of annoyance. Slade apologized without words, and then carefully, with the rune still in his hand, laid his fingers on the fox's head.

Slade found it unpleasant to try and fit human thoughts around fox perceptions. However, before long, he could see the world differently, and he could sense things that were not natural. First came a mishmash of information like how the prey had run, how the humans tramped through, and upset everything. And then something more; the fox had been hiding in the bush when the enemy went by.

Slade caught that memory and watched the tramp of booted feet. There, the blue of a tattered robe. The fox looked up at the priest, feeling a bit of kinship with the person who went by. Koya stood on his own feet but looked haggard, bruised, and miserable.

And just behind him walked a Dragonkin. At first, Slade thought that meant the others were Dragonkin as well -- but no, they were Norters from the looks of it. They must have taken another prisoner. Perhaps the Dragonkin was that touch of magic that Slade could feel, out of place and unsettling --

Not.

And then, just off the side of the trail, came something else.

Huge, earth-colored, a face that turned towards them and startled Slade out of his contact with the fox, who yipped and whined, and then quickly retreated again.

Slade sagged back against the tree, trembling and uncertain if that came from exhaustion, the work, or what he had seen. It had been a nightmare, that creature.

"Slade?" Malin asked very softly.

"We have a problem, Malin. The Norters are traveling with something ... something magical and out of place, and I don't even know what it was. I did see Koya, briefly, in their ranks. And another prisoner, it seems. Someone of the Dragonkin."

"Making enemies of everyone."

There was an interesting observation, and Slade gave the

boy a quick nod of agreement as he tried to figure out what they should do next. That thing was what he could feel in the woods, full of latent power, darker and tainted with blood. Not the blood of the hunt, but rather of something killed for him. Sacrificed.

They had to reach Koya and get him to safety.

Koya, who had felt something dark and dangerous here in the north.

Slade started to stand in haste but then settled back on his knees. Rushing now would be no better than rushing before. It was still just Malin and him, and they had to think this through and work carefully.

And pray -- *truly pray* -- that creature didn't find them first.

CHAPTER

SEVENTEEN

They unexpectedly came upon a fort.

Koya knew there shouldn't be anything built here in the backwoods so close to the Dragonkin border. The humans had small villages nearby (like Ziven), but they only hunted in this area, and by treaty, no one settled in this strip of land. These Damarians who had built the fort came from farther north, beyond the triangle where the three territories joined at the edges of the great Meyoman Lake. That location was a place with bogs for miles on all sides, and a perfect border for three angry groups that fought whenever they came too close to one another.

This fort posed a new problem. The walls stood straight and tall, cut from hundreds of towering ash trees, the trunks stripped bare and shoved back into the ground to form three sides of the protective barrier. The fourth wall was a natural cliff that rose high over them, the surface pocked with holes where birds and bats swept in and out. A watch tower and smaller wall stood up there, as well. Koya couldn't see through the massive iron-shod gate yet, which had just started to open, but he caught a whiff of humanity: food, decay, and a poorly maintained latrine.

The Dragonkin prisoner moved up beside him and shook his head in mute surprise as he looked over the walls. This seemed something they could share, the shock and mistrust over yet another strange Damarian move. Koya saw his own emotions mirrored in the Dragonkin's face.

"They should not be here," the Dragonkin said.

"I know."

The narrow face turned to him. Koya hadn't noticed the thin cut and darker bruise along the right side of his face, nor the blood on his right arm. Whatever wound the Dragonkin had there, he didn't seem to notice it much.

Someone shoved them from behind, and neither thought to argue. However, Koya saw the way his companion looked off to the side of the trail, toward the wider woods and darker shadows. If he could get free and run while these Norters were intent on getting inside --

The creature rose up right there at the edge of the trees. It stared as though daring either of them to try. The Dragonkin drew in a hissing breath, and his step faltered, but he turned his attention back to the path and the last distance to the fort. They had not opened the gate wide, and the others were moving faster now --

"What enemies do they have here?" Koya asked aloud.

His companion gave him a wary look and said nothing.

"None of my people know they are here," Koya said, ignoring the second glance of mistrust. "And I suspect the same of your own. So why are they afraid to open the gates? What is out there that might be our ally?"

"Nothing we could deal with," the Dragonkin finally said.

The guards were too busy spreading orders to their own people to pay attention to what they said. "There are wild things here, some of them magical. They live in the woods and do their best to avoid all two-legs. They would be no friends of ours, but they may have caused trouble to these Norters."

"I am a priest of The Ten," Koya said and put his hand on his chest where his emblem should have been hanging if that chain had not broken. "Sometimes, that can help."

His companion turned a glare on Koya, who supposed he either didn't believe or that being a priest was not any better than just being a human in general. Koya tried to curb his frustration with the one person who might have been an ally but who refused to give up his own bigotry.

They passed through the gate and went inside. Shadows seemed to live here in a place perpetually shaded by the cliff and the tall wooden walls the humans had built. Koya was not surprised to find such a rude habitation inside, with only a single flimsy building up against the cliff and a plethora of hide-covered tents in a haphazard array nearer the walls. Koya saw a stockade without any horses and knew they were headed there to wait judgment in the open and the cold.

Koya didn't care as long as they could stop for a while. He'd kept himself going, even when the pain in his leg grew to a new agony with each step. He had blocked that pain away as best he could until he faced the hope of rest.

He went down on his knees, right there inside the gate. One of the Norters kicked him, which didn't help. He tried to get back up because he hated to show weakness. The staff no longer helped. This was worse than it needed to be thanks to that damned Most Holy --

He stopped the thought before it drove him to rage. Maybe he was being taught something. Humility? Oh yes, quite humbling to have to crawl when he wanted to stand --

A hand caught him by the shoulder. He hissed in pain, but

then realized his Dragonkin companion was helping him up.

"We don't want to annoy them," the Dragonkin said, his eyes narrowed as though he still suspected Koya of some subterfuge. Koya stumbled to his feet and stayed there the last few yards to the rough walled pen. The Norters grabbed the staff and then pushed them in, growling words in anger as they shoved the gate closed.

Koya saw no cover and nothing but dirt and mud. He took a step to the side of this final gate, leaned against the nearest post, and slid down.

"I don't see any reason to go any farther," he said, looking up at his companion. "It's not as though we'll find better accommodations on the other side of the pen."

The Dragonkin frowned, and then gave a little shrug of agreement, and chose the next post down, landing on the ground with less grace than even Koya. The trip hadn't been easy for either of them.

Koya wanted to ask questions. He wanted answers. He wanted ... some clue on how to get them out of this place. He didn't want to face anger and bigotry of the Norters, nor did he want to go into the care of that beast, whatever it might be.

Koya glanced at his companion and wondered if the Dragonkin, being tied to the world of magic, knew what the creature might be. He didn't ask anything with the guards patrolling unhappily just outside the stockade. Koya would have to observe what was going on through his own eyes and find answers his own way.

He did notice that no one was happy here. The Norters didn't act as though they had made a conquest by taking this bit of land, but rather as though this was the last place on earth that they wanted to be assigned. The glares Koya saw turned his way made him think that the people somehow blamed the prisoners.

Or what they represented: Kasprians and Dragonkin.

There had never been any love between the magic-less humans of the north and the humans and others who used magic in the south. The hatred had led to a religious war and an ongoing battle between good and evil -- with both sides defining evil as the other people's beliefs. Koya saw the remnants of that war everywhere, like the reaction of the Most Holy to his light hair and the way people had run from the Dragonkin when they marched through a village.

Koya shivered a little, remembering the Lesslings. That the Dragonkin could deal with those creatures -- and humans could not, marked the differences between them far more than any outward differences. Even so, Koya wished that this Dragonkin had a least one around to help them.

Koya glanced at his nameless companion, hoping for conversation. Although exhausted, he wanted to talk with someone who might help keep this nightmare at bay for a little while. The Dragonkin never looked his way, though.

Koya finally closed his eyes, letting his head rest back against the hard, rough bark of the stockade fence. He had to find a way out, but he could hardly think at all. He drifted to sleep for a while and awoke with a shock of pain as someone grabbed him by the arm and propelled him to his feet. He didn't stay there. The guards cursed, dragged him up again as they took him out of the stockade.

He thought he saw his companion-in-misery give a worried glance -- just a moment of shared commiseration. Then the guards shoved Koya forward, pushing him all the way to the rough-walled wooden building that sat up against the cliff. The guard knocked once and then pulled the door open and shoved him inside.

Koya found a room covered in thick but worn rugs of muted, time-worn colors. They spread from the floors to walls -- and yes, even across the ceiling. The coverings did not keep out the damp or the cold. Smoke drifted around in curls from a badly kept hearth on the sidewall. The furnishings were nothing more than a rough-hewn table and chairs, and a bed on the floor in the corner. Even that was covered by another dirty, old rug.

The guards shoved him into a chair opposite the door. They saluted a man who stood by the hearth, something Koya hadn't seen them do to anyone else. The man waved the guards away, and they left in haste.

Someone of importance. Koya did not bow his head when the man looked his way, though perhaps that was just stubborn stupidity, considering what had happened with the Most Holy. The two guards had left. They did not, obviously, take Koya as much of a threat.

"We live like barbarians, you know," the man suddenly said.

Those were not the words Koya had expected. He weighed them for a moment and then finally looked up to find the man watching him.

"I grew up in the north. I chose not to be a barbarian."

"And went to the evil and cursed south, instead."

"Where you appear to be heading as well," Koya reminded the man and decided that being daring was better than cowering. He doubted there would be any difference in the outcome, but at least he felt better for it. "I was Called by the Gods. You come only to destroy. You cannot judge evil."

The man looked shocked for a heartbeat, and Koya knew this one -- like the Most Holy -- wasn't used to people talking back to him. The Gods were toying with him again. Koya wondered what he had done to deserve another confrontation like this and vowed to make amends if some God would be kind enough to get him out of this mess.

The man stood taller than most Damarians Koya had seen, his hair cropped short, but his face was nearly covered in a bushy and unkempt beard. When the man finally stepped closer, Koya saw eyes of a colorless grey and piercing as they measured him. Koya could not guess what the man wanted, although watching those eyes, Koya knew he dared not show weakness. Koya sat up straighter and did not wince, even when the man came and put a hand on his shoulder.

Oh, the man knew it hurt. And that brought up another aspect of this madness.

"You deal in magic," Koya said, looking him in the face. The grey eyes blinked, and the stranger took a step away. "You deal with whatever creature that is out there, and you know it's not natural. How can you accuse people of a crime and think yourself without taint?"

"Use the devil to catch a devil," he said with a little quirk of a smile.

"That's a very convenient lie to tell yourself."

The man backhanded Koya, though not with much force. He blinked and stared back at the man, not offering anything more. The truth had been spoken, and this Norter leader knew how he'd be judged.

"I will wipe magic from the world and make it pure again." The man leaned closer and looked Koya fully in the face this time. "I will use a devil to kill a devil."

"You are trying to make it look as though the Dragonkin are raiding villages along the borderlands in hopes of getting the southerners to go to war with them. Then you will let both groups annihilate each other."

"And I'm sure you think I couldn't do such a thing," he replied. He leaned back against the table, so seemingly at ease now. "But I can. Your people -- your adopted people -- and the Dragonkin don't trust each other. There will always be an easy excuse given to go to war with one another. You've been waiting for it for decades."

Koya hoped not to be a part of those plans, even though he had inadvertently started the people on the path this man wanted.

"I know your secret," the Damarian said, leaning closer over Koya again.

"I know."

He smiled with a show of yellow teeth behind the beard. Then he grabbed Koya by the arm and threw him to the ground and kicked him. Agony raced up through his body, and he expected another kick, but instead, the man caught him by the arm and dragged him across the carpeted floor and to the back wall where he jerked one of the rugs aside, showing a wide cavern mouth. The cave stank of decay. Something moved farther in the depths.

"I have brought him for you," the man said.

"Mine," it whispered. "Mine."

"Yours, like the other, to play with for a while. I want this priest back."

A sound like dark laughter came from the depths of the darkness. The face appeared -- huge and frog-like. Koya tried to scramble back, but the man caught him by the arm and dragged him a little farther and then quickly moved away when the creature reached out with a claw, snagging Koya's robe.

The man retreated, and the rug fell back into place, cutting off almost all the light.

The creature dragged Koya into the depths of its hole, heedless of rocks and debris. His head hit a rock, and blood ran into his eyes. He choked on dirt. When Koya became wedged between boulders that the creature had stepped over, it dug claws into his leg and jerked him free.

"Why ... why help them?" Koya asked though breathless, and hardly able to form a coherent thought. "They are not ... not your friends."

The creature laughed, that dark, deep sound that came from nothing natural. Koya felt a rough, massive tongue lick blood from his leg. Koya choked, trying desperately not to be ill. A huge hand poked at his leg and then grabbed him again, pulling him onward.

"Give me toys. You give toys?"

"No."

The movement stopped, which didn't help, and the creature let him go. The little light that came into the cavern, through some high crevice, didn't do more than show shadows moving. Koya shivered, cold and aching, and waited for the creature to come for him again. He thought he should try to crawl away, to hide. He knew, though, that it would do no good.

"Others lie. Others say they will give anything."

"I will not."

The thing grunted, no doubt annoyed -- like the Most Holy and the man up there, the one hiding in his hut and pretending to be in charge. Koya knew differently. This thing, here in his little hollow, controlled the humans.

Koya tried to use a little magic, anything that might help him escape, though there wasn't much he could do without his runes. No matter; the creature breathed the magic in with the air and the power did not affect it.

"What do you want?" Koya whispered.

The creature laughed with delight as it threw Koya onto a bed of rock and began to poke small holes in his skin until Koya whimpered and finally fell into blessed unconsciousness, no longer caring if he awoke again.

CHAPTER

EIGHTEEN

Malin sat guard by the opening to a little cave which was really hardly more than a depression in the ground. The boy remained silent and still, though Slade could tell Malin stayed fully awake and alert to everything outside. The slightest flutter of a bird in a bush drew his immediate attention. The whisper of a breeze drew his eyes to the sky to check the weather.

Slade knew he could sleep with the boy as a guard. And he tried, he really did. However, he also started at every sound, and he stared out into the night, looking for ... something.

He napped, awoke, napped again -- and somewhere around midnight, Slade heard the soft whisper of his name, startling both Malin and him. He scrambled upright, hitting his head and elbow on the rough walls before he grabbed at the chit out of his pouch.

"Kenning, sir?" he said as softly.

"Is it safe to talk?" Kenning whispered.

"Yes, sir." Slade sat up, though the low rough-walled cave still made him hunch forward. He spoke just a bit more loudly. "We're held up for the night and far away from others. Is all well with you?"

"The Most Holy is a problem," Kenning said, and even snorted at his own polite choice of words. Slade shook his head, trying to decide if he should be amused. "I've slipped out of the Temple grounds and gone most of the way across town to speak with you. I dare not stay long. Tell me everything."

Slade reported what had happened over the last few hours, including the view of the creature walking with the Norters. He shivered at the image the fox had given him.

"A rockling?" Kenning asked, his voice soft and worried. "This sounds like a rockling, but I didn't think they existed outside of the Dark Gate and into the Forbidden Valley. Rocklings are legend. Surely, one wouldn't be with the Norters who have no use for magic."

"No use for magic, but they have captured a Dragonkin, and they have Koya. I wouldn't be surprised to learn that they'd seized Ziven's last priest as well, sir. They seem to have fallen into magic in a big way."

"So, they have," Kenning agreed, sounding even more troubled. "I will think about this. Keep watch, Slade. Be careful, you and the boy. I have a mess here, thanks to the Most Holy. He's already sent word to Tralista that the Dragonkin are attacking. I'm doing my best to counter it, which is difficult since he is my superior."

"Sir, if it's not the Dragonkin people --"

"I know. We should have listened to Koya. We should have --"

"Even if you had, you still would have had to go through the Most Holy, and he would not have been swayed by any proof."

Kenning said nothing. Maybe it had been too much truth to say aloud, and Slade regretted it. Then Kenning gave a little sigh. "You're right. And since there had been no attack before this, it would have been difficult to get any backing anyway. Gods all, what a mess. Do you have anything more on Koya?"

"Nothing."

"I have to get back." Kenning sounded frustrated and a little angry, neither of which Slade had heard from him before. "Take care; both of you take care. Get Koya out if you can, but also remember this trouble includes matters of far more importance than just our friend."

Malin turned his way, his face hidden in the shadows. Slade wondered if the words bothered the boy or made him angry, but he couldn't tell.

Slade, though, had another thought on it. "I think if these people want Koya, then it's essential that we get him free, sir."

"Oh Gods, yes," Kenning said, sounding startled again. "But carefully, Slade. Very carefully."

"Yes, sir."

"Contact me when you dare. The Most Holy is leaving to head to the capital at first light -- which, in Most Holy terms, should mean sometime in the afternoon. I intend to leave shortly after him and take a more northerly route to the city. I'll have runes for communications to keep in touch with you as best I can. Just be careful of any contact until after tomorrow, lest the Most Holy is still lingering around Templeton. I'm going to spend as much time away from the Most Holy as I can, but if I'm with him, I'll pretend you are someone else. There is no reason to encourage his bad behavior."

"Yes, sir. I'll be back in touch."

The rune went silent and cold, and Slade put it away with some trepidation. He thought they should have discussed several things, not the least of which was what Slade should do next.

"Sir?" Malin asked softly.

"We're on our own, my friend." He stretched out his legs and winced. "And I'm awake now. Do you want to rest?"

"No, sir. Not yet."

"Then let's go do a little scouting while it's still dark," Slade suggested as he crawled to the front of the cave and looked out into the night. He rifled through his runes until he found what he wanted. Malin watched, intrigued.

"Cow," Slade said, holding up the rune.

"Cow?" Malin looked around, as though he expected such an animal to show up at the cavern entrance.

"The chits not only link to the animal but also represent some aspect the animal portrays. In this case, it's a sense of being uninteresting. Cows are, for the most part, placid creatures and not given to sudden alarm. Except for farmers, no one pays them much attention. We don't want to alarm anything out there as we wander around. So, I'm going to lay a bit of dullness around us. I hope that the animals which usually take fright at humans lumbering through their woods in the dead of night will stay calm and not give us away."

"Oh." Malin looked intrigued, but in a way that made Slade think he wanted anything to keep his mind from remembering the horror of Ziven. Slade carefully placed the little spell in a full circle around them. Soon, the two moved along the edge of the trail, not quite in the open but still in an area that allowed them swift movement. Slade had the feeling they didn't have very far to go because he could soon smell the cook fires. He didn't need to tell Malin to slow down.

They found a fortification that was backed up against a high cliff, almost lost in the trees. Slade stared for several heartbeats, watching guards on the cliff that towered over the walls, and fearing they would be spotted. He hadn't expected to locate something like this, and he could tell the sight startled

Malin as well.

Slade gave a little signal -- a military sign, but the boy understood. They backed up and kept retreating for some distance into the trees before Slade felt safe enough to even whisper.

"There is no way we can get Koya out," he said with a shake of his head, feeling the weight of the words as he spoke them aloud.

"What are they doing there? Why do they have the fort?" Malin asked. "This can't be good, sir. They shouldn't be here at all."

"No, they shouldn't."

"You have magic. Can't you use it to help get Koya free?" Malin asked.

"Maybe. But I'm not very powerful. Not like Koya. Unfortunately, Koya doesn't have his runes."

"We can't abandon him." Malin stared at Slade, daring him to say something to the contrary.

"No, we can't," Slade agreed and saw the boy's shoulders relax. "We'll need to do this carefully, though, my lad. We need to think everything through and not do anything that either gets us killed or perhaps gets me caught as well. They are gathering people of magic ... and other things with magic."

"Oh." Malin stared back at the trail, though he couldn't see the fort from here. Whatever happened, they didn't want to make this situation worse.

Though Slade suspected that would not be in their control.

What was going on here? He couldn't feel it out. Did the Norters really want a war between the two groups? If they had a magical war, it was likely that the powers used would devastate the land.

They would also destroy each other and take all the magic with them. Maybe, in the end, that was all the Norters really

cared about. Fanatics. Fools.
  And dangerous.

CHAPTER

NINETEEN

The guard pushed Koya into the chair while another threw the first, and then a second, bucket of water over him. The icy shock startled him fully awake as the water washed away some of the stink and the blood, though it puddled on the dirt floor -- the rug beneath him had been removed. The water sank into the ground. Koya blinked at the man who stood by the hearth again, waiting for him to speak.

The box of runes -- the ones he'd seen on a shelf in Ziven -- sat on the table before him. The man crossed to the table and tapped the lid, drawing Koya's attention.

"You will help us now," he said. "Or else you will go back to the rockling."

"I will not help you."

Koya surprised the man, who looked startled for the first time. "You cannot mean that," he said, leaning down and starring into Koya's face.

"I will not help you," he repeated, the words a little stronger despite the rapid beating of his heart. "I will not use the gift the Gods gave me for evil."

"You pious fool. I'm only asking that you call a few animals and set them to some specific jobs." He waved back to the table and the box again. "The last priest was no fool. He gave me what I wanted, and he survived."

"Not for long," Koya said and tilted his head. "He's dead now."

"Oh yes, he is dead, though only because he was old and weak from the start." The man tapped the box once more and a little more forcefully. "Do this, and you go out into the stockade. Don't, and you go back to the rockling. It will not kill you, but eventually, you'll wish it did."

"I will not help you."

The man snarled and grabbed Koya by the arm, dragging him out of the chair, cursing --

Someone knocked at the door, drawing a growl of a curse before the man nodded to the two guards. Those guards, Koya noticed, did not go near the rockling's cave; this was the commander's pet and his work alone.

One of the guards opened the door, and a large, burly man with unkempt hair stepped in. He looked at the scene with a scowl, and then belatedly saluted.

"General Bertand," he said, his words almost a growl. He might have been half bear from all Koya could tell. "The guards thought they spotted someone on the trail and looking at the fort. Shall I send out a party to investigate?"

"Yes," Bertand said, his hand tightening on Koya's arm -- a sign of worry, he thought. "Make certain they're well-armed."

"Yes, sir," the man cast one quick look around the room and retreated in haste.

Bertand -- good to finally have a name -- stared at Koya with one eyebrow raised. Koya wondered if he should be tempted to ask for mercy or to give in and use the runes. After all, they were not his own, and he'd have very little ability with them. At best he might call up only a half dozen or so animals --

Then Koya thought about the rats that were already dead because of this man and he knew no other creatures were apt to come to a good end. He would not do it.

Bertand saw the resolution in his look. "You are a fool, priest."

"So, I've been told."

Bertand snarled and dragged Koya to the rug-covered opening. He could hear the rockling on the other side, waiting. Good to have a name for that thing, too.

He would endure this and not give in.

The rockling grabbed Koya as soon as Bertand pulled aside the rug. It dragged him away, laughing, laughing...

Koya awoke in the cold, with the fresh air blowing over him, and the feel of a light rain against his face. He blinked at the grey light, not understanding any of what he saw and felt. What happened to the darkness and the stink?

Someone had brought him back outside. He turned his head and found his fellow prisoner sitting beside him, staring toward the hut. However, Koya suspected the Dragonkin's mind wandered elsewhere. Koya tried to move, which set everything aching.

"Careful, priest."

Wise. Even a slight shiver set some wounds bleeding again, a flash of warm blood against his chilled skin.

"They will take me in next," the Dragonkin whispered.

Koya looked at him, blinking, and then understanding. Bertand would give the Dragonkin to the rockling next. For now, though, the Dragonkin would dread what was to come. He would be in worse shape mentally when they dragged him into the cabin and through no fault of his own. It was in the nature of man ... and of Dragonkin apparently -- to imagine the worst and let those fears grow.

What could his companion do for these people? The same that Koya could if he gave in? Worse? The Dragonkin people had remained when the others retreated into the Forbidden Valley with magical creatures like the tiny fairies and the human-like fae. Koya might call animals and do a few other little tricks. What could they win from his companion if they broke him?

"We need to get out ... out of here," Koya said softly. He tried to sit up and failed.

"Oh, yes. We'll just do that now, shall we? Get up and leave?"

"I will find a way out." Koya meant those words. "Help me sit up."

The Dragonkin shook his head but did as Koya asked, even though it was difficult with his arms still secured. Koya almost couldn't breathe as the world swirled around him in black and grey, but everything settled after a couple of breaths. They were just inside the gate to the stockade, and though there were no guards nearby, Koya saw no way out without drawing Damarian attention. Even if they got to the fortress walls, they would never get the fort's gate open. Go up over the wall? He couldn't climb, not in the state he was in. Maybe he could get his companion out. That might count for something.

"We need to bind some of these wounds." Koya's companion -- he decided to just think of him as DK -- began to tear cloth from the rags of his own tunic. "Unless you wish to bleed to death?"

DK asked this as a legitimate question, and Koya supposed it was, under the circumstances.

"I want to survive, at least for a while longer," he replied. DK seemed to take that as a good answer. "I will find a way out."

"I think you are delusional," he said.

"Yes, I probably am. Right now, though, I don't think delusional will hurt us. At least it promises hope still."

"True." DK began to wrap bandages around the bleeding cuts that were mostly on Koya's legs and arms. DK worked with a far gentler touch than Koya had expected. Koya settled his wounded arm at his waist --

And felt something in the fold of his belt.

He pulled out the rune -- his rune. Rat. He had been using it to try and clear the rats from Ziven, and he hadn't put it back with the others.

His own chit. His own power. Koya could do something with this rune, though he wasn't sure what yet. The gate to the fort would remain closed except when guards went out, and they couldn't fight their way past them. He hadn't the power to use magic, either, even if he could pull up something helpful. They couldn't climb. They couldn't dig their way out --

Tunnel.

The rockling's cave had to open to somewhere else since the creature hadn't come in through the gate. Koya looked at the makeshift building, which carefully hid the opening. Rats? Oh yes, he thought he might still call enough rats to make this work.

When he looked at DK, his companion must have noted the difference in Koya's attitude. For a brief moment, Koya thought there might be hope in those dark green eyes.

"We are going to get out." Koya held the rune out where only DK could see, though his companion didn't appear to understand the significance. Koya carefully folded the rune back inside his aching and bruised fingers. "This is power, my friend. This might be our way out ... but this won't be easy."

"Nothing here is easy. If you can work some of your Gods' magic and get us free, I'll do my best to help you."

How odd. The promise had a little power of its own, as though DK used magic with those words. Koya wondered if he did it on purpose, or if this was part of being one of the Dragonkin. Humans knew so little about DK's people. Koya suspected he might be given a chance to learn more -- if they survived.

CHAPTER

TWENTY

Slade watched as Malin finally slept, the boy too exhausted to stay awake, and even too drained to succumb to nightmares. Malin had stretched out on the hard ground, his head buried in the crook of his arm, and fell to sleep within a half dozen breaths.

Slade remained awake and even dared a little magic to banish his own fatigue. He used the fish rune this time; moving, moving, along the streams and rivers, moving to breathe and stay alive. He paced around their new little camp and quietly kept watch.

The night had turned bitterly cold. Slade dared a touch more magic to help keep them both warm -- no rune for that, just an increase in his body's temperature. He did the same for Malin, and then he prayed to the circle of Gods that no one with power looked this way. Slade wished Kenning would contact him, though, despite that risk. He almost dared make contact himself, but he had nothing new to report. Besides, it might wake Malin.

Slade passed a long night, and one filled with all the worries he had tried to keep from Malin during the day. The worst concern, of course, was that he didn't know what they should do. Slade had no idea how he could rescue Koya from a Norter army. He feared if things turned worse, they would have to abandon the priest to the mercy of this enemy that had already massacred one village.

Something dark and dangerous was happening here, and it was going to spill out of the borderlands and into Kasprin. Slade had to think of all those people and not just Koya. He knew it. Kenning knew it as well, but for now, they still had hope of rescuing their friend.

Clouds obscured the faint light of the moon and made shadows move. Slade wanted the daylight to return. He prayed now and then, his hand brushing against his pendant and feeling a little answering warmth there. It helped --

And then he felt magic moving through the world.

Slade suspended his own powers so quickly that the displaced magic made a snapping sound, and a small flash of light brightened their little area, startling Malin awake.

"Wha --"

"Quiet," Slade whispered and tried not to sound as worried as he felt. He dropped down on his heels beside the boy. "Magic out there."

More than magic: Slade felt the rush of life that came when animals were compelled by magic to do something against their nature. Slade stood and lifted his hands certain they were about to come under attack. Rats! Rats moving couldn't mean good --

Malin saw the creatures and scrambled back, his breath catching in a gasp.

The rats didn't seem to notice them at all.

"They're not after us," Slade whispered, putting a steadying hand on Malin's shoulder.

"What are they doing?" The boy's soft voice trembled. "Rats -- rats going to some other village. And the Damarians will follow, won't they? We have to warn them!"

Slade caught Malin's arm and held tight when the boy tried to go ... somewhere. "There are better ways to warn them. Where's the nearest village?"

Malin blinked several times, and then looked out at the rats again. The numbers were growing, a surge of moving shadows in the night. "They're not heading in the right direction. There's nothing up here, sir. Nothing this side, anyway. The nearest village was downstream from Ziven by almost two days' hike. Where are they going?"

Slade watched for a moment and then nodded. "They're headed toward the fort."

"Are they calling them in, getting them ready for an attack?"

Slade slid forward to the edge of the trail and dared lift his hand and test --

"Koya's magic!" A thrill passed through him as he spoke. Rats glanced his way but kept moving. "Koya's alive, and he is calling the rats to him."

"Maybe they are making him do it," Malin said.

Slade felt a little shiver at that idea, but he felt out the magic again. "No. There is nothing but the feel of hope in Koya's magic. It's him doing this for whatever reason."

"I wish ... I wish he wasn't calling rats," Malin whispered and moved farther back into the edge of the bushes.

Slade said nothing. Instead, he felt out the magic, making certain he was right. The rats headed for the fort, but he could feel Koya start to weaken, to lose them --

He dragged out his box and quickly found the rat rune. With a silent prayer to all the Gods that he was right, he added his help. Then he gathered up his pack while still carefully holding to the rune.

"We have to go and help Koya," Slade said softly, and then looked back at where Malin huddled in the shadows. "I have to go. You can stay here, and work your way back down --"

"No." Malin looked steady when he stood. "No, I have to go with you. It's not their fault, the rats. I know it."

"You're a brave lad," Slade said and put a hand on the boy's shoulder as they started down along the trail. A half dozen rats shied away to the side, but the animals kept going with no other notice. Malin shivered for a moment, but then took better control.

They followed the path with the rats, and Slade hoped he was doing the right thing. He hoped Koya was acting wisely as well.

CHAPTER

TWENTY-ONE

K oya felt his power start to slip and knew he would lose the rats after all. *Failed.* DK would go to the rockling next, and they would both die here --

Magic swept in around his own, supplemented what he had done, and took over, carefully pushing the rats towards the compound. Koya gasped, for a moment dismayed, and then felt weak with the relief.

"Help," he whispered to DK, who reached towards him, worried. "No, I found help. Another priest is out there. I think he must be hunting for me, praise all the Gods. He's taken over the rats. They're still coming. I couldn't have done the work alone."

"I feared as much," DK admitted and bowed his head. "But any hope was better than none. They are coming, these rats?"

"Yes." Koya still held carefully to the rune and hoped he

had enough magic of his own left to direct a few once they got here. "They're already close. Be ready. Run if you can."

"I will not leave you behind." DK looked straight into Koya's face for the first time. He could hardly see the Dragonkin's features in the pale, misty light of the cold night, but he thought he could feel something determined. He also felt something magical in the statement.

"Please --"

"I am decided."

Arguing would waste energy, and Koya had none to spare. Instead, he gave a nod and closed his eyes, knowing the rats drew closer. The rockling would likely notice them and the magic first. Koya hoped Bertand wouldn't pay the creature much attention. The rockling seemed excitable.

One of the guards shouted in fear. Koya opened his hand to drop the rune to the ground and grind it into the dirt. DK caught it in mid drop -- very fast, and plainly with good night sight.

"I will keep this, which may be of use to you later. And the soldiers will not find it."

"Yes. Good."

Another shout. Koya heard the first wave of rats already scrambling down the incline beyond the fort and heading towards them. A moment later, he heard startled cries and clawed feet on dirt and wood. Humans shouted, and he caught the rumbling sound that had to be the rockling.

Bertand burst out of his hut and rushed towards them, his tunic unlaced and his feet bare. He cursed as he tripped on a rock, but the pain didn't slow him.

"What have you done, priest!" he said, grabbing Koya by the arm and yanking him upward.

The world went black, though not for long. Koya came back with Bertand shaking him in anger, though the man looked towards the walls and a few rats climbing over. The man stank of fear, and it did not make him any more reasonable.

"What have you done!"

"I -- I did nothing. Rats. Rats coming -- backlash to whatever you did before," Koya gasped.

"No. No. The rockling said we were safe --"

"And you trust such a creature?" DK asked with such obvious contempt that Bertand let go of Koya and backhanded his companion.

More of the rats had reached the fort and surged up over the walls. Koya made a show of panic and trying to escape, and that ruse set Bertand running. The General would have gone to his hut, but several of the soldiers rushed towards him, shouting for orders. Their presence stopped his inelegant and panicked retreat. Bertand knew that if he ran, then he would never get his men back under his command.

The panic and diversion gave Koya and DK their only real chance to escape.

"Go," Koya said, struggling to keep to his feet. "To the hut!"

DK didn't argue. He caught Koya by the arm, though DK was still hampered by having his arms secured at his sides and just above the elbows, he all but dragged Koya along.

They headed straight for the still-open door as the rats swarmed into the camp behind them, and men screamed in terror. Koya heard someone shout about abandoning the fort. He couldn't be sure those words came from Bertand, but he did clearly hear Bertand shout another order.

"To the army! Leave the fort and get to the main camp!"

"Damn," Koya whispered, gasping as they finally reached the door. "They have more troops somewhere!"

"I -- I heard!" DK got them inside, the small room lit by a flickering lantern.

The bedding had been thrown hastily aside. The General's

boots sat half beneath a blanket. Koya grabbed them, hoping they were close to the right size, though he could do no more than shove them into a pack he found and hanged it on his shoulder. The pack had some food, a rope -- he hadn't time to check for anything more. Koya saw something else far more useful on the table -- two small boxes of runes. Neither were his, but he might be able to use them to some degree. He shoved them both in the pack as well. Then he stopped long enough to untie his companion's arms. DK nodded his thanks and grabbed food from the table, wrapping it in cloth, expertly tying that into a sling that he slipped over his shoulder. His arms clearly hurt to move, but he was not slowed. DK hurried to the door and started to throw it closed, but Koya stopped him.

"No. Stand behind me. The rats won't hurt us. We need -- we need them to do one more job."

DK nodded, watching as the first rats reached the doorway and scrambled inside. They came straight to Koya, gathering around him like dogs begging for dinner scraps.

"I need your help. I need you. Forgive me."

He waved his hand toward the blanketed wall. The rats turned and started that way, rushing forward even though he had imparted to them how much danger they would face.

Moments later, he heard the new battle enjoined, and the rockling screamed with such rage that the ground trembled, and the walls began to crack. Koya braced himself and sent as many of the rats as he dared back out after the soldiers. The animals were safer outside where the men were running in terror.

None of the soldiers were used to magic. Mistrusting it, and no doubt believing it would turn on them, made this so much easier. Bertand couldn't erase generations of fear just to raise this army and attaching a rockling.

"General Bertand is heading this way," Koya warned,

watching the man with worry. "We need a weapon." He began to look around frantically.

"The man is a coward. I think there is a better way," DK said. "Can you bring more of your friends at a run ahead of him?"

"Yes. But Bertand doesn't seem to fear the rats as much now --"

"But he will."

Koya didn't ask what DK intended. He called more rats to him, and they scrambled inside --

A moment later, DK let out a blood-curdling scream that startled Koya, rats, and apparently even the rockling. Bertand stopped where he was, and through a crack by the door, Koya could see the horror on his face.

Koya nodded appreciation and signaled the rats to go back out and after the man. He watched the general turn and run for his life. The sight gave Koya a moment of satisfaction, though not for long. They could hear the rockling growling in anger, a sound he hadn't heard before. Koya could tell that it had begun to scramble up the cave towards the cabin.

Rats poured out of the hole ahead of it. Some of them looked as though they intended to turn back and fight, but Koya waved them away. They left reluctantly.

"Once we get past the rockling, we must hurry -- down through the lair and out wherever it leads us. The rockling comes in from below. There has to be a way out as well."

DK nodded, though his eyes flickered a little with worry. "How do we get past?"

Koya had been looking for a weapon, but he grabbed the lantern instead, checking to see how much oil it held. Not much -- but placed in the right spot --

"Let me," DK said softly and took the lantern. "The face?"

Koya nodded and moved so that he didn't get in the way.

They had no time for any more plans.

The rockling reached the opening, shredded the rug covering with one huge hand, and rushed forward, clearly intent on reaching his enemy, whom he must have realized was Koya. The thing could feel magic.

DK stepped forward, right into the path of the enraged creature, which swept out a clawed hand to brush him aside. DK moved just as fast, and the oil splashed across the rockling's face, and the fire followed.

The rockling went mad with the pain. A claw caught DK in the side, entirely by chance, but he leapt away, grabbed Koya, and kept going. Before they even reached the cave, the cabin had started to fall around the flailing and screaming creature.

Rats retreated with them, rushing down into the dark depths. Koya could hardly breathe, but he held to consciousness and kept moving. He would not slow DK, though he wasn't moving as fast as Koya expected. When his companion stumbled and went to his knees, he knew there was something seriously wrong.

"Go --" DK said, trying to push him ahead.

"No."

He heard his companion hiss in anger and try to push him away, but Koya wouldn't go. "I wouldn't get far anyway, you know. We might as well stand together here. I am not abandoning you."

The cabin had caught fire, and flickering red light bounced along the rock walls, partly illuminating the area where they had stopped. Koya could clearly see DK look up at him with shock and surprise on his face.

Koya met the look. "Humans are not evil or cowards, you know."

"I did not know." He struggled to his feet with one arm wrapped around a badly bleeding cut across his chest. "My only experience with your kind had been our friends up there. And my people do not say good things about any of you."

Koya wished they had time to discuss such matters. He had hoped the rockling would either die in the flames or go out into the compound, but clearly, the creature meant to retreat into its hole. They could see his bulky shape stumbling their way.

"We should go," DK said. "We should go for as far as we can."

They'd both had a few moments to recover. They moved on at a steady but slower pace. Koya expected the rockling to catch up with them at any time, but apparently the injuries slowed the creature as well. Sometimes the rockling howled though, and he knew it had their scent.

"Not far," DK whispered. "Not far to the opening. I can smell the fresh air."

So could Koya. They hurried, though they knew reaching the outside wouldn't mean safety. The rockling would follow them, and there would be soldiers around as well. Koya could hear the sounds of humans as the two came closer to the opening, but they had no choice except to stop and wait for the rockling. Koya led them out along the ledge, remaining as far back in the shadows as they could. The men were on the higher ground, panicked still.

A stream cut across the landscape about a dozen yards away. Koya glanced left and right, frantically hoping to see a place where they could climb the hillside or ford the water. He located what must have been spots where the rockling had clawed into the cliff as he clambered up and down, but they were in no shape to attempt that kind of climb.

"The stream," DK said. He started that way, a hand on Koya's arm and pulling him along. Koya wanted to protest. The stream was broad and turbulent, and they'd never survive trying to ford their way across.

No choice. The rockling stumbled out of the cave behind them, bellowing in rage. If the creature had been a thing of nightmare before, it was far worse now. Oil still burned in rivulets down the face, a sullen glow that showed one ruined eye and the other damaged and blinking with pain. Parts of the face had melted and reformed. He didn't believe the creature could see them, but it knew they were there. With a scream of rage, it leapt forward.

They reached the water first. DK, his hand still tight on Koya's arm, leapt into the stream and dragged Koya along. Koya never got his feet under him once they went in, and he suspected DK didn't either.

The current caught them as they went under. DK never let go. Did the rockling follow them in? Koya couldn't be certain. They might be getting away if they didn't drown. Koya forced his way through the frigid water to reach the surface, and he dragged DK up as well, both of them gasping for air before they went under once more. Koya scraped along rock and then surfaced yet again. With a combination of stubbornness and the last of his magical reserve, he fought his way towards the far side of the water. He hoped they survived.

CHAPTER

TWENTY-TWO

Slade stood by the tree, safe in the shadows while watching the chaos that spread below in the fort. Slade thought he saw Koya before the young priest rushed into the cabin at the far side of the fort -- he and the Dragonkin, obviously working together. There was a sight to see. Slade wondered if they would be safe inside, though.

As Slade watched, the building burst into flame and began to fall so quickly he barely had time to catch his breath and lift his hands. The rockling charged out through the wall, howling in pain and anger, fire burning its face.

"They're trapped! Do something!" Malin shouted, panicked enough that he took a step forward, as though to throw himself down the hillside and into the camp.

"No -- No, they're not trapped. Look -- there's an opening in the cliff. That would be the rockling's lair."

Malin took in the scene and then nodded, though he still

gasped with worry. "The rockling is starting back in after them--"

Slade had time only for a quick wave of magic, hoping the act would go unnoticed in the larger mass of trouble. He didn't even have time for a rune. He simply waved magic at the fire below and blew it back up into an inferno, slowing the creature again.

"Where will they come out?" Malin whispered, craning his neck as though he could see past the burning building and into the cliff beyond it.

"I don't know. I can't tell. We need to get away from here, though. The Norter soldiers are scattering."

"We should try to help!"

Slade also wanted to see Koya again and know he'd escaped that inferno. "We will. But we won't be any help if they spot us. We're still a secret resource."

Malin considered the words. "We need to get away," he agreed though there was still reluctance in his voice.

As they turned away, Slade thought he felt a little whisper of magic that could only have been Koya's work. He took it to heart and tried not to doubt his friend's survival as he and Malin hurried back into the woods.

The rats began dispersing since they were let free of the magic that had drawn them here. They seemed far more anxious than the humans to get clear of the area. In an odd way, they seemed to help. The rats retreated into the woods in the same general direction that he and Malin took, and that kept the soldiers from heading their way as well.

They reached a little cave, found it empty except for a couple startled rats who took off again, and they took the place over. Slade took the time to pull some brush across the front and waved a bit of magic to cover any prints they had made in the area.

The woods were alive with sounds, but none of the

humans had come any closer to them.

"They got away, didn't they?" Malin finally asked, still breathless from their run. "Koya and the other -- the one from the Dragonkin?"

"I think so. I thought I felt a little of Koya's magic as we were leaving. We still need to help if we can. We just have to wait through the rest of the night and be careful tomorrow."

"Are you going to contact others?" Malin asked.

"Not yet. Listen. The rats are upset. I think something is coming our way."

Malin went still. The rats beyond their covering of brush squealed and growled in anger as they ran past. Slade soon heard voices. That relieved him of his one fear. He didn't want the rockling coming this way, but he could deal with men if he had to. The two men muttered and cursed, though Slade didn't understand the words. Not happy men. They didn't linger.

After a while, the area grew silent again.

"I understood most of what they said," Malin whispered. "We pick up some of the language, here on the border. The first one asked what they were going to do if they ran into more of their men. The second said that they'd just say they got lost in the woods, but he shouldn't worry because everyone else had headed for the army camp."

"Heading for the army camp?" Slade said, startled and worried by the words.

"Yes, sir. It sounded as though they meant another camp and not just an outpost."

"That complicates things, doesn't it?" Slade patted Malin on the arm. "Thank you. I wouldn't have had any of that information without you. Get some rest."

Malin huddled back by the wall, and he might have slept for a little while. Slade did not. He listened all through the night, marking the passage of other men and animals. By dawn, the forest sounds had almost returned to normal, and he slept, leaving Malin to keep watch.

They crawled back out well after the dawn, both stiff, sore, and worried. Slade covered the little cave over again on the slight chance they might come back this way.

Slade had asked a rabbit and several squirrels about any humans around, and they'd seen no one at all. He seemed to be getting better at dealing with the smaller animals. Maybe that came of need, or perhaps the Gods had taken notice and were doing their best to help him out.

"What now?" Malin asked. He sounded tired, confused, and worried. "That creature from last night --"

"The rockling has gone in the same direction as the soldiers. The rabbit told me so."

"Ah."

"You can trust rabbits, especially when it comes to things that might be risky in their woods. They keep track of dangerous creatures and where they might be hunting."

"The rockling has gone hunting in other places. Hunting Koya."

"I suspect so, though the creature was injured, so that might slow it some." Slade stared down the dark path and frowned. "And we'll be hunting Koya as well, so we best be careful."

"Can you ask the animals to find Koya?"

"I'm trying, but they're mostly too afraid to go in the direction the others have gone. We'll do better to get past the fort and into the areas beyond before I ask again."

"What if Koya came back this way?"

"If he did, then he's pretty much safe. Nearly everyone else went the other way. I suspect that's where Koya and his companion went as well, though. He'll be hunted, and they won't want him to reach anyone and report what he has seen."

"The person with him is from the Dragonkin."

"Yes. Is that a problem for you?"

"I don't know. We always lived in worry about them," Malin said, and then stopped and closed his eyes for a moment, obviously at the memory of all he had lost. Slade touched his arm, and Malin finally sighed and began to move once more. "I suppose none of that matters now, does it? It wasn't the Dragonkin who attacked."

"No, it wasn't, but that doesn't mean they aren't dangerous."

"There are lots of dangerous things in the world," Malin said and shrugged. "They aren't all my enemies."

"You've got a good head on your shoulders," Slade said. The boy looked embarrassed, so he didn't say more. Slade suspected they'd have time enough to talk on the trail. The journey wasn't getting any shorter. "I'm going to try to reach Kenning since there isn't anyone else around."

Slade pulled out his rune. He was tired and short on energy of all kinds this morning. Walking while trying to reach Kenning at all proved to be difficult, and Slade wished he had better news to report. As soon as he heard Kenning's voice, he quickly told the story of the night before and what he'd learned so far this morning -- nothing but what the animals had told him.

"This worries me. This worries me on many levels," Kenning replied and paused for a moment. "The Most Holy is still packing, but he will be gone before too long. I'll leave no more than an hour later. I'll be taking the longer path to the capital but given that I will not be traveling with an entire retinue of people, I might make it there ahead of him, or at least no later than a day afterward."

"Sir, that's dangerous. He'll have your post, if not your life, once he learns what you're doing."

"I can't stand back and let him start a war, Slade. And I can't send anyone else to the authorities and put them in danger of his wrath. If I don't survive this, it's on my own head. However, I have faith in the Gods to see me through and make certain this trouble doesn't get worse."

"But sir --"

"I'll stay in touch as best I can," Kenning said. "I need you and Malin to keep up the work, Slade. You are my true eyes and ears on the border where things are happening. I need the truth to battle the Most Holy's lies."

"I should be with you! I know --"

"No, Slade. You are where I need you most. I must have the truth, and you can keep supplying the news for me. I need you, Slade. I need your keen eye and your military background to be able to decipher what is happening."

"Ah." It made sense, finally. He took several deep breaths and looked around again, as though he could see answers in the trees. Time to truly put those old skills to work.

He saw Malin look startled as he stared at Slade, and Slade had no idea why.

"Be careful, Kenning. Be very careful. You're going straight into the jaws of the beast with this one. The capital is filled with people whose entire existence is balanced on the fine line of making points and winning fame before the Empress. The person who should have been your most powerful ally and protector is going to be your worst enemy. I suggest you go to Lord Oak. He's no friend of the Most Holy, having gone up against him a few times in years past."

"Thank you. I'll remember that name," Kenning said and sounded profoundly grateful. "You two stay safe. I mean that, Slade. I need to have the ability to reach you, to get real answers. We must hope that Koya has gotten away. This has gone far beyond the worry just for him."

"Sir --"

"Keep after him, help him if you can -- but remain safe."

"Yes, sir."

"I must go. The Most Holy will expect me to attend him

as he leaves. I must go play the meek, loyal servant. Gods all, he is making this far worse than it need be."

"Be careful, Kenning. Be very careful."

"I will. Once I am away from the Most Holy -- no later than this afternoon -- it will be safe to contact me at any time. If he does not leave for some reason, I'll let you know somehow. Go with the Gods, Slade."

"You, too, sir."

The rune grew cooler to his touch. He looked at Malin and shook his head in disgust.

"How does such a man as the Most Holy become so powerful?" Malin asked a question that went straight to the heart of the matter.

"By not being faced by any real crisis while he rose in the ranks," Slade replied. They walked along the path, talking quietly. The animals remained calm. Nothing dangerous roamed the wilds just now, and Slade felt the panic of the last few days finally starting to ease. Good. He needed a level head.

"Were you really a soldier? It wasn't just stories to tell me?"

He glanced at Malin, startled by the sudden question. Then he remembered the boy's look when he had been speaking with Kenning.

"Yes. I was an officer in the Empress's Own."

"Really?" The boy's eyes lighted, just the way he had seen other boys react back in that different life. He forced himself not to smile, though the reaction did lighten his mood, even if he did not really like to talk about his days in the army.

"Really. Being a soldier is not all glory, you know," Slade said.

"Oh, I know," Malin said with a quick nod of his head. "My uncle died in the army, and my brother died in the border guard five years ago. But the Empress's Own -- that's something else, isn't it?"

"Something very much different from the rest of the forces," he agreed. "The elite. We guarded the Empress, but we also went to battles where they didn't think anyone else could handle the trouble."

Malin nodded and then stopped walking, turning to him with a different look on his face. Dread edged up through his brown eyes. "When I was five or so, there was a battle, and the Empress's Own fell nearly to a man."

"Very nearly. There were only twenty-three of us left in the end, out of five hundred. It was a bloody battle, there at Caris Crossing."

"Is that why you became a priest?"

"No, but it is why I left the service. A person can only see something like that once. Afterward, he is forever changed. But you understand that truth."

Malin stared. "It wasn't noble like your battle --"

"No battle is noble. No death at the hands of others is ever right. Sometimes you must do such things for the sake of those whom you protect. And sometimes, if you are fortunate, you learn that you can help in other ways. I left the service and headed west. I had gold in my purse, and nowhere I had to be. Then, months later, I wandered into Templeton and met Kenning. He was the first interesting person I'd talked to in years. I told him of my past. He invited me to stay at the Temple as his guest. I don't think either of us expected me to take vows."

"Why did you? I wouldn't think a soldier would find that kind of life very fulfilling."

"I never liked being a soldier. I was good at it, though." Slade gave a shrug that helped to ease the growing tension in his shoulders again. "I did what needed to be done, but I was glad to leave it behind. I was rich enough, with my stipend, that I might have just taken a cottage in some village and lived well for the rest of my life. But..."

He stopped, and Malin glanced at him and away. "I don't mean to pry."

"You aren't. If I didn't want to tell you, I wouldn't. I didn't want to be useless, Malin. I didn't want to live my life sitting in a cottage garden, pulling weeds, and watching everyone else go on with their lives. Kenning never suggested I join the order, but the Gods called to me. So, I went to them, and I did surprisingly well. The Gods smiled on me and showed me my gift of magic. Not nearly as strong as Koya, but still more than a soldier would expect to find."

"Did you know Koya?"

"I was there when he first came to the Temple, a ragged young man running for his life and arriving in the dead of night. His presence awoke all of us. I had thought we were being visited by a God because he was so strong in magic. The moment he walked through the gate, he set every bell in the Temple ringing. By the time he reached the Temple, his magic had made every candle blaze in the sanctuary."

"Koya," Malin said, looking confused again. A rabbit darted across their path, startling them both -- but it was a good sign that there were no other dangers in the area.

"Koya, a ragged-haired young Norter who couldn't even speak the language. You cannot imagine what a shock his arrival was to us. Kenning took Koya under his wing, much as he had me. I was almost ready to move on by that point, so I didn't spend much time with Koya, but I did see him now and then when I came to visit at Templeton."

"But you liked him."

"Oh, yes. Once Koya stopped fearing that we would turn him out or that someone from the north would find and kill him, he became quite likable. He wanted to know everything. After Kenning was able to teach him some control in magic, we all realized he was far more powerful than anyone we had seen."

"Including the Most Holy?" Malin asked.

They headed off to the right, away from the abandoned fort, which they could sometimes see between the trees and down below their hill. There didn't seem to be anyone around, but they kept their voices low.

"Is Koya more powerful than the Most Holy?" Slade said with a shrug. "That's always been the question. I don't know if any of us ever asked it aloud, though."

"But the Most Holy hurt Koya, right? So, he must be stronger."

"No. Koya wasn't ready for such an attack. No one was prepared for what the Most Holy did. I don't doubt Koya could have held it off, but the Most Holy took advantage of the fact that no one would have thought of doing defensive magic at a meeting with him."

"You don't like the Most Holy."

"No, I do not. He's blind and bigoted -- but he is the Most Holy. I think Kenning is far more holy and blessed by the Gods. However, the Most Holy has a knack for gathering power. In a reflection of that ability, he has made the Temple far more potent than it was under any of his predecessors."

"Is that good?"

"Yes, it is. We help people, you know. Now that we have a power that puts us on a level with the local lords, we are no longer controlled by them. In the past, the Lords could tell us who was to be helped and who wasn't. We were political tools. It's much better that we are powerful enough to have those decisions and control in our own hands."

"Even in the hands of the Most Holy?"

"The Most Holy usually stays in the capital and plays at politics there," Slade replied. He didn't try to cover his words with platitudes. Malin was smart, and he already knew the answers to most of this anyway. "It is where he does his most good."

"Except now."

"Except now, when he needs to be wise and is not," Slade agreed. They took a path that would take them wide of the fort in case anyone lingered there. "He is going to be the only voice for what is happening here until Kenning arrives. We have to hope that the right people will listen to Kenning instead."

Malin nodded and walked on in silence again, obviously thinking through what he'd learned. Slade wished he knew what went on in the boy's head. He would have helped Malin through this hard time if he could have.

Although, maybe, he had. He didn't lie to Malin. The truth may not always be pleasant but lies did more harm.

They moved well to the south as they went past the abandoned fort. None of the animals he approached could tell him where the rockling had gone, and he feared the creature might still be close by. It wasn't something he wanted to face, so they went farther afield and well away from the majority of the Norter troops who were all heading northwest.

They'd have to go in that direction soon as well. However, a day of calm and feeling out the limits of this situation wouldn't hurt. Slade needed to get his balance back. He needed to find a way to do what Kenning wanted and to help Koya if he could. Even though his heart pulled him in that direction, he didn't go searching only for the young priest and ignore all the rest of the trouble.

The Gods would keep Koya safe. Slade believed it, even now.

CHAPTER

TWENTY-THREE

Kenning didn't want to leave for Tralista on that long, northern journey. It was not the lack of amenities that bothered him, though he had looked forward to having his place back once the Most Holy left. It was not even the fear that he would find trouble he couldn't handle at the end of his path.

Kenning's real worry was that he was leaving the area where problems were bound to erupt, and all too soon. Ziven had been a border town, but even Templeton sat well within reach of the mountains. Partha was even closer. He had already heard rumors of people panicking there with the thought that the Dragonkin prepared to descend and kill everyone, just as they had in Ziven. The Most Holy had spoken to few outside the temple, but his people had spread the news through Templeton, and from there it had spread elsewhere.

Kenning had quietly prepared to send his priests out to the villages -- all but a few of the eldest and Armath would scatter along the trails not long after he and the Most Holy left the town. They would do their best to quell the rumors and allay the fears of the others.

Kenning also sent word to the Cloud Temple up in the rolling hills not far away. The priestesses who kept a hospital there were capable of taking care of themselves when faced with trouble, but he wanted to make sure they knew the situation. None had come to see the Most Holy, so Kenning assumed someone there knew him too well. Kenning took that as a good sign.

The Most Holy had finally moved off on his own journey not long past noon. Before Kenning started his travels, he had sent all the messages he could to commanders in the territory, to headmen, and lords, and friends, telling them the truth of the situation. The truth didn't mean they were not in danger, only that the threat would come in a form they might not recognize so easily at first.

"I don't want to go," Kenning said, to no one in particular, although every priest still at the Temple stood in the courtyard with him. He saw worried looks, and he couldn't tell them to be calm and that all would be well. He couldn't lie. "I don't want to go because there is so much that needs to be done here. But I have faith that the rest of you can do this work. Yes, faith. The Gods are putting us all in our places."

"Even Koya?" Armath asked.

"Oh yes, even our Koya. He knows the ways of the Norters and is doing what he can to help." Kenning kept the fear for Koya's life from his face, even if it had lodged in his heart. He didn't know if Koya lived, and he didn't want the others to doubt the Gods. He looked at the faces around him and then gave a sudden nod. "I must go, my brothers. I must go now and ride hard. Do well. Do the best you can. These will be dark times. We dare not fail."

Maybe they hadn't really thought that so much would rest upon them. Kenning saw shock and fear renewed. They needed to be wise. He trusted them.

And he needed to leave.

Kenning pulled himself up into the saddle of the Temple's best mount, Glory -- a chestnut gelding with a small white star on his forehead. Kenning patted the little bundle of supplies the others had gathered for him -- riding light and fast -- and then turned the horse towards the gate.

"The Gods go with you, Kenning!" Armath yelled as he rode away. Those were good words to hear.

Kenning went out of the Temple's horse gate a moment later and into the streets of Templeton. His passage didn't go unnoticed. They were not used to seeing him on a horse, and the locals knew it meant he was going on a journey. Scurrying out so shortly after the Most Holy's departure couldn't look proper.

He didn't stop to explain himself, especially since these people were mostly believers, and had been honored that the Most Holy had been in the town. Most Holy had at least given them a sermon and a good show on his way out, complete with bells and drums. Handling these people would be in Headman Fywarth's hands -- and there was the man now, giving a nod to Kenning as he rode by.

Kenning moved through the streets, waving toward the people who called to him, and passing on without pause. He faced the more curious guards at the gate, but they didn't try to slow him. Kenning saw the worry in their faces as he headed out, and he paused the other side and looked back, lifting his hand in a quick blessing of guards, gates, walls, city, and the people within. He hoped it helped.

The others might think he was trying to catch up with the Most Holy, and he didn't dissuade them of the idea. The worried people of Templeton didn't need to realize there was a problem within the religious circles as well as problems on the border. The trail he would take, which was not the same as the Most Holy, was not visible from the town, and he had to ride several hours to reach it. He hoped to reach the crossroads before dark.

He dared not ride too fast before the point where the roads diverged, though. The Most Holy might have slowed. He might even have turned back -- or sent some of his men back. Kenning used subtle magic to feel out the trail ahead, and he went slowly. By the time he reached the different road, he could feel the Most Holy barely five miles ahead of him, making steady but slow progress.

Kenning turned his mount off to the side trail with a genuine sigh of relief. He almost immediately urged Glory to move faster, though he did not use magic. Kenning was already sore; he'd been far too long from the saddle, and he was going to pay for that now. He'd gotten soft and complacent in his lovely Temple.

Kenning had held his panic at bay. However, riding alone down the trail, he felt as though time slipped away like sand, and something dark built like a storm behind him, ready to break upon the land in a swath of destruction. Kenning didn't know if he could do anything to stop the storm. He did hope, at least, to make sure that if the people of Kasprin went to war, it was against the proper enemy.

Kenning rode into the night and stopped only for the sake of the poor horse. They made camp by the side of the trail, and he fell into a restless sleep, hoping for the dawn.

The next six days passed with little change, except that he rode through increasingly larger villages as he neared Tralista. Many had heard the rumors of trouble, but the people didn't seem as panicked as they had been nearer the border.

On the sixth day, Kenning had begun the long curve

down from the northern trail and headed to Tralista. If his calculations were right, and the Most Holy had kept mostly to the same speed of travel, he would barely be in the city now, even though the man had taken the far shorter, southern route. How long would it take the Most Holy to reach Empress Silana? Worse yet, how long would it take Kenning to get an audience since he had no ties to the court? He would have trouble finding a way to contact anyone of importance.

Lord Oak -- the name Slade had given him -- seemed the best answer. He wasn't sure how he would find the man, though. The mere idea of trying to locate a single person in a city the size of the capital suddenly seemed far too daunting.

Ah, but surely finding a Lord wouldn't be like tracking down a common man. Good. He could do this. Then he could sleep for a while. All he had to do was deliver the truth to someone who believed him.

Kenning pushed that worry away in a haze of exhaustion. Get to Tralista first, find Lord Oak, and then see what happened from there. He might not have to go to the palace at all.

Maybe the Most Holy would come to his senses.

And pigs would fly.

He looked up, half-hoping...

They had told him at one village that he was only a day's ride from the city if he pushed hard. Three villages stood between him and it, but he'd passed one quickly -- or had that been two? Gods, he needed to get his mind in order before he faced anyone at all. Sounding crazed was not going to help the cause.

Kenning even slowed the horse, who turned his chestnut-colored head and blinked in what could only be a show of surprise. The reaction made Kenning grin, who had not grinned at all since he started this journey. He touched the circle symbol of his Gods, bowed his head, and prayed for help and wisdom. He calmed, knowing the Gods approved his work. He wasn't bothered by the fact that the Most Holy should have been the one with the ear of the Gods. He had known the man lost his sanctity long before he created this problem.

Calm helped.

Unfortunately, it didn't last for long. Kenning found chaos when he reached the fields beyond the next village.

Kenning had heard the muffled shouts as he passed through the last line of the trees and thought he saw something running through the woods -- deer he supposed a first. The horse had nearly bolted in surprise.

Then he found the battle and realized Lesslings were running free. That sight frightened him -- though not so much as the scene of a dozen soldiers bearing down on a troop of Dragonkin, who turned to make their stand even as he neared.

Kenning yelled and, with a slight touch of magic, forced the reluctant Glory forward and rushing through a band of Lesslings and then right past the Dragonkin and into the face of the oncoming soldiers.

He had startled everyone, and a little bit of whispered magic scattered the soldiers' horses and left many of them rider-less. He didn't dare look back to see what the Dragonkin were doing, but since none of the famed Dragonkin arrows had taken him in the back, he hoped for the best.

"What the hell --" a soldier shouted, scrambling up from where he had been thrown and grabbing his sword. He looked at Kenning and grimaced a little. "What are you doing, priest?"

"Saving you from starting a war."

"The war's already begun, man! They've attacked along the east --"

"They have not! I am Kenning, High Priest of Templeton. I know what is happening in the east!"

"But the Most Holy -- he told us -- he sent us to chase

after them --"

"The Most Holy was mistaken," Kenning said and tried to keep the surge of rage out of his voice. "We are not under attack by the Dragonkin. A group of Norters, pretending to be Dragonkin, set this in motion. Do you really want to be the ones who truly start the war with these people? Do you want to be the ones in the wrong?"

The man blanched. Then he looked around as though he wondered what in hell he was doing out here. Kenning sat up a little straighter and lifted his hand, testing ... yes, magic. The Most Holy had sent these men rushing to this battle by using his power, and Kenning feared the soldier may have figured the truth out as well.

"I suggest, sir, that you and your men grab your horses, turn around and head back to the city and wait for word from your commanders," Kenning advised. "They'll know better what needs to be done than the Most Holy does, don't you think?"

Kenning did not make the words into an accusation, but the man winced and looked back at his men. "Get the horses! Prepare to ride back to the city!"

"Sir," one of the men said. "Lieutenant, the enemy --"

"We must go back and await orders from those in command!"

Faces paled, and Kenning could almost feel the magic dissipating around them. The soldiers obeyed their Lieutenant, but that man moved closer to Kenning. "I have a question. Did the Most Holy send us by using magic?"

"I fear so," Kenning admitted. He could not bring himself to say he knew that was true, but mostly for fear that it would upset these people even more. The Lieutenant gave a hard-eyed nod, though. "How far am I from the capital?"

"Barely five miles," the man said. He looked past to where the Dragonkin stood and then away again. "But the trip is going to be dangerous, so you had better ride with us. The Most Holy has been urging everyone who would listen to him to embrace the war. That anger will be spreading outward -- even without other help."

Kenning bit down on his lower lip to keep from saying something ruder about the Most Holy than he wanted heard from a priest. The Lieutenant must have caught the gist of Kenning's thoughts in the look on his face. He gave a short nod and turned back to his own people.

Kenning finally dared a glance behind him. He had expected the Dragonkin people to have moved on, but they had stopped, settled into a protective line, and waited. They did not have their weapons drawn. If Kenning had not happened along just in time, there would have been a hell of a battle. The Gods were with him still.

A Dragonkin woman stepped out of the line, waving the others back, and saying something exceptionally sharp and hissing to the Lesslings when a few tried to move up with her. They slinked away, but not without hisses of their own.

The woman came forward a few more steps and then paused a couple yards away when Kenning's mount took exception. Horses disliked the presence of the Dragonkin. One of the soldiers took hold of Kenning's mount, giving both him and the woman looks of worry. Kenning didn't know what to make of this approach, except maybe he'd had far too little sleep; for some reason, he felt amused.

The woman bowed her head when he neared. She looked annoyed, spotted in dust, and even her bright green crest had fallen a little to the side.

"Why did you stop them?" she asked before he could bow his head in greeting.

"I knew they were in the wrong. I know what's going on at the border, and it has nothing to do with your people. The Norters are trying to push us into a war."

"Are they?" she said, her eyes narrowing. "You know this for certain?"

"I've had reports from two different priests in the area. One, unfortunately, is now a prisoner of the group that attacked Ziven. I think, perhaps, you even met him."

"I know no -- " She stopped, and her eyes went a little wide. "The very brave one who stood his ground while the others ran for cover. The one who looked far too much like a Norter himself."

"Yes, that would be Koya," Kenning said with a sigh while he tried to hide his fear of loss.

"And you trust his word."

"Oh, yes."

"But your leader, the Most Holy --"

Kennings lips curled back into a little snarl. He had not meant to, but it proved a good reaction. The woman nodded again. The soldiers had prepared to leave. Kenning wanted to ride back with them, suspecting it would be the fastest way to get through the gates. One of them should be able to tell him how to get to Lord Oak as well.

"Go carefully. I fear the Most Holy has perhaps spread the word about the supposed war between our people already, and I think..." Kenning stopped, then stepped closer and lowered his voice. "I think he did it to make certain it came true. Don't let him win."

"Ah. Then we do not ride the trails. We'll be longer getting home, but we can stay out of sight. We have done it before."

Oh, now there was a bit of news that got a quick look from him and a feral smile from her at the secret she gave, trading for his own report. Thank the Gods he had such faith in the truth, or else that look would have worried him far more than it did, which was bad enough.

She bowed her head to him and turned away before he

did. He felt a little shiver, watching her walk away and back to the others.

Gods give them quick and easy paths out of Kasprin.

He turned to the soldier holding his horse and mounted. In a moment, they were riding towards the city. He had stopped one small bit of trouble. Could he stop the war?

CHAPTER

TWENTY-FOUR

oya and DK did their best to avoid even the deer trails where the guards might spot them. They hiked through brush and past ancient trees, scuffing the dirt, and sometimes pulling dead branches down behind them. Late in the day they forded two small streams and finally climbed down a steep hillside and then up again to a flat outcropping above a rocky cliff. The last climb had left even DK winded and glad to rest at the top.

Koya ached in every muscle. He felt the effects of the Most Holy's damned spell worse today, and he'd had to walk with a makeshift cane most of the time, slowing them --

Or not. DK walked with a hand on his side and wincing at each step. He hadn't looked as though he could move much faster anyway.

They'd heard no one in hours, praise the Gods. So now, with the sun nearly down, they could rest for a while. The cliff had a good view of the valley below. He could see a herd of elk in a glade about a mile away, grazing calmly enough that no one could be near.

This had been a damned long, hard day after too many other damned hard days.

"Do you have any idea where we're going?" Koya dared ask.

DK looked at him, startled by the words. "You think I would wander blind in these lands?"

"I have no clue," Koya replied and tried not to sound annoyed, especially since he realized that meant DK did know where he was taking them. "I don't know where we are, but I don't know this area at all. Do you?"

"Well enough." He put a hand to his side again. Koya could see some blood, which he hoped was not bad. They would likely have to move again soon. "I came here to do my honor hunt. They caught me with magic. I had not expected it, but it is still a dishonor."

That didn't sound good. DK looked embarrassed and angry, and Koya decided he best not to ask what all that meant just now.

"We have both been tricked," Koya pointed out. He desperately wanted to rest. "Many people have been tricked, and it's going to lead to far worse if we can't find a way to stop it."

DK agreed with a nod of his head. "Since you have asked, we are heading towards the border, which is no more than four days hiking from here."

There were words to bring him out of his stupor "The border? The Dragonkin border?" Koya said, shocked by the idea.

"Yes, to Synetha. There is another border you would prefer? Head to the Norter lands instead, do you think?" DK said, looking annoyed now.

"No, of course not. It's just that --" He waved a hand

towards his body. "I'm human. Worse, I'm a human priest. We aren't allowed --"

"You are allowed as a guest. You need not fear that part, Priest."

"Good. I like having a direction and a destination -- especially one where I think the Norters would be slow to follow."

"Oh, let them try," DK said, his eyes narrowing this time. "Let them try. My people patrol the border. They'd be glad to have such a visit, especially after they hear our tale. Rest, Priest. I fear we can have no fire up here on the cliff tonight. But it is not a cold night, at least, and a few hours here will give us a better chance in the morning."

Stay the night? He thought to argue with DK about staying. They needed to keep watch, and he could do it as well as DK --

But he made a spot for himself on the hard ground, brushing away some pebbles, and laying with his head on his arm. He didn't care. He wanted to sleep. It came quickly and he awoke again only when DK touched his shoulder, sending a surprising shock of pain through his body.

"Magic," DK said softly, pulling back in haste. "Someone has done this to you by magic."

"Y-Yes." He sat up slowly to find a dark night, the moon hanging overhead behind wisps of gray clouds. "The Most Holy."

"The head of your Temple."

"Yes."

"Why?"

"He didn't like what I told him," Koya replied. Maybe he shouldn't have said anything, but he didn't stop. "I felt magic growing out here in the wilds. Now I am sure it was the rockling drawing closer to the border. I knew trouble was coming. I even said I didn't think it was from the Dragonkin."

"Ah. And this man disliked that you said such truths to him?"

"He disliked *me*. It hardly mattered what I said to him in the end. However, if I had been wise and listened to Kenning --" He stopped and stared out at the world for a long, silent moment.

"Yes?"

"The Most Holy said the Gods placed the spell on me, not him."

"And this is not blasphemy?" he asked, plainly very confused now.

"Oh, from anyone but the Most Holy it would have been. But he is the man closest to the Gods --"

"And you believe this of a man who would curse you so?"

"No, I don't believe it. I didn't then, either. Still, sometimes the Gods move in ways that we don't understand. And I am here, I think right where I needed to be."

"Ah. I wondered." DK shifted and looked uncomfortable. His hand went briefly to his wound, but he pulled it away again. "I must rest now."

"Sleep," Koya said and stood slowly, stretching some of the kinks out of his body. "I'm awake. I'll keep the watch until dawn."

DK looked at him for a long moment, no doubt measuring many things.

"You are resourceful for a human."

That must have been a considerable compliment. Koya bowed his head in thanks and hid his smile. He turned and sat where he could easily watch over the lowlands that spread out in grey and black shadows below them. After a short while, he could hear DK's rhythmic breathing and knew his companion slept.

Koya let his shoulders sag a little then, the weight of the last few days bearing down on him once more. So much gone wrong, and so little he could do about it. He wanted to turn around and head back for the Temple. He wanted to lay this trouble at Kenning's feet. Instead, he could not even talk to his friend. He had only DK for a companion and as good as they had worked together, there was still a wall between them.

Kota wanted to go home. That sounded childish in his head, and he brushed the thought away and straightened his shoulders again, staring out at the darkness. The world looked lovely out there. The wild woods were bathed in bright moonlight, and he could see far down the side of the cliff where moose moved through the glade. He could hear other animals nearby, and wished he had his runes --

He didn't have his own, but they had taken out two boxes of runes from the Norter's camp. With a start, he looked around until he found the pack they'd carried away. He crossed over and knelt by it, drawing DK's attention for a moment before his companion closed his eyes again.

Koya took the boxes back to the edge of the cliff and knelt there where he could watch the world below them and study the runes as well. The first felt cold and unresponsive, except for the distant feel of another priest. They didn't want to answer him at all. The second was a bit better. These had been Galt's, and when he brushed his hand over the top of the box, he felt a shiver of fire through his fingers. The runes protested, but not much.

Koya paused and looked out over the landscape again, taking note of everything in its right place. Then he lifted the lid and studied the runes inside. Galt's work had been crude compared to his own, and it took him a moment to realize that the moonlight was showing him the rat rune, there at the top, and to the right.

He shivered a little at the sight of it.

Touching the stone confirmed that it still held far too much power. Koya didn't disturb it but turned the box a little and looked at the other three runes that were on top, hoping they might tell him something.

One was a bird -- a raptor of some sort, he thought, from the look of the crudely carved talons. The other looked like a bear or a raccoon. Koya didn't think he would dare try to use that one. Bears were trouble, but raccoons were often worse if for no other reason than they like to follow along and get into things. The first time Koya had called a raccoon, he got a whole family of them, and they were still terrorizing the Temple garden several years later.

Koya smiled and believed he would soon go back to the Temple. He knew so in his heart. He just had to survive this, and end a war, and -- best not to think beyond that work.

The last of the runes stacked at the top was a fish. That might be useful later for food. Koya didn't like to use his gift from the Gods to draw unwitting animals to their deaths, but the priests had all found that fish proved the least bothered by it. Besides, he had dreamed once that the Gods gave them this gift to help in times of need. Koya liked the omen and seeing the fish rune on top gave him some hope again.

He looked down the cliffside towards a distant pond. It would probably take them all day to get there, but they'd have fish for dinner tomorrow night if all went well.

He tried to believe that it would.

Koya carefully lifted the bird rune. The stone stung his fingers. He'd felt far worse pain lately, and he held on, grimacing and silent, his eyes staring at the world around them. His mind concentrated on overcoming the feel of the older Priest. Galt hadn't been strong, but he'd held these runes for decades, and they remembered him very well.

Perspiration formed on his face and ran down the collar of his tattered robe despite the chilly night. He wanted to brush at it, but he shook his head, ignored that feeling, and focused on the rune again.

Koya still wasn't sure what type of bird the carving had meant to be. No matter, really. Since he had to take over the rune, he would reshape it into what he needed. At first, he thought he wanted an eagle, but then quickly changed his mind. Eagles were big, strong, and might be more than he could handle in his current state. A hawk would be better. A small one, in fact. Koya formed his thoughts around a peregrine and fed that into the rune while he worked to subvert the stone to his own needs.

Galt, he decided about dawn, had been a stubborn old bastard. The rune reflected him. It did not want to give way, and every now and then, the stone gave off an exceptionally sharp sting, like a schoolmaster slapping the fingers of a recalcitrant student. The moose had gone, and deer had slipped into the glade. A pack of wolves had chased them off. The deer ran very well, and the wolves must have already been well fed. Koya didn't think they were going to catch the deer today.

He heard the cry of a startled loud screeching of a peregrine hawk.

Koya found the creature high up over the trees to the south, circling, then coming closer, then circling again. He felt the first welling of hope he'd had all night. He called to the little bird, softly but insistently, pulling it closer and closer to the cliff where he sat.

DK sat up, and for a moment, Koya feared he would say something, and Koya would lose his feel for the bird -- but DK must have felt the magic or seen that Koya was doing something important. He remained very still.

The hawk landed on a boulder beside Koya, dancing back and forth, his eyes bright with anger and curiosity.

Koya wanted only a moment, only a thought or two. Humans, strangers --

Evil thing.

Rockling. Koya could see the creature far too clearly through the hawk's sharp eyes. The bird hadn't gone too close, for the thing grabbed, killed, and ate everything in its path. Hawk had also seen humans. Many humans, off across the trees and down the riverside -- not so far away really --

Koya caught a glimpse of them through the bird's memories. Soldiers in Norter uniform. A thousand, and a thousand more, and more still --

"Gods of all," he whispered and nearly lost his hold on the hawk who didn't like humans being there any more than Koya did. DK moved slightly, obviously worried. "Anything else, little winged brother?" Koya asked while still holding tight to the rune for one more moment.

The hawk protested and then gave way out of curiosity. There was more: another set of soldiers were making their way up the hills not far from where Koya and DK were camped.

"Thank you, friend. Good hunting." He let the bird go and afterward felt a shiver of cold and exhaustion wash over him.

He carefully unfolded his fingers from the rune.

"Trouble?" DK asked softly.

"Afraid so. The rockling is a few miles in that direction," he waved a hand toward the right. "A Norter army so huge I could not guess the number is over there." He waved to the left. "And soldiers, I think from the fort, seem to be coming up quite close above us."

DK looked from one direction to another and frowned. He appeared more bedraggled than Koya had expected after the rest, and he stood slowly, a hand still on his side. "We must go."

"Where?" Koya asked. He dropped the box of runes back into the pack. "They're everywhere out there."

"Straight down," DK said, looking over the cliff.

"I can't fly."

DK smiled a little for the first time. He looked young, though Koya couldn't be certain since his contact with Dragonkin people had consisted of that one meeting at the crossroads. Koya wanted to ask things, even now, but he kept his questions to himself. The last thing Koya needed was to step over the boundary of common politeness and annoy the person who had helped keep him alive. Best, instead, to stay silent.

Except when he went closer to the edge where DK stood and looked down.

"Is insanity common among your people?" Koya asked.

DK made a little sound of amusement. "It is said that it only comes from prolonged contact with humans. It's why we do not keep you as slaves."

"And nothing to do with how dangerous we are."

DK looked at him, head tilted to the side, as though he had not considered such a thing, but Koya could see the ruse in the little smile at the corner of his lips.

"How are we supposed to get down?" Koya asked.

"Vines, handholds, and the luck of the Gods," DK said, waving his hand downward. "I suggest you pray."

He did. And then he followed DK over the edge of the cliff. Vines did cover some of the cliffside, though they were not very strong, and the two of them dared not use the same ones for fear of yanking them out of the ground and one or both of them falling. The covering of the cliff, which had looked smooth in the dark of night when they'd settle in, now showed bumps and indentations. It looked almost easy.

It was not.

CHAPTER

TWENTY-FIVE

Kenning had spent an uncomfortable night in a small stable near the edge of the city, sleeping in the same stall as his horse since the inns he'd found had no rooms. He'd woken at dawn, grabbed his small travel pack, and left the horse in their care. He went on foot to find Lord Oak's city home, following the directions he'd gotten the night before.

Getting through the front door had meant only a quick check of the pack by the doorman. Kenning hadn't argued. When the doorman returned, Kenning stood from the bench in the entryway.

The man frowned but gave a polite nod. "Lord Oak will see you."

"Thank you," Kenning said, which seemed to surprise the man. Since the head of the house was on the outs with the Most Holy, maybe they didn't expect any priest to be polite.

Kenning brushed a hand through his hair and grimaced as he found a twig and pulled it free. His clothing showed dirt and mud, and he stank of horseflesh and unwashed human.

Lord Oak sat at his breakfast table. He wasn't a glutton, at least, though a big man. The food smelled like heaven, and Kenning feared his stomach would grow louder than his voice.

"Sir," he said and bowed.

"Priest." Kenning heard more than a little disdain in the voice as Lord Oak lifted a piece of apple towards his mouth and paused, glaring as his bushy eyebrows drew down into a V. "Why has the Most Holy sent you?"

"He hasn't. He doesn't know I am here in the city."

Lord Oak put the apple back down on his plate. His eyes grew a little wider, and he finally nodded to a servant. "A chair and a plate for our guest. I can see he has traveled far and hard, and I get the feeling that he might have something of great interest to tell us about this new war with the Dragonkin."

Kenning stepped forward, put his hand on the back of the chair for support, and nodded. He didn't think he had the strength to go any farther.

"Sir, I can tell you that the war is not with the Dragonkin, though the Most Holy wants everyone to believe so. I am, Kenning --"

"The High Priest of Templeton, where Most Holy had been staying just before this trouble," Lord Oak said, his eyes narrowing again. "It was good to have the old -- to have him out of the city for a while. I was sorry to see him come racing back, and especially with the word he brought. Oddly, though, I did not mistrust his news. Sit down and eat a little before you faint. And tell me the truth."

They had an interesting breakfast.

"This priest of yours --"

"Koya, sir."

"No, the other one. The one who suggested you come to me. That would be Slade, yes?"

The man knew a considerable amount about what was going on in Kenning's far corner of the empire than he thought possible, and he found himself giving a short, nervous nod.

"Slade served under me in the last war," he said. "I kept track of him after that last, lamentable battle. The one where we stood the battlefield, despite my misgivings, because the Most Holy had said the Gods had told him that we could not lose."

Kenning looked up, his eyes gone wide, and a piece of bread forgotten in his hand. "I never heard that."

"There are very few people who know that piece of truth. I'm not certain Slade knew the reason we went to battle, despite being so severely outnumbered. If he had, I would be doubtful of this news, Father Kenning. Instead, I am tempted to think the Gods have honestly looked upon us again, despite the sanctimonious bastard who runs the Temples."

Kenning only nodded.

"We must go immediately to the Empress with this news before the Most Holy can get things moving in a way we can't stop." He clapped his hands and gave a series of orders that included, praise the Gods, water and soap, along with carriage and guards.

By the time they left Lord Oak's townhouse, the sun had inched toward noon, and the city had come alive. Kenning had arrived in the city the night before, just before gate close, to find things loud, stinking, and filled with fog and shadows. Now, with the morning light full up, the fog was finally burning off, though it lingered in ghost-like tendrils along the edges of the streets and in dark alleys.

People moved along the edges of the street while carriages, horses, and wagons -- drawn by animals and by humans -- moved along the middle way. Lord Oak looked like a horse rider to Kenning, and he was surprised when the man had his carriage brought out. It seemed a surprise to his servants as well.

He patted the emblem on the door and waved to the banner flying from a pole at the top. "We're going to the Imperial Palace. I need to make certain they know who I am and not to give me trouble."

"Ah. I am grateful for the carriage, sir," Kenning admitted and allowed a servant to help him up the step into the closure. "I have had enough of horses for a while."

"You must have ridden with the wind to get here so quickly, especially since you came by the longer route," Lord Oak said as he settled onto the little bench across from Kenning. He tapped the wall, and the carriage moved with a little jerk. Kenning could hear the driver calling out to make way for Lord Oak, and it must have been magical words because they were not slowed at all.

Kenning only glanced occasionally out the window, though he really wanted to gawk like a country bumpkin. He kept his decorum as best he could, but it didn't last very well when the carriage finally came to a stop, and they alighted in the First Courtyard of the Imperial Palace.

Kenning had seen pictures drawn of the magnificent palace -- but nothing prepared him for the real sense of grandeur. The stones beneath his feet were made from slabs of marble, white-streaked with gold alternating with black-streaked with gold. Tall trees and stately flowers -- the imperial roses, which were not allowed to grow anywhere else -- lined the edge of a path leading to a large, ivy-covered trellis. Beyond that opening, the long, wide stairway was lined with pale orange roses and statues.

They started out at a moderate walk, and just inside the trellis a servant in imperial clothing appeared and silently bowed. However, his arched eyebrow said a great deal about the surprising company Lord Oak kept today. Lord Oak made nothing of it.

"A message for her," Lord Oak said, and handed over an envelope sealed with his emblem. He must have written it while Kenning cleaned up and changed into his better robe. The servant looked startled this time, then bowed and raced away, taking the first set of stairs two at a time.

Kenning started out at a brisk walk, but Lord Oak caught him by the arm. "Slow and steady here. We'll get there in good time. The Empress doesn't like to be rushed into things, which is good for us, since the Most Holly arrived last night, but will not have gotten an appointment with her until this morning. Chances are we're not long behind him."

"And we will get in without an appointment?"

"If she thinks I've brought her something important enough." He leaned a little closer. "I should have said before, but the Most Holy sometimes annoys her, and she might take this as a pleasant opportunity to cause him some discomfort. I'm counting on it. All I said in the note was that I had someone who thinks the Most Holy is not telling the full truth. I hope she finds those words intriguing enough to get us past the usual problems of gaining an audience. If not, we'll be camping out in the main hall for a day or two. And yes, I have had to do that before, too. So, there is no telling, especially given the situation."

"Ah."

"But, none the less, I think I am the best chance of getting to see her as quickly as possible. Many of the Lords would not even make it within the gate without an invitation, but I have some clout here."

"I thank you, sir. I didn't know what I would do, especially if the Most Holy learned I was in the city before I could speak to anyone. He does have the power to order me."

"Good point."

They kept heading upward. Kenning could see flashes of the Imperial Palace above, and occasional smaller buildings -- huge things, but tiny compared to the palace. Those set off along paths to the right and left. Lord Oak named them as they climbed, acting like a tour guide. Perhaps it kept him calmer.

Kenning silently prayed all the way up the stairs.

CHAPTER

TWENTY-SIX

Malin grabbed at a stout bush and slowed his descent on the treacherous hillside as he came to a panting stop by Slade. He put his hands on his knees and took short, quiet gulps of air while they listened.

Animals still shouted in wild protest not far away. Something louder growled about the tumultuous sounds. The ground seemed to tremble with the noises.

"Rockling for sure," Slade said and looked wildly around. "I don't think he has caught sight or scent of us. We must keep moving. Into the stream. Can you swim?"

"A bit. Never liked it much," Malin admitted, still gasping, but then he shivered at the sound from off to the west. "But there are things I like far worse, so the water looks good, sir."

"Yes, it does. It's going to be cold, though. Hold on to my belt. We're going to head downstream."

Slade had already begun mapping their way down the fast-flowing stream. He could see huge boulders in the middle of the water, and two fallen trees that had been caught there. It wasn't far to that refuge.

The rockling came closer. Birds flew overhead, screaming warnings to everything within range. Slade took the caution to heart and pulled Malin straight into the water. An otter swept past them, frantic to get away as well, while four foxes raced along the edge of the stream on one side and deer fairly flew over the ground on the other.

Malin kept tight hold of his belt. The stream bed was both rocky and slick, and the water felt as cold as ice. Slade didn't dare use magic to help them right then, not with the rockling so close.

So close, in fact, that he could see the movement of the trees behind them.

"Make no sound," he whispered and drew them faster to the rocks and the fallen trees. He pushed Malin down under the water, and he went as well, and then up again into the mass of dead branches. Twigs tore at his face, and he felt Malin give a shudder and nearly slip away, but he caught the boy's arm. Malin caught his belt again.

The world trembled around them, and something huge blocked out the light of the sun. Slade peered through the branches and rotting leaves, but he could barely make out the shape of the creature.

"I smell it," the rockling growled. Everything else alive had either disappeared from the area or had gone as still as Slade and Malin. Even a dozen frantic fish had taken refuge with them beneath the tree. "I smell it close!"

Something slapped at the water and sent a wave that nearly brushed the trees away, but they held -- the Gods on their side, Slade thought and silently said a prayer to the Ten. *Please, Gods, stand by us.* Please help us. He could see part of the rockling face now: burn marks and frog eyes, damaged and squinting into the gloom around him. It sniffed and sniffed again, and Slade wondered if he could call upon any magic that would help.

Then the creature stepped back from the stream edge. "Not the one I want. Not."

The rockling moved again, a stamp of feet, a constant growl. It went past where Slade and Malin hid in the stream, and he could see the shape of the rockling now. The creature was more massive than even he had imagined it would be.

"Will find it."

The rockling trampled bushes and pulled down good-sized trees. It kept going, along a path it made, regardless of what stood in the way. They kept quiet still. He didn't trust the creature at all, and it was only when he heard the return of a heron flying through the trees and across the stream that he really thought it had gone.

Malin began shivering so hard he had no control over his movements. Slade was a little better, but he kept hold of the boy and dragged them both out on the opposite side of the stream from where the rockling had passed. The amount of damage the creature had done was incredible. It looked as though a small tornado had passed through the area.

"We need a fire," Slade said, and the words startled Malin, who looked around -- frightened, but unable to speak yet. "It's gone. The birds are coming back. They'll give us a warning if it returns. Just sit here. I'll find us some wood."

"S-sir --" he said and tried to stand but couldn't.

"Just stay. I'm not going far."

Malin appeared almost blue with the cold, and he shook like the last leaf on a tree at the onslaught of a winter storm. It was impossible to tell where the cold ended, and the fear began, and Slade suspected the boy might be facing more than just what happened here.

Slade felt sick, and his legs didn't want to hold him either, but he forced himself to gather a little wood -- enough to start a fire and begin to get warm, and then he would get more. He didn't want to go too far from Malin because the rockling could come back.

He didn't think they would survive if it did.

Slade gathered an armload of wood and came back, clearing a spot near the stream so they could leap back to the water if they needed to. He pulled his runes out and found the one for fire -- a rare, non-animal one, like the one for the Temple. His fingers brushed the Temple one as well, wondering if he should try to contact Kenning -- but no. Fire first. That magic might take most of his strength, and better they were using it for survival.

The fire came unexpectedly quickly, in fact. Need could do that for a priest, and in a moment, even Malin lifted his head, pleased as he moved closer to the little warmth. It wasn't a really cold day, either. They were going to survive this encounter.

"It's hunting Koya, isn't it?" Malin asked softly.

"That would be my guess," Slade agreed. He dug through his pack and found some bread, still wrapped in cloth and nearly dry. They shared it. "We can follow and probably find Koya as well, though I don't know what we'll do then since the Rockling will also be there."

"But better to have more people against the rockling when it finds Koya."

"True."

"Kenning doesn't want you to go after Koya, though," Malin said and looked at him with a frown. "We can't go and help him, can we?"

"We are scouting out the enemy," Slade answered. He held his hands closer to the fire and knew he needed to stand and get more wood. He felt weary. "The rockling is not only an enemy but one that has been in the company of the

Norters. We'll follow it for a while, Malin. I don't know that it will help Koya. We may find that we need to go elsewhere."

Malin accepted the answer.

When Slade shoved the last little branch into the fire, Malin stood and patted Slade on the shoulder. "I'll get more wood. I won't go far, sir."

He nodded, grateful for the help.

The sounds of the forest were already nearly back to normal. The rockling was making good time, and it would be miles ahead of them before they started out again. He hoped the rockling didn't find Koya. He hoped it wandered on and on and left this battle with the Norters behind because they had enough trouble without the creature.

CHAPTER

TWENTY-SEVEN

DK reached the bottom of the cliff first and hurried into the underbrush just as Koya put his feet down on the ground. He limped over to the place where DK sat -- his companion with a hand plainly on his side and blood seeping through the cloth.

"That doesn't look good, friend," Koya said.

DK frowned and shook his head. "I can still go on, and we must keep moving. You saw the birds flying? Something is heading our way."

Koya looked up as a flock of crows flew across the sky, shouting in protest.

"I fear the rockling is near," Koya admitted. "I don't think we can outrun it, either."

DK frowned. "You are right. We need to find some cover. The stream, I fear, is too far away."

"We probably should have stayed on the cliff."

"To avoid the rockling? No, not a good idea. Rocklings are at one with the ground and the rocks. It could have waved a hand and brought us to our deaths."

"Then anywhere we hide isn't going to be safe."

"Trees," DK said. "Off the ground, up high as we can get."

Koya made a frantic, quick search of the area as sounds grew closer and more ominous. A tall pine stood off to the right amid a cluster of smaller trees. "There?"

"There. And quickly."

Koya wanted rest: his legs and arms already ached, and he feared he would not have much luck climbing, but like DK, he wasn't ready to give up. Koya followed his companion, both of them limping, and DK apparently cursing in his own language. Koya decided to try praying instead. He hoped it helped.

When they reached the tree, Koya looked in shock as DK started up without any trouble at all. Claws: he saw them dig into the bark and hold the Dragonkin as he pulled himself upwards.

DK climbed a few yards and then looked back down.

"Blunt-fingered. I forgot. I'll get up higher and drop the rope."

Koya had forgotten the rope in the pack. "Good. Quickly. I can hear it coming."

DK scrambled on, reached the first large branch, but it creaked ominously when he put any weight on it, so he went up higher, and higher still. The rope finally dropped downward, and Koya could barely reach the end.

Koya grabbed hold and started climbing up, hoping his hands didn't slip on the rough rope, which was burning his fingers and palm already. He'd done this sort of thing with his family, working the trees near their holding. He'd even done it a few times at the Temple when he pruned trees on the grounds. Out of practice, but not impossible. It would have been better if they'd had a chance to tie knots along the length, though. He would start to slip soon.

Koya heard the rockling coming -- a growl of sound, a steady heavy beat of feet against the ground. It helped propel him upward with a surge of adrenaline. He hadn't thought he could call that much energy up again. Fear proved a great motivator.

DK caught his shoulder, and with more strength than Koya thought possible, pulled him up to the branches and swung him towards the right. He caught hold of a stout limb and settled in -- quickly and as silently as he could as DK drew the rope up.

He could see the rockling through the boughs of the trees, ungainly and huge, and the thing moved through the land like a small walking hill.

It grumbled, groaned, and growled -- the only sound except for the breaking of branches in his path. It came on, then paused to sniff, and then came on again.

"Smell, smell --"

Koya could see the running wounds on the creature's face, the one ruined eye, and the burn marks everywhere, which made him a little ill to think he'd done that kind of harm to any living creature. He feared he might have to do more.

The rockling came closer, slowing. Koya suspected they were not going to get away, despite DK's work. However, the creature did seem confused.

"Gone?"

The rockling shuffled forward a few steps and stopped again, the colossal head ranging back and forth, turning as it looked at the ground and sniffed. Koya had the feeling it was not really smelling things in the same way that he did. He could, in fact, feel the little bit of magic that came every time the creature sniffed.

When the rockling came towards the tree, he lifted his hand and wished more than whispered magic that diverted the creature away from the trees and back towards the trail. He sent a scent of he and DK on ahead of the rockling, and it followed, sniffing and sniffing -- and gradually disappearing. He didn't think the magic would last more than a mile or two, but it got the creature away from them here.

"Well done," DK said softly. "But let's rest here for a while."

This seemed as good a place as any to rest. Koya wrapped his arm around the rough trunk and leaned his forehead against it, taking long, deep breaths and fighting off the urge to either sleep or run. Neither would be a good idea just yet.

He glanced a little to the side and saw that DK had stretched out across the branch, and though it had bent a little, it didn't seem to be a problem for him. It looked, in fact, to be comfortable and natural, but Koya knew he'd never be able to rest that way. He stayed and held tight where he was, content for the time being.

Koya could hear animals in the woods now that the rockling had passed. He listened to the sounds of birds, the bark of a nervous fox and the whisper of the stream not far away --

And then he heard something far more ominous.

"DK," he whispered.

"I hear. I think this must be soldiers. Very many soldiers," he said. "It is well that we're still in the tree. Be still. They may have scouts."

"Norters," Koya whispered. "No magic of their own. I can keep us safe."

This wasn't going to be easy, though. Koya thought he should have practiced more with the runes that belonged to the other priests, but there wasn't time, and he had great need. He pulled out what plainly must be an owl and wrapped his fingers around the protesting rune. It stung at his rope-burnt fingers, but Koya held on and felt for the owl in the stone. He wasn't calling for an owl but instead looking for the essence of the bird to fill the air around them. Quiet bird. Unseen in the trees, natural, calm in the light of day.

Nothing to look at up here. Not worth checking.

The scouts went past first, not very close to the tree, which was just as well since Koya didn't have full control of the rune yet. The scouts moved on, plainly tracking the rockling.

They were fools to chase after the creature, but Koya didn't tell them as much. He stayed still and concentrated. He could already hear the rest of the soldiers.

They'd made good time if they'd come from that vast army the hawk had seen. It was not the entire army -- but there were at least five hundred of them, and they ranged out, many of them passing right below the tree. A few started to look up and didn't. By the time the last of them had passed, Koya was holding tight to the rune with his eyes closed. He breathed softly and slowly let go of the magic.

And nearly let go of the tree. Koya had no strength left at all, and he feared he would fall. DK must have realized. He swept around and caught him, and quickly wrapped the rope around his chest, securing him to the trunk.

"Rest. Rest here. Safer, I think, than on the ground."

"There might still be others," Koya agreed, but he hardly had the strength to get the words out. "We must be careful."

"Careful here in the tree," DK agreed.

With the rope around him, Koya felt secure and even safe. He kept the rune in his hand, even though the stone still stung with a touch of anger if a little piece of rock could feel such a thing. Or maybe that was Koya, feeding his own emotions back into it and creating a bad echo. He was angry, though he tried to bury that reaction.

The rest would help. Koya clutched the rune tightly and closed his eyes, soothing both he and the stone towards peace and sleep.

CHAPTER

TWENTY-EIGHT

The seemingly endless stairs finally gave way to a long path through another lush garden. Kenning could see a substantial and ornate door ahead, set into a wall of perfect white stone. He self-consciously brushed at his robe glad he'd had the foresight to pack an extra that he hadn't worn on the harrowing journey.

"Yes, we're finally there," Lord Oak said. Though an older man, he was clearly still in good shape. Oak glanced back over his shoulder. "You should take in the view. Not many get this far to see it."

Kenning turned and froze at the sight of staircase and landing, staircase and landing, all the way back to the courtyard where the carriage waited. Even as he watched, someone came to take a fallen leaf from the steps.

However, the view beyond the staircases was truly spectacular. Kenning could see the city laid out along the

Royal Way, with huge buildings flanking the road all the way down to the azure sea where a single sailing ship moved leisurely with the wind.

The Great Temple, which Kenning had not dared to go near, stood midway between the palace and the sea. The colossal circle gilded in gold and inlaid with silver stood on a pole above the roof and caught the sunlight like a new sun in the sky.

"Ten Gods watch over us and keep us safe in this time of madness," Kenning prayed and made a circle in the sky with his right hand. He dared a little magic in it, and for a moment, the small ring of magic glittered.

"Well." Lord Oak looked a little surprised and then gave a somewhat embarrassed smile. "My apologies. You are the first truly devout priest I've met. I don't think I've ever heard the Most Holy pray, except as part of a show for the Empress."

Kenning winced and reluctantly turned away from the view. "May I be so bold as to ask if she likes the show?"

"Oh, yes. Quite entertaining," Oak said, and then his face split into a big smile. "Especially when she tells the Most Holy no to his latest request."

"Ah."

"It won't help you much either way, I'm afraid. The Empress isn't going to be taken in by priests these days. However, your tale transcends your calling."

"If she will listen to me."

Lord Oak looked worried for a moment. "If she does not, we'll try again. The army cannot be raised in a day. We have time, praise the Gods, since you were wise enough to race here yourself and not trust such dire news to a courier. He could have waited a couple weeks to see even a minor functionary in the court. "

"It's a wonder that anything gets done," Kenning said with a look of astonishment at the area around him.

"It is, sometimes."

They reached the ornate wooden door carved in trees and flowers and those inlaid with gold and gems. Lord Oak pulled a bell, and someone lifted a bar and swung the portal open. A dozen guards in royal green and blue stood on the other side and eyed the two suspiciously for a moment.

"I bring grave news for the Empress," Lord Oak announced.

"The Most Holy is already in session with her on important matters," one of the men said. Gold adorned his uniform. He was obviously of rank.

"We must see her for that very reason," Lord Oak said, gave a little bow of his head -- which seemed to surprise everyone. He looked up again at the man with gold trim. "Captain Epodca, there are matters we fear the Most Holy will hide from the Empress. We fear he may be leading her toward his personal Holy War. He has been trying to force an attack against the Dragonkin before."

"Every time he comes here," Captain Epodca added with a snarl. Kenning must have looked as appalled as he felt. Captain Epodca looked him over and then signaled the two intruders to follow him.

"You don't normally stand guard duty at the door," Lord Oak said, walking to the side of the Captain.

"I heard you were arriving with a priest. I had to see this wonder for myself," Epcoda admitted.

Lord Oak gave a little chuckle. Kenning walked behind them with guards at his sides and another three at his back. He didn't feel comfortable enough to make any comment. Instead, he took in the view, which was magnificent enough to almost keep his mind off the fact that he was going to the Empress. Kenning had thought he would send word to her. He thought he would talk to others, and they would take the message to the Empress.

He brushed at his robes again.

Colonnades had taken the place of the tall trees they'd passed outside, and those alternated between white marble with darker versions, some black, some green. The stone-lined path had given way to mosaics of what Kenning hoped was glass and not gems. He didn't stop to find out. The effect was incredible, and he felt as though he walked among living rainbows where the light touched the surface.

At the end of the entry, they went up a broad set of stairs and into a darkened hall. People sat here. Many, many people. All of them held scrolls that must be petitions of some sort. He thought there must be over a hundred, and they remained incredibly quiet, with only a whisper of sound as they passed. All of them had food hampers and blankets. Lord Oak had not been exaggerating about camping here until their turn. He felt guilty as he passed through the line without taking his turn, but Kenning knew that the news he brought was too important to wait.

Captain Epodca signaled them to wait in an alcove, and he went on to another door, talked to the guard there, and then pushed it open. For one brief moment, Kenning heard the thunderous voice of the Most Holy -- "Enemies of our Gods!" -- and then the door closed again.

"I feel bad about them," Kenning said, waving a hand towards the benches where people waited.

"Don't. The news you bring is far too important to keep you sitting out here with the others. Besides, it's not as bad as it looks. They sit through some part of the day, and if they need to wait through the night, not only are they paid a silver coin for the inconvenience, but they get to attend the nightly feast. Many people spend months trying to find a cause important enough to get them this far. The Empress enjoys their company, too."

That eased a good deal of his guilt. Besides, the worry about the others had only been a momentary diversion at best. He looked towards the door, dreading when it would open because he had no idea what he would really say to Empress Silana.

Except that he would say the truth, of course. He had to get over his fear of speaking before the Empress and deal with the trouble at hand. He had dared the Most Holy's wrath by coming here -- and he had no doubt the payment would be harsh. He would do what he must to tell the truth to the one person in the Empire who had more power than his spiritual leader.

Still, when the door opened, his heart sank to the pit of his stomach, and he probably turned as pale as snow after a storm. Captain Edpoca gave a quick sign for them to enter, and Lord Oak gave a slight nudge. Kenning walked forward like a poorly handled puppet as he stepped into the single most famous room in all the Empire, and maybe in the world.

The Empress's throne room was long and narrow, the roof high and pointed, and filled with light from the translucent stone that covered the rafters. Rows of carved cherry wood benches held a dozen or so petitioners along with clerks, servants, and specially appointed barristers who spoke with the petitioners to help them make the presentation. He had read about the room and knew that it usually was filled with whispers that almost rose above the sound of the current petitioner.

There were no whispers today, not with the Most Holy at the podium which stood sideways to the throne and the crowd giving everyone a view of the petitioner. Oh yes, the Most Holy no doubt loved that all the work of the Empire came to a stop for him. He stood, leaning against the podium with one hand raised as though to strike the wood, his face flushed --

and his mouth opening like a gaping fish when he turned slightly and saw Kenning.

It was not a good sign.

Kenning looked past the man and to the Empress herself as he bowed. He had only seen sketches of her, and they did the woman no justice. Her hair, now as much silver as brown, had been worked into braids and curls so that the strands looked very much a part of the crown of silver she wore. Her face was thin, the eyes large and bright, and the lips held tightly closed, though he couldn't guess if that was against anger or mirth. She glanced his way as he bowed and gave a little flick of her hand. Captain Edpoca led them to the podium.

"This is an outrage!" Most Holy yelled. Kenning, crossing the area, saw many of the people on the benches flinch at the sudden, thundering sound. "Kenning has no right to be here and speak against me --"

"How very odd," the Empress said. She had the voice of a purring cat -- soft against the Most Holy's harshness, both powerful and soothing at the same time. "How odd, Most Holy, that you know what this man will say before he says it."

The Most Holy turned a glare in her direction, and then quickly turned away again at the lift of her delicate eyebrow. He didn't apologize or admit to any wrongdoing despite being rude to the Empress.

Kenning really couldn't decide how the man had survived this long.

"Lord Oak?" Empress Silana said with a wave of a long-nailed hand in his direction. "I am surprised to find you here, and in the company of a priest. My guard says that you have things to say that I will want to know?"

"Yes, Your Grace," he said, bowing his head again before he spoke. He put a hand on Kenning's shoulder, probably to offer him strength. "This is High Priest Kenning, of Templeton."

"Is he, indeed?" she said and sounded a little surprised at last. Kenning wasn't confident that helped. "And he has brought me news?"

"Yes, Your Grace."

"Then let him speak it to me," she said and waved a hand again.

Before Kenning could even open his mouth, Most Holy pounded the podium three times, so hard and loud that he thought the wood might break under the blows. The Most Holy's face had gone bright red, and his eyes nearly disappeared behind the narrowed glare of rage.

"This is my man. I do not give him permission to speak -- "

"This is not your place to say," the Empress replied, quiet but forceful still.

"He has left his post without permission. He has come here --"

"To tell me something. *Be silent*, Cedric the Benevolent."

It was an order. Kenning thought the Most Holy would not obey. The man's mouth opened once more, and Captain Edpoca took a step closer to him. The mouth closed.

"Kenning of Templeton?" she said, looking back at him. "Tell me what you think I need to know."

"There is trouble along the border, as the Most Holy has told you and others. It is not, however, with the Dragonkin. The Norters are trying to maneuver us into a war with the Dragonkin. My priest, who was present at the attack on Ziven, sent me word that it is so."

"And you believe him?"

"Yes, Your Grace," he said with a bow of his head. His heart pounded. "Besides, I sent another priest to help him, since Koya had fallen into the hands of the Norters. This one confirmed that there is a Norter army in the area, and they are in league with a rockling."

The Most Holy snorted this time. "Norters working with a creature of magic? And you believe these lying priests of yours? Even though one of them is a Norter bastard himself?"

"Koya came running to the Temple from the north, yes," Kenning said and didn't allow his own anger to fill his voice. "He was not the first to come seeking sanctuary from those who would kill him because he had the gift of the Gods."

"Lies, all of it lies. I never trusted him."

"Yes, I know," Kenning said and fully faced the man. There was no hope of recovery from this slight, so he need not hold back. "Your bigotry has blinded you, Most Holy, to some crucial points. Not the least of those is that if Koya was working with the Norters, he certainly would have continued to support their efforts to get us to attack the Dragonkin. Instead, he has risked his life, and for all I know might well be dead already, to get us the true answer."

"It's all lies," Most Holy said, his voice growing to the sound of thunder again. "Lies, and more lies."

"Yes, but who is lying?" Lord Oak dared to say.

"You are damned beyond all redemption," Most Holy said, glaring at his old enemy. Kenning was glad enough to have the attention taken from him. He suspected he felt a little as Koya must have during that ill-fated meeting with the Most Holy back when all this madness started. Kenning just wanted to tell the news and make certain things were done right, but it seemed he would have to work hard to prove himself first.

"I had not heard that you were the one who judged the worthiness of a soul," Lord Oak said and didn't look in the least bit contrite or worried.

"Begone from my presence, you and that perfidious man who claims to be a priest. Be gone before you feel my wrath --
"

"This is not your place to order who is welcome here and who is not," Empress Silana said, and the purr was gone from her voice as she leaned forward on the throne. "One more word, and someone will certainly be leaving. I think you can guess who it will be, Most Holy."

Most Holy turned his head slowly back to the woman. Kenning saw a little flicker of anger in her face, and the Most Holy must have seen it as well since he took a step back from the podium, as though to put more distance between himself and the Empress's rage. Kenning suspected, the way even Captain Edpoca straightened, that it might not be something commonly seen.

"Is this priest of yours a Norter?" she asked, looking at Kenning.

"Yes, Your Grace, in that he was born there. But he has a true man of the Gods."

Of course, Most Holy could not keep quiet, though his voice did not rage quite as loudly this time. "The Gods cursed him before I left your Temple. I saw it myself."

"You cursed him, Most Holy. We all saw it. He still went on with his work, despite being in great pain because of you. He tried to tell you that he could feel some sort of magical trouble coming. He even said he didn't think it came from the Dragonkin. You wouldn't listen."

"He does that well, the not listening," the Empress said and almost won a grin from Kenning.

"I hear the voices of the Gods," Most Holy replied, and stood straighter, trying to throw the mantle of sanctity over himself again. "I do not need the word of Norters to tell me any truth. He claimed to feel things that no one else did. And now, after he has gone to this place, trouble has fallen. Do you really think that a coincidence? Maybe I have mistaken his allegiance. I think it might be worse than I believed. He is not working with the Norters. He has given up all ties to humans, and now he works with the Dragonkin. What better way to ruin all of us than to get us fighting, human against human so that they can rush in and kill us all?"

It was, as things went, far better rationalization than Kenning had ever heard from the man before now. Granted, before this, Most Holy didn't have to do anything but bluster and order people since he was of the highest rank present. Before Her Grace, however, he plainly had to think.

"Should we trust this priest?" The Empress asked with a frown. "Someone not of our people -- no matter if he is graced by the Gods or not. It is not an easy matter --"

"There is the other priest, Your Grace," Lord Oak said.

"No doubt in league with Koya and Kenning here," Most Holy replied. "I will cleanse all the east of heresy and traitors before I'm done --"

"Your Grace," Lord Oak said, and something in his tone silenced even the Most Holy and everyone else. "I think you can trust this other priest. It is Slade."

Her face showed a moment of surprise, not lost on anyone in the room. "Slade, the former Captain of my Guard?"

"Yes, Your Grace."

"I had heard he entered the priesthood. This is, surely, the work of the Gods," she said, and Kenning felt an odd shiver at those words. The Empress believed the news he had brought! She leaned forward, anxious this time. "Tell me more, Father Kenning. Captain Edpoca, you have my permission to escort the Most Holy from the room if he interrupts again. Step away from the podium, Cedric. I have a need to hear this tale, and I will have questions."

The Most Holy stepped away, red-faced with anger, but silent at last.

CHAPTER

TWENTY-NINE

Slade and Malin kept far back from the soldiers, watching one group head towards the rockling -- and good luck with that duty, Slade thought. Most of the men broke camp and headed southward. Slade knew they needed more information about the soldiers. He and Malin followed the larger group, relying on animals to scout for them and gathering whatever clues they could.

It made for the most pleasant day they'd had so far, even with the occasional scare of stragglers from the troops. A couple bands of men moved through the thinning woods gathering wood for fires and doing a little hunting; by those signs, the two knew the troops had made camp.

Slade and Malin left the area as quietly as they could and found their own place for the night. It was early afternoon, which seemed far too soon to stop, and that made Slade think there was something else going on.

He wondered if he could get close enough to find out.

Slade and Malin hiked back over a low hill and then found a narrow crevice for their own camp. They'd been gathering a few berries, roots, and mushrooms all through their hike -- plants disdained for mistrusted by the Norter army. Slade suspected the later, and that meant the army was in a territory they didn't understand at all.

He and Malin ate well, though he suspected the boy might be more used to meat. They'd try for a little fish, maybe, tomorrow night.

Slade was glad to sit back and relax. He placed a little perimeter spell that would warn them if anyone came close tonight. A short conversation with a squirrel convinced him that the army had settled in, and they would be safe enough for now.

"The world seems very different today," Malin said, leaning back on an elbow.

"A moment of peace between the battles," Slade said. "I remember these times too well from the days when I was in the army. These are rare days. We learned to treasure them."

"I hadn't really thought about it, you know," Malin said with a little frown.

"About what?"

"That there is going to be war. I keep thinking of this in personal terms. I don't know why they destroyed Ziven and killed the people there. It makes no sense to me. We were no one, you know."

"You were citizens of the Empire," Slade corrected. "But unfortunately, you were in an area where any number of things could happen, and no one would know about it until far too late. Secluded places like that are hard to protect, and far too often the target of trouble."

"I'd heard such things from the past. Tales --" He stopped, no doubt remembering the people who had told him such stories, and that they were all dead. "Tales told around the fires at night. Gloomy stories to frighten little boys who wanted to run wild."

"So true. I'd heard such tales as well, but sometimes they have a kernel of truth in them. In a hundred years, it's unlikely that either of us would recognize the tale of what happened in Ziven."

"Maybe that's all right," Malin said. He shrugged. "Maybe they don't have to know the truth because no one would believe it anyway, would they?"

"That depends on what happens next." Slade leaned back, letting the sense of peace take him, at least for a while. "If this goes to war, then Ziven becomes a rallying cry for the troops, and what happened there will be a major part of the history of the land. That means your name will be there as well, for all the rest of the time that the Empire thrives, and perhaps for a long time afterward."

The boy sat straight up, his eyes wide and his face paling a little. "I can't be part of history. Not me."

"You already are -- and like most common people caught up in the flow of events, you did nothing to put yourself there. It's only the nobles and high officials who have purposely placed themselves in the way of history, and all too often they find that they are caught in matters that those people cannot control and that are not working the way they had hoped."

"I never would have wanted to be here. Even if I can help to save the Empire, I would rather have been back home, hunting and working with Master Alcrew."

"I know. I'm sorry it worked this way, but I'm glad to have you as a companion. You've done very well."

Malin shook his head. "I've sleep-walked, sir. I haven't really been here at all."

"Your subconscious has made the choices for you while your mind rested. You still made all the right choices. I won't say it will be easier now but --"

"Slade?" a voice whispered.

He gave a little jump and then laughed, and Malin with him, as Slade pulled out the rune. It felt a little cool to the touch, which meant a great distance stretched between him and Kenning.

"Sir?" he said, feeding his own power into the connection.

"Is it safe to speak?" Kenning asked, his voice a little hollow with the distance.

"Safer than it has been for days, sir."

"Good. I am in the Imperial Palace, in the company of the Empress, Lord Oak, and the Most Holy. There are questions that they would like answered."

Malin had jumped to his feet and stared wide-eyed at the rune. His lips formed a single, silent word. *Empress?*

Slade looked at Malin and nodded, and though Slade didn't get back to his feet, he did sit up straighter: an old habit, to come to attention in her presence.

"Ask anything, sir. I'll answer what I can."

Lord Oak asked most of the questions, and he didn't hear the Empress at all, though he did feel her presence. The questions were basic things about troop strengths, positions, movement. He fell back into the old terms with an ease that made him shiver slightly and wonder what Gods had put their hands on him to place him where he could do such good.

The Most Holy protested when he said there were no Dragonkin to be seen.

"You cannot know --" he bellowed so loudly that it startled a bird in a nearby tree.

"I know what I have seen, Most Holy," Slade replied, his voice still calm. "And that is what I have reported. Tomorrow, the Norters may join up with a Dragonkin army the size of a mountain, but at this point, they have not. They have worked to make us believe the Dragonkin people are attacking. I think it obvious that they are trying to create a fight between our two people."

"You have no right to give such opinions --"

And then, finally, the Empress spoke. Slade found himself smiling at the tone, too, which he remembered far too well. "Slade is in a position to say what he has seen, and he is well-trained, so his opinion gives it merit, Cedric. He has put himself in danger to help us. You could have been there, sending information to me instead, but you ran for the capital as fast as you could as soon as trouble arose."

"It is not my place --"

"No, it is not," she said, cutting him off. "Be silent, or I will again have you removed."

Malin looked delighted. He suspected the boy had just been won over to Empress Silana, body and soul. Good. The boy desperately needed somewhere to place his honor, and Empress Silana wouldn't betray it -- not the way that the Most Holy did with his priests.

"What do you think, Slade?" Empress Silana finally said.

"Your Grace," he said, and bowed his head the way he had so often in her presence. It was an old habit, and it made him feel oddly better. "I think Malin and I should continue to work as scouts. The Norter army is not marching hard, which makes me think they are either near to their destination, or else they are preparing for a hard march --"

Malin looked up, startled, and then looked towards the south with his eyes narrowed.

"Malin?" he said.

Malin looked toward the rune, obviously speechless in the presence of the Empress, even in the shape of a little piece of stone. He opened his mouth a couple times, and his face flushed.

"She won't bite you, boy," Slade said, and the Empress laughed.

It was a delight to hear, something she so rarely did.

"Y-Your G-Grace," Malin said and bowed his head. Then he looked away from the rune, and his voice settled. "There is a narrow, dangerous path through the mountains about ten miles to the south of us. It leads to the backside of the Forbidden Valley, though you won't see any way in, of course. It is very dangerous, and few people will take it, because being so close to the valley, there are sometimes still trolls and such creatures lurking around."

"Like rocklings," Lord Oak and Slade chorused.

"I'd never heard of such things, sirs," Malin said. "But there are tales enough of other creatures hiding there, caught between the Dragonkin lands and the world of men, and sometimes they slip out from the Valley to their old lands."

"Child's tales," the Most Holy scoffed.

"Yes, much like the story of the rocklings," Lord Oak added.

Malin was at least a little less spooked by the discussion, but Slade was running out of energy to hold the connection. He hoped this ended soon. He didn't think there was much more that he could add to the discussion at this point.

"It's said that a person needs a guide to go through the Forbidden Valley," Malin said. "A magical guide. And they have the rockling, don't they?"

Silence on all sides.

"The boy's right," Lord Oak said softly and with obvious worry.

"You said the rockling went off in another direction," Most Holy replied, obviously ready to dismiss the idea.

"And we said that soldiers went after it. There's a good chance it will be coming back to join the army. That could well be why they camped so early," Slade said.

"And that means it will come this way, sir," Malin added and looked nervously out through the trees.

"He's right." Slade got to his feet and waved away the little magic barrier he had built, fearing it might already have drawn unwanted attention. Malin began grabbing up their few supplies. "Your Grace --"

"Go, Slade," she said, her voice filled with a touch of worry that he found shocking. "Be safe, both of you. Learn what you can of what the Norters are doing but do so with care. You are the only eyes we have there, Slade and Malin. I am sending a contingent of scouts riding out today, but by the time they get there, I fear everything will be in motion. Give me news, Slade, when you can."

"Yes, Your Grace. I am still your man."

"I know you are," she said more softly. "And I think the Gods have moved to put you where I most need someone I trust implicitly. Be careful. Kenning, say whatever you need to, and let them go."

"Be safe, Slade," Kenning said. His voice sounded shaky, plainly a sign of stress from the connection.

The rune went silent and cold. Slade pushed it into his pouch and looked around with frantic haste. "This way," he said, and started out at an angle away from the army camp. It was not an easy climb, but Slade thought that best as they scrambled over thorn-covered hillocks and up boulder-strewn hillsides, trying desperately to stay in the shadows for fear of what might look their way.

They kept moving for the rest of the day and stopped only when the sun had started to go down and made the climbing more treacherous. Even Malin, who was as sure-footed as a mountain goat, had slipped on one of the shale-covered hillsides and twisted his knee. They were both happy to rest afterward, there on the dark side of a huge boulder. Slade had chased out a couple poisonous snakes and dissuaded an opossum from trying to take the place instead.

This was not as comfortable as they had been in the glade, but he was glad for the rest.

"I'll take the first watch, sir," Malin said.

He didn't argue.

CHAPTER

THIRTY

L ord Oak led Kenning out of the building and into the grounds with night nearly upon them, the dusky light gray with a pale fog. Kenning looked around, blinking several times and feeling as though he walked covered in cloth. Everything felt distant, out of reach.

"I think you had better sit down for a few minutes, priest," Lord Oak said, and caught his arm, taking Kenning to a bench beside an ancient willow. Kenning settled there without comment and then looked around, still blinking.

"This can't be real."

"I fear it is." Lord Oak settled beside him and leaned back, looking weary for the first time. "The trouble with the Most Holy is bad given his bigotry. You must be careful now. Most Holy will be coming through here soon, and not in a good mood."

"We shouldn't be where he can find us."

"You don't trust him."

Kenning looked at the man, his head tilted and shaking his head. "Of course, I don't trust him. Why do you think I raced here to counter what he said?"

"Well yes, good point," Lord Oak replied and sounded amused. He glanced around the area, perhaps looking for spies. Kenning didn't care. He hadn't lied, and he wouldn't do so now. Let anyone hear the truth. "But I meant in a less obvious way, Kenning. You don't trust him to deal fairly with you, now that you've been proven right."

"Have I been? I'm not even sure Empress Silana is fully convinced yet. As far as the Most Holy is concerned, I am just another priest from the east, in league with that Norter bastard that he hates so much."

"Ah. And he does hate this man?"

"Koya. Oh yes, very much so. And why? Because he is from the north, of course. But worse than that, Koya has the blessings of the Gods. He's a very powerful priest."

"Powerful?" Lord Oak asked and cast one look back at the palace.

"Yes, he is more powerful in magic and gifts from the Gods than the Most Holy."

"Ah. A threat to the old bas – too Most Holy's place in the world. Here they come. I think it time to slip into the shadows, my friend."

Lord Oak led him quickly behind the huge willow to a hidden path amid some tall trees, where the shadows covered them like the darkest night. In fact, Lord Oak moved so smoothly that Kenning could tell he had done so often enough that this escape was second nature to him.

Peering through the leaves, Kenning could see the Most Holy in a sedan chair as he was carried down the steps. The priests labored under the weight, already gasping. They had a long walk ahead, most of it down the stairs that lead to the level of the street. Kenning seemed to remember hearing that priests had to do penance by carrying the Most Holy.

All of it needless work. With a touch of a rune, and a wave of his hand, the Most Holy could have made himself as light as a feather. The man enjoyed the suffering of others far too much.

Kenning saw the Most Holy as the pale light caught him; his face was set in dark rage, and his lips moving in what clearly were not prayers. The man leaned forward, nearly unsettling the sedan, and the men beneath him gasped and fought to keep the Most Holy from tumbling. He didn't seem to notice.

"Where have those two traitors gone?" he demanded. "Where are they? Still in the palace, telling more lies to that woman?"

"They -- they left, Most Holy," one of the men said, fighting to shift the pole he held. "We watched. They left. They must have rushed ... rushed ahead to avoid your wrath."

"Oh yes." Most Holy leaned back. "Wise to fear me and the power of the Gods. I have already struck the Norter pretending to be holy. Kenning will not be far behind. And then Oak. I'll have even him before I'm done. And more, if I have to."

They were moving on to the first set of stairs and heading downward, the Most Holy's voice slowly fading. Lord Oak did not move yet, though, and Kenning soon saw the reason. Another three priests finally followed. Plainly they were guards to make certain no one came up behind the Most Holy.

"Well, I think you had best avoid crossing paths with that man while you are here," Lord Oak said. "We'll just stay here and enjoy the garden for a bit more and give him plenty of time to get away, shall we?"

"Yes, that sounds wise," Kenning agreed. He wanted to sit down again. "I'm exhausted. That kind of communications takes far too much from a person. I hope Slade is all right. He's in far more a dangerous position than I am."

"Oh, I wouldn't count on that," Lord Oak said, his voice dropping a little. "The Most Holy is dangerous enough, of course, but he has allies. No one that pompous and disliked could have stayed in power here without help. Even if he is the head of the Temple, that doesn't mean he would have political power as well."

"I am not well-versed in such things," Kenning admitted. "I have even stayed out of politics back in Templeton when I could."

"Wise man," Lord Oak said and herded him back out and to the bench. "Sit down. It will take them a while to get down the stairs, and there's no reason to rush after them. It's a nice night to sit here for a while, don't you think?"

"Nice to sit anywhere," he admitted and leaned back.

"Cedric could have helped you out with the power it took to talk to Slade, right?"

"Oh yes, of course. I didn't expect him to help, and quite honestly, I don't know if I would have trusted him. He's done things already that make it hard to believe the man would do anything for good."

"Ah. Excellent point. I know Cedric has powers, and I admit they worry me -- and others -- sometimes. It's troubling to have him working against you and have things start going wrong. You wonder how much of it is bad luck, and how much of it is him nudging the world to suit him."

Kenning frowned and glanced towards the stairs and back at Lord Oak. "It's not easy for me to speak about him. He is the head of the Temple."

"Ah, yes. My apologies."

Kenning lifted a hand and silenced what more the man was about to say. "It's not easy, but I think I best get over such feelings. I have known truly holy people, and Cedric is not one of them. I wouldn't doubt that he uses his powers to influence things in ways that suit him. He's bigoted, bad-tempered, and a bully. He's a dangerous man. I believe the Gods will deal with him eventually. I also believe the Gods expect us to help ourselves in such situations. We are tested, even if he has already failed."

Lord Oak gave him another odd look, his head tilted and something close to a smile on his lips. "It's been a long time since I've been in the company of a true believer, let alone a priest. My faith failed when I became far too aware of what kind of man Cedric was. How does such a man gain power like he has?"

"I think that's more in your realm than mine," Kenning said with a grin. "The power he has here may be facilitated by his magical power, but a political status doesn't come from the Gods."

"Now, there is an interesting point I really hadn't considered," Lord Oak said. He looked content to stay and talk, and Kenning didn't complain. He'd had a difficult few days and resting in the shadow of the palace seemed both odd and welcome. Kenning was no longer in a hurry to get somewhere. That came as a bit of a shock, too. He had done what he needed to, and though there might still be more work, the harder and more important part was done. He had told the truth before the one person who needed to know it.

Kenning and Lord Oak talked, mostly about the city, politics, and things that Kenning didn't understand well, so he welcomed the knowledge. He wanted this to go right, and it was becoming increasingly apparent that just getting the accurate news here was only the start of a long battle. The discussion made him wiser, but it also left him weary in mind and body.

They took their time going down the long stairs and enjoying the view of the city and the sea. The Most Holy had long since left by the time they took the last staircase down to the carriage. Several stable boys were already harnessing the horses, likely having watched them come down the steps. The city seemed no less alive as the night came on. Maybe even more so, and Kenning stood on the final step, staring out at the long street where it seemed as though fairy lights came on as he watched. This place enchanted him, and he found that he liked the city better for it.

"Kenning?" Lord Oak said and turned back to him. "I haven't asked you to be my guest yet --"

Kenning turned, smiling at the offer -- and saved their lives. If he had been walking closer to Lord Oak, Kenning would not have seen the men on the top of the carriage aiming crossbows --

"Down!" he shouted and dove for the cover of the trellis.

Lord Oak dropped and rolled towards the carriage, putting him too close for the enemy to get a good aim with the crossbows. The driver had been sitting on a bench. He yelped and scrambled under it, though an arrow caught the man below the knee.

"Son of a bitch that was stupid!" Lord Oak yelled, and Kenning couldn't decide if he meant them or the attackers. Lord Oak rolled fully under the carriage and then snaked out to the horses, spooking them. They bounded forward, and three men on the carriage top tumbled and cursed. By the time the carriage had slipped aside, Kenning could see Lord Oak facing three men with swords drawn.

Kenning was not about to lose his only offer of a place to stay.

He only had a little magic of his own without the runes, but he called up what he could and sent a quick, strong wind that knocked all four men down. He wished he could have spared Lord Oak the tumble, but he didn't have that much control.

The use of that much magic nearly sent him unconscious this time, and started an odd ringing in his ears as he leapt forward to help --

But no, not ringing in his ears. An alarm was sounding, and it brought soldiers at a run. He had barely tackled one of the attackers before a squad of soldiers arrived and grabbed the men.

Lord Oak stood, brushing at his clothing and looking around with a frown. The soldiers were already transporting the wounded driver away, and a dozen more had taken positions at the gate. Captain Edpoca arrived, quite breathless and flushed. He had plainly run all the way down from the palace.

"Hell," Edpoca said -- the only word he could gasp out as he looked at the three men who were held. They were silent, and their eyes glared like fanatics. "How... How did they get in here?"

Fanatics.

"Priests," Kenning said and saw at least one man's eyes flicker with a little worry. "Check them for runes, or else it's unlikely you'll be able to hold them for long."

"Traitor," one of them said and spat.

Kenning helped the soldiers find the runes before they took the priests away. By the time they were done, Kenning became aware of something that made him shiver. The city had been loud before the battle but now had gone silent as a tomb. Kenning spun, looking towards the long street. He could only see a short distance from this lower ground, but it seemed that everyone had stopped and turned toward the palace.

"I better get that handled," Captain Edpoca said, waving a hand toward the city. "Masday! Get out there and tell people it had nothing to do with the Empress, and all is in hand!"

"Yes, sir!"

People moved on all sides, rushing about in a dizzying array of colors. The sounds seemed to echo oddly. Kenning stumbled across the courtyard and found a bench, feeling more than a little ill. He had no doubt that the Most Holy had set the assassins to kill him and his companion.

It made this entire situation far more real and dangerous again.

It also made Kenning feel an unusual surge of righteousness. Even if the Most Holy had been right in his assessment of the situation, he should never have turned to attempted murder to get his way.

Lord Oak settled on the bench beside him. "Thank you, Kenning. You saved my life. I wouldn't even have gotten my sword drawn before those jackals were on me, crossbows, or not."

"I'm glad I could help, sir, though, in truth, I brought the trouble as well."

"I suppose so, in some ways. However, that doesn't mean you are the one in the wrong, priest."

"No. No, it does not." Kenning took a deeper breath finally. "Slade knew I had to find someone to help me in order to get the news to the Empress in time. I'm glad it was you, though I am sorry to put you in such danger."

"I'm glad you came to me as well," Lord Oak said and plainly meant those words. "Slade is a good man, and he knew you could trust me."

"Yes, sir."

"We'll be here at the palace for a while still. Perhaps the whole night. But we'll be safe for it, too."

"Does that mean we're going back up the stairs?"

"I fear so."

"Damned inconsiderate people to wait until we're all the way down here before they attack," Kenning said. He started to feel a bit giddy and light-headed. He shook his head and then stopped abruptly because strange lights played across his vision, and a headache had started to build at the base of his neck.

"Can you make it that far?" Lord Oak asked. He looked worried.

"I'll make it."

He did, too, though Kenning didn't remember anything that happened after they stepped back into the palace. Sometime later, he found himself sliding into a soft, comfortable bed.

"What --"

"It's all right, Kenning," Lord Oak said from the door. "I'm just across the hall, and we have a contingent of the Queen's own guard to watch us. Sleep well. You'll need a clear head in the morning."

He grunted some answer and dropped his head down on a softer pillow than he'd felt in years, and he slept like the dead.

CHAPTER

THIRTY-ONE

Koya and DK traveled that night since both had rested during the long day. Koya felt as though he had been bruised by the tree and abused by everything else. He limped worse, and the pain that had come from the Most Holy seemed to have grown again. He bit at his lower lip and said nothing as they made their way through the dark woods. At least they didn't rush.

DK moved very well in the dark of night. Koya felt awkward and loud, which bothered him, though he knew he only used that worry to mask all the other problems. He wanted to stop and talk to animals, but Koya didn't think he had the strength left to overcome Galt's conditioning of the runes. A shame, because they could have used a little guidance on a night like this.

Though, to give him credit, DK did well enough anyway. His companion was a hunter and knew how to handle himself in the woods.

Koya had begun to think himself a fool in far too many ways. He'd been lulled into believing he'd found his place at Templeton, and that he could live out his life in peace within those quiet walls. Now he remembered something Kenning had once said, very early in their acquaintance. The older priest had told Koya that men gifted with power never have quiet lives. The Gods had always meant them to fix things.

Now he realized he had only been resting at the Temple, learning more about life and the Gods, and it was time to use what he knew to help others. He knew he had been blessed by the Gods. He hadn't really thought much about why or what that meant until now.

And the problem, of course, was that he couldn't help much at all.

"Rest now," DK suddenly said. "We made excellent time."

"Did we?" Koya asked, stunned by the words. He looked around, but they might as well have been in the same place where they started. The woods, filled with shadows, looked very much the same, and for an insane moment, he thought DK had led them in circles.

"Rest, human," DK said again. He slid down with a tree at his back, plainly exhausted. "We shall have hard climbing tomorrow, but afterward, the True Lands will be in sight."

"True Lands?"

He saw a little flash of a smile in the moon-lit darkness. "That is the place where the Dragonkin lives -- the True Lands."

"And where do the humans live?"

"The Stolen Lands."

"Ah."

"It's an old war. Your people don't have the same sort of names for where the Dragonkin live?"

"I've only ever heard them called Synetha," he said with a little shrug. "There are probably other names, but I never heard them."

"Because you are a priest?" he said, a little hint of curiosity in his voice.

"Yes, mostly that. And because when I was around, people mostly talk about Norters."

"I see. It was not easy to fit in?"

"No, not considering I came from the north."

"We always think of humans as if they are all of one kind," he said. "I suppose you think the same of us."

"Yes, but it's for the same reason -- we don't know any better."

"You shall learn, I think. And will you then teach others?"

"If I have a chance. And if I think it will do no harm."

"How can truth do harm?"

"Are we really prepared to tackle this kind of philosophical discussion tonight?" Koya asked and won a barking little laugh from his companion.

"Perhaps not," DK agreed. "We need to rest."

"Sleep for a while. I'll keep the first watch this time."

DK gave a little bow of his head and leaned back, his eyes closing. In some ways, Koya regretted it. He would have liked to talk for a while longer. In another way, it made him feel oddly satisfied to know that DK trusted him so well.

The silence left Koya alone with his thoughts. He worried what might be going on out there where they could not see and wished he had the strength to try and call to Kenning, even using Galt's runes. He prayed instead, hoping that his warning about the Norters had gotten through.

What did the Norters truly want, besides the war between the people of the south and the Dragonkin? Did they think the two would wipe each other out and leave the Norters with the spoils? That didn't seem likely, and he couldn't believe the people would think so.

And what were they doing in the company of a rockling? There was the real question that needed to be addressed, and the one that he thought would cast more light on this matter than any other.

The night had turned too cold. While they'd walked, Koya hadn't noticed the breeze. Now, he felt the cold, his aches, his hunger, and his growing anger. Koya tried to tame the last back, knowing it wouldn't help. He concentrated on the sounds of the forest. He could read them somewhat, though not as well as he could have read the natural sounds around the Temple. When something substantial moved not far away, he almost woke DK, but a moment later he knew it to be a bear, and not moving towards them, so he let his companion rest.

It couldn't be long until the dawn again, either. He would rest a little while in the light, and then they would go on --

And he would go to the True Lands. How odd.

Koya was already learning how little the humans knew about the Dragonkin. If he survived, this was going to be an interesting trip. At least he finally had something to look forward to.

CHAPTER

THIRTY-TWO

The days in the palace soon took on an air of the commonplace, if not outright boring, except for the times Kenning found himself called before Empress Silana. Kenning never felt less than awe for the woman, and that awe grew as he watched her in the Royal Hall and in Council Chambers with her advisors.

The advisors had mistrusted him at first and Kenning quickly realized it was not really him, but of his station. They had no reason to think priests would understand anything about war, and that belief had not been helped by the Most Holy's attitude towards them.

It also didn't help that the Most Holy had sent a group of soldiers off to kill an ambassadorial party, news that did not even come up until the third day.

"Even -- even if the war had been true, we never kill ambassadors, Cedric," Empress Silana had said. She came half out of her chair as though she would cross the room and strangle him herself.

The Most Holy scrambled backward half a dozen steps in shock before he caught himself. He cast one warning glare at Kenning and then straightened his shoulders again. "You can't prove anything."

"However, that doesn't make it untrue. Just as we can't prove that the priests who tried to assassinate Kenning and me were not here at your orders," Lord Oak said and won a snarl from Most Holy. "Kenning says there was magic, and I believe him. And we have more than a few witnesses who say you called the guards to you, and that they then took off at a run after the ambassador and her group."

"If they did, maybe they were only wiser than others," Most Holy answered, though did not dare a look at the Empress. "If there was magic, it came from the Gods."

"All magic comes from the Gods," Kenning dared to say. He had lost his fear of the Most Holy, along with any patience for the man's tirades. "And by saying those words, you do not deny you directed it, or that you misused the power to your own gain."

Kenning had never before been quite so open in his distrust and dislike of the Most Holy. He and Oak had discussed it before they came to the Council Chambers and had agreed that holding back would not help. Kenning knew that no matter what he said, it would not help with his position in the Temple. He regretted that he would be stripped of his robes and symbols -- but better to give them up than to lie.

Oak had said Empress Silana would agree. Kenning suspected, in fact, that Lord Oak had discussed the matter with her already.

The Most Holy stared at him, eyes narrowing, lips in a tight line of anger. His pudgy face grew redder, and his hands began to move --

"Don't even think of cursing me the way you did to Koya," Kenning warned. He brought up his own hand, and magic already played at his fingers. He didn't need time to call up magic, and he thought the Most Holy looked a little startled this time. "And don't pretend that it would be the work of the Gods, either."

"I am your spiritual leader, the head of the Temple."

"Yes, you are the head of the Temple. You lost any spiritual sanctity long ago when you started to take politics more seriously than the work of the Gods. We knew it even in the East, Cedric the Benevolent. But we were unwise, and shrugged our shoulders, saying it's good that he's out of our hair. We were all fools to let you play so long in places you never should have gone."

"Too true," the Empress said. Everyone in the room looked at her, startled by the words. "We let Cedric into our councils because it kept him busy and out of trouble. We were all unwise, Priest Kenning."

"Not priest any longer," Cedric said, his voice a mere whisper. "I strip him of his powers, of his place in the Temple, and of the gifts of the Gods. I make him banished from the grace of the Gods, an outcast, and a traitor to all that we hold Holy!"

Kenning had expected the proclamation, of course. He also knew that before the Most Holy's anathema against him could take away his right to be a priest, there must first be a Temple council. However, the Most Holy had effectively removed him from his position until then. Kenning thought he ought to feel something at the words -- dread, perhaps, or remorse, or loss. Instead, he felt strangely elated.

"Odd, but I don't seem to feel the Gods have turned away from me," he said and laid his fingers on the symbol of his office. The circle glowed slightly, and that was not his work.

He looked down, startled, and he thought that reaction must not have been lost on the others.

"Tricks. You can't fool me --"

The Most Holy took several steps forward, grabbed at the circle --

And leapt back, yelping as he held his fingers.

"I didn't --" Kenning said, feeling odd and shaking his head as he backed away as well.

"I would say the Gods have spoken," Lord Oak said and sounded more startled than pleased.

"You won't get away with these games, Kenning," Most Holy said. He still held his injured hand and had gone more than a little pale. "You have made some pact with a dark God, and you are subverting the Empress with your powers --"

"I have come here to tell them the truth. I have done so. I will gladly leave now if that will make the others more comfortable. I will go back to the East and help there as I can, whether as a priest or not."

"Not quite yet, Kenning," Empress Silana replied. He tried not to sigh. It would have been nice to go home, even if it was to face a war. He had not been made of the stuff that could stand here in the capital and deal with politics on this level. "We still need you to keep in contact with Slade, and we must have what information he gives us."

"Another could reach him," Kenning said.

"Maybe so, but whom should we trust?" she asked and gave a nod to the Most Holy as she spoke. "One of his men? Like the ones he sent to kill you and Lord Oak?"

"I have not -- You cannot prove --"

The Empress looked at Most Holy, silent this time, and he fell quiet as well. He still held the hand. Kenning suspected that the Gods were truly had been out of sorts Cedric the Benevolent, and the man would suffer from that displeasure for a while.

Empress Silana looked back at Kenning, who bowed his head, remembering his manners even while he tried to sort out precisely what was happening. He had not called upon the Gods for help, and yet he felt the exquisite touch of their presence, far more strongly than he had in a long time. It felt like coming awake.

"Now that we have gotten past the dramatics, perhaps we can deal with the true trouble at hand?" she asked and looked towards General Stanmark.

The General had been called in from the south where he'd handled a minor insurrection by a local king and some hired mercenaries. Stanmark had dealt with them quickly and had been setting things back to order when the Empress called for him. Kenning had been standing at his window and watching when the General came striding up the stairs with guard and clerks rushing to keep up with him. He hadn't looked particularly tall -- and standing now before the man, Kenning could see he wasn't more than middling height, and yet he did have an incredible presence. When the man leaned forward over the long table before which Kenning, Oak, and the Most Holy stood, he could almost have out shown the Empress herself.

"You have contact with someone, a priest who is checking out things?"

"Yes, sir. One of my priests, Slade, is there."

"Slade," he said with a little start and a glance at Oak.

"Yes, that *Slade*," Oak said with a bit of a grin.

"The Gods are with us then," Stanmark said. That surprised Kenning, who wouldn't have taken the man for someone pious. "I had wondered what became of Slade after he left us."

"He's a good priest, sir," Kenning said. "Careful of the people's welfare."

"He always was," Stanmark replied. "I had never considered how much alike such work might be, on one level at least, between us. You can contact Slade?"

"Yes, sir. We have to be careful, though, because there is no telling what situation he might be in."

"Can you do it now?"

Kenning nodded and pulled out the rune. It already felt warm, and he had the feeling talking to Slade was not going to be too much trouble, at least on his side.

CHAPTER

THIRTY-THREE

Slade stretched out on the stone slab and watched the clouds drift across the sky as he nibbled on berries. Malin slept curled up like a cat in the sunlight. This had been the most peaceful day they'd had since they undertook the journey. A shame it was not going to last.

Slade had expected the pulse of the rune and had it in hand and heard a slight whisper of his name. He sat up slowly, reluctant to leave the peaceful afternoon behind.

"Sir?" he said softly. He didn't like to speak loudly, even when he didn't think anyone lurked nearby to hear them.

"Is it safe, Slade?" Kenning asked with the concern -- as always -- plain in his voice.

"Yes, sir. We've camped a few miles off from the army, and it's as we feared. They are heading into the Forbidden Valley. I haven't seen the rockling yet, but the group that went after it haven't returned either."

Malin sat up, stretching, and blinking at the bright sunlight. He looked rested, which he hadn't in a few days. They'd bathed in a hot spring the day before and feasted on fish from a nearby stream for two days. The berries and roots made a nice change, though Slade looked forward to reaching civilization and clean clothes again.

He hoped they both lived to see it.

"Have you noticed anything we should know about?"

"Another five hundred or so soldiers came in from the north yesterday. They appear to be far more nervous than those who we'd already been following. I couldn't get close enough to learn anything important, but I think there might be some question about the command."

"That could help," a new voice said, and one Slade recognized.

"General Stanmark, sir?"

"Yes. Never trusted this magic stuff, but it is helping us now, isn't it? Did you see their banners?"

"No, sir. I've been watching for them to unfurl when I'm close, but the countryside here is tree-covered and hilly. I haven't seen the command tents at all, but I thought I saw a glimpse of a Bear Banner yesterday."

"Yes, that would be right," General Stanmark said. "The little bit of information I've had out of the northlands in the last year showed the Bears were getting restive and preparing for something. We thought they planned on attacking some of the other northern tribes."

"I think they're here, sir. But it's more than Bear, since my count is about 8,000 troops right now, almost all infantry with very little horse and no heavy weapons. I suspect they plan on surprise and numbers."

"Gods all," Stanmark said. Slade could almost see him starting to count his own troops and figure out where he was going to get more and quickly. "And you think they are going to go through the Forbidden Valley? How? Those in the valley aren't going to just let them march through!"

"With a guide, sir -- which is why they are still tracking the rockling. Or maybe, if we're lucky, they plan to fight their way through."

"Oh yes, that would be far better," Stanmark agreed with a gruff laugh. "I don't think we'll get that lucky, though."

"It occurs to me that if they have a rockling as an ally, they might have contact with other magical beings, and maybe they don't need the rockling for a guide."

"Oh, now there's an interesting thought," Lord Oak said. "This is all so new that it hadn't occurred to us there might be more magic involved. I wish I knew what had set them on that path. I never would have thought the Norters would turn to magic."

"Me either, sir. I suspect that most of them are not happy about it, either. The few words I've heard have often been curses about magic."

"But they follow anyway," Stanmark added, and sounded thoughtful.

"Yes, sir -- so far, at least. And they're not tied by magic as far as I can feel. It might not be the same for the commanders, but the regular troops are just following orders, sir."

"Good point. Excellent point. I'm damned glad -- begging your pardon Empress Silana, Kenning -- I'm glad you are there, Slade. We need someone we can trust in these observations."

"I've thought so as well, sir. I'm glad those of you in the capital are noting what I'm saying, too. This is a dangerous position for all of us. If they break through the pass without anyone moving to stop them on the other side, it will be catastrophic."

"Yes, it will. Empress Silana, I believe I need to start moving troops."

"It will cause a panic," the Empress said softly.

"Yes, it will. Far worse will happen if we are not there to stop the Norters -- and their allies."

"You are right. I give you leave --"

"And what will you do when the Dragonkin stream over the border, hundreds of miles from where you are?" Most Holy demanded, his voice almost thunderous. Even Slade gave a start and looked nervously around before he cupped the rune, in hopes of muting some of the noise. "What will you do when they lay waste to all the land and march upon the capital?"

"I have spies in the Dragonkin lands, you know," Stanmark replied with a sound of contempt. Slade looked at the rune, startled by the sound of the general's voice. "We move on the things we know are happening. 8,000 troops are standing at one side of a pass, and we have nothing on the this side. I am not going to send troops to watch for Dragonkin when we know we have a real enemy at the gate --"

"The Dragonkin will always be our enemies! We cannot trust them or any man who does not stand up before them! You are blind to turn your back to them, for they steal the magic of the Gods --"

"Be silent!"

In all the years that Slade had served Empress Silana, he had never heard that tone before. Neither, apparently, had anyone else. Slade felt as though the entire world went silent at that order. Slade felt afraid to move, even though he was not anywhere near where her wrath could strike, even if it had been aimed at him.

The silence held. Slade wondered if anyone in that room dared breathe just then. The Empress was known for being caring, willing to listen, and stern when she needed to be. He had seen men hanged for treachery, and it seemed to him that the Most Holy might not be as safe behind his holy robes as he thought.

No, Empress Silana wouldn't do that and risk turning the believers against her. He took a deep breath at that thought and wondered how he could deal with the Most Holy in the future. He feared his life as a priest was over.

"I will go and gather what troops I can here in the city and send riders to the camps and through the countryside ahead of me. I will have to arrange for supplies. Slade, have you seen what they are doing in that respect?"

"Mules and wagons. Miles of them, sir. I think those supplies are supposed to hold them through the pass, though. Some of it looks like reasonably fresh produce, so I suspect they stripped the fields in their lowlands to get this far."

"I dare not do the same," General Stanmark said and sounded worried. "I won't leave devastation behind on our own side --"

"I'll start work on getting supplies," Lord Oak said. "If I move quickly enough, I can buy up grain in a wider path than the one you'll march, and not leave any one area at risk of starvation."

"The royal treasury is open to you," Empress Silana said and drew some startled gasps. "It is all that I can do to help. Lady Martin, I want you to serve as an aid to Lord Oak if that is not too much trouble."

"None at all, Your Grace," a woman said, her voice steady. She had come to court after Slade left, and he didn't know her, except by reputation. She'd done well in her own lands.

"I'm grateful for the help," Lord Oak said. He sounded anxious and with good cause. "With your leave, Empress Silana, I will get straight to work."

"You are free to come and go as you need to, Lord Oak."

"Empress, if I may be so bold," General Stanmark said. He sounded a little uncertain for the first time since Slade had ever heard him. "If you can spare him, I think that this priest should ride with us down to the pass so that we might be better informed of what is going on as quickly as possible. Will Slade follow the troops into the pass?"

Slade looked over to Malin, who gave a quick, decisive nod.

"We will try. I don't know if it will help since we will not have anyone to guide us."

"It will be very dangerous," Empress Silana said. "Go with my blessing, Slade, both of you. Stay safe. And when this is done, come to see me again, you and your companion. I would like to meet Malin."

Malin looked startled and a little pleased. Slade silently prayed to the Gods that he had a chance to bring the boy to see the Empress. It was the least he could do for the boy who was working so hard to help save them all.

"I think that's all for today," Slade said, feeling the drain of power again. "We'll see what we can find out about the troops tonight. I'll talk to you either tomorrow or sooner if I learn anything of importance."

"Good luck," Kenning said. "Is there anything more to ask him?"

He heard faint sounds in the background.

"The Gods go with you, Slade."

The rune went cold again. Slade stared at it for a long, silent moment.

"This is all more trouble than I thought it would be," Malin said softly.

"I feel the same way," Slade agreed. He stood and slowly stretched, staring off into the distance, as though he could see the troops where they were camped. "This is going to get even more dangerous, my friend."

"I know -- but I couldn't turn aside now. I've come too far into it."

"We'll stick it out together," Slade said. "We have a long way to go. I fear we won't have much rest after this."

Malin nodded, but he wasn't slow to follow.

CHAPTER

THIRTY-FOUR

The long days of hiking had been difficult, but not dangerous. DK had finally stopped putting his hand to his side, and he looked ahead in a way that made Koya think they had almost reached the place DK wanted to go. Koya even began to feel safer.

It didn't last.

Koya saw the first wave of birds go overhead flying fast and shouting in protest and warning. DK looked up as well, cursing aloud, though in his own language. There was no doubt about the tone.

"You were right," DK said, looking back at him. "It is still following us."

"I admit I had hoped we'd lost the thing," Koya said with a sigh. "I can't run anymore, DK. I just can't."

"We are no more than five miles from the border and the watchtower, Koya." He looked at the priest, frowning at Koya's distrust. "I would not lie to you."

"No, you would not. I'm sorry. Let us keep going. We might still have a chance -- but I cannot run, DK."

DK looked at the cane Koya had fashioned from a branch two days before, and how Koya leaned more heavily on it today. He nodded. "I will stand by you. We'll make it."

"If it comes --"

"I will stand by you."

There it was again, that little whisper of magic that he had felt back at the fort. This must be something innate to his companion and had to do with promises. Interesting -- but also a problem Koya could not argue around.

Koya tried to move more quickly, but his body ached, and wounds he had taken at the hands of the rockling felt as though they still tore at him. He knew a fever had set in and used what little power he could to fight the weakness.

DK had given him hope with the knowledge of how close they were to the border. Koya used the knowledge to fuel his movement. The power wouldn't last, but he'd do his best to make certain DK was not caught because of him.

So close. They didn't have far to go. Just a few more miles.

Another flock of birds -- mixed breeds, loud and frightened -- cut across the path. The rockling was apparently coming from the left and a little behind them. The creature was likely still slowed by the forest, but once the rockling found the trail, it wouldn't take long to catch up.

DK caught hold of his arm. Koya hissed in pain, but his companion didn't let go this time. "Forgive me. We must go faster."

DK pulled Koya along now, even when he couldn't quite keep his feet under him and nearly went down. His companion didn't allow Koya to fall. Deer outstripped them on the path, and then foxes and rabbits passed them as well while they ignored each other with a worse enemy coming behind. Trees crashed not far away, and in the next moment, he could hear the howl of the rockling. The sound shook the leaves from the trees around them.

"We can't --" Koya whispered, gasping for breath while pain hazed his vision with red and black. "*I can't.* DK -- for the sake of both our people, go on! Spread the news about -- about the Norters!"

DK continued for another three steps before he stopped. His face looked white, his eyes huge, and sounds came from his throat that must have been genuine distress.

"Go," Koya said, pulling free of him. "Go now while you can."

DK turned and sprinted away at a speed that even amazed Koya as he watched his companion, and his only hope, disappear up the trail and around a curve.

So close.

Koya walked after DK left him rather than wait for the rockling. Maybe he should try to get off the path -- but no. It was possible the rockling would miss that he had slipped off, and then it would go on after DK. At this point, he had only one purpose, and that was to make certain DK got through and warned his own people of the real trouble at hand.

Koya walked a little more and then stopped and prepared to make his stand. He wouldn't use any animals against the rockling this time and put them in danger. He had only his own inner power. Though Koya felt weak, he thought he might still have enough magical ability to at least slow the enemy.

He could see the first real hint of the rockling now, a dark shadow still in the trees. Branches cracked, and smaller trees fell before the creature. The ground began to tremble, and he heard a continual, angry growl that sent goosebumps up his arms.

Koya held his place.

The rockling came out of the forest and onto the trail no more than a quarter of a mile away. The creature stopped there, head bowing to the ground as it sniffed. Then the colossal head swept from side to side. Koya stood still, realizing that the rockling hadn't seen him yet. Every moment it stayed confused was a moment longer that DK had to reach safety. If it did kill him, Koya thought it might turn aside.

Koya shivered at that thought of dying alone in this place he didn't know -- but no. The Gods were with him. They did not promise him victory, but they would not forget him.

When the rockling turned his way, Koya stood ready.

It howled this time, and raw magic swept through the air, hitting him like a bolt of fire. Koya staggered back two steps, but he held to his cane, and he didn't go down. The rockling looked like a crazed wolf, the head lowered as it stalked forward, teeth bared, and a low growl erupting from the throat. It had come more than halfway before Koya could hear that it actually spoke words in the snarling sound.

"Enemy, caught, enemy, dead --"

"Not quite caught or dead yet," Koya said while trying to force a façade of bravado. He had nothing more than the cane and a failing core of magic that might slow the creature but wouldn't kill him.

Koya braced his feet in the dirt. He had never felt so helpless -- or so determined -- in his life.

"The Gods guide me," he said a quick, soft prayer.

The rockling surged forward.

Koya brought up the cane, infused it with a bolt of magic, and struck the creature across the face. He could see it was blind on one side where a wound from the fire had never healed. He moved a little in that direction and struck again, across the tender part of the wounded nose.

The rockling bellowed in anger and took a swipe at him, but Koya had backed up, barely out of reach. It hardly mattered. His leg started to give way, and he would have gone down anyway if he hadn't stuck the cane back to the ground and balanced himself. Koya had enraged the creature. At least it would not play with him this time. He watched it prepare to leap forward, the good eye glowing with a lambent red light, mouth foaming with anger. It crouched and --

"Down!" DK's voice, fool to have come back --

Koya dropped to the ground.

Magic flashed over him, and caught the creature in mid-leap, slapping it back in the air. An arrow followed, and another -- Dragonkin arrows, burying themselves even in this rock-like skin.

Koya turned his head enough to see that DK was not alone. Six other Dragonkin people stood in a line and pulled more arrows, though they didn't fire. DK sprinted forward, caught Koya by the arm, and yanked him back to his feet.

"They -- they had heard a disturbance, came to check," he said, gasping still. It must have been a hard run there and back.

Koya couldn't decide why they came to rescue him. The others stood, ready with their weapons. They shouted to DK in a language Koya didn't understand, and DK grunted an answer. Then he grabbed Koya up and threw him over his shoulder and began to run once more.

Koya lifted his head. Arrows flew past them, two embedding in the rockling's right shoulder. The creature shuddered and leapt forward but lost its balance.

"Going to fall on us!" Koya warned.

DK tried to leap to the side, but the rockling still caught them, falling forward with his teeth snapping far too close to Koya's head. They all three rolled, and Koya lost any ability to breathe as a sharp pain spread through every inch of his body, paralyzing him. He heard DK give one cry and go silent, and though Koya tried, he couldn't lift his arm or call up magic --

Shouts rose all around them, a strange echoing sound that made him feel ill trying to sort it out. Koya still couldn't move, but he did notice when the rockling finally slid off of them, half-crippled by arrows. He could finally breathe a little though it caught in his chest with piercing pain. His arm twitched, and then his head --

He turned and found DK face down in the dirt ... and unmoving.

"No!"

Koya forced his own body to move, rolling over and grabbing hold of DK's arm. He found no response at all, nor any movement that indicated breathing. Koya pushed DK over onto his back and stared in shock at the blood seeping from his open mouth.

DK's eyes fluttered open, but the pupils were large and unfocused. He didn't move except for his eyes and then, slowly, his lips.

"I am Takkatia," he whispered. "Tell them that I died well."

He closed his eyes.

No feeling of life anywhere.

"No! We did not come all this way for you to die here!"

Koya took hold of DK's head and forced magic into the body in a way that he had never done before and knew this was dangerous for both of them. He hadn't any power to spare, and he couldn't be certain DK wasn't genuinely dead already, though he refused to believe it. Perhaps it was that belief that gave him power.

Koya became aware of a glow that surrounded them, a rare show of magic that few priests ever achieved. This was power pulled to him from elsewhere, and he had never known anyone to do so without runes. The glow almost distracted him, but Koya refused to take more than a passing notice. Instead, he spread the magic down through his friend, as he thought of healing, of a cease of pain, of life made right -- all the things that would help someone recover.

He wouldn't give up, even when it seemed the magic took life from him. Koya had already prepared to die, but he would not let another be sacrificed in his place. He would not give up.

DK took a short, gasping breath and would not have taken another if Koya hadn't held on and forced the next. Then another. DK moaned, but each breath grew easier, as the magic healed along the paths it took through lungs, bones, organs. Slow work and Koya moved carefully, aware that he gasped far more than DK towards the end. He held on for another moment, a little more--

DK unexpectedly reached up and caught his arm.

"E -- enough before you kill yourself," he said, his voice shaky and soft, but the grasp firm. "Enough, priest."

DK's own magic swept up and cut him off. Koya cried out in dismay because DK wasn't fully healed --

And coming back from the power made him all too aware of his own injuries. They were not anywhere near as extensive as DK's had been, but he could feel a cracked rib and a leg twisted in a way that meant torn muscles and perhaps worse. The light died like the scattering of glowing dust around them, and with it gone, he felt very, very cold.

DK sat up and looked startled, and he brushed a hand across his chest where blood showed, but no wound was left. Then he looked past Koya, and his eyes went large.

"Oh, hell," DK said with a frustrated sigh.

Koya turned to see.

The rockling charged their way again. The people who had come to help beat at it with swords, the arrows spent and sticking from the creature in various places -- but not slowing it as it rushed past them and straight at its enemy -- Koya.

DK grabbed him again.

"No! Go, you fool --"

DK was no more going to listen now than he had the last time. He didn't have the strength to put Koya over his shoulder, but he did drag him off the trail and to a stout tree. The rockling ran straight into it and bellowed as long-clawed feet reached around -- but DK had already pulled Koya towards the next one, and at least the creature slowed in the maze of trees.

"We can't kill it," DK said, wonder in his voice. "The thing will not die, and even our best arrows only pierce the -- the rock skin and do no real harm."

"It wants me."

"It can't have you."

"DK --"

"I gave you my name," he said. "You may use it now."

"You gave it under duress. You thought you were dying."

"I was dying," he said and grabbed Koya to another tree, but too small -- the creature nearly knocked it down. The others still tried to attack it, and he could see that they had taken wounds as well, but none of them slowed. "You saved my life. You can use my name."

"Takkatia," he said, speaking the name aloud.

His companion smiled brightly. "Takka, for short."

"Takka," he said, breathless still.

Takka nodded, grabbed a branch that had fallen, and slapped at the side of the rockling's face as it came near. It howled and backed away.

"The face is sensitive," Koya said.

"Ah. Yes." Takka whistled, and then shouted something in his own tongue. Others answered, but Takka didn't translate. He and Koya kept going, though more slowly now. Koya wouldn't have been moving at all except for him.

They reached a glade, which was bad luck Koya thought, until he saw the others there, waiting. He saw grim looks on the three who had their bows up, and it was apparent the others chased and drove it on while he and Takka led the way.

Takka's hands tightened. "When I say to get down --"

"Just drop me. I won't have a choice," Koya said as they moved out into the tall grass.

Takka nodded.

They took another dozen steps before the rockling charged out of the trees. DK didn't drop Koya, but they both went down. DK -- Takka -- rolled with him, out of the way of the charging creature. It wouldn't work for long, though the tall grass did help cover them. However, the rockling would find him anyway, scenting the magic.

The others leapt in for an attack. Arrows flew, and they shouted as they rushed past, swords swinging. One of the Dragonkin, a deep cut across the woman's shoulder and arm, stopped by the two and pulled Takka to his feet. She handed him a long-bladed knife. He bowed his head, kissed the blade, and said something that must have been a thank you.

It didn't look like much of a weapon, but it was better than none at all.

They had beaten the creature back to the edge of the woods, and for the first time, Koya thought they were going to survive. It took him by surprise, and from the fierce grins on the faces of the others, he thought they felt the same.

Another jab and the rockling howled and backed up --

The Norter soldiers arrived.

Koya gave a shout of dismay all his own. Although they were no more than a dozen, they caught the Dragonkin people by surprise, and he saw one killed straight out, and another go down before the rest could rally. Two tried to hold back the rockling while the others brought their weapons around to the new enemy.

"We must --" Takka began.

Koya let go of him, shoved him towards the trouble, and tried to follow himself, though he could barely stumble a few steps before he went back to his knees, an intense pain through his legs. Darkness tried to take him, but he refused to give up and let these people fight and die for him. He forced himself to his feet and took a few more steps.

Whistles filled the woods.

More Dragonkin appeared, and this time from the direction that the rockling and the Norters had arrived. With them came the fierce little Lesslings, who leapt at the rockling, driving it back just by their persistence. The Norters shouted and retreated from the new force. In a dozen heartbeats, the battle had moved back into the woods, the more significant army of newly arrived Dragonkin warriors taking up the fight.

Takka limped back to him and settled on his knees beside Koya, gasping and putting a hand to his chest as though he felt his heart would burst.

"You bring miracles, priest," Takka finally whispered. "We had no chance until the ambassador arrived. It's a wonder she found us."

"Ambassador?" he asked.

And then Koya saw her. Jade, without a doubt. He stared at her, startled -- and only at the last moment saw the Lesslings bounding through the grass toward him.

Show no weakness.

He surprised Takka when he got to his feet nearly as fast as his companion. Takka shouted something and even jabbed his knife at the nearest Lessling that came at them with teeth bared and ready to bite. Jade arrived, yelling her own orders, and the creatures slowly backed away, hissing and growling as they went.

"I had not thought to meet you again," Jade said, looking at Koya with a shake of her head. "You are a long way from home, priest. And you seem to have had a most harrowing Honor Hunt, cousin."

"We have news, Ambassador," Takka said. He spoke rapidly in his own language. The woman nodded, her green eyes flickering from Takka to Koya. She didn't seem very surprised by anything that Takka said.

"We had heard some of this from another priest who saved us from a battle. Kenning worries for you, Priest Koya."

"You know Kenning?" he said, startled by the words.

"We met, travelers passing on the road," she answered. Then she whistled with a loud piercing sound that startled him and made his headache. Others came at a run. She gave orders. Takka protested something, but she stopped him with a shake of her head. "No. We will carry you both for a while, Takka. We have a great distance to go."

"The border isn't -- the village --" He stopped and sighed. "We're going to follow the rockling, aren't we?"

"Yes. Because I have had guards out, scouting the area. The Norters very badly wanted the rockling and are taking it away to help them. They are massing at the gates to the Hidden Rock Pass."

Takka growled out some curse that Koya didn't understand. He wanted to rest, and it seemed they were not going to let him. He wanted to go even into the Dragonkin lands if it just meant he could sleep somewhere safe for a few hours. They couldn't intend to take him somewhere else again.

"Your people call the place the Forbidden Valley," Jade said, looking at Koya.

"Oh, then they're fools," Koya said. "They'll never get through there. The creatures that live in that area won't let anything pass."

"Not without a guide," Takka said.

"Well, yes, but --" Koya stopped and looked past Jade, fallen trees, and where they were digging a grave for one of their own. He tried not feel despair at that loss. "The rockling. It's their guide. That's why they wanted it back so badly."

"Yes, we think so," Jade agreed. She looked bothered. "Why else would they hunt so hard for it? And why else would the troops still be standing at the gateway?"

"We need to get word back across the mountains to Kasprin," he said, frantic already. "They won't know -- they won't expect it --"

"We cannot get across fast enough if they go through the pass," Jade said, shaking her head. "We will do what we can, human, but we cannot fly, and only those with wings could get the word there quickly now."

"Your runes?" Takka asked.

"Too far. If I had my own I could -- but I'll do what I can. I might get a warning through to someone."

"We make stretchers to carry you both -- and neither of you will argue because we haven't the time to waste," Jade said and looked straight at Takka. "Or we could send you on with the Lesslings. I thought I might try to send them back to the lands because they have become too wild on this trip, and I do not trust them."

Takka looked surprised by that news, but Koya didn't know enough to ask what it meant. Maybe that was just as well. He didn't want to annoy anyone.

When they brought the stretchers, made of limbs and cloth, he didn't argue. Takka still looked annoyed and embarrassed. Koya saw the pallet as a chance for at least a little sleep. He laid down as Lady Jade instructed him, and he closed his eyes and hardly cared what happened next.

CHAPTER

THIRTY-FIVE

Kenning had never traveled so much in his life, and he suspected he would never want to go anywhere again. The long days on horseback took him farther and farther away from the lands he loved. He found some consolation in the small Temples that adorned some villages. General Stanmark didn't mind that Kenning went there to pray whenever they stopped. At least the General knew where to find him.

Kenning prayed a lot during those days. He contacted the priests at Templeton and learned the news from them. Everyone seemed filled with unrest, but there had been no visible sign of trouble.

General Stanmark gathered troops where he could as well as some supplies, though he would not strip any area bare. He was caught in the troubling situation where either the soldiers or the commoners would have to do without -- unless Lord Oak came through with a miracle and quickly.

Kenning prayed for one.

Every night as they made camp, Kenning sat down with General Stanmark, and they contacted Slade.

"Nothing new," Slade reported for the fourth day in a row. He sounded considerably calmer and more rested. Kenning felt the opposite. "No more troops have arrived, I'm glad to say. Some scouts came and went more frequently this afternoon, though. I think something is about to happen."

"We're closer to our position," Stanmark said. "I don't know that we're ready, but it will take them a few days to get through the Forbidden Valley, I hope."

"Yes, sir," Slade answered. He sounded more like a soldier and less like a priest, but Kenning didn't say so aloud. Slade was whatever they needed right now; Kenning only hoped that he didn't lose the good man back to the army when this was done.

He hoped they didn't lose Slade at all.

"I've just had a scout from Lord Oak. The supplies and more troops should reach us in two days," Stanmark said. He always stared at the rune in Kenning's hand as he spoke, as though he could see Slade on the other side. "And here's the good news: if the Norters haven't started moving, then we're going to be camped and rested when they push through. I can't believe they'll have an easy march of it through the Forbidden Valley, whether they have a guide and allies or not."

"True enough," Slade said. He sounded relieved at the words. "Malin and I will keep a close watch tonight, and if anything happens --"

They could hear Malin saying something urgent nearby, though Kenning couldn't make out the words. Stanmark frowned and leaned closer to the rune, but he shook his head as well. He started to say something and stopped, though impatience showed on his face.

"Sorry -- sorry sir," Slade said. He sounded a little breathless, and Kenning realized he was running while he spoke. "Malin had been watching the camp. He says the rockling just came in with a group of scouts, and it looks like it took some wounds from Dragonkin arrows. It must have tried to get over the border."

"Why?" Stanmark asked. He shook his head with disbelief.

"Who knows, sir? I can't begin to understand this creature at all. Malin says there was a lot of activity at the camp as soon as it arrived. It's late. I can't believe they'd start marching at night."

"Unless they had a good reason to hurry," Stanmark said. "How badly injured was the rockling?"

"Ah ... maybe that's it. Fear that their key through the magic lands will die before they reach the other side. That might get them moving," Slade agreed. "Have to go silent now, sir. We're getting closer. Don't want to give ourselves away to the guards. I'll contact you again after I've had a look."

"Take care," Stanmark said and nodded to Kenning to close the link.

Kenning would have listened for a while longer, just to make sure Slade remained safe -- but what good would it do, except to waste power? He couldn't help from here. Finding himself relegated to a communications link started to annoy Kenning, though he buried that unworthy thought.

Kenning stared at the mountains. The last of the sunlight touched the tremendous shape towering over them. They looked dark, foreboding, and far more dangerous than the gentler edges of the range up by Templeton. Here the earth had shoved these mountains straight up into the sky, like an impassable wall. However, even as he thought it, Kenning could see the fissure in the surface that looked like a crack through the otherwise dark surface. It ran halfway down the mountain, a wound that didn't look natural, because it wasn't.

Long ago, a battle had been fought between the human mages and the creatures of natural magic. The humans, being tenacious and unforgiving, had pushed the others all the way to this valley below the mountains where they had no chance to escape.

The enemy had pooled their magic and cut a path straight into the mountains. They escaped through a portal they made there, leaving a few guards behind so that the humans could not follow. Anyone foolhardy enough to try had died.

It was heresy, of course, to wonder why those same creatures hadn't turned such devastating power against the humans instead. Surely a spell that could cut through the mountains could have destroyed the enemies pursuing them. Kenning thought that choice might be a sign of their true nature.

Now it wasn't the creatures coming back for revenge, but rather other humans -- the ones who considered any magic evil -- who apparently planned to attack.

And they came with magical help.

Kenning still hadn't figured out what had brought that unexpected change. It made no sense at all. The Norters had rarely even come close to the borders. They hated the people of Kasprin as well as the Dragonkin.

Hated them enough to take up with other magic to defeat them?

This trouble made no sense.

"You look bothered, Kenning," Stanmark said.

"I am, but that's nothing new. What I am thinking touches on nothing that helps us, except I still can't figure out why the Norters took up with magic. This change makes no sense, sir. None at all."

"No, it doesn't, but then people do odd things without reason," Stanmark said and made a quick glance around where others still set up camp. "I was not ready for a war. I still haven't gotten used to the idea. I want this to be some mistake, but I trust Slade too well to take his observations lightly."

"Yes, sir."

"Dinner should be ready." Stanmark nodded toward his tent, which had gone up first. "Let's eat and relax, Kenning. We are going to have a long night, I fear. Slade is a thorough man, and it will be a while before he contacts us again."

Kenning stood from the fallen limb where he'd been sitting. The camp had been falling into place around them, and he'd gotten used to the frantic work, which had looked crazy the first few nights, but now seemed well-managed.

"You don't think of Slade as a priest, do you?" Kenning asked.

Stanmark gave him a startled look, and then his brows drew down in the familiar sign as the man considered the idea. Kenning had never thought he would be so at ease with a man of war. They were more alike than he would have thought a few weeks ago when he still sat safe and comfortable in Templeton.

"You're right, I don't." Stanmark frowned again and then shrugged. "But I think that's good. No offense, Kenning, but I need a soldier keeping watch on those bas-- on those Norters. I wouldn't know what to make of a priest reporting these things. I wouldn't know if I could trust his judgment, even if he told me the same things I've heard from Slade. I need to believe in that trust, Kenning. We're basing the entire throw of the dice on what your priest is telling us."

"True," Kenning said. He gave a little shrug. "If I hadn't known about Slade's background, I would have worried myself. So, I guess we're both lucky. I don't want to lose Slade,

General Stanmark. Just so you know, I'll fight to get him back when we're done."

Stanmark stopped by the entrance to his tent and gave Kenning a very odd look, which passed to a bright smile.

"Sir?"

"Interesting to see where your passions fall."

"My passion is my religion," he said.

"Oh, yes, that too. However, you have another, you know. You are incredibly protective of your people, from Slade to that other priest --"

"Koya," he said, and for a moment, he closed his eyes. "The Gods protect him and see him safely back to the Temple where he belongs."

"Yes, exactly."

Kenning gave a little bow of his head in agreement and followed the General into the cool blue of the tent interior. Food sat on the table, including bread and cheese and some cold meats. The makeshift desk not far away stood topped with a stack of messages that the General would look over. None of them were essential, or else his men would have taken them straight to the General. Stanmark seldom had time to rest. After dinner, he would go and speak with the top men in his command, who, in turn, would go to the next level down, and so his orders would pass down through the ranks.

For a few minutes, they could eat and discuss other matters and not really worry about a war that was virtually on their doorstep. These quiet days would pass. Kenning didn't know what he would do when the war came upon them.

"Maybe they won't get through," he said suddenly.

Stanmark didn't think the statement odd at all, even though they had been discussing the local plant life a moment before.

"I hope -- I even pray -- that's true," Stanmark agreed. "I don't want to go to battle again, Kenning. I want the world to be calm and quiet, and for the years to pass with nothing worse than a border skirmish -- but here we are, the two of us, waiting for the enemy."

Kenning nodded and bowed his head, whispering another quick prayer asking that ... that everything worked out well. Sometimes he tried not to be too personal in his wishes. The Gods saw the wider world. Maybe there was a reason that the Norters should attack them, but Kenning didn't think so. He couldn't make himself believe this was right, and it had nothing to do with magic --

"Have you had any sort of indication that there was any trouble at all in the north?" Kenning asked, suddenly leaning forward. "There has to be something, General. They can't have suddenly decided to join forces with something they despised – something that their Gods say will damn them forever. It makes no sense!"

"I have people in the northern capital," Stanmark said, frowned again, and then shrugged. "Nothing changed there -- no sign of a sudden shift in such a fundamental part of their beliefs. No sign at all."

Stanmark stopped and stared ahead, his eyes blinking. Kenning waited in silence, listening to the soldiers outside, and feeling the darkness pressing in on him like something alive. He wanted to hold the day a while longer. Kenning wanted everything to stop here, and the war that was standing on the other side of the mountains never to press forward and reach them.

"I never saw anything coming," Stanmark said after a moment's silence. "Not a sign more than the usual disputes they have between various lords. I do realize that more of those disputes were with the tribes along the border, Kenning. I suspect the people in the Damara capital might have no idea of what's going on in the outer reaches of their own lands, especially considering how fast everything has happened."

"Sir --" Kenning began but could only shake his head.

"It is audacious, but it fits. What if someone, literally crazy, teamed up with the rockling? Someone of at least moderate power? I had heard the Chieftain of the Bear Clan had wild aspirations. I thought it was only a Damarian problem, and happy to see them fighting among themselves. Maybe we had better send them word of what's going on, don't you think?"

"Send word to Damara itself?"

"Turn their own against them," Stanmark said. He pushed away his plate and grabbed quill, ink, and paper from the nearby desk. "It won't get to them quickly enough to help here, but it might make a difference later. No war is ever won or lost in one battle. Remember that, Kenning. No matter what happens here, win or lose, it's unlikely to be the end of the trouble. Better to see what we can do to make trouble for the enemy." He leaned over and wrote a quick note on a sheet of paper, paused, and then put his official seal on it and waited while the wax dried. He looked at Kenning again. "It can hardly matter, you know. Either they know, or they don't. If they don't, we may be able to turn an old enemy against a new one. I think that's been our mistake, you know. We think of them as Norters, but if these are the border lords moving against us -- yes, they might be more tempted to magic, which they see more than the people of the far north do."

Kenning nodded. "True enough. We sometimes have contact with Norters up near Templeton. It's why Koya was not such a problem there."

"I have to send this off," Stanmark said and stood. "It's only a little thing, but I'll take any hope I can find."

He sounded like a desperate man.

When he left to find a messenger, Kenning prayed again.

CHAPTER

THIRTY-SIX

Malin sat on his heels next to Slade. The boy remained silent, knowing not to utter a whisper as they watched the Norter camp. They were well within the guard line already. The scent of food made Slade's stomach growl with far too loud of a noise. That made Malin grin, though.

The people below moved like frantic ants. The soldiers ate in haste, and men shouted orders all around -- so many voices that even Malin couldn't pick any out and could only catch a few words about preparations.

It looked like madness down there.

Slade signaled to the right. They snaked along the edge of a rock outcropping, careful not to disturb the loose rocks. There were no creatures nearby to startle, at least. They'd all taken off when the army arrived. If any had remained, the rockling surely sent them racing away.

Only fools like the two of them tried to get closer.

They were rewarded at last. They moved down to the edge of the next rock, and below this outcropping, they finally had a view of the rockling. The creature sat still and remained uncommonly quiet. Men crawled up over it, pulling out arrows. They must not have hurt the beast, though Slade thought some wounds on the face must have been worse.

Then he saw something that made him catch his breath. The reason the rockling was so cooperative was that a troll, unmistakably huge blunt-faced, and long furred, stood before it and held rough hands to the vast, ugly face.

Magic.

Slade blinked. Another troll stood behind the first, and then he could see another few in the shadows --

This was not the place he and Malin should be. He tapped Malin on the arm and gave a frantic nod to go back the way they had arrived. His heart pounded so hard that Slade feared the trolls would hear even the sound. He thought the only way they would get out of this was if the Gods stood with them.

They inched backward -- and he saw a troll look their way. He didn't have to warn Malin to stay very still. Trolls had exceptional hearing, but poor eyesight. The huge creature stared for a dozen heartbeats and then looked away again. Malin started to move. Slade stilled him. The troll looked back but plainly didn't see anything amiss, and finally went back to work with the rockling. Huge dark fingers brushed with unexpected kindness over the rough skin, and the rockling gave a little sound like a purr of a gigantic cat. The noise was their best chance. The two of them scrambled away, and then hurried out of the area. They made it past the guards without a problem.

Slade didn't speak for a long time. Malin walked silently beside him. Ah, but General Stanmark would have plenty of questions, and none of the answers he could give would please the man.

"This is not good, Malin," he finally said softly.

"No, sir, it isn't."

"We thought they might have one ally in the rockling. If the trolls are working with the Norters as well, it may well mean there are others. If that is so, though, why did they work so hard to get the rockling back?"

"Maybe they brought the rockling back just to prove they had not killed him. I think maybe he was loaned to them, sir, to help with the magic out here," Malin replied.

"Damn, that's a perceptive idea. Now I wonder if they have an army of magical allies. What is waiting inside the valley?"

"We'll have to find out," Malin replied and turned to look towards the dark slit in the mountain, barely visible in the night.

"If we go in, we aren't likely to come back out the other side."

"I know," he said. He sounded far too old for his years.

"We better get some rest while we can. And I have to contact the others." Slade drew out his rune and held it for a moment. "Things are going to get worse."

Malin winced -- things hadn't exactly been easy until now -- but he nodded and sat down.

And he watched the mountains.

CHAPTER

THIRTY-SEVEN

No matter how rough the journey became as they headed back toward the Kasprin border, Koya reminded himself that he was at least heading closer to home.

Koya had thought going to the Dragonkin lands would be an adventure, but he was far past the point of wanting anything exciting. Koya wanted to rest now, and he fell almost instantly into a fitful sleep each night when the others made camp. At first, he could barely walk, even with the cane, though he grew stronger by the third day. Even so, he wanted nothing more than peace, at least for as many hours as the others would allow it for him. He trusted these people with his life.

Koya did become aware when something bothered them. He heard the worried sounds of their voices, although he couldn't tell what they said. He noticed the unease in the

Lesslings -- those animals had not yet been sent back, although Takka hinted at it often.

Koya had started to notice that the Lesslings sometimes acted like a pack of barely tamed dogs, and other times like poorly trained servants. They did not always listen to the Dragonkin orders, which only made matters worse because Koya could tell the Lesslings didn't like him or having him around.

Show no weakness. Koya sat up straighter when any of the Lesslings came sniffing too close. As much as he would have loved to shout and send them scurrying away like the Dragonkin did, he suspected such a move would more likely send them into a killing frenzy.

This time DK -- Takka -- came along and snarled a few words that sent the creatures slinking back to their part of the camp. Takka watched them with a glare.

"They've no love for humans, even when we say we are allies."

"I noticed." Koya accepted a cup from Takka. It held a sweet tea that he'd come to appreciate. He had some bread, too. Koya found that harder to eat, though it tasted fine. He just didn't have the strength for it.

"You look somewhat better," Takka said, dropping down on his heels beside him. "And this is good, human friend."

"Things are looking worse, aren't they?"

"The scouts have found the path of an army. A large one. It is between us and the mountains, not far away. They sit below the entrance to the Forbidden Valley."

Koya looked towards the mountain ahead. It rose towering above them, the early morning light catching the tip. "They're ready to go, and they have a guide, don't they? They have the rockling."

"This is a good observation, human," Jade said as she crossed the small area and stopped beside them. "It's good to see you have your wits back. I think you may need them soon."

"You intend to leave me here and go back to your land," he said with a nod. He understood.

"We intend to leave you here and follow the army," she corrected.

The news startled him. Koya frowned, then sipped at the tea again, trying to make some sense of what was going on this time.

"I'll go with you. I can walk now. You will need me if you make it through to the other side. Unless my being with you is a problem, and you will not have a guide to get through because of it?"

"No, that is not the problem," Jade said. She settled to his right, just as Takka had to the left. "We have treated you well in hopes you will survive, not to throw you into a worse danger -- and this is far worse, human priest."

"Worse all the way around." Koya sat his cup aside and tried to think everything through. "The army is from the Norter lands, right? Then they are going through to attack the human lands beyond. Is there a reason you don't want them to make it?"

"They still have disguises. They still pretend to be us," Jade said, and with such a snarl that she almost looked half-Lessling herself just then. The change startled him, and he went still. He had gotten used to them being human-like. "We choose our own wars. We will not have these liars choosing it for us."

"How big an army is it?"

She gave a little half-grin this time. "Thousands."

"And you'll do what to stop them?" he asked.

"We do not know. I've sent four of my fastest, and most eloquent, runners back to the True Lands to tell the tale of what has happened, in hopes that they'll do something more than we can manage with so few. We must go on, though, human. We must do this for knowledge others will need and for the hope that we can stop these Norters from starting a war we do not want."

"And that's why I must go with you as well," Koya said. "I must try to find a way to help. If I can get closer to the other side of the mountains, I might be able to use the runes I carry to contact priests on the other side. They are not my runes, but I can force them to my control. It might help."

"It might," Jade admitted with her own glance toward the mountain. "Though dangerous again, you know. We will be in an area where magic rules, and the use of magic there will be noticed by the inhabitants. It may not be safe to draw attention."

"I will work at your discretion only."

She tilted her head, green eyes blinking. "Takka said you would not be left behind. I should have listened and remembered what a brave human you are."

"Brave and a fool, I suppose," he said with a little smile.

She laughed. "We have a saying: A coward learns nothing, human. The only problem is that a brave person may not learn quickly enough to survive." She looked at him for another four heartbeats. "You walk today, for the whole day. If you stay on your feet, you come with us. If not, you will stay behind and Takka with you. We would not turn you out helpless after you did so much to spread the word about the lies against us. And you saved Takka's life. Still, it would be better if you can come with us, so be strong and brave, human priest."

Koya nodded as though he could affect such things at a thought. Jade stood again and headed back to the others, although she did pause long enough to snarl orders to the Lesslings who were starting to creep closer again.

"They're going to be trouble," Takka said with a shake of his head as he watched the creatures retreat.

"You can't send them away?"

"They do not want to go. We think they sense a battle and are not easily turned away from it." He frowned a little but continued. "In the last generation they've attached themselves more closely to the clans, and now they go wherever we go, sometimes whether we like it or not. The only way to be rid of some is to kill them, and that would be cruel to reward such loyalty, don't you think?"

"Yes, of course."

Koya had hoped for a different answer and one that sent the creatures elsewhere so that he felt safer. He'd just have to be careful. The journey would soon become more difficult if he stayed to his feet all day. While they carried him, there were always people of the clan there to send the Lesslings away. He looked at where the creatures huddled together in their own camp, a whispering hiss of sound coming from that direction, and he did not feel safe.

"Do you understand what they say?" Koya dared to ask.

"A little," Takka replied. He looked toward the camp as well. "It is said that we were much like them before the change. It makes me ... uneasy to think such things. I don't want to be an animal. There are some among my people who think being like humans is far worse. I don't mind it."

"Is it a choice?"

"I've heard tales," he began, then shrugged. "Children's tales -- that some have wished themselves to be dragons again and have sailed away into the sun. Maybe that would be a great adventure, but I don't know. This is what I am," he said, waving a hand towards his body. "I know this existence. It is adventure enough for me."

"I've no choice in what I am," Koya said and looked at his companion. "I know it bothers some of the others to have me with them, but this is not my choice."

"Not until now, when you choose to go on with us," Takka pointed out. "I cannot say if that will make a difference to the Lesslings, but don't worry. They are under the Lady's rule, and they'll abide by her decisions. She is the one you must always obey."

He'd already figured that part out, but it didn't hurt to have it explained aloud.

A few minutes later, the others broke camp. He saw covert glances his way, but he stood on his own, using his cane for balance and walked down to join them before they were done.

Koya had been walking for some parts of the last three days anyway. He tired quickly, but he knew how to pace himself for the long day, and he was not going to slow them. Determination would be the most critical part of this decision.

Koya looked up at the mountains rising over the forest. The tallest peaks in all the land stood there. He was farther south than he'd ever been, well away from his beloved Templeton. Koya thought of his home with a sigh of regret and gave a silent prayer that what he did here would save that place from any trouble. That, too, was reason to go on.

They made a few miles before the Lady Jade called for a stop again. She sent some scouts on as the others rested. They passed around canteens of water, and Takka shared his with Koya. It seemed that perhaps the others were less unsettled by him now. Maybe being able to walk made him less of a problem for them to worry over.

Or...

Koya gave one quick glance to the Lesslings, just to find out where they were, and then back at the rest of the people around him. If -- if the people of the Dragonkin had once been more like the Lesslings, how much of their old instincts did they bring with them?

Show no weakness.

He remembered how much effort Takka had put into ignoring and hiding his own wounds when they had escaped from the fort. He hadn't thought it more than a typical show of being strong. Maybe it had been something entirely different. Did the Lesslings go for the kill, even among their own, if they found one of them weakening? He'd heard of such creatures, and though he didn't think the Dragonkin people were that driven by instincts, he did wonder if there weren't some of the same motivations that created their own reactions.

Should he look more to the Lesslings to judge what he should do? Maybe, on some levels. However, he would trust to the Dragonkins' good sense.

The guard came back. Whatever they said, it didn't look good.

Takka gave a grim nod. "The Norter troops are already on the move into the pass, and trolls are leading them. Trolls are not our friends."

"Trolls are no one's friends," Koya said. "I've read that they even fight each other."

"Yes, true," Takka agreed and looked distracted. "It's odd that they would lead the humans through the passage then, isn't it?"

"Unless they don't intend for the humans to survive?" Koya asked. He tried not to hope for such a thing to happen, and the people to die. However, better there than in a battle on the other side. If it was a choice between evils, he would rather see the one where the invaders never reached their destination.

"We could hope for such," Lady Jade agreed as she neared. "But I fear it is not so. We are going closer. We will not follow into the Forbidden Valley, though, until they are well away."

"And we will have guides?" Koya asked. "Or do we need them?"

"We will ask for guides," Jade said. "I don't know if we will get any. If we do not, we will go anyway. It is not forbidden of the Dragonkin to go here, but we have not taken the journey for hundreds of years. These are not our kind, and some are old and bitter with the lost wars, even now."

"Bitter enough to set the humans against each other and help to blame it on your people?" he asked. "Because, in that case, they aren't going to want the Dragonkin to go through and learn the truth."

"Yes, I have thought so as well," Jade said with a nod of appreciation. "But we have to go. We have to know."

Koya nodded, but it didn't make the journey seem any better.

At least they didn't race ahead, so he had very little trouble keeping up with them the rest of the day. He tired, but he kept going, and after a while, even the others stopped looking at him as though they expected a problem.

The Lesslings snarled more often, though, until even Takka looked at them with a frown. "They're bothered knowing there is trouble not far away, and we hold them back from the fight. The Lesslings like the battle; they look for it even with us when they think they can get away with it."

Koya had come to distrust Lesslings more with each mile they traveled together. He didn't like the way their yellow eyes looked to him, or the way their lips drew back, and the long tongues flashed out between pointed teeth. He didn't like it most of all when they stood up like humans. It felt wrong in ways that still made his skin crawl.

Koya walked with a feeling that a vicious beast followed a few yards behind him. Not keeping track of them seemed the worse folly. He did feel better when Takka walked with him, though. The Lesslings kept their distance then.

"The others," Takka said, waving a hand toward the rest of the group, "They can't decide if you are very brave or very crazy."

"Crazy."

"Yes, that's what I told them," Takka said with a nod. Koya thought he caught a slight glimpse of a smile at the corner of his friend's lips, but he couldn't be sure. "They have put me to keep watch with you. I am to make certain you understand what is being ordered, since the Lady may not have time to talk with you directly."

"And the others don't speak Kasprin," Koya said. They started to move again, and he forced himself on without slowing, even though he had the start of a cramp in his right leg. "And that's odd since they were part of a group that went to the capital."

"The Lady speaks the language. The others didn't need to."

"And you speak the language. A hunter."

"You never asked me what I hunted." Those words startled Koya, but Takka smiled. "I came in search of knowledge, and I learned your language because I was on the border between our two lands. If I was to learn anything, I had to be able to understand what the people were telling me."

"You hunt for knowledge."

"I also hunt food, but hunting knowledge is my goal." He unexpectedly touched the blaze of multicolored hair on the top of his head, as though that should mean something.

Koya didn't ask. Maybe he should have. Perhaps, because his companion hunted knowledge, he could do the same. They might be able to trade information.

Later. This wasn't the time. Koya could start thinking up questions.

Koya did note when the others began to slow. They'd made a reasonable distance, and he ached in every bone and muscle. He had not hindered them, though only because they weren't ready to rush into danger.

They took another break and Takka settled by a tree with him. His friend looked exhausted, reminding Koya that he wasn't the only one who had been injured. They had not spoken about what Koya had done when Takka had almost died. The people of the Dragonkin didn't appear to be bothered by it nearly as much as Koya.

Had he done what the Gods wanted of him, or had he stepped between them and Takka's fate? He tried to believe that he hadn't the power to contravene the acts of the Gods, but it troubled him, and Koya wished he could speak to Kenning.

Koya was glad to have Takka alive -- especially when his companions once again ordered the Lesslings away. That drew Lady Jade's attention, and she came and chased the Lesslings off to their own little section of the camp. They hissed and growled, but they went.

"They know better," Jade said, frowning. "I think this area where we are, so close to such magic, bothers them."

Koya looked towards the mountain, which blotted out all but a bright blue corner of the sky. He nodded. "I think I feel it a bit as well. It worries me."

"Good. You are not a fool. Some of my own are anxious to get there to see this wondrous land of magic." Lady Jade waved a hand toward the others who sat eating dried bread and cheese. "They are fools not to think about the consequences of such a place. They still believe that all creatures of magic are brethren."

Takka made a snort of derision and then bowed his head in apology to the Lady. "Sorry. I just had not thought they were so blind."

"They don't want me to go with you," Koya added, which suddenly became apparent to him.

"Some do not. This is not their choice. You need not worry about them. They are civilized. The trouble with the Lesslings, though --" Jade stopped and looked at the little camp where the group remained huddled together, snarling softly. "Beware of them. When we get closer, I'll send the Lesslings out as scouts. They'll like that work, and they're good at it. If they continue to create more trouble, I'll order them back home, and if they do not go, they'll learn who really is in charge."

Koya saw the creatures' heads come up, and they looked back at her, eyes blinking. They understood what she said, even though she spoke in Kasprin. He didn't know if the threat would help or not, but he could tell that the idea of going against her bothered the group. It might be enough to keep them away from him for a while.

Takka shared food with him again. He'd plainly gotten it from the others.

"I wish I had something to share as well," Koya said, nibbling at the cheese, which was richer than he usually ate, so he went easy with it. His stomach was already protesting the odd food again, so he countered it with the coarse bread, which he liked better. Takka even cut an apple in half for the two of them, but he looked at Koya with a little frown.

"What?" Koya asked

"You have fallen into this trouble with the rest of us, and you came the least prepared for such a journey. That isn't your fault, you know. The Norters wanted to use you to create even more of a problem. I think they wanted to draw notice to areas like the village with the rats and away from the Forbidden Valley, but you denied them that ruse. You have stayed alive and kept with us, even when some of our own would have gladly stayed behind at some camp until they were well enough to go on again."

"I want to see this through," Koya said. "I want to make certain there are no problems if we meet up with my own people."

"You do not heal yourself as you healed me."

Koya saw the concern and question in Takka's eyes. He gave a slight nod before he explained. "The gifts that the Gods give us are to help others, not ourselves. I can use little magics, usually, with the help of my runes, that might make my own journey easier -- but I don't have my own runes, and I don't have the time or energy to expend trying to tame the runes that are not my own."

"You did not use a rune when you healed me," he said, and put a hand on his chest, as though to feel the wounds there.

"That was -- unusual. The Gods stood with me then," he said and felt the truth of those words, and his own doubts leave him again. "I could not have done it without their aid."

"And your Gods would save me?"

"Yes," Koya said. "Yes. You are a good person. We've worked well together, and we still have more work to do."

Takka gave a slight nod, though Koya thought the answer didn't really appear to settle well with his Dragonkin companion. "As much as I like still being alive, I think the idea of foreign Gods interfering in my life bothers me."

"I'm not happy about them interfering in my life, and I serve them," Koya replied with open honesty.

That won a bright laugh from Takka. They settled into a more companionable meal afterward. Maybe he had shown a little more sanity than Takka had expected with that last line.

They talked about the world around them, about plants and what they knew about them, the names according to Dragonkin, Kasprin, and Norter wording, though he hadn't spoken that last language in a long time. This was, really, the sort of exchange of information Koya loved, and he would have gladly sat there all afternoon if Lady Jade hadn't come to stand over them. Koya glanced up and saw the amused look on her face and the shake of her head.

"Two of a kind," she said with a rueful shake of her head. "I should have known. We're ready to go if you two would care to join us?"

The others were standing and waiting. Even the Lesslings had already taken their places along the line.

"My apologies!" Koya started to rush to his feet, but the wave of her hand slowed him.

"All is well. Teach each other. We all need knowledge."

Talking with Takka almost helped him forget where they were going, though every time he looked up at the mountains, the reminder struck him again. He wondered why the Gods had set him on this path, and knew he could not begin to understand.

Koya had heard about this area in the mountains near the Forbidden Valley. Humans -- whether priests or not -- were warned not to travel in here because sometimes one of the magical beings would come through to see the world they'd left behind. Koya had thought the area would be a dreadful, scary place with the feel of magic washing over him, but this was the opposite.

A human could get to like this feel and not want to leave again.

A dangerous place and they weren't even to the area were the lands trapped in magic remained hidden. Oh yes, it was useful to remind himself of the danger ahead, including the Norter army moving into the Forbidden Valley. None of them, least of all the lone human, were safe.

CHAPTER

THIRTY-EIGHT

Guards had arrived at the tent with a surprising rush of whispered words and worried glances in Kenning's direction. Stanmark gave a signal, and Kenning followed him out of the comfort of the tent. The late afternoon sky had darkened, and a slight breeze kicked up the inevitable dust.

They watched as a dozen riders and a wagon festooned with bright cloth and bells rolled forward amid the sound of flutes.

The last thing Kenning had expected -- or wanted -- was to see the Most Holy riding into camp atop the fancy wagon. Cedric the Benevolent arrived with dozens of his own people and enough panoply to make a royal procession look dull.

"Gods all," Kenning muttered. "We do not need this!"

Stanmark nodded, his mouth clamped shut against anything he would have said, which probably would have been far less civil. Then he glanced Kenning's way and bowed his head. He spoke softly. "I told you Empress Silana wouldn't let him back into the council meetings. We should have expected him to trail after us. I suspect she doesn't know he's left the city, though it would be hard to miss this show. I don't know how he got this close without warning --"

"He used magic," Kenning replied. "Both to leave Tralista and to get close to us. He can pull some magic from the seal on the Forbidden Valley."

General Stanmark gave a snarl of agreement. The Most Holy's wagon rolled closer with him sitting atop, his rotund body draped in cloth and bolstered by pillows. Riders flanked the wagon on all sides, and soldiers who had been sitting at their camps were forced to scatter out of the way. They lost some supplies and probably a couple weapons as well, which were all things they could ill afford to lose before the coming battle.

The sight angered Kenning -- so much so that he marched right with General Stanmark to the wagon, forcing the Most Holy's people out the way, and making the wagon stop. The driver hauled back on the reigns, and the Most Holy nearly toppled from his throne-like spot. The music died away in a shocked silence that swept over everyone.

Both the Most Holy and General Stanmark glared; Kenning fought to get his own emotions in control. He would need to be a calming influence here if he could manage the work for himself. The disgust on the Most Holy's face already set Kenning's blood boiling, but he did his best to keep that reaction from his face.

"You are not welcome in this camp," General Stanmark decreed.

Those words won gasps of surprise everywhere around them, and even Kenning winced at the straightforward and cold statement. The Most Holy's eyes went wide in his flabby face, and then his lips tightened, and his eyes narrowed. He lifted his hand --

"Don't," Kenning ordered. He saw disaster about to strike on all sides. The troops were already uneasy at the confrontation. If the Most Holy hit the General with a spell, there was going to be a severe falling out among the people.

The Most Holy even knew it. He knew what he was about to do, and Kenning's single word was not going to stop him.

Kenning moved between the High Priest and General Stanmark, drawing a warning hiss from Stanmark but only a little nod from the Most Holy.

"You show where you stand," Most Holy said, his lips curling back in something close to a smile as he lowered his hand. "So be it."

"Yes, I stand with General Stanmark and Empress Silana," Kenning replied loudly and with more daring than he had expected. "As will any sane man in the Empire. The threat we face --"

"Is all based on lies!" The Most Holy bellowed so loudly that his own horses tried to bolt, and Stanmark himself had to stop them. The Most Holy surged to his feet, ignoring the danger, and Kenning could have wished for him to fall and take injury -- nothing serious, but enough to silence the man. "These are the lies of a devil-worshipping Norter who is trying to direct us away from the true danger!"

"Koya, may the Gods protect him wherever he is, has not had contact with us since the fall of Ziven," Kenning reminded the man. He tapped General Stanmark on the arm, hoping the man kept quiet a little while longer. "Slade, on the other hand, was a member of the army, and he knows what he's talking about when he reports to us."

"And for all we know, that Norter bastard has control of him!"

This was, as things went with the Most Holy, an almost logical statement.

"You put a lot of belief in the power of this Koya to manipulate everything to his supposed choices," Stanmark said with a tilt of his head. "However, I personally know Slade, and I trust him. If you do not, you need not be here. Go stand guard where you think the true trouble will be. I'm sure your sanctity will hold back any enemy army, right?"

"Don't mock me," the Most Holy warned, leaning down toward the General. "I will not give my blessing to this army -- "

"Well, now there's some good news," Stanmark answered, and won a whisper of shocked dismay from everyone again. "I remember the last time you gave your Holy Blessing to an army. Not ten men in a thousand survived the battle, Cedric. Slade was one of the few to walk away from that field. I trust him far more than I trust you."

"Unbeliever --"

"I believe in the Ten. I pray to them every morning and every night. I offer at the Temples on the Holy Days. What I don't believe in is your ability to determine what the Gods want, let alone what is happening on the other side of those mountains. Your hatred of a single priest who happens to be of northern blood has blinded you to anything of importance, just as your hatred for the northerners has fueled all the rest of your career. You used your sacred station to start a Holy War once. It will not happen again. You can play at politics all you want, but you will never have any control over the army. That was decided long ago, Cedric. We will not trust you with the lives of men."

"If I say that they should not follow you -- if I declare you an enemy of the Gods --"

"You had better have some unequivocal evidence of it," Kenning replied, his voice harsher than he had expected. "And if you don't, I suggest you don't push this any farther, Most Holy."

"You -- you are no longer a priest --"

"I was not brought before a Temple court. I was not stripped of my symbol, though you tried," Kenning replied. He found himself growing increasingly ill-tempered with the man who obviously wanted to cause trouble. "You saw what happened when you tried to remove my symbol of The Ten."

For some reason, his words seemed to have struck the Most Holy worse than the General's statements, which wasn't for the better, of course. Cedric the Benevolent (Gods all, who gave him that name, anyway?) grew red-faced, and his hands moved --

Kenning had been ready for the attack, and he created a ward that covered not only him but also the General and several people who stood close by.

Fire hit the shield and bounced in several directions, though Kenning captured some of the power to limit the damage to others. He had anticipated that whatever the Most Holy did, it would be dangerous to everyone in the immediate area. The light blinded him for a moment, and he heard startled shouts all around. He blinked, still holding the ward in place and trying to see if the Most Holy meant to do more.

The Most Holy was down on his knees, holding his hand to his chest, white-faced, and making a soft keening sound. Kenning winced when he saw the red, blistered fingers, though the wounds did not look serious. There were burn marks on the Most Holy's perfect robes, and even some of his hair looked singed.

"Oh hell," Kenning whispered and let the ward go down at last.

"Serves him right, you know," Stanmark said though quietly. There were shouts, and no one heard the two speaking. A few others had been injured but not seriously. "He would have killed us with that fire, right? Us and anyone who happened to be near us."

"Yes. But still --" Kenning began and winced when the Most Holy looked his way. The man's eyes protruded from the flesh of his face, red circled and filled with such rage that Kenning really could feel it like a wave of magic -- aimless, without purpose, but real.

"You dared -- you dared to attack the head of your own Temple --"

The sounds of shouting died away in the crowd. Kenning glanced around and saw the surprise in almost all the people, including some who had come with the Most Holy. For the first time, people apparently realized the man was not reasonable. Kenning even considered that he might not be sane.

The Most Holy struggled up from his knees. It wasn't easy, and no one moved to help him. Kenning felt the world coming apart at that moment. This was more than he had ever meant to see happen, even if he didn't agree with the politics of the man who headed the Temple of the Ten. This couldn't be good, and if he hadn't known better, Kenning might have suspected magic working against them all.

Unfortunately, the Most Holy alone had brought this trouble down upon himself. They needed strength. They didn't need this madman to try and dictate the situation and set them on a war against the wrong enemy.

"The gods will see you pay for what you have done," the Most Holy said. His voice sounded calm this time, but his eyes showed his rage. "You have attacked the head of the Temple, and I'll see you brought up on charges --"

"You do that," Stanmark said. He dared a step forward and Kenning almost stopped him but realized that wouldn't be good in front of the troops. Besides, he suspected the Most Holy could not call up another spell because of his injured hand. "You put him up on charges. I'll come to the trial, and I'll bring everyone here who saw what happened. I'll call on the Gods themselves to bear witness that you tried to kill us and were injured by your own spell."

Most Holy looked shocked. Then he shook his head and glared at Stanmark as though the man had been purposely trying to confound him. Kenning realized that the Most Holy was beyond any hope of understanding. That only left the problem of what to do with him.

"I suggest that you head back to the Temple, Most Holy," Kenning said. He kept his voice calm and tried to sound differential. "This is not where you want to be. If there is to be an invasion elsewhere, you will need to be ready for it."

"I came to order you back to the Temple where you belong."

There is was, finally. Kenning had feared this moment an order would come from the man, but facing it now, he had no trouble making up his mind on what to do.

"I will not go," Kenning said. "I will not leave this place where I can help in whatever way it pleases the Gods."

"And I say the Gods are not pleased with you at all, false priest. I say --" His voice caught as he moved a hand, but his face had taken on the look of a fanatic again. "I say that the Gods will strike you dead."

"So be it," Kenning answered. "If I have displeased them, they can, and should, strike me dead at any time. But until they do, I will stay here."

"And you will go," General Stanmark added. It was not a request, and Kenning decided he had better not try to get the General to be more discreet, not with his own soldiers watching this show. "You will leave this camp and not interfere with our work again, Cedric."

"I am the Most Holy --"

"You can be whatever you want, but not *here*. This is an army camp. This is a place where I must weigh how best to put these men to fighting and consider every life that will be lost. I will not have matters made worse by your intrusion and your bigotry. You hate the Norters, and that has warped everything you are doing. I won't have that bigotry affect what I will do."

"You cannot order --"

"I will have you removed if I must," he said.

Several soldiers moved forward as though to do that work. Kenning hadn't expected it, and he wondered if Stanmark had arranged this somehow. Others looked uneasy, though not too many.

"I will not remain in a camp with disbelievers and those disowned by the Gods. Those who do not wish to share the fate of the damned should leave with me."

"Anyone who believes that the Most Holy is right should go with him," Stanmark agreed with a glance around at the others. "Those who believe that we are here to protect the Empire from the threat of invasion should remain."

Stanmark walked away. Kenning thought the man was crazy to put the Most Holy at his back, but he hurried to go with the General, and after a few steps, realized this was wise. Neither man could dare show weakness now, and Kenning needed to make the Most Holy's appearance less important, so that his own refusal to obey was only a minor insurrection in the confrontation.

"Some of the troops will go with Most Holy. That was bound to happen the moment he showed up, but his own actions have limited the number who will stand with him now."

Kenning waited until they were inside the tent before he spoke again. "I think that sometimes Most Holy has no control over his rage, and he might not even remember the actions. I don't think he knows he tried to kill us, and he believes that I injured him."

"Hell," Stanmark said, looked out the opening. The wagon was starting to turn. "He can't really be that far gone, can he?"

"I don't know. I don't like to think so, but the man lives in a world of his own making." Kenning slowed, starting to feel the loss of the energy he'd put into that shield. "He says that it was the Gods who put a spell on Koya, not him. Maybe he really thinks so."

"He'd believe the Gods would purposely make someone miserable?"

"Oh yes, if he deserved it, and the Most Holy believes that Koya is the enemy. He's blind to everything else. Just as he's blind to his own actions. The man is far more dangerous than I thought, General. We need to get him away from here, or I fear what will happen when the real battle does arrive."

"Do you have the power to send him away?"

"No."

"No. There's only one person in all the world who might have the power to command him, but only if he listened to her. I'm going to get a messenger to the Empress. Maybe she can send someone to convince him to return to her. It would save a lot of trouble."

"We might not have time."

"True, but we have no choice. You better rest, priest."

Kenning nodded and went back outside where he found a place to sit by a fireside where other soldiers gathered, speaking among themselves. He paid them no attention. The General's tent would be too busy for rest, and Kenning knew he needed to think.

He watched the mountain, fearing the attack would come at any moment, though his mind was only half on that problem. He thought more about the Most Holy and what needed to be done about him. Those thoughts went far beyond the current challenge to the future of their Temples. The man could be removed, but it would take a vote of priests throughout the Empire to make the decision, and Kenning didn't think that was going to happen. They would, he feared, be forced to wait out Cedric's natural lifetime and hope the man did nothing that would put the Empire in any worse danger.

Hope?

Kenning rethought that idea; he prayed instead.

CHAPTER

THIRTY-NINE

The last of the troops moved down the side of the hill ... and disappeared into the darkness, like all the soldiers before them. Slade could hear nothing at all but the passing wind and the distant call of a hawk. They could barely see the cavernous opening past a tumble of huge boulders.

That unnaturally dark shadow must be the gate to the Forbidden Valley.

"That's eerie," Malin whispered, remaining careful despite the silence. "It's as if they've disappeared into nothing. We should still hear them, shouldn't we?"

"Yes," Slade said. They'd moved closer to the troops as the army headed into the Valley. "We should hear an echo of sound. Something. I don't understand where they went, but I think they're not in a natural cave. We should have realized there would be magic involved."

Malin nodded, eyes narrowed again. "And we will follow, right?"

"Yes. But first I need to contact Kenning. We might just disappear, Malin, and never come out. The Gods alone know where we'll be if we don't."

"That's fine." Malin gave a little shrug and looked back at Slade. He saw loss in the boy's face again, a look that he had hidden over the last few days. "It doesn't matter where I go, Slade. You realize that, right? I can't go home. I might as well go somewhere else."

Slade wanted to dissuade the boy of those thoughts, but he nodded. "I know. I felt much the same as you when I left the army. I found the Temple -- or maybe the Gods just kept me there until they needed me again."

"You truly think the Gods are responsible for you being here?" he asked, his brow drawn down as though he hadn't thought about it.

"Yes."

"And me?"

"No. I don't believe the Gods would willfully do something this awful simply to move one person in the right place. Humans do evil, Malin. So, sometimes, do the darker Gods that others follow. Our Gods only pick up the pieces and give us new choices."

Malin nodded, but Slade suspected he neither believed nor understood the words. Slade wished he could have offered more, but maybe what Malin needed was the same as him. They would help to save the Empire.

Odd pair to have such a job, he supposed. But then who would be a better choice?

He stood and took a step forward -- and something moved in the shadows at the bottom of the hill.

"Troll," Malin hissed.

The creature knew they were there. While it might not have the best eyesight, it hadn't missed the two of them standing up. It lifted his head and turned their way with a growl of anger. Slade glanced frantically around for a place where they could take cover -- where they could hide and be still --

No, it wouldn't work. The troll had their scent now. They'd have to fight.

Slade fumbled through his pack and runes, trying to come up with something that might help get them out of this mess. He and Malin retreated, half falling on the loose shale. The troll had dropped on all fours and bounded upwards like an enormous, ugly dog. The growl grew closer to a howl, and the two barely escaped the first strike when Slade shoved Malin ahead of him. They both slid downward where the enemy had been heading up a moment before. They reached a small stand of trees before the troll turned to follow them.

Malin grabbed a branch and whacked the charging creature across the face with enough force that the limb broke, and the beast howled again and staggered, though he kept to his feet. It looked groggy, and Slade found another fallen limb and hit it as well. Malin had done the same, but the troll didn't seem any worse for it. They just needed to slow it so they could escape.

To where? To the dark cave where the troops went? As good as any --

The troll leapt at Slade, a wide clawed hand swiping across his leg and putting him to his knees with the sudden pain. The next blow would have caught him in the neck, and he wouldn't have survived it, but Malin charged the creature with enough force that it sent them both tumbling.

He feared for the boy's life. Slade used the limb as a crutch and rushed after the two, yelling and calling up what magic he could. He struck with a blow that nearly left him senseless, but the troll fell back, scrambled to his feet, and swayed again.

Malin got up, though his chest and arms bled. Damn! Their enemy wasn't down, and it was enraged now.

"Go, Malin," he said. "Go quickly."

"No, sir. You're the one who should go. You have a duty to contact the others. I can't do that."

Malin took a step closer to the troll, obviously intending to throw himself on the creature.

Slade grabbed him and dragged the boy back a few steps.

"Sir --"

"No. I have some magic yet -- "Slade stopped and almost cursed. He could hear sounds in the woods -- the growls of more creatures coming quickly towards them.

Malin tried to push him toward the cave, but Slade shook his head. "No. I can't run. I won't get clear in time."

"Sir --"

"I'm sorry, Malin," he said. He grabbed out the rune and ran magic through it, reaching for Kenning. "Kenning! Do you hear me!"

"Slade --"

"We have problems. Troll. We won't make it --"

"No! Slade --"

"Listen! The army has gone -- gone into the Valley!" He leapt aside as the troll tried to swing at him and hit it across the nose with the limb. Malin battered it a couple times again. "They went over the hill and disappeared, and I -- what the hell! Those are Lesslings!"

"Slade?"

The large lizard-like creatures rushed out of the woods and up the incline, nipping and growling.

The troll looked as surprised as Slade, tilting his enormous head and growling deep in the throat. A few Lesslings backed away, and it almost appeared as though the growls they made were answers. The sound made Slade nervous.

Malin caught his arm and pulled him toward the cave, hoping, no doubt that they'd get to cover before the battle broke out. Some Lesslings looked their way, yellow eyes blinking, long narrow mouths opening to show rows of teeth. They were no safer than the troll --

Dragonkin came at a run, shouting and with weapons ready. The troll ran straight for the cave, scrambling into the darkness before the Lesslings could catch up.

"Gone," Slade said. He still had the rune in hand. "The Lesslings, sir, held it off. Now there's Dragonkin people here. I don't know how this will go --"

He stopped again at the sight of Koya coming from the trees, leaning on a cane and looking battered and exhausted but moving.

"Slade?" Kenning said, sounding distant and worried.

"Koya," he whispered, barely getting the word out before he took another deep breath. "Koya is here!"

Malin let out a shout of surprise and pleasure and started down to greet their friend. Koya hurried towards them, a young member of the Dragonkin helping him along. The other people were calling back the Lesslings, which seemed to be difficult. Slade didn't care. He had limped over to Koya and stopped just short of embracing him, only at the last moment, remembering that it would be painful for him.

"Praise all the Gods," Slade said. "We feared you were dead."

"Near enough, sometimes," he admitted with a surprisingly bright smile.

"Koya!" Kenning shouted, so loud it drew the attention of the others.

"Sir?" Koya smiled at the rune. "I'm glad to talk to you again!"

"You -- you are the priest I met on the road, yes?" a Dragonkin woman with shocking green hair and eyes asked as she came closer.

"Ambassador? Yes, I am. How did you come to be with Koya?"

"I would say luck, but I think your priest has mumbled about the work of the Gods now and then," she replied with a surprising smile of her own. "And now I have found another of your people at a fortuitous moment for him. I think I shall have to say something to your Gods about using us as agents."

But she laughed and moved away again, going to help with her people. Another had bandaged Malin as though it was normal for these people to take care of humans.

"Slade? Koya?"

The link to Kenning had faded. He forced it back with a start. "Sorry, sir. Just shocked. Amazed. We've survived. I don't know what's going on, though."

"Sit," Koya said, waving toward boulders. "We need to sit for a while. This has been a long journey."

Koya looked tired, battered and worn, reminding Slade how he felt as well. The humans moved out of the way of the Dragonkin and Lesslings, all of whom seemed in great agitation over something. Slade wished he understood what they were saying.

"What's going on with your companions?" Slade asked.

"I don't know," Koya admitted. He sat down and looked relieved to have the rest. "I don't know what will happen next, but from my perspective, it's bound to include a lot of travel and more excitement than a priest should probably have."

Kenning laughed with a pleasant sound through the rune. "I am glad to find you have survived, Koya. I worried."

"We still have another odd journey ahead," Koya said. He patted Malin's arm as the boy sat by Slade. "There is a problem and one that we need to address right away. An army of

Norters is heading through the Forbidden Valley towards Kasprin --"

"We have our forces here and waiting for them, Koya," Kenning answered. "Slade and Malin have been tracking them."

"They've gone through, sir," Slade reminded him. "There's no telling what will happen now. There's magic involved, so we cannot trust time or distance. They could be to the other side in moments."

"Excellent point," another voice said.

"The general has rushed off to see to the matter," Kenning explained. He sounded relieved and worried. "We have problems here. The Most Holy has arrived, and he's on the rampage about this not being the actual battle. We've had a serious confrontation, and I suspect it will get worse."

"We don't need more trouble," Slade mumbled. He could feel himself weakening. "I fear -- I fear I must rest, sir. We'll be back in contact when we have some answers."

"Rest," Kenning agreed. "The Gods keep you safe."

The rune went silent and cold. Slade looked up at Koya and offered a smile. "Sorry. I just couldn't hold for any longer."

"I was glad to hear from Kenning at all. And knowing that they're prepared for trouble makes me far calmer than I've been in days. What do we do now?"

"I think, perhaps, that's more in the hands of your friends than in ours," Slade said. "For the moment, we can rest."

CHAPTER

FORTY

K oya noticed that Takka kept his distance while the humans spoke. He glanced their way with some trepidation, but he did not come near until Koya waved him to join them. Then he crossed to them with apparent nervousness.

"This is DK," Koya said, introducing him. DK looked startled and a little pleased already. Perhaps he had feared his name being given to others. "He was a captive with me, and we escaped. We were within a couple miles of the Dragonkin border when the Lady caught up with us. It was a welcome meeting since we were under attack by a rockling. Then the Norters arrived and took the rockling, so we followed."

"Malin and I spotted you at the fort," Slade said as he rubbed the cloth around his leg. Koya would try to heal the wound before they went on walking. "I helped with your magic to draw the rats, but we had to keep watch on the

Norters, especially when we found out that there was an even larger section of the army here in the mountains."

"It's been a long journey for all of us," Koya admitted. He wanted to rest, but the Dragonkin people were preparing to go again. "I fear this next trek will not get any better."

"We're going into the cave," DK said with a nod. "The Lady convinced the others that since so many humans already went inside, that our human allies must come along. This will be up to the three of you to continue. We cannot say what kind of reception we will receive."

"Malin and I were about to go through anyway," Slade said. "I would be glad for some company, as long as we aren't a problem."

"Everything is a problem," Takka said and glanced at Koya. "You?"

"Oh, yes. I've come this far. I want to see this through."

"Good then. I shall say so to the Lady." He bowed his head and hurried away.

"You make him nervous," Koya said with a little smile. "But I'm sure he'll get used to more humans. We will be leaving soon. Let me deal with your leg, Slade, and your wounds, Malin. I don't have my runes, but --"

"I brought your runes," Slade said and waved toward his pack. "I picked them up in Ziven."

Koya felt as though something had gone right for the first time since the battle in that unfortunate village.

Malin handed over the box of runes with a smile. The boy knew what they meant by now, after all this time with Slade. Koya took the box into his hands and held it for a long moment, savoring the ambiance of his own magic. He grew stronger, just holding the runes again.

"Thank you. This will help. I tried to use Galt's runes. He was a stubborn old man, I fear. The runes didn't much like me.

Would you carry Galt's runes, Malin? I fear to place the two boxes too close together."

"I would be honored," Malin said. He paused and sighed. "He's dead, isn't he?"

"Yes, he is."

"You and I are the only ones who survived from Ziven," he said and looked lost for a moment. Koya had suspected it was so. The boy took the box he held out and nodded. "I'll be happy to take these for a while."

"We can't do anything that will make up for what happened in Ziven," Koya said. "We can only do our best to see that the people responsible don't win the larger battle."

Malin nodded, but those words didn't erase the bleakness in the boy's eyes. He brushed his fingers across the top of the box before he put it away. Koya suspected he had given the boy something precious.

Kenning might want to reclaim the runes later. Runes let loose without a priest to control them could sometimes be dangerous.

Slade had watched the boy, but he looked at Koya and gave a brief shake of his head. It would not be easy for Malin, no matter what the future.

"Let me deal with your leg," Koya said, and opened the box, smiling as the power of the runes reached for him. Slade had started to argue again, but he changed his mind. "Ah, you found my temple rune! Thank you. I had dropped it during the attack."

Koya searched the runes and found the one for cats, which he had always associated with nurturing.

The magic didn't come to him as quickly as it had in the Temple before his encounter with the Most Holy. However, it still felt good, and he could seal the wound closed and make sure Slade bled no more, which would have been dangerous.

He took a deep breath before he looked toward Malin, wondering how he might help there --

Lesslings rushed at them, their teeth barred, hissing in anger.

"Look out!" Koya threw out a wave of magic that shoved some Lesslings away, but four came through in a rush, and one grabbed Malin by the arm, teeth ripping into the skin while the boy shouted in dismay.

The others dashed straight for Koya and Slade. Takka yelled and leapt into the fray with his drawn knife, and other Dragonkin people rushed to help. The Lesslings never slowed. Slade grabbed a large rock and pounded it against one Lessling's head as it grabbed Koya by the leg. The bite had been sharp and was quickly released, but another moved to take the same place.

Slade had another of his own, but he caught it by the tail and threw it aside and then snatched the one attacking Koya --

More charged for them --

The Dragonkin arrived. Lady Jade half severed the neck of a Lessling that had attacked Malin, the creature falling dead at her feet. She spun and shoved her sword into another, and Takka had killed two more. Three other Lesslings died by the hands of the others, and the Lesslings were backing off, slinking away and snarling as they went back to the shadows of the nearby trees.

"I'm sorry," Koya said, looking around with shock. "I don't know what we did --"

"Be at ease," Lady Jade said. She cleaned her sword and looked at the dead with a shake of her head. "This is not your work. They were unhappy, and perhaps the magic here has affected their thoughts, but they would not listen to orders. Lesslings that go wild are very dangerous, and these would not be the first ever to die at our swords because they became senseless killers. I am sorry for it, but I do not blame you."

"Thank you," Koya said, still shaken. He looked at the other Lesslings, worried because they were too close.

Malin was the worst hurt, and he turned his attention to helping the boy, even while Slade did some minor work on Koya's own leg. Lady Jade spoke for a moment with her own people and then headed toward the Lesslings. It frightened Koya to watch her march right up to them, but Takka put a hand on his shoulder.

"It's what she has to do to test them. We're prepared if they turn wild."

"Do they just hate humans?" Malin asked, holding his still aching arm, though he had gotten some of his color back. "Is that the problem?"

"Some of it," Takka agreed. He seemed to look the boy over for the first time. Koya wondered if he found some kinship with Malin at that moment because he looked more at ease. "Lesslings are strange creatures, and they turn for reasons we cannot name. They are talented hunters and scouts, and when one is out in the wilds, they make fit companions for certain travels. We do not keep them in the cities."

Koya felt a little better for that knowledge, though he still didn't like to watch Lady Jade going down to talk to the creatures. However, as soon as she neared, they stopped their restless prowling. At a growled order from her, all the remaining Lesslings stood up on their back legs, looking as though they had come to attention in the military ranks. It would have been amusing if it still hadn't bothered him so much to see them stand like humans.

And worse when they suddenly, after some words from Lady Jade, bowed their heads to her. It sent a chill up his spine, as though he knew they lied in that move of submission.

He looked away but chanced to spot Slade looking at the Lesslings with distrust, and he wondered if they both thought the same thing. He didn't ask it aloud for fear of upsetting the Dragonkin people, though.

"We'll be going in soon," Takka warned, watching the cave.

"Do you know what we'll find?" Koya asked, glad for the distraction. He looked towards the darkness as well and shook his head with shock. It was easy to forget what a strange next step they were about to take.

"None. This will be dangerous, though. The tales of old say that even time sometimes plays games in the Valley. There are creatures there of all sorts, who stayed in a place they created in a way that it is not fully a part of the actual world. We don't know what's in there. A few of our people thought to scout ahead, but the Lady fears they might not come back out again. She thinks it wiser if we all stay together. We could very well face enemies the moment we walk in since the troll will have given a warning."

"Is there another way in?" Slade asked.

"Not on this side of the range."

"I'll contact Kenning this time," Koya said. "Once we go inside, it might be harder to reach him."

"I've thought the same," Slade agreed. He leaned against the rock, looking more relaxed. "At least we know where we're going from here. It's been too many days since I had any true idea of what would come next."

"I think that's the definition of an adventure," Koya replied with a slight sigh. He pulled out the Temple rune. "I'd like to return to the calm of the Temple now."

"I suspect we have to take another long walk, my friend," Slade said with a wave of his hand towards the mountain.

"An exciting one, I'm sure."

Even Malin grinned at that pronouncement. Koya turned his attention to the rune. After the fight he'd had to try to do anything with Galt's runes, the ease of working with his own seemed almost unnatural.

He hadn't much to tell Kenning, and little time anyway, because the Dragonkin were ready to go.

"We're heading in now, sir," he said and stood, wincing, and nodding his thanks to Takka, who handed him the branch he'd been using as a cane. "The Dragonkin can't tell us what will happen inside the cave. Chances are that you'll see the Norters coming out the other side before you hear from us again, but we might learn something helpful."

"Take care," Kenning ordered. "Move carefully, even when you come through to here. The Most Holy is..." Kenning stopped speaking, and it made Koya a little nervous, waiting for the words to continue. "Koya, we think the Most Holy might truly be insane," Kenning continued softly. "We're doing what we can to negate his influence here, but it will be perilous for you when you arrive."

"I'll remember that, sir," Koya said. He hoped the anger and bitterness didn't show too much in his voice. "I'll talk to you soon."

The rune cooled. He put it away and watched as the Dragonkin people lined up, putting Koya, the humans and Takka in the middle. He wondered how his young friend felt about being pushed in with them, though he didn't seem to mind much.

Lady Jade walked at the lead, her hand on her sword. The next four held bows, though they didn't have them up and ready. They moved over the broken ground, toward the cave.

Koya had a real look at the darkness ahead; it seemed like a half-circle of night set into the mountain. This was too perfect and too dark to be natural. He thought the entrance swallowed both the light and the surrounding sound.

Koya cast a glance at Takka, but his companion only stared and shook his head, no more certain about this place than he was. They didn't have to go. The Dragonkin knew the troops were in there, and would come out the other side and --

He had almost slowed, intending to turn back, when he heard something strange and extraordinary.

He couldn't tell if the sound came from a flute or a bird, but the bright tones sang out of the darkness with a sweet tune. The others had stopped, even Lady Jade tilting her head a little. Takka, though, looked uneasy.

"Is it a problem?" Koya whispered.

"I don't know. I've heard nothing like that before, but I mistrust anything that comes from that place."

"Why?" Slade asked. "I would have thought, being people of magic, you would have felt safe enough inside there."

"Magic doesn't mean we're all alike," Lady Jade said, looking back at Slade. "We created wars among ourselves before we took to our battle with humans. Some things inside here will make you and I akin, human, despite that you don't have magic." Then she stopped and smiled, a flash of bright teeth, some of them far too sharp looking. "Well, except that you priests have a magic of sorts, and that ties us even closer together."

The tune came again, and with a shake of her head, Lady Jade started forward. After a couple footsteps, she and the first line of Dragonkin disappeared into the dark.

And fools, all of them -- the rest of the group rushed to follow.

CHAPTER

FORTY-ONE

Kenning watched the campfires where the Most Holy and his men had made camp. They were far too close, which left him uneasy. However, maybe they wouldn't be a problem. Perhaps the Most Holy would be content to rant and rail about the evils going on around him. He liked a sympathetic audience, and the people who had followed him had nothing better to do than to listen.

"Kenning?"

Kenning turned with a start to General Stanmark. He'd been too intent on the other camp. "Well," he said with a bright smile. "Good thing I'm not on guard duty, isn't it?"

The General gave an appreciative laugh but looked toward the distant people as well before he frowned again. "I should have chased him off farther."

"No," Kenning said and surprised Stanmark. "We want him where we can see him. He's happy enough to have people who will listen to his lecture. In fact, I would suggest you send him a few more."

"Ah, now there's a good thought," he said and looked around. "A few more followers for him there and a few more guards for us, if he does something more insane."

"Even if he doesn't, it won't hurt to know what he's saying. If we survive this battle, we might have to deal with anything he starts."

"Ah. Another excellent point, and one to keep in mind. I am so focused on struggling to decide what kind of war we face that I had considered nothing beyond that future trouble. Your people might be within the Valley by now."

"Yes, sir. I thought about attempting to reach them, but they're in such a dangerous position that I don't think it wise."

"True."

He looked from the fires of the Most Holy's camp to the darkness of the mountain. "It doesn't help that we do not understand how long it will take them to get through. Come away, Kenning. We need to rest. As troubling as the Most Holy is, he's nothing more than a distraction, and we don't need such a thing. I'll send a dozen soldiers slipping over to him tonight. We'll monitor him. But you and I have to rest."

"Yes, sir. I understand." Kenning cast one more glance at the camp and shook his head as he turned toward the tent. "The Most Holy is dangerous, but as long as we're ready for that kind of trouble, we can deal with him. He is not subtle. We should have plenty of warning."

Stanmark nodded and walked through his own camp. Kenning went with him, though he felt the hair on his neck stand on end as though he left a treacherous enemy at his back. He didn't like the feeling, but Stanmark was right.

He could see agitation in the army camp as they went toward the General's tent. People shifted around the fires, and no one appeared to settle down. Words whispered around the two, and faces looked their way with worry.

"Supplies are getting low," Stanmark said a bit more loudly. "But Lord Oak is only a day away with more, so I'm not worried about that now."

That seemed an odd thing to say to him until Kenning realized the General did so on purpose so that the men of the camp would spread the word without Stanmark having to tell them officially.

"That's good to hear, sir. Lord Oak seems an honorable man to have put in charge of requisitioning for the army's needs."

"He is. He understands what we need. We'd have done better with a little warning, but we'll get by. And we'll have rested while the enemy did not. We can hope, even, that the Norter troops, being human, will encounter some trouble on their trip through the Valley. Maybe we'll turn out to have an exciting field exercise and no combat at all."

"True, sir," Kenning said. He silently prayed to the Gods that the madness resolved that way -- and also prayed that Koya, Slade, and the others didn't run into the same problems.

They reached the tent with no one bothering Stanmark with anything more than regular reports. Stanmark waved Kenning on inside and talked to an officer in a soft voice -- no doubt arranging for a few defections during the night. He came inside only a moment after Kenning had sat down on one of the folding chairs. His legs ached, and he still felt weakened after the encounter with the Most Holy.

That trouble would haunt him after they survived the rest of this madness. Kenning feared he would not be going back to Templeton.

"You look worried," Stanmark said and poured them both some watered wine.

"Nothing to do with this matter." Kenning took the cup with a nod of thanks. "I just realized that I won't return to Templeton when once we've finished this trouble, which is unfortunate for me. I liked it there. But maybe the time had come for me to move on. A man can get too complacent sometimes."

"And sometimes a man can never find peace, even when he's given the perfect place. Cedric strikes me as that last type. He always wants something more. You would think someone chosen by the Gods to head the priesthood would have enough to keep him busy. He wanted to rule the Empress and control the country as well."

"Excellent point," Kenning said, then looked with a start as the tent flap came open. Few people just walked in --

Lord Oak stopped inside the opening and grinned when he saw them. "All's well," he said. "I have supplies that will be here by morning. I road ahead to make certain you were prepared to receive them, but I see you have an area already marked off."

"Yes," Stanmark said and poured a cup of wine for the man. Lord Oak crossed to the table and dropped into another of the chairs. It creaked ominously under his weight. "I'm more than ready for you and your supplies. I don't want there to be even the slightest hint that anything could be wrong here."

"Tell me that wasn't the Most Holy Bastard camped just to the north," Oak said, looking that direction as though he could see through the tent.

"Oh yes, Cedric rode in this afternoon and put on quite a show trying to kill Kenning and me."

"You're joking."

"No, afraid not. The ploy bounced back at him in more than one way. He's accusing Kenning of attacking him. However, the people who were there know Cedric threw the fire, and only Kenning's quick work saved us, and accidentally sent the magic back at the maker."

Lord Oak looked startled for a moment and then shook his head. "You know, I almost wish I had been there to see it happen, but the wiser part of me says I would have made the situation worse."

"I don't doubt that at all," Stanmark replied with a guffaw. "But it's done, and we'll find out what happens next with the Most Holy. This has put Kenning in a difficult position, so he's staying close to me."

"Or me, now that I'm here," Lord Oak said with a nod.

"I feel like a puppy being passed around," Kenning said and laughed at the looks the two gave him. "Don't worry, I am grateful to know I have people watching out for me. But remember one thing: if there is a confrontation between the Most Holy and me, I am best suited to deal with him. I stopped his magic this time. I don't want others getting between us if it comes down to a duel."

"Oh, now there's an excellent point," Lord Oak said and slapped him on the shoulder. "You're a wise man, Kenning. And I never thought I would ever say such a thing to a priest, you know. Cedric has made it impossible for me to look at a priest with an open mind."

"There must be worthy priests in the capital," Kenning said. "They can't all be like the Most Holy."

"He has the choice of who serves with him," Lord Oak replied as he leaned back. "He keeps those who either think like him or are more interested in power than sanctity. This never occurred to you?"

"I knew the priests that served closest to him had to share his views -- or keep quiet about their own. I never thought beyond his small circle. Even on the rare occasions when he traveled, he never brought more than a handful of his men with him."

"And he remained safe among you?"

"Of course," Kenning replied. "We took our vows seriously."

"Oh, good point, priest. Very good point. The peasants and townspeople, they'd just be awed at the sight of him, I suppose."

"Yes, they are happy to see him. Even when we had trouble with him at Templeton, we tried to keep the news from the others, because there was no reason to bother them with Temple politics. People do like him because he looks and acts the part."

"And what is it the Gods think of him, then?" Lord Oak asked. He said it with the air of someone who really wanted an answer.

"What makes you think I would know such things?" he asked, his head tilted.

"Because, Kenning, my friend, you are a man far closer to the Gods than anyone I have ever met."

He laughed before he saw the man's face and knew that Lord Oak was serious. Kenning took a breath and tried to contemplate the question. This was one he had thought of before, but tonight it seemed to take on a new meaning.

"I cannot say what the Gods may think of Cedric the Benevolent. Except consider this: he is losing ground at a time when he should be a beacon to everyone. If the Gods stood with him, we would perceive their influence. If you want to meet a truly holy man, hope that Koya comes through that pass. Then you'll see someone whom the Gods bless, and help, even against their High Priest."

"I don't know that I could live with such faith," Lord Oak said and leaned back. He looked tired but thoughtful.

"That's why I'm a priest, and you are not. Part of my job is to have such faith in what happens. Thank you for reminding me of my place in the world." Kenning stopped and sipped his watered wine, thinking about what he needed to do. The others watched him. He sat the cup aside and leaned back to relax. "We must do our best, and hope that the Gods side with us in this. There are so many things I don't understand about what's going on. What role do the Dragonkin play since it's obvious they have been drawn into the web as well? After all, they keep meeting with priests -- three times now, at key points in this trouble."

The two men appeared shocked by that idea. Kenning suspected they had not really considered the Gods' involvement in this matter, even with the priests playing important parts at so many levels. He looked from one to the other and nodded at their worried stares.

"The Gods rarely step into the wider sphere of human troubles," he said. "And I suspect it is something we should not be glad to see, to be honest. It means there is far more trouble out there than what we can perceive with our limited mortal eyes. Expect things to get worse, gentlemen. I suspect that something is playing with the balances and that it does not like humans very well at all."

"Some God?" Lord Oak asked.

"Maybe, though, not one of our Gods. It could be a creature of magic that found a key to cause trouble. That's happened in the past. Look to our myths, and you'll see the tales where things went out of balance under those kinds of circumstances."

"But myths -- just stories for children --"

"Like rocklings and trolls, and things we know are real, but we relegate to the myths."

"What are we going to do?" Lord Oak asked, looking confused for the first time since Kenning met him.

"We will stand here with the army and fight in ways that we can," General Stanmark replied, recovering from his own shock. "Whatever else is going on, this coming battle is real and dangerous."

Kenning nodded. Lord Oak looked a little relieved at that idea, as though he feared that they would find themselves drawn into some metaphysical war with things he didn't understand.

Kenning didn't mention that he feared it might still come to that as well, or even something worse.

CHAPTER

FORTY-TWO

S lade watched as they lined up and prepared to move forward, but suddenly the Lesslings let out a startled, hissing yell and surged ahead ... into the darkness and gone.

The Lady held up her hand, listening for a moment. She shook her head. "I can't hear anything from them. They will have much to answer for before we're done."

She signaled, and they walked into the cave, a black space that seemed without sides and without end.

He heard no sound of the Lesslings or even the footsteps of those beside him in this unnatural place. Slade doubted that he could feel anything real beneath his feet -- and that brought on such overwhelming vertigo that he felt sick and almost went to his knees with a soft moan.

"Slade?" Malin asked with hardly more than a whisper.

The boy's voice echoed through the black, strangely warped as though the sound undulated. Maybe pride alone made him stand straighter and keep going again now that he knew another walked nearby.

"I'm all right," Slade replied, though he hated how his words moved through the darkness.

"We are almost there," the Lady advised, and her voice sounded assured.

Slade didn't understand how she could tell such a thing, but he tried very hard not to doubt.

He forced himself forward, one step after another. Within a dozen steps, he thought the black felt less oppressive, even if he could still see nothing.

The music started again, somewhere not far away, and that drew the others into a faster walk as they headed for those beautiful notes. Slade heard the unmistakable sound of blades being drawn from sheaths, a noise a soldier knew very well, and a reassuring one under the circumstances. He saw a hint of greenish light ahead, glimpsed through the shadows of moving figures at the opening.

At least forward looked like a pleasant spot. He could see that the green came from grass, and the beautiful music still beguiled them, which was better than the wail of fighting, he supposed. He didn't trust the music any better, but this could have been worse.

"Careful now," the Lady said as she slipped out into the light and looked around, sword in hand. Her companions followed close on her heels with their weapons drawn as well. Slade wasn't too far behind, because he wanted out of the black tunnel.

He stepped into paradise.

Green trees stood down the hill from them, and lovely flowers dotted the hillside. The air itself tasted sweet and a slight breeze blew across his face. He blinked, getting the place in focus after the darkness. A broad and well-worn stone path led downward toward a distant pond, and he could see many trampled blooms along the edges of the rocks. That would be where the Norter army had passed.

Slade found no other sign of Norters or Lesslings. Neither of the groups should have crossed that distance in so short a time and disappeared into the woods beyond. However, they were not here, and open ground stood on all sides, except for a few boulders behind him that framed the dark cave.

"Where did they go?" Malin asked as he moved up closer to Slade. The boy glanced around with worry.

"The flowers are dead," Koya's companion said as he bent and lifted a crumbling flower in his hand. He looked bothered. "Time passed differently for them. The army must have gone this way at least two days ahead of us. I don't know what became of the Lesslings. Maybe they didn't make it through at all."

"Damn," Slade whispered, then shook his head, half in apology as he glanced at Koya.

"Oh, I was thinking much the same thing," Koya answered. He frowned as he lifted his cane.

"What's wrong?"

"More of what's right. I don't feel the Most Holy's curse here, though there are aches and pains enough without it."

"We're shielded here from the magic that exists outside this place," the Lady explained.

She lifted her hand and felt out the world more easily than Slade could have done, even with runes -- which he suspected would not work here. "I think we had better move on. Nothing is here to stop us coming through, so we should be wise and not to wait and see if something bothersome happens along."

"Lead the way, Lady," Slade said, bowing his head in agreement.

They could soon hear the music again, and this time from farther away. The Lady started down the path, careful not to tread on the flowers, and signaled her people to keep to the inlaid stones.

They moved forward at a steady pace, but not too fast. Slade hoped that confidence might help. Slade could see how Malin took in the view with apparent surprise and pleasure.

Bright birds of red and orange dipped into the pond and out again, and rabbits moved towards the edge of the water, sipping, and bounding away. The sounds of the place seemed natural enough, but when he looked upward, Slade felt a little shiver again.

"Where's the sky? Where's the sun?" he asked.

Heads turned toward the sky all along the group, and he heard whispered sounds that might have been curses from several of the Dragonkin. The others stopped, and the Lady lifted her hand and reached up into the air. She turned back at him with a frown.

"This day is made of magic. We should expect such things and not be surprised -- or distracted -- by them."

She spoke to the Dragonkin in their own language, apparently repeating the same words. They didn't look any happier than Slade. He found it odd to feel so at ease with them.

They hiked down closer to the pond. The distance seemed greater than it looked, but at least it was a pleasant walk.

"Careful when we near the water. There were once things that lived in such ponds, and they were not friendly to anyone who came too close without permission," DK advised.

"Wise to mention such a possibility," the Lady agreed. They moved within yards of the pond, and she signaled the others to slow. "And since we are not here with permission at all, I should not wish to be careless. Perhaps this is the place to rest, though, and get a better feel for the area. Sit, but stay to the path. Destroy no more of the flowers than the damned Norters have."

Slade nodded and started to settle --

"Smart, to stay to the path," a voice said from behind them.

They spun, weapons in hand, ready to face --

A single young man with pale skin and long brown and gold hair. He held a long-stemmed flute, and a multicolored bird sat on his shoulder.

Had he followed them down? Had they never looked back? Was he dangerous?

Oh, yes, dangerous.

Everything here was dangerous, even if it did not look so.

The Lady waved the others to hold and moved through the group to stand in front of this stranger.

She bowed her head to him, and he returned it, though the bird seemed unsettled by her presence.

"You are brave, Lady of the Dragons," the man said. His voice sounded like music, and his clothing glittered, though not with gems.

Magic, Slade thought. Magic flittered around him like fireflies gathering in a field on a warm summer night. "You and your companions show uncommon bravery to have visited here, uninvited and without a guide."

"We come of necessity, sir," she said. Her words seemed to surprise him. "We come to keep evil from befalling the outside world, brother Fae."

Slade had always heard they were human-like, but they seemed more akin to the Dragonkin because of he magic that seemed a constant part of their existence.

The Fae tilted his head and looked at Lady Jade. "Should I care about what happens outside?"

"Oh yes, because if the Norters win out there, then some will stop turning a blind eye to you and your lovely land here. They despise all magic."

"And you think we could not defend ourselves?" he asked. With a brief wave of his hand, magic brightened and formed into a long, sharp blade.

"I'm sure you could. Do you want that war in this lovely land?"

"Ah. No." A flick of his wrist and the weapon disappeared again. "I do not want the battles here. But neither do we care to have humans here."

"The three of us will go," Koya said. He bowed his head, part apology when the Lady looked at him with a frown. "If we are to be any point of contention, then we can remove ourselves. But the Norter army is human, and yet you let them pass?"

"They had allies," the man replied and frowned. "Allies and guides and such have not made many happy here. You have not come at a good time."

"No, we have not," the Lady agreed. She seemed to have relaxed, though Slade couldn't decide why. This was a dangerous man, without a doubt. Maybe she had expected no one to talk about the situation, and he gave her a little hope. Slade wasn't sure if he liked Koya stepping in like he did, either.

However, Koya had always had a knack for knowing things that needed to be done, and he had that look now as well. Slade, who had almost reached out to take hold of him. Koya took his place beside the Lady, and it seemed natural that he should stand there with the Dragonkin.

The Lady gave him one glance and then nodded and turned back to the stranger.

This man had the oddest reaction. He stepped away a pace, but not in fear. There was a look of shock on his face and then surprise. His hand brushed over the air around Koya -- and some of those magic fireflies swarmed around the young priest.

Slade felt a new shiver of astonishment.

"You are blessed with magic," the stranger said.

"Yes, literally blessed," Koya agreed with a bow of his head. "I am a priest of the Ten Gods, and they have shown kindness to me in that respect."

"This is good." The man turned his head to the side as though he heard something else.

He looked back at Koya. "I am Thatyn, Guardian of the Gate, maker of music, and, it seems, your guide through the Exiled Lands. Be at peace, my friends. I'll do my best to help you through the lands, but there will be danger. We are not of one accord about the current troubles. The rocklings, trolls, and their allies have unsettled many by taking in the human army that has -- as you can see from this path -- no care for the land. But then the rocklings and the trolls are often the same, so they could not learn manners from them."

"The Lesslings that went ahead of us -- what happened to them?" The Lady asked, looking around as though she expected to see them arrive.

"I saw no Lesslings. Someone diverted them in the tunnel. We may find them yet."

And with that, he walked past the Lady, Koya, and the rest of them and started down the path again.

They followed.

CHAPTER

FORTY-THREE

Koya had heard something magical whisper to Thatyn. It had given them permission to enter, pleased with the magic Koya held and found them acceptable. He couldn't say why.

This didn't guarantee their safety. The place lured Koya into feeling as if he could relax, and he knew better. There were enemies here. The Norter army could be anywhere along with the creatures who had sided with that army. There might be others who simply disliked humans for all their own reasons.

"Your war," Thatyn said, frowning over the word as though he hated to even pronounce it. "Why do you fight?"

"Not our choice," Koya answered. This was a human conflict, and the others had dragged the Dragonkin into it against their will. "The Norters attacked, but I'm not sure what drove them to this madness this time. Now, either we fight to protect ourselves, or else we let them destroy everything."

"You," Thatyn said, and reached out, brushing a finger along Koya's hair. "You are a Norter."

"By birth," he agreed, surprised that the people here recognized such differences. "I left because the Gods called me, and the Norters would have killed me when they learned of my powers."

"And they would kill you even now for it."

"Oh, yes. I stand against them in the war as well as in religion and magic. I don't understand why they are here, Thatyn. In the world outside, these people are sworn to destroy everything associated with magic. And now we find them trafficking with rocklings and passing through the Forbidden Valley without trouble. It makes us uneasy."

"With cause." Thatyn turned his head slightly, and Koya knew he listened again to someone else. Once more, Koya almost heard the words, and then he saw Thatyn looking at him, a little surprised. "You can hear the call."

"I hear something, though not clearly. My apologies. This is unintentional."

"I'm sure," Thatyn said with a grin. "It is annoying to those of us who pick up the whispers when we don't want to. You are human, and it is a wonder to see such a thing. Do you hear it, too, Lady of the Dragons?"

"Only faintly," Lady Jade admitted. She moved up to walk beside Koya, looking him over again. "I knew you were unusual from the start."

"I had that feeling as well," Takka added and drew laughter from all around. The sound shocked Koya, who gave a nervous glance at his companions.

"I shall want to know the tale of how you came to be together, though not yet. We go to meet more of my people.

There are many decisions we'll need to make about things than I can agree to on my own."

Koya and Lady Jade nodded, and he felt a kinship with her again. How odd.

Koya worried about those who would stand up to the Norters when they crossed through the other side.

Would they have rocklings and trolls with them? The Kasprin army wasn't ready to face that kind of trouble. It would help that they had Kenning with them, who had considerable power. Maybe even the Most Holy would see the genuine danger, though Koya didn't count on it.

Koya had to drive the thoughts away, at least until they were at this meeting. There he might dare more, depending on how these people reacted. Or perhaps he would get Lady Jade to ask the questions he so desperately wanted the others to answer.

He turned to Slade and saw a grim stare as the priest glanced around, plainly not impressed with the beauty of The Forbidden Valley. Koya suspected that the former soldier hoped to find the enemy and settle the trouble. Koya hoped he would remember his priestly patience.

The boy appeared just the opposite. How odd that Malin should be entranced with this strange world of magic. Maybe it helped to blur the horror of what he had lived through. Koya had not been in Ziven long, but the remembrance of those kind people, now all dead, burned him with unexpected sorrow.

If this place was a balm for Malin, Koya would accept it as a pleasant place, no matter what other troubles haunted him. Someone owed the boy a little joy in life again.

The Dragonkin studied the area with mixed emotions as smiles changed to frowns and back again. No one knew what to expect. They reached the pond, and Thatyn moved close to the edge, so the others did as well.

Faces looked out of the water -- Norters, still in uniform, and quite dead, their faces contorted in shock more than fear. Koya started to back away.

"You're safe," Thatyn said. "They angered Ala -- this is her pond -- with their disregard for the plants and animals that showed no fear of them. A soldier reached down and broke the neck of a rabbit, shoving the body into his belt -- I believe he is that one in the middle."

Koya took a quick look and then away again, hoping the sight of those men didn't haunt his nights forever. Thatyn watched Koya, his eyes narrowed this time, as though he couldn't quite understand the reaction.

"I would rather no one died," Koya whispered. "Even the enemy, if he would just turn around and go back to his own place."

"We thought all humans were bloodthirsty."

"I suspect there are myths we have about your people that are not all true, either," Koya replied. "We are individuals. Most of us seek peace and a chance to live our lives without fear. We're willing to work hard for such a life, but there are always others who want to do little and have much, and they're more apt to violence because it's easier than work."

"Ah. Interesting concept, and one that can, to some degree, even apply here. We might find we have concepts in common."

"Many things," Koya agreed, glad that they were passing beyond the water. "I wish we could have met under better circumstances. I would have found this place fascinating and want to stay for a while to learn more."

Thatyn said no more.

They left the pond behind and moved on into the forest. Peace spread around them, and except for their footsteps, he heard only the call of birds and the sound of a small brook rushing over stones. Tall ash and pines vied with each other for space, and where the sunlight -- or whatever lit this place -- peeked through the shadows, bright flowers caught the light and held it with a gentle glow.

They had walked some distance into the woods before Koya noticed the first small face peering out from the v of a tree trunk and watching them. He gave a startled cry and stepped back before he passed too close, and the small figure grinned and dropped out of sight again.

"Wee folk," Thatyn said with a brief laugh. "They're insatiably curious about everything and afraid of very little. Except that they love to play pranks, they would make wonderful companions."

Bright laughter echoed from the trees all around, and Thatyn smiled but didn't slow.

"Not today, friends. We head to the council, though you are welcome to come along. But no tricks. This matter concerns the lives of many, and if we slow now, it will bring disaster to some.

"No fun then, no fun," a gruff voice said from straight above them. "But I'll travel with you. I'm curious, I am, to know what comes of this strangeness."

A small figure, no more than a foot high and dressed in forest green, slipped over a branch above them, and dropped onto Thatyn's shoulder, opposite the bird, but beside Koya. He had the look of an older man with a neatly trimmed gray beard and bushy eyebrows. He took hold of Thatyn's collar as they moved away again. However, he watched Koya with narrowed eyes, plainly mistrusting him.

Koya gave him a bow.

"Sir," he said.

"Oh, polite enough for a human, at least."

"And what would you know about humans?" Thatyn asked.

"I've heard things," the newcomer replied, settling more comfortably on his companion's shoulder. "Enough to know, for instance, that the humans and the Dragonkin people should have knives at each other's throats, rather than walking so calmly side-by-side."

"Times change," Lady Jade answered. She seemed amused and enthralled by the wee man. "And we have found that we have a common enemy trying to trick us into war with one another."

"But you are too wise to fall for the tricks," the little man said with a laugh, and perhaps made a joke although Koya didn't think even Thatyn could tell.

Koya could hear voices ahead, and they didn't sound at all calm and welcoming. He cast a glance at Thatyn, who gave a slight shrug, nearly unsettling both man and bird.

"They are not happy with all that has happened of late. Armies should not pass through our lands, but they at least came with guides. You, though -- your group, walking in as though it was your right --"

"Far better than trying to sneak in," Slade replied from behind them. "That would have been the worst ploy. We had to follow the army, that's all. We just need to know what they will do."

Thatyn nodded but said no more as they came through the last of the trees and into a glade.

In the center stood a circle of substantial white stones with stone benches along the edge. People milled about already, most of them dressed in the same forest greens as Thatyn, which made Koya think this might be a uniform of sorts, and some carried bows, swords, and shields.

Everyone turned and fell silent at the approach of the group. Oh, this could not be a suitable place for the three humans, Koya thought. They should have let the Dragonkin go through without them. He trusted Lady Jade, Takka, and the others to do their best, and could have convinced Kenning to do the same.

But they came in.

Why? Why, when they knew it would be trouble --

Everything was trouble.

"Sit here, in the place of honor," Thatyn said, waving to a set of benches made of lovely green marble. Koya gave a silent nod, happy for the chance to get off his feet again --

A woman snarled when Koya started to sit and marched toward them with her hand on the sword hilt at her hip. She looked much like Thatyn except for shorter and curly hair, and a snarl on her thinner face.

"You will not treat them as guests," she said, her words sharp and her look filled with rage. "Not here, in our place --"

"They were called to this meeting, Reed. We have not brought them as prisoners --"

"They should be locked in chains, shoved into a hole --"

"They were *invited* here," Thatyn repeated, and this time his own voice took on a bit of anger. "We do not mistreat people we invite as guests, even if they are enemies. Take your seat, Reed."

Reed showed a little surprise and then reddened with embarrassment, which could not have improved her feelings toward the group. The others, at least, had kept back from the confrontation. It could have turned bad because Lady Jade appeared ready to cause trouble as well. Takka looked worried when he glanced her way.

Koya settled on the bench, and Lady Jade looked at the bench and then sighed and dropped next to him. She gave a swift set of orders to her people. They didn't look thrilled either, but they sat on nearby benches, while Takka, Malin, and Slade joined the two of them. They made, he supposed, a rather impressive looking group.

"In council back in the True Lands there is often a confrontation to decide who has the place of honor and the right to speak before the others," Lady Jade explained aloud. Reed at least looked worried this time. "I had thought, for a moment, that this might be like home, and I admit that I welcomed it."

"We are civilized here," Reed said, scowling again.

"But not very polite," Slade answered and surprised them all. "There. Now we have insulted each other, and we're all equal. I think there is more important business at hand, and quite honestly, the sooner we're on to it, the sooner you will no longer have to deal with us."

Koya had expected the woman to go for her sword. Instead, she gave Slade a somewhat more civil bow and retreated across the circle, sitting down with some others.

The rest did the same, except for Thatyn, who placed the small man and the bird on a bench and then moved to the center of the circle. He unexpectedly pulled up the flute, and the soft and beautiful notes filled the area and silenced everyone. It would have been worse than impolite to talk during such music.

Magic. Koya realized Thatyn played the essence of pure magic in the sound, and it must have taken a master craftsman to shape the powers as well as he did. The notes calmed them all, though not through a spell forced on them. The music soothed and refreshed. By the time the notes slipped gently away, and he lowered the flute, everyone looked calmer afterward.

"There," Thatyn said and sounded out of breath. "That's better. We need clear heads and cool tempers for this, my friends. There is far too much going on. And while none of us wants humans crossing into our land, these three are not the worst of it."

"And they don't trample the flowers," the little man said, almost a shout in the near silence. The bird beside him jumped and then gave him a reproachful stare. "They don't trample flowers, and they don't kill the little wild things. The trolls and the rocklings -- they don't care about the joy of life either. They brought the evil humans in."

"And you know more about it than you've said so far, don't you, Pine?" Thatyn asked.

"Oh, yes, oh, yes. The Wee Folk have gone skipping over the highland rocks, much to our own peril. We told you, trail walkers, that things were happening that boded ill. We said it, didn't we?"

"Yes, you did," Reed agreed, and she even sounded a little contrite. "But we didn't listen. Forgive us, Pine. We thought it just more of your jokes."

"Well, well," he looked down at his feet and shook his head. "I suppose it were hard to know the difference sometimes. But I can tell you, this is more than the rocklings and trolls. It's all the things that live in the ground and the dark -- those beings have always lingered up in the highlands and never come down to join the rest of us civilized folk."

That brought a whisper of laugher, which must have made it some local joke. Koya was just glad to everyone had calmed, though he fretted about what Pine had seen.

"Please, tell us more," Thatyn said, nodding Pine.

Pine looked more serious, and Koya noticed how worried that made Reed. The others grew increasingly upset. This likely meant more trouble than Koya wanted, but better to hear it from this group rather than run into something later.

Most of what Pine said made little sense to him. The Wee Man named places and gave the designations of creatures and even some personal names. Those won hisses of surprise now and then but nods as well. The tale took the interest away from the humans and the Dragonkin. Lady Jade seemed surprised to see how they had all but been forgotten.

Shock, Koya thought, had won this reaction from the locals. They listened to Pine's tale with growing dismay.

"There have been other humans, too," Pine said and drew Koya's wandering attention and found Pine staring at them. "And humans they were, not Dragonkin, though one pretended to be. I don't think the dumb rock eaters knew the difference, either. Just a bit of colored hair, and a bow, and the man bought the rocklings with a promise of freedom to do what they pleased beyond the pass."

"There, that's what won them," Thatyn said with a nod. "In all the ages we've been here, those who dwell in the highlands have always chafed that we don't allow them full reign to do what they please because they would tear down the woods and make rock piles of everything."

"And they are stupid enough to believe that some outsider would give them that right?" Reed asked.

"There was a rockling," Koya dared say, his voice trembling with the memory despite himself. "It traveled with the Norter army, helping them. It knew they were not Dragonkin. But it seemed ... maybe not sane? I don't know if I could judge such a thing, but I had an odd feeling from it."

"Basher, I bet," someone offered. "I told you a while back that he was hanging about the tunnel. We chased him away. I think we were all fools, my friends."

"And now we're all paying for it. An army of humans is in our lands, which makes these three and their almost-human companions hardly worth our notice," Reed said, still sounding contemptuous. "And I wonder, I do, what the trolls and the rocklings intend to do because they will know we won't accept this treachery."

"Oh, now there's a dark thought," someone added, and others whispered agreement.

"And one that makes me think we're wasting time sitting here."

"What about these humans?" Reed asked, waving her hand towards them.

"Send them back out, take them on -- it hardly matters. They aren't the problem," Pine said.

No one argued, although that didn't explain what would happen with them. Koya looked at Lady Jade, who shook her head as if she did not understand. That made Koya feel not quite as stupid.

"Will you give them over into my hands, then?" Thatyn asked, glancing around the group.

"Oh yes, you take them," someone answered. The others even laughed a little at the haste of the words.

"This is serious trouble, my friends," Thatyn said, looking from face-to-face. That stopped them again. "This is not, as we first thought, just a business of outsiders moving through places they ought not to have been. There are groups on the move within our own lands, and we've been blind to them. Complacent. I think we shall find ourselves tried over the next few days. I want to know where the Norter Army is. It marched out of the cave and went -- where?"

"The highlands, I'd guess," Pine said.

"Perhaps so, but here's a thing to consider: The path the humans took to Ala's Pond was narrow. There is no print of troll, let alone rockling, along the way. I suspect something else led them through, and I fear it might be one more akin to us."

"Oh, now there's another dark thought," Pine said and shook his head. "You may be right, Thatyn. And that makes this even more difficult, doesn't it?"

Nods again, and then it seemed they had some signal that the meeting had ended. The others stood, gathered into small groups and headed away ... and stopped at a soft trill of sound from Thatyn's flute. He played only for a moment and then lowered the instrument again.

"Be careful, my friends. Be very careful. We have not faced this kind of trouble in centuries, and we did not come into it aware and prepared. If we had known, there would have been more guards on the watch. Pine, did you see anything more we should know about?"

"No, I fear not," the little man admitted, still standing on his bench. "We were trying to track the highland creatures, and we didn't even hear about the human army until they were well beyond our usual range. A few of my people have tried to follow, but I haven't heard from them yet."

"You are wiser than the rest of us, Pine," Thatyn said and bowed his head.

Pine burst into bright laughter. "Now, there's a line that's bound to go down in legend!"

Even the dour Reed laughed this time. She had, Koya suspected, realized the full extent of the trouble and knew she would find true enemies. She didn't need to focus on the three humans and their Dragonkin companions.

The others had turned to leave again, but Reed stayed by Thatyn, who gave her an odd look.

"You'll need help shepherding them through this," she said with a wave of her long-fingered hand and a slight smile.

"You're right," Thatyn admitted. "I think it best if we head after the army -- it appears both their trouble and ours align with that group."

Reed nodded and looked back at the group, her eyes lingering on Lady Jade.

"We go where you think best," Lady Jade said with a gracious bow of her head. "But after the army seems best. They mean harm. Maybe not to this place, though from what I've seen, they've done it no good so far."

"True."

Reed looked at the humans and Dragonkin over again and nodded. "I think I will find it interesting to travel with outsiders. We live in a little world here, no matter how perfect it might be. I would like to know more about the Outer Lands."

"I'm going back to my woods," Pine said, walking in among them and nodding up towards their faces. "We'll do some scouting and see what we can learn. I'll talk to you later, Tha."

"Be careful," Thatyn warned. "Say the same to the rest of the Wee Folk."

"We will, friend. You do the same. You make far larger targets."

Koya watched the small man bound off into the woods. Then Koya and the others stood and followed Thatyn and Reed, no doubt heading toward new adventures.

CHAPTER

FORTY-FOUR

The night passed in relative quiet. The Most Holy had shouted and railed at the world for a while, but he must have screamed himself hoarse, because he fell silent before midnight, and everything settled down.

Kenning slept through almost until dawn, curled up safely in a corner of the General's own tent, well-guarded by the soldiers. At the same time, he protected himself, Lord Oak, and the General from anything magical. Something tried to brush against his ward late at night, but he pushed the magic aside.

He waited for a while, and when nothing more happened, Kenning went back to sleep. He needed rest. They all did.

Kenning thought the prod might have been from the Most Holy, but it hadn't been powerful. He considered the incident when he awoke and headed down to the latrine. Kenning knew the Most Holy would not be up this early. He saw only the flickering of a few watch-fires at the edges of the other camp. They didn't need trouble from that quarter.

When he returned, Kenning stopped outside the tent and turned toward the Forbidden Valley -- and froze in shock, his breath held.

A light flickered over what had been midnight black until now. It had only just started, he thought, or someone would have seen and given a shout. The glow -- blue and green and a hint of red -- moved like lightning caught in a cloud, dancing across the wall of darkness. Beautiful, but he knew this show meant trouble.

The cry went up. He could hear the General and stepped into the tent, lifting his hand in a gesture of peace when both he and Lord Oak reached for weapons.

"It's all right. Something is going on, but it's at the entrance to the Valley, and I don't think we can do anything about it. Lights playing over the black. Pretty, and maybe dangerous, but they're staying there for the moment."

"We don't need anything like this," General Stanmark grumbled and ran a hand through his matted hair. He still looked half asleep. "It will spook everyone."

"Most Holy Bastard is already on the move," Lord Oak said, looking out the tent opening.

"Well, there is a miracle all of its own, to see the Most Holy awake at this hour," Kenning offered.

The General grunted, and the two older men headed out toward the latrines.

Kenning kept watch on the Most Holy's camp, wishing he could go back to sleep. He also glanced at the strange magic. They didn't dim in the brighter light of dawn and had not changed at all by the time the General and Lord Oak returned.

"Priest?" Lord Oak said, dropping a hand on his shoulder.

"They're pretty lights. But they do nothing except --" Kenning stopped and looked back at Lord Oak. "Except they distract us, my Lord."

"So they do," General Stanmark replied, and gave a quick look all around. "It might just be a coincidence, but it won't hurt to keep watch elsewhere, too."

Lord Oak nodded, his eyes narrowed, and as he stared towards the place where he obviously expected to see trouble. Kenning glanced at the Most Holy's camp as well.

"I've infiltrated four men into his followers," General Stanmark said with his voice soft. "I have heard nothing from them yet, though. My people were told to be discreet, but I believed they would get some word to me by now."

"Do you think he has them held prisoner?" Lord Oak asked, frowning again.

"Maybe something else," Kenning began and moved so he could lift his hand discreetly and test the magic of that camp. "Something far worse. I believe he's used a spell on everyone there to keep them in his control."

"He's what?" General Stanmark said, his face going red. "He can do that?"

"I haven't heard of such a thing in our times, and it's forbidden in Temple scripture except where a group of people might need forcibly calmed to save them or preserve the peace," Kenning replied. He mimicked Lord Oak's move running a hand through his hair. " The Most Holy probably convinced himself that there is cause for using such a spell."

"What should we do?" Stanmark asked.

"Nothing at the moment," Kenning answered with a quick nod. "It would take magic to break that spell, and it might not be safe for the people involved. Wait and see what the Most Holy does. If he moves against us, then I'll do what I can."

"You stood up to him yesterday. Can you do it again today?"

"If I need to," Kenning replied, giving General Stanmark a nod and showing no doubt. "But it's those lights that really bother me, sirs, and what they might mean."

General Stanmark nodded. He turned to go, pausing for one suspicious stare at the other camp before heading off to his own work. The soldiers were uneasy, and they needed their leader. Lord Oak stood by Kenning. He stared at the entrance to the Hidden Valley and shook his head.

"This might be nothing, you know," Kenning said and wished he could believe those words.

"Oh, but that's not true. This is something, even if it isn't a problem for us. I don't remember hearing about such a display before, but this is a desolate area, with no one eager to settle below that mass of magic."

"I haven't heard of anything, either." Kenning stopped and then nodded. "I think I'll put some of the good brothers in Templeton on this to find any information they can locate. We've quite a few books there. They might come across something."

"Oh, excellent plan, my friend. I'm not much of a book person myself, but I can see where such knowledge would help in this case."

Kenning headed into the tent and his supplies. Others began cooking breakfast, and he heard a steady whisper of worry as they went about their work. Kenning contacted the Temple and enjoyed talking to his friends, though he didn't dare waste too much power. They sounded happy to hear that Koya was alive and with Slade. They were eager to do the research and curious about when he would be back home.

"I don't know, my brothers," he said, giving a brief sigh of regret. He saw General Stanmark had come in and looked at him with a nod of commiseration. He hadn't considered that even the general might want to be somewhere else. "I'll return when I can, but the matters here need my attention. Do you still have calm there?"

"Yes, sir," Armath said. "We've dealt with some worried people, but nothing has happened, so they've all gone back to their lives. Some from the various towns escorted two of the brothers to Ziven so they could say a chant for the dead and get everyone buried. It cannot have been a pretty place, but they got the work done."

"Praise the Gods for that."

"We wish you were back with us, but we understand that the needs of others put you elsewhere. Take care, sir."

"I will. Let me know if you learn anything."

The rune went cool. Food sat on the table, and Lord Oak came to join them. The two men looked glum.

"It's not all that bad. Here's a thing to consider: The lights are only lights so far. They are distracting, but that may only be a side effect and have nothing to do with us at all."

"And what about the Most Holy and what he's doing?"

"He's spending considerable magic on something that won't win him anything in the end. He'll tire out. The work of controlling those people will keep him busy. I don't like that he's done, but there is far worse he could be doing."

"Yes, I suppose so," General Stanmark agreed. He grabbed an apple and a small knife, attacking the fruit rather mercilessly. "I don't like this sitting and waiting. I want to know what's going on."

"As do I," Kenning said. "But I can't reach Slade or Koya. I feared I wouldn't. They are now inside that shell of magic, and nothing is getting out. Which is good, you know. There are things we would not want to have loosed on this part of the world."

"Why are you so damned logical, and especially at this time of day?" Lord Oak asked with a laugh.

"Years of morning prayers and dawn meditations," Kenning replied and grinned to see them both blush.

They had a pleasant enough breakfast, broken at the end by the announcement that the Most Holy was on his way, with a trail of followers. Kenning stood.

"Maybe the two of you would rather not be there for this confrontation," he said. "He will not be in a congenial mood."

"Has he ever been in a good mood?" Lord Oak asked.

"Not that I remember, although he could occasionally be almost cheery as long as he was getting his way. Too bad we can't throw him something to keep him pleased now."

"You two go meet him," General Stanmark said. "I don't want him to think I'll come running every time he shows his head. You shouldn't look as though you have no backing here, Kenning."

"Lord Oak, if you would care to go with me?"

"Oh, why not? At least this is something to do."

They had no trouble finding the Most Holy and his followers. They chanted as they walked, the Most Holy in the lead. He wasn't moving fast, which only made Kenning think he was right about the magic. This spell had to take considerable power to keep those people in line with him, even if he only brought a dozen.

Kenning decided not to allow the man to have the first words. Perhaps that was petty, but he stepped forward, a hand waving Lord Oak to stay back. Kenning stared the Most Holy in the face without even a bow of his head.

"I know what you've done to these people. It is an abomination in the eyes of the Ten Gods, and you know it."

The Most Holy had not expected an attack. His face, as expected, grew red, and his mouth opened and closed several times. Then he glanced past to Lord Oak and smirked.

"You accuse me of doing wrong when you have done the same? Or is it that you pretend the Gods are on your side, and that's how a backwater priest drew the attention of a Lord?"

"I am now convinced of how delusional you are."

Even Lord Oak made a slight hissing sound at those words, but Kenning meant them and watched how the Most Holy reacted. There was no comprehension in the stare he gave Kenning, only contempt and hatred.

If they had been back at the Temple, and Kenning had seen that look, it would have quelled him. It had not done so for Koya, which reminded him of what had befallen his friend. Better not to push this or be ready for an attack.

"Is there a reason you came to the army camp?" Kenning asked. He even kept his voice somewhat calm this time.

"I am not here to speak to you," Most Holy said, his head lifting. "I am here to see the General. Bring him to me."

Kenning almost said he was not the Most Holy's servant boy -- but in fact, on one level, that was a position he held. If he refused, there would be those in the army who would mistrust his humility, if nothing else. He didn't want to create distrust.

So he bowed and turned away, shocking Lord Oak, who moved with him.

"Why would you play lackey to that man?" he whispered fiercely as they slipped out of range of hearing.

"Because this was a test. If I had said no, Most Holy would have pointed out that I was not a priest, because all priests are answerable to him on that level. It would have been too easy of a win for him, Lord Oak, and just led to more annoying posturing. Besides, I want to know if he really has anything to say to General Stanmark."

"True on all accounts," the man agreed, though he didn't look any better for understanding. "But the next time he'll ask you to do something more difficult."

"Oh, yes. Most Holy will keep pushing until he learns my breaking point and then uses it against me. We can play these games for a few days. I am only keeping momentary peace."

"Yes, you're right, but I just hate to see him win at all. Ah, but that's petty of me, I suppose. However, I suggest, friend Kenning, that you don't rush off to greet him every time, either. Don't let the Most Holy think he automatically has control of you, because General Stanmark and I might have to step in to correct him."

"You shouldn't --"

"Kenning, you are our only hope of contact with Slade and Koya. You are helping us through this trouble, while Cedric is creating more problems. Why should we allow him to control you when you're the one we need?"

"Ah. But I can't reach them now --"

"That doesn't mean you never will again. And Kenning, you've offered more help even outside of that magic than anyone else. I'm curious to learn what your priests have to say about those lights. I don't want to ride all the way to Templeton to find out."

He nodded, realizing the man was right, but it didn't make his position any easier.

Except he knew the Ten Gods stood with him and his allies.

CHAPTER

FORTY-FIVE

K oya awoke to the sound of thunder rumbling overhead in the clear blue sky. A bright light flashed, but not like normal lightning. It played through the air, darting and circling and casting off trails of rainbow colors. He sat up and noticed the others were doing the same. Rain had begun to fall in a splatter of cold against his face.

"Ah," Thatyn said with a shake of his head. "This is not usual in the valley. We have storms now and then, but rarely of any power."

"I think we best find some better cover," Reed suggested.

Thatyn agreed with a quick nod, and everyone gathered up their supplies. If these two suspected something was wrong, Koya and his companions would not be slow to follow orders. Koya thought Reed looked relieved to see them get straight to work.

"This has an odd feel," Thatyn admitted as they hurried out of the glen where they'd gone to sleep a few hours before. A sort of twilight had come -- Koya had been glad of it since it gave some sense of time passing. "I have the impression this is the nature of the place reacting to something it does not like."

They headed for the nearest trees, though Koya wasn't confident that would provide safety. The wind had picked up --

Glowing lights darted straight at them. He backed up in haste.

"Pixies," Reed said. "They're just frightened."

The small, winged creatures swarmed Thatyn and held tight to him. Their little wings glowed, and now that they stopped, Koya could see they were clothed mostly in flower petals and bits of leaves. He barely heard their high-pitched voices above the storm, though.

Lady Jade looked bothered. "I think they're saying something about the Lesslings," she said with a worried glance at the woods and another at the sky. "If they are nearby, I hope I can get them in hand."

Thatyn seemed to have calmed the pixies that held to his clothing as they entered the covering of these trees. The pixies showed a sudden fascination in Malin, probably because he was the only one with no magic. Before too long, he carried a few of his own. They clutched at his shirt and his hair. He looked delighted.

"Pixies are born new to the season," Thatyn explained, smiling at the little things that climbed on his arms. "When the days grow colder, and winter is coming, they find safe places, spin cocoons, and sleep. They are reborn in the spring, so they are always children."

Koya wondered what that would be like. A blessing? You would not remember the evil of the year before. Was there wickedness here? He supposed so since they had trouble with the trolls. But not recognizing past problems also meant that they couldn't learn from them, and every danger would be new and frightening.

Thatyn found one of Lord Pine's people, an older woman who took the pixies into the hollow of a tree. Thatyn had smiled and bid them farewell, but as soon as they disappeared, he seemed to turn serious again.

"I don't know if we can help, but we need to find out what's gone wrong," Lady Jade suggested as they huddled together near the edge of the trees. "If this is something that our presence has set into motion, then we should figure out how to make it right."

Thatyn and Reed both nodded. Koya didn't believe this trouble was their fault, though. He couldn't feel any of the magic directed at them. Besides, they were not the only strangers in the Forbidden Valley. He wondered what the Norter army was doing.

Where were the Lesslings?

They hurried onward, Koya expecting to find trouble. Then, as they came over a slight hill, they discovered the scene of a battle that could not have been more than an hour old, though the living had departed the field. The fighting must have been furious and fast. Bodies of several types littered the ground, many that Koya couldn't name. Thatyn and Reed stared in stunned disbelief, but it was Takka who said something Koya had not noted.

"Lesslings," he said and stood from the body of one of the fae and pointed to the wounds. "Lesslings were a part of this attack."

Lady Jade whispered beneath her breath and nodded agreement. "This is worse than I expected of them. They were a problem outside, but I never imagined -- Gods, what is going on?"

If Reed had meant to say anything about the Dragonkin and control of the Lesslings, she changed her mind at Lady Jade's grief. Thatyn had gone around to the other bodies, his face set in anger that Koya didn't like to see. He didn't want to know what magic the piper would play if he took up the instrument now.

"Not just the Lesslings," he said. "I've found signs of trolls, ogres, rocklings ... and humans."

"This is madness," Reed added and shook her head, looking around as though there might be enemies here still. Koya considered it lucky that she didn't turn that look on the Dragonkin and the humans in her company. Her anger, though, covered loss that Koya could feel, being closest to her. He suspected, from the look of despair, that she knew these people. After all, this was a small valley, even if magic seemed to make it larger.

"Why did they fight here?" Slade asked, looking the scene over from the point of view of a soldier. Koya appreciated that part of the man's background just then. "Was this a chance encounter, or was this something planned?"

Reed and Thatyn both stopped what they were doing and turned to him. This wasn't a question Koya would have thought to ask. Lady Jade might have if she hadn't been thinking so much about the Lesslings.

"The trails cross here," Thatyn said, his voice softer and shaking now. He waved to the right where a path came from more woods and crossed their own. He took a deeper breath. "It might have been chance but --"

Thatyn stopped again and turned to the right, his hand lifting towards the storm that was still raging, though it had turned off in that direction. Reed moved up beside him and shaking her head with worry.

"What is the problem?" Koya dared ask. "I can almost feel a touch --"

"Something draws me," Lady Jade said with a tilt of her head. Koya noted that the other Dragonkin were much the same.

"This path," Thatyn said, waving a hand to the trail that led toward distant hills. "This one will take us to the Well of Power. The place is guarded by dragons, the most magical beings in all the world. They chose this valley for our sanctuary because the Well is one of the few locations where the magical energy of the earth is close to the surface. The Well keeps us safe here. But the storm -- I think it is a sign of a true battle at the Well where the dragons guard."

"We must go help them," Lady Jade said. "We must save the dragons."

Koya felt a chill at those words and the look on her face. The others didn't argue as they started down the path. They wouldn't be too long in finding trouble, and the Lesslings would not find him weak or forgiving this time.

CHAPTER

FORTY-SIX

Kenning found a quiet place by the General's tent where he could sit and pray and meditate on all that troubled him. Mostly, though, he considered the problems with the Most Holy. Kenning accepted terms like unsettled when Kenning thought about the man. Now he tried new thoughts and unwelcome ones.

Insane was one of the worst. Demon-possessed also played in those thoughts, though Kenning considered the second unlikely.

Demons had a signature that anyone with power could feel, or so he'd learned from the books. There hadn't been demons in the land for centuries.

Insane seemed far more likely.

That didn't make this any better. A person like the Most Holy with his power and no link to reality? Gods help them all.

The trouble with Cedric at a time like this was catastrophic for everyone, not just for the Temple.

He prayed again for the Ten Gods to aid him.

Instead of help, he found another problem heading their way. As the pretty magic lightning at the entrance to the Forbidden Valley grew more powerful, it drew a natural storm to it. He could see the clouds starting to build over the plain and felt the first cool breeze. Magic and nature interacting often created trouble, and he feared this would get dangerous.

Kenning reluctantly left his little spot of tranquility and headed off to find General Stanmark and Lord Oak. The guards said they were examining the supplies, and he turned that way, though the wind grew so swiftly that everyone had taken note and realized it was not natural.

The Most Holy hadn't missed the incredible speed and strength of the changing weather.

"Devils!" Cedric shouted into the wind, so loud that Kenning heard him though the dust obscured the view. He turned towards the Most Holy's camp, where he could already see people moving frantically and not in any way that would help.

Cedric rushed straight for the military camp, and Kenning could hear him shouting to get to their weapons and prepare because they were under attack.

"What in the name of all the hells is he doing!" Stanmark demanded as he caught up with Kenning.

Lord Oak followed and cursed enough that Kenning gave him a shake of his head.

"Don't do that.

We have enough troubles."

Lord Oak started to say something and stopped. "I'm not used to working with priests. What do we do?"

"He's spreading panic," General Stanmark warned, grabbing at one soldier and shaking him before he let go. "If we don't get everyone in hand, we will lose the battle before it happens!"

The General was right. Kenning didn't think the Most Holy intentionally tried to create trouble this time, but his emotions were out of control, and so was his power. Kenning had to step in and do something.

Calm. Kenning had to counteract the Most Holy's panic with his own composure and magic, and he wasn't confident he was up to the battle. He stepped forward. If they didn't get control, then they had no chance of surviving whatever might come through the magic wall. This was not the battle they came to fight, but it might be the most important one. Kenning hoped the Ten Gods stayed with him as he rushed to fight the leader of his religion.

CHAPTER

FORTY-SEVEN

The devastating emotions Slade had felt at the battle site had hit him far harder than he'd expected. He'd frozen, hardly able to even breathe when he first saw all the dead. Slade had left the army, walked away from the killing, and found a place where he could help rather than destroy. He wanted nothing to do with this --

Slade had taken a breath. Another.

He didn't look at the bodies. Instead, he focused on his companions and refused to show this weakness to them. Koya would understand. Slade didn't think the Dragonkin people would, and he wasn't even certain Malin would comprehend the horror this scene brought to him.

The boy looked pale, though, and he kept silent.

He couldn't escape, so what could he do that would help instead? He was their human guard, he supposed. That purpose settled his nerves and gave him the strength to go on.

He'd already pointed them towards the more critical battle by asking his question about why this one had happened.

Koya was having trouble keeping up with the others. He was weaker than Slade had expected, and even without the Most Holy's curse, he had taken injuries enough. Malin and DK had already slowed to stay with him, despite that he tried to wave them on. Slade put a hand on Koya's arm.

"Slow," he said. "Let the others rush ahead to engage. We are the reserve."

"That doesn't bode well if they need us," Koya mumbled, but then he took a deeper breath and kept going.

They didn't have far to go. Slade could hear the battle as they topped a rise and saw the fighting below. Reed and Lady Jade fought side-by-side against trolls, and the rest of the Dragonkin had spread out and attacked anything that fought against them. This included the Lesslings, and many of those creatures had already fallen.

Then the green hill behind the battle moved.

Slade had not realized dragons would be so massive. The creature gave a shout of anger, and the world trembled around them so that even the trolls and rocklings retreated in haste from the snapping teeth and loud roars that shook the ground.

Beyond the dragon stood a column of pure power, the light flashing with rainbow colors. Another dragon stood guard there, this one blue rather than green, and an apparent last line of defense.

Slade thought everything was going well until more trolls, rocklings and other creatures arrived at a run from the right -- along with the damned Norter army, still fighting with their unlikely allies. He watched them and thought he saw more madness than intention in their movements.

Slade and Koya used what magic they could to beat the newcomers back, but it wouldn't hold for long, and Slade feared that if they had allies of their own, they would be late to the battle.

"We can't -- we can't hold them," Thatyn said. He'd retreated to where Slade and the others fought. Blood ran down from a wound in his shoulder and had shoved the pipe he played into his belt. He had a sword in hand instead and used it to kill a Lessling that leapt at them.

"I don't know what to do.

They dare not take command of the Well from the dragons! If they do, it will be a disaster for everyone, both here in the valley and outside!"

"Whatever they promised the Norter Army, I think this was the actual reason to draw them in.

What can we --" Koya began, but then stopped speaking.

The dragons no longer gave roars of anger. Nor did they snap out with their long necks and kill enemies with a single bite. The green dragon stood beside the blue, and the soft humming sound they made had been lost beneath the battle. Magic moved in threads from the column of power and intertwined into a flat circle on the ground, like a lake made of light. Slade thought he saw shapes within it.

Lady Jade and Reed had retreated, and the Dragonkin came with them, many wounded and a few dead left behind.

"Magic," Reed gasped. "Powerful magic. I don't know --"

"Portal," Lady Jade replied, equally winded and worried, but her fingers felt out the magic. "They're creating a gate that links to the barrier and straight out into the human lands. We need to push the enemy through and get the battle away from here. If the others take down a dragon, they could wrest control of the Well from the other. Nothing would stop them from ruling all the world."

"Then we do it, with all the magic we can shove at them," Slade said and brought power to his hand. He would do this right. "Koya, be ready to warn our friends on the other side. I suspect trouble is coming their way."

CHAPTER

FORTY-EIGHT

T he magic dancing on the surface of the barrier had changed. Kenning noted the surge of colors in passing, more concerned with the trouble of the massive storm on their side. The lightning and rain had become erratic so that everything might be still in one moment, and powerful winds would take down tents in the next. The soldiers had rallied behind their General and Lord Oak, though.

That helped to save their lives as the spell Cedric had used to control people finally failed. The looks some of them gave to the Most Holy sent that man backing off in haste.

Just in time.

The storm died down for a moment, but in that stillness came a loud boom, and a rift appeared in the magical block on the edge of the Forbidden Valley. Things flew out as though they'd been thrown through, and at almost the same time, Kenning heard the frantic voice of Koya.

"Are you there?" Koya shouted.

"What in the name of the Gods --" Kenning demanded, pulling out the rune from where he kept it close.

"Kill everything except the Fae and the Dragonkin and anything they protect!" Koya shouted -- an extraordinary order from a priest who typically erred on the side of kindness to the point of making life difficult for himself. "We dare not let them get loose in the human lands!"

"Kill the Lesslings!" a woman yelled. Was that the Dragonkin leader he'd met? "They're far too dangerous, and they know too much of the land. They'll help the enemy."

General Stanmark had been standing close by. He looked at the rune in no little dismay. Then he shouted orders for his people and led them into the attack. The storm swept back, adding to the terror and confusion. He couldn't see the Most Holy, but he didn't expect the man to be helping.

Kenning was the only priest here who could help get the more massive creatures in hand. After he saw one of the rocklings kill several soldiers in one swing, he had no qualms about holding them still with magic while the others did the work. He did not want these things loose in the human lands.

He hadn't expected the Most Holy to attack him. It almost worked, too, with so much power in the air. Kenning didn't notice the attack coming straight at him at first. He spun in that direction to meet the power -- almost too late, and the surge of energy he used left him dizzy.

Cedric rushed toward him with fire in his hands and a look of madness on his face.

Kenning had no choice but to fight back, magic against magic. The Most Holy could still call upon the power latent in the area, but Kenning ... Kenning felt the touch of the Gods themselves as he moved and stood before the man who should have been an ally.

Cedric had chosen. Even with all the creatures around them, he refused to see the true enemies.

Kenning didn't regret his own decisions as he prayed to the Ten Gods for their help and guidance amid all this madness.

CHAPTER

FORTY-NINE

K oya did his best to push the enemy into the portal. Slade worked with him while Malin stood at their backs, providing protection with a sword he had gotten somewhere. Takka stayed with Koya. They helped shove the creatures through the portal with both weapon and magic.

Thatyn had fallen with a cut across his back, but Koya grabbed him out of danger's way and even used magic to stop the bleeding. Koya faced troubles of his own, though. With the connection to the other land open, Koya felt the curse again, and probably worse since the Most Holy was close.

They'd taken the enemy by surprise at first, but they were rallying behind Bertand now. Koya was surprised to learn the man had survived this far.

"Takka," Koya said, almost breathless. "Do you see --"

"From the fort," Takka replied with a hiss of anger that attracted Lady Jade's attention.

Takka spoke something in a rush of words that Koya didn't understand, but he also pointed to the figure.

Lady Jade pulled down her bow, drew an arrow, and aimed. The Dragonkin had not used their bows much since they were useless against rocklings and trolls. She waited, just waited while the others fought around them -- until Bertand looked her way and froze at the sight. The man knew from where his death would come, and in the next heartbeat, the arrow went through his chest, and he died. She had handled it well, that bit of revenge by the Dragonkin.

The enemy army fell into disarray as the Norters yelled out in anger and fear at the death of their leader. Others moved in to take advantage of the change, but the chaos didn't help either side.

Thatyn fumbled at his belt and brought up the pipe. "This should help, but I can't hold them for long," he admitted.

Lady Jade nodded.

Her people had used their bows to take down several of the Norter army -- another act of revenge against those who had pretended to be Dragonkin to start a war.

Thatyn played a beguiling tune that reminded Koya of the rush of water along a brook on a warm summer day. For a moment, some of the more massive creatures seemed to pause. Koya found the music enthralling, but he kept his head, and when the others stopped fighting, he used his magic to shove all the harder.

By then, they had more help. Lord Pine arrived with many of his people, more fae, and other beings, all of whom rushed into the battle. Unfortunately, more trolls appeared as well and cut off Pine and his companions.

Thatyn continued to play, but soon the music faltered, and he almost went to his knees, helpless as the battle raged around them.

"Only one way out of this," Lady Jade said. She had hold of Reed, who had taken a wound across the chest, but still held her sword, ready to fight. "We have to pass through the portal, pull what enemies we can with us, and go out into the human lands."

"This will not be good. The humans might panic," Slade warned, but they all knew it. "Let's go."

They linked arms and leapt.

Koya came down hard on the ground, his leg giving way from under him. He fell and Thatyn with him, though the others remained on their feet and got the two of them up. There was no time for more. They'd landed in chaos where battle and storm swept over them. They had brought their own enemies as well. The others fell quickly into fighting once more.

"Kill him!"

The shout from the Most Holy's familiar voice brought Koya's head up with a start. He could feel the taint of the Most Holy's magic around them before he saw the lumbering man standing not far away, his head turning left and right -- from Koya to where Kenning stood. They had arrived amid that more personal battle.

The Most Holy still held powerful magic. Koya felt the energy he wove as he pulled people in to do his battle, a line of soldiers whom Kenning tried to avoid, unwilling to do them harm.

"This is evil!" Koya shouted and moved forward, ignoring weakness and pain. Slade, Takka, Malin, and even Lady Jade fought the other creatures, but he lifted his hand and sent a spell out to sever the Most Holy's link. The spell had been crude, and Koya had no trouble freeing them of the compulsion.

The soldiers hurried away in haste and turned to the other battle.

Koya moved to stand by Kenning, who appeared as though he was barely able to stay on his feet.

Most Holy, seeing them side-by-side, looked around as though to find allies, and then cast again. The magic swirled out from him, dark and unstable -- and moving toward the mass of creatures that had found themselves on this side of the Forbidden Valley. This time the rocklings went crazy and killed everything they could reach: trolls, humans, horses, fae, and even a few hapless birds.

Koya prayed that the Gods would help him as he moved to stop this evil man.

And they did. Koya felt the power surge through him and then spread out to Kenning, Slade, Lady Jade, Reed, Malin, and Thatyn. At his quick orders, they formed a circle around the dozen creatures still fighting and the remnants of the Norter army. Koya wasn't even sure what happened next, but magic surged into a bright ball that encompassed the enemy ... and then they were all gone.

The last troll died with a shout of anger. The Dragonkin dealt with the Lesslings.

And his other enemy?

Koya looked frantically around and found the Most Holy still retreating -- and saw him fall, floundering in the mud.

Another larger man had been following and moved in with soldiers to quickly put him under guard. Koya knew that could not be safe. The Most Holy would recover.

"Kenning," he said and smiled as they embraced, though Koya pulled free first.

"I think you need to go help that man with the Most Holy. He's not going to stay helpless for long."

"Lord Oak.

"Yes," Kenning agreed and started away almost at a run, though he staggered with weakness. With a nod from Koya, Malin went with him. The boy looked stunned, and still too unsure to trust the fighting had ended.

The storm disappeared, leaving a clear blue sky behind. Koya let the others deal with the aftermath of the battle, and he watched as the tear in the magic wall began to heal. Thatyn and Reed stood on this side of that older barrier, but they could get home by the longer trail back into the mountains. They worked with Takka and Lady Jade -- and Slade and General Stanmark.

No one seemed likely to attack each other. Koya suspected this might be the start of a new age.

CHAPTER

FIFTY

Slade stepped into the ornate office and bowed to the man behind the desk who busily went over the piles of papers before him, shifting sheets from one stack to another with a growing frown.

"Most Holy?" Slade said softly. The man didn't look up. "Most Holy? Kenning?"

Kenning looked up with a start and shook his head. "My apologies. I can't get used to it."

The change had been quick. Once the Empress stepped in and strongly suggested they should not allow Cedric back into power, it became only a matter of who would take his place. Kenning proved by far the best candidate.

"I came to tell you that we're ready to go," Slade said.

"Thank you," he said and stood. Kenning brushed down his plain blue robes, at odds with the splendor of the room. Neither spoke of it as they walked out into the enormous courtyard. The Temple at the capital rivaled the palace in size and glitter, and Slade knew Kenning felt no more comfortable with this show of power than he did.

By the time they reached the stables, Koya and Malin had already mounted. Both looked anxious and perhaps even excited. Kenning smiled, which he had done little of during the last few weeks.

"I went to see Cedric in his cell this morning," Kenning said and shook his head, "and tried to talk some sense into him, Koya, but he still won't remove the curse. I'm sorry."

Koya reached down and put a hand on Kenning's shoulder, drawing the man's look. "I'll be fine. It is easier, farther away from him. Besides, Gods forgive me, he is old, and he will die within a few years. The magic will fade with him."

There was no arguing with such logic.

"Good luck on your journey," Kenning said. "I might envy you, traveling to the Dragonkin lands. You had better leave or Lady Jade and her people might go without you. I'll miss your excellent council, my friend."

"We'll stay in touch," Koya reminded him with a hand on the pouch where he kept his runes. He frowned though, and Slade wondered what was on his mind. "I want to tell you something, Kenning. Do with it what you will."

"Yes?" Kenning said and looked curious.

"Don't lose yourself here, in the games of power and politics. My suggestion is to move the High Temple to Templeton, far out of this playground. Have this place torn down and the riches dispersed to the poor. Remember what we are, which Cedric forgot, and even others before him had let drift away. Being here makes the Temple part of the political world. Go back to serving the Gods firsts. Besides ... I think everything might be better if you and the force of the High Temple are both closer to the border. There will be more trouble from the north."

Slade felt an odd whisper of worry thinking that Koya might have seen something coming again. He saw how Kenning nodded. They both listened to him.

Slade mounted his own horse, gave a nod to Kenning, and rode away with the other two. They'd leave the horses before the day was out since the animals didn't much like Dragonkin.

They were about to have an adventure. Slade hoped they survived this one, too.

The End

ABOUT THE AUTHOR:

Hello!

I am an eclectic and prolific author who has published in several genres, including Young Adult Mystery, Contemporary Fantasy, Epic Fantasy, Science Fiction and many works on writing. While I started on the outer edges of traditional publication with sales to small press and magazines publishers, I have since moved most of my work to the Indie world and I am madly in love with the new world of publishing and the direct contact with readers.

I live in Nebraska with my husband, my cats and a small but entirely useless dog.

I also own Forward Motion for Writers and the ezine, Vision: A Resource for Writers.

Connect with Zette:

Web Site: http://lazette.net

Facebook: http://www.facebook.com/lazette.gifford

Joyously Prolific Blog: http://zette.blogspot.com/

FIND WORKS BY

LAZETTE GIFFORD

ON

SMASHWORDS

BARNES & NOBLE

AMAZON

AMAZONKINDLE

LAZETTE.NET

www.ingramcontent.com/pod-product-compliance
Lightning Source LLC
Chambersburg PA
CBHW061510020726
47502CB00006B/2013